The Last King
of the Neverland

S.C. Poteet

DEDICATION

This is dedicated to my wife, children, and those who never want to grow up.

Table of Contents

Fo'w'd viii

I 1

II 10

III 22

IV 37

V 49

VI 61

VII 82

VIII 101

IX 123

X 137

XI 152

XII 153

XIII 167

XIV 181

XV 196

XVI 204

XVII 218

XVIII 227

XIX 245

XX 258

XXI 276

Acknowledgements 282

ABOUT THE AUTHOR 284

The Last King of the Neverland

"Ambition:
It is the last infirmity of noble minds."
— J. M. Barrie

Fo'w'd

This book was a passion project since the moment the idea sprung in my head. It was a story I wanted to tell, using my favorite subjects as the narrative. It took me far longer than I anticipated to complete and took many more turns than I initially planned. I had an idea. I had a concept. In going through the process, I found myself in corners and dead ends at times. However, I believe the story that is told is one that shaped itself as the plot unfolded, collapsed, and found ways to leak out of its own cracks at times. It does not go where I first envisioned it leading, but I enjoyed finding other ways to pivot and develop the characters.

I love the story of Peter Pan. There are many of versions of this story, and while mine may pale in comparison to some, I wanted to write this story with the education, adoration, and passion for both historical piracy and the "story" of Peter Pan. I did this, and I am proud. I have loved every minute of this, even when I was frustrated, stuck, and losing interest for those reasons. When I was "on a roll" it was a high. I felt incredibly free and full. I thoroughly enjoyed writing as an outlet, and this has sparked something in me I hope to continually pursue. This may never be a best-selling novel, but it is mine, and I did it. I will always have that, and I will always be happy I wrote it.

I have visited the Caribbean islands extensively, and can say without question, it is my most favorite place on this spinning rock. It is my Neverland. I say this because, in my descriptions of the island, I took intentional time researching, educating, and learning what I could (from a historical time period's perspective), to do it justice in my descriptions and scenes. I learned more about the actual history than I already knew, which I prided myself on being a geek about to start. I learned even more about events and stories throughout this writing, that it sparked a deeper passion for these subjects and the original story. I am certain there is much I likely got wrong, and for that I apologize to anyone who wishes to protest any of that… So, I will lean on "creative license" to tell the story I wanted to, in a place I wanted it set.

Lastly, I started writing this during a time in our modern history, where civil unrest was and remains a very real situation in this country. Racism, xenophobia, homophobia, and sexism have become prevalent issues, and the source of extreme, sometimes deadly violence. I have written this story to include historical subjects and behaviors that are things that happened. I do not support or promote slavery, but it was a very real aspect of colonialism, particularly in time frame this is set, specifically in Jamaica – *England's sugar pot*. In telling this story, I have taken intentional efforts in my language to use terms and phrases to knowingly exclude the "N" word but have used other terminology which some may find offensive. I feel this was necessary to tell those parts of the story, given the characters and their histories. At no point do I believe those instances to be gratuitous, rather were crafted to be a part of the storyline.

I

Notoriously abysmal, crewing a merchant ship was quite possibly the most undesirable employment available in England. So bad so, that to even have enough hands for a ship, officers resorted to preying on drunkards in taverns, rendering them unconscious, stealing them on board the ship. Often, these men woke from a hard night with a blistering headache, and miles from land aboard an unknown vessel, with no option but to work. As if that weren't enough, the captured men were almost always tortured or killed; and if lucky enough to survive the voyage - abandoned without pay in some remote location with no prospects to improve their lot. This was the way of merchant ships, and even the tavern keepers were in on the cut.

These trans-Atlantic trips were routinely parceling, where the ship would be laden with provisions and other amenities from England to use as trade items once the ship made port in Africa to re-provision or take on bartered cargo. The journey would continue onward through the equatorial middle passage toward the Caribbean. This leg was roughly a 6-week jaunt to complete and was notoriously known to induce extreme nausea and sickness due to rancid holds, packed tightly with livestock and people. Ships on this route were unmistakable because of the emanating stench, that other ships could detect their presence from the scent on the trade winds. As well, these weeks were so monotonous, crews and captives often mutinied because they were fed up with the seemingly gainless progress and detestable atrocities.

However, this venture was apt to be different. This commission was backed almost fully by a gentleman, with whom his wife and daughter were also in tow. They were enroute to America on account of his employer, and had amassed the necessary funding to charter reliable, safe, and appropriate passage. Therefore, those selected to sail were enticed with hopes that this endeavor would reward their willingness to sign on. This commission came with the relative - though unsubstantiated - assurance of remuneration on account of the privatized duty of transporting the wealthy family across the Atlantic. Because of the detail, most assumed the captain would be forced to treat the crew kindlier than usual, as the price for secure delivery relied upon the family arriving safely. This meant the crew could bet that they wouldn't be swindled and left penniless in some foreign port. Thus, the roster to crew the ship witnessed no shortage of interest.

George Darling, the financier, had taken employment with a firm in America, and was transplanting himself and his family to Virginia. Average in stature, he was neither large nor small, but rather common. He had been subject to difficult circumstances as he had lost his family at a young age. An orphan, he was driven by necessity and desire to regain the life he once knew. Fortune granted him an opportunity when he stumbled into an apprenticeship for a fledgling operation managing goldsmithing wealth. Because he was educated, he was eventually entrusted with counting and ledgering the stores of gold. Over time, civil strife, colonial expansion, and pressure from the crown, the business had to adapt, which was no easy transition. Those in the firm were edgy and invested in themselves to succeed. Tobacco and cotton were the new gold, and they were turning profits hand-over-fist.

Haunted by losing everything as a boy, he was constantly striving to better his position and ceaselessly working to earn as much as he could. In turn, this, and a lack of any family modeling for George, trained him to be practical yet assiduous. He worked hard and grew into a trusted partner in the firm. He was prudent and lived his life modestly while simultaneously providing a comfortable and bounteous life for Mary and his daughter Wendy. They would want for naught. When he learned Mary was with child, he became so parsimonious, he nearly went mad, worried that he could not afford to care for the child, or that it would become orphaned like he had been. Knowing the struggles of London, and the tumultuous changing of the houses in the monarchy, George sought for what was suggested as a more secure life in the American colonies. With his family's interests in mind, he set forth in securing passage across the Atlantic.

Mrs. Darling, was a proper lady, dressed in fine fashion with heels lifting her above the mire of the wharf. She was quietly precise in her manner. She knew her place in society and her marriage to George and was always alert to her surroundings. She was not aloof as many women of her class appeared to be. She was smart, strong, and attractive in a non-descript simplicity; admired by most who knew her. She was always to the point in her conversations, though had a gentle approach that made one not feel slighted by any indiscretion directed toward them. People liked Mary Darling and often wondered how she managed to go about so assertively carefree.

Wendy Darling had come of age by the time the family was positioned to make the journey to the southern colonies in America. She was a radiant woman, taking after her mother in grace and beauty, but from her father, she inherited his hardy frame. Her cheeks rosy, nose cutely buttoned, dimples and a smile that would stop gentlemen in their tracks, and eyes of piercing aquamarine. She wore gowns of the highest fashion afforded, and her caramel brunette hair was dressed up neatly, with slight curls bouncing upon her shoulders. As a lady, she was demure and polite; trained in propriety and grace. However, due to character traits learned from her mother and father, she had an underlying current of curtness for those that crossed her.

At Wendy's age, she should have been married off to a husband of status and security. However, George, knowing his plans to relocate to America, had not devoted any effort in his duties to arranging her marriage. This did not stop would-be suitors from calling and negotiating for an opportunity. Wendy was a prize none could win. Subsequently, this had an unfortunate effect on her over time, as she grew older and was still unwed. Circles of the aristocracy began to murmur and whisper when they saw her, spreading undue gossip and rumors. It was not her fault, but her father's; preoccupied with his plans. Mary urged her husband to take notice of their daughter's declining station, but he was too invested in their new life and a chance at growing their estate. He would find her a husband once in Virginia; a good, wealthy plantation owner or servant to the crown in the General Assembly. At that, Wendy's prospects dwindled sharply, and she had no choice but to accept her unmatched destiny.

On an early morning in the overcrowded landings of London, ships were busy with loading and unloading of various cargoes destined for - or returning from - trade routes. One ship in particular, the *Eagle* laid alongside the fray, filling its holds with the personal belongings of an exceedingly wealthy family. The *Eagle* was a merchant ship making ready for the colonies in America. She was a stalwart 3-masted Dutch ship captured during a privateering raid off the coast of Portugal. The *Eagle* was a fine ship, in good repair, her lines sleek, her sails proper, and her deck as neat as Sabbath supper. On board, her crew scuttled about, the boards creaking beneath their hurried stamping.

Captain William Smythe commanded the *Eagle* and saw to her fittings and her readiness for sail. He was a coarse and stoic man, who rarely engaged in trivial ordeals. However, it was not uncommon for him to lay down swift, and often egregious punishments when the occasion necessitated. Because of his family lineage, experience, and historically profitable transatlantic voyages, he was enmeshed among high society, which allowed him the benefit of not taking opportunities unbefitting of his status. He was adept at commanding a ship for lucrative business ventures and was paid handsomely as a result. Accordingly, his reputation proceeded him and is how he came to contract this specific passage. He had hand-selected his officers, whom he trusted to enlist the crew. Any deviate member assigned to the *Eagle* would face severe consequences as a result of their infraction, as would the officer who signed them on.

By mid-day, the heavily laden ship squatted in the water nearing ready for sail as the cargoes were securely stowed below decks. Casks of water, wine, ale, salted meats and biscuit were stacked tightly in rows. Livestock, fowl, and hogs were led into cramped pens and left to confused confinement. Heavy rolls of canvas were lashed together. Cords of wood piled high for cooking necessity. Weaponry, cannon, powder, and shot were affixed into their respective stations. Typically armed to fend off would-be assailants along the route, the *Eagle* required extra space for the family's property therefore some cannons were removed to make extra room for the additional freight. As a result, the subtraction of firepower put the heavy ship at risk, should they encounter any nefarious characters on the open ocean such as the Spaniards, or worse, pirates.

The tediousness of loading the ship vexed George, though he was rarely ever at ease. Mr. Darling was an impertinent man, always on the move, mind racing, brash in his manner. Vainly, they were suffering the arduous process of the loading the *Eagle*. The ship's needs were priority for the passage, followed by the Darlings' household property. Portmanteaus and chests lay strewn about containing their wardrobes and personal effects which were manhandled with what seemed no regard for the fragility nor the expense of the items. Everything had a place, and everything was to be fit in that place accordingly for smooth sailing.

Impatiently, George barked at the ship's men as though he in charge, orchestrating the chaos. From the onset, this irked the crew, and they quickly became agitated toward his presumptuous presence. Captain Smythe approached Mr. Darling as he irritably paced the deck. Having much to attend to, this was not a task the captain cared to devote effort toward so soon before leaving port.

"Mr. Darling, I trust that you mean well and have the best of intentions toward my men, but if you would please be reminded, they are under my charter, and they are atask in the manner as I see fit," the captain calmy, yet assertively addressed George.

"And I will remind you Captain Smythe, I have paid my fare to have myself and my family delivered to Virginia post-haste. All this knockering about is consuming valuable time, for which we could be asea!"

"Yes," Captain Smythe replied, already exasperated. "You're a practical man, a banker of some sort, am I correct?"

"Yes, yes! What of it?"

"Then it is reasonable to assume, you are no man of the sea, nor have you commanded a ship in practice?"

"To what purpose does this inquest serve, sir?"

"As a man of the sea, and captain of this ship, I will once again request of the gentleman that these are my men, and they are attending to matters I deem appropriate to take him and his precious family across the sea. If he has any qualm, he can be forcibly restrained below decks until such a time is found appropriate that he be unchastened. That will be everything and all on the matter."

Captain resolutely turned, and left Mr. Darling fuming to the effect his ears burned with indignant rage at having been so contemptuously regarded. To make matters worse, Mr. Darling was accustomed to always having the last word, but at the captain's dismissal of himself, he was unable to land a final barb. This frustrated him riotously, and so he stamped bitterly back down the gangway to where Mary and Wendy awaited permission to board.

"Miserable cur," He griped, pacing, wiping his brow with his kerchief.

Mary paid little mind to her husband. She was used to his petty tirades and knew well enough to mind her business. She sat, fanning herself, growing weary of inaction, though never breaking repute. Wendy sat primly as well, taking in the bustling theater before her. The cacophony of the wharves became oddly melodic while all manner of man, woman and beast functioned in an unscripted performance. There was a method of mayhem on the docks, and barring any significant disruption, everything operated fluently day in and day out. It was truly a sight to behold.

However, the Darlings did not belong there sitting idly by in the throes of such clamor, but they had arrived earlier than expected, and awaited access aboard the ship longer than they'd hoped. Captain Smythe was preoccupied with ensuring everything was safely stowed before granting them access, despite Mr. Darling's impetuousness. The dangers of passengers in the way of the crew posed a risk he was unwilling to chance. So, they sat in relative purgatory until such time they could consign themselves to his charge.

Though the activity may have appeared rote, the docks were infamously dangerous, filthy, and reeked of foulness. Fetid seawater and excrement putrefied in the mid-day sun. As thousands of bodies jostled about, the mire was stirred constantly, ceaselessly rancid. The air was choking, and no breeze abated. Even in the stillness of night, a stench hung like a fog, emanating from the polluted river, mildewing lines, rotting produce, sodden timber, and carcasses of the dead. Rats fed on the decay. Cats preyed on the rats in the continuous circle of life; or death as the case may be. Only to be reprised the following day, and the day after that, and the day after that; relentlessly.

After hours of restless idleness, Captain Smythe finally permitted the family to board the *Eagle,* and the ship was made ready for sail. The fat hull listed as the moorings were cast off, and the ship waded apart from the docks. The crew scurried about pulling lines, hoisting canvas, shouting commands, and falling into their stations while the helmsman piloted them along the current of the filthy river. The city rolled by Gothically as they progressed along the Thames. A collective of rowhouses and spires paraded by against a dull gray sky. Mixed feelings stirred within the Darlings as their history, familiarity and home faded away behind them. They shivered in the chilly damp air as the distance increased, and the *Eagle* set a course for the new world. Night fell that evening with bittersweet emotions, and the family took to their quarters below decks, and readied themselves for the long voyage ahead.

Not being permitted to roam freely about topside, the family was relegated to their quarters below deck. Consequently, the Darlings spent their time lying in their bunks, wracked from sea sickness. George seemed the worst off, followed closely by Mary. Despite his physicality, he was not accustomed to the motions of the sea and succumbed to retching nausea. He was determined to best the malady, however being unable to rid himself of the sickness angered him, which did little to improve his countenance unfortunately. The dizziness had come on quickly as the first night shifted into waking day. To the contrary, Wendy seemed the least afflicted and was left to spend her time attending to the other two. Whether she was or not, she had little time to notice any seasickness of her own, other than the sympathetic reflex induced by the next bout of vomiting from her parents. Caring for them throughout an unremitting affliction was demanding and utterly exhausting. Trapped in cramped space, she yearned for fresh air, or even just reprieve to see the sky above. For hours on end, she nursed her parents, washed away bile, emptied chamber pots, and eked out what sleep she could.

Soon enough, the *Eagle* wrapped around the southerly bend of Africa and made port along the Gold Coast. The winds settled, the ocean surface calmed, and the sun bore hot. Once at anchor the Darlings were permitted liberty from their squalid bunk and for the first real time since departing home, they were able to walk about topside in the fresh air. Exceptionally weak from malnourishment during their sickness, both George and Mary looked gaunt and peaked. Lacking in any strength and still reeling, they carefully hobbled along the deck and occupied a section along the aft railing out of the way. From here they gazed out across the bay, their eyes adjusting to the brightness of the reflecting African sun. Before them was a spectacle of scenery, so foreign to them from their norm of London-town. A fortress in the distance stood like an ominous guard, glowing white against the brown terrain. From the comfort of the ship, the Darlings basked in the sun's blessings, revitalizing in its gleam.

Captain Smythe greeted the Darlings, and inquired to their health, seeing their pallor. There was no denying, nor was he not unaware, of their state during the first leg of sail. The pleasantries were cordial, and the fresh air renewed the Darlings' sociability.

"Ahh, Mr. and Mrs. Darling," he chimed. "How is the warmth finding you?"

"The sun is an afront, and quite searing," George complained. "However, it is a welcomed adjournment of the dreadful torrent from whence we have come."

"Yes, that is a reasonable sentiment. Though I will caution you, we have yet to see the worst of it, I'm afraid. The passage from here to our destination can be a proper tumult. But I hope that we will be fortuitous in our crossing that we may be blessed with fair winds and avoid any tempest that be capable of deterring our path."

"You mean to tell me we are yet to be free of these dreadful conditions?" George's head reeled at the thought of further suffering.

"Aye. The currents from here the Carib are oft quite a stir. The trades can blow hard, which aid us in our speed across, but also make for a mess. It is hard to say for certain, but I expect we shan't see any harrickins, as we've set off ahead of season. One can never be too sure. But for the sake of my ship, crew, and your family, I'll be intent to get us along as right as I can make so. Though, ye should be thinking positive, sir."

"And what, pray tell, might that mean?"

"Gen'rally speaking sir, those who've not fared well to this point, make the best of the idleness while at anchor here, and seem to be fit as the rest when we make way."

This gave Mary hope, as she was not interested in spending weeks on end in the same state of malaise. George on the other hand, continued to dwell on the potential for misery, and spiraled into an aggravated self-deprecation. Wendy, who was no-worse-for-wear, quietly stood among them allowing the hot sun to warm her porcelain cheeks.

As George attempted to compose himself, he redirected the conversation, "Captain, what is our business here?"

"This is a port-of-call for refitting, refilling our casks and food stores, and making trades and purchases for items of high value in the colonies."

"What artifacts might those include? I would quite like to partake if that is the case."

"Well, I'll be taking on a variety of property, sir, but that of interest to you might be silks, spices, or other sundries in the markets. However, I kindly insist you not go ashore, so as you are not jeopardized in the transport."

"I say, it would do me well to get off this god-forsaken ship and plant my feet upon terra firma! Now, if you'll be so kind as to get us to land, I would like to walk around and peruse the markets of which you speak!

"Again, Mr. Darling, this port is not quite what I think you'll find to your predilection, and…"

"Captain," George rudely interrupted, "If I am to be subjected to your lectures about what is good for me, I shall see to it this is the last passing you will command. Furthermore, I will be damned if I am to be cooped up aboard this wretched vessel for weeks on end with no recess while we lie at anchor!"

Captain Smythe, glared at George, then at Mary and Wendy. Mary, embarrassed at the outburst, looked back at Captain Smythe with apologetic eyes, though not daring to impugn her husband. Captain Smythe caught her look and comported himself. "As you wish, sir."

At this, he turned and withdrew to the main deck to make arrangements for the family to be rowed ashore.

"Leftenant, the Darlings wish to adjourn to the markets. I have made my argument to them, that this is not in their best interest. However, this may prove to my advantage. See that they are taken ashore with a company and that they are shielded from my business. When I have concluded my affairs and loaded the cargo appropriately, I will raise the signal flag upon the mizzen. Upon that you may return with them. Keep them distracted, and should you see that they enjoy a bit of drink, that will be all the better."

"Aye, sir."

Soon enough, skiffs were set from the *Eagle* and rowed to shore; five to six men occupied the small boats apiece. The crew going ashore for provisioning, clustered together, and pulled hard the oars to expedite their landing ahead of the Darling's expedition. Captain Smythe, with the group of skiffs, eyed the departure of the Darlings with three of his men in a separate boat. His eyes burned at the irritating man sitting awkwardly in the bow, as though impersonating the captain himself.

II

In the dusty streets outside the fortress, Lt. Allain chaperoned the Darlings through the exotic market. Vendors offered spices, wines, artisanal wares, silks and dressings, carpets and tapestries, and all manner of fish, fowl and produce. They perused the tables intrigued by a variety of tribal headdresses, weapons, jewelry, and more. The craftsmanship of the items was exquisite. So often, similar items could be seen on display in the wealthy homes back in England - and the Darlings certainly may have owned similar items themselves - but it was a sight to behold in the places of origin. When the products are unloaded at home, they don't hold the same mysticism, since they are carted off a ship in crates or rolls and installed as a fixture or display in a home. So much of the specialty is wasted on the wealthy, that it only becomes a showpiece, which is merely meant to impress the other wealthy in a game of impersonal collecting. Seeing such pieces outside of gray-street London, the flare piqued a more personal connection.

When they grew hungry, the food stalls offered no shortage of cuisine, influenced by English, Portuguese, and African recipes. Daringly, they partook of a strange meal involving a doughy lump with a spicy soup. They were instructed to pinch a portion of the mixture, dip it in the soup, and eat it. At first, their unversed palate wasn't prepared for the texture nor the spice, and the locals found this to be quite entertaining. However, it tasted distinctively enjoyable, so they continued with the meal. This also made quite an improvement to the empty stomached visitors' countenance and bodily nourishment.

"I say," George smacked, as he sucked his fingers, "this dish is divine. What is it?"

"Fufuo and Nkatenkwan," Lt. Allain replied. "It is a favorite among the locals and those of us who have had the occasion to share. They make it of cassava, which we find akin to potatoes. The soup is made of groundnuts and spices and is a delicacy. I can tell you this recipe has made it across the ocean and has become a favorite in Virginia. You'll find it commonly on the plantations and is quite a nicety on those long December days."

"This? In Virginia?" George asked. "The name again?"

"Nkatenkwan, sir. Though, you will find it simply called 'peanut soup' in the colonies. They don't tend to keep the negro names of things over there.

Not many can reproduce the inflections or phrases of the Africans, nor do they care to. They take what they want and make it their own."

"Peanut Soup, eh?" George continued, pawing at his bowl, paying no mind to anything else Lt. Allain had to say.

When they had finished supping, they felt revived and much more able to operate and move about. The food had filled their empty stomachs and quelled them of their agitated state. They continued about the market until Lt. Allain guided them into a den which was darkened and smelled resinous and thick of incense. Inside, dark faces skeptically eyed the guests, and mumbled to themselves, attempting to not attract attention to themselves. Strange white faces in these places often came with floggings, and other punishments. In a gesture of comfort, Lt. Allain approached the owner, and spoke quietly while the Darlings waited, equally as apprehensive as the locals. After a short bit of hushed conversation, Lt. Allain came back to the Darlings.

"It is normally not custom for outsiders to partake, but I have arranged for you to enjoy the treatment of the proprietor in his establishment here. Come, sit."

Feeling privileged at this gesture, the Darlings sat low on the floor on bolsters, surrounded by a mixture of heavy rugs. Lt. Allain took leave and stood watch outside the door, so as not to cause any further discomfort for those inside. He was also minding the signal from the ship that it was permissible to take the Darlings back.

Inside the smoky den, the Darlings were presented with a few crude vessels by Addae, the owner. He sat with, poured some milky liquid into three bowls, and motioned to them to drink. Curiously, they took the bowls in hand, and raised each raised them to their lips, almost in following each other's movement. The concoction was sweet with a tinge of bitterness, and when they had taken their sip, they again looked at each other awkwardly. Addae smiled a toothy grin, his white teeth contrasting his dark face, "Akpeteshie," he spoke, still smiling, gesturing for them to drink up.

Sensing the relative safety, they all relaxed a bit, and the Darlings continued to imbibe while Addae attempted to speak to them in broken English and hand motions. Each of them got the gist of the conversation and participated comfortably. George and Mary continued to drink the alcoholic concoction, but Wendy had politely refused any more after a second bowl was dished out to her. She felt the dizzying effect setting in, and this made her uneasy. She had never been drunk before, and she had the wherewithal to know she did not like the feeling in such an unknown place. Her parents, the socialites they were back home, continued to drink without realizing they were loosening their inhibitions as a consequence of the alcohol. They were giddy and enjoying themselves, for once, since setting off from home.

After a strategic duration of time, Lt. Allain entered to find the Darlings where he'd left them, no worse for wear; only inebriated as intended. Pleased, Lt. Allain palmed Addae a purse of coins, thanking him for his attention to his customers. Addae took Lt. Allain's hand and bent in gratitude to the handshake, touching his forehead to the clasped hands. Returning to his original posture, Addae spoke in his native tongue, a blessing, and again touched his forehead to Lt. Allain's hand. Satisfied, Lt. Allain again thanked Addae, and loosed his grip signaling the end of the exchange. As Addae cupped his hands toward his forehead now, Lt. Allain collected the Darlings and began to usher them back outside.

While waiting, Lt. Allain had espied the semaphore from the *Eagle*, indicating it was admissible to return to the ship. Captain Smythe had procured and secured his cargo, and therefore it was time to return with the Darlings. Once aboard, they would very likely be setting sail posthaste, as it was dangerous to idle in the bay with the cargo aboard. Lt. Allain was expected with some urgency and knew not to dawdle. Fortunately, the signal had come while he had his charges in the shebeen, so they would be fully liquored up when they arrived back at the ship; all, save for Wendy, to which Lt. Allain was unaware of her ceasing to imbibe.

Once they had arrived at their rowboat, Lt. Allain carefully loaded the Darlings, and shoved off with the oarsman pulling hard against the crashing shore break. Now past the tumult of the breakers, they were on their way back to the *Eagle*. From the fo'csle deck, Captain Smythe peered through his spyglass to see that they were enroute. Additionally, he could see the insufferable George darling bobbing and waving as though singing some tune to his company.

In fact, he was. George was so gay with liquid jubilation, he had begun singing an old society melody, hoping to carouse the others to join in. Mary, silently enjoying inebriation and her husband's glee, held on to the gunwale to steady herself against the jostling. Wendy, embarrassed by her father, gazed far out at the retreating castle back on shore. Lt. Allain and the oarsmen eyed each other, speaking to each other telekinetically, thinking the same thing: the man is an ass.

Captain Smythe shut his spyglass resolutely at seeing the return of the family, and barked orders to make ready for sail, and to prepare for the re-boarding of those they awaited. By the time the Darlings arrived back at the ship, the crew had neared ready for departure. Once safely on board, the anchors were raised, and the *Eagle* began drifting lazily with the current. The crew then scrambled up the lines to unfurl the sails, and the ship puffed into motion. The movement of the heavy ship cruised with what little breeze there was, feeling quite splendid on Wendy's cheeks. She closed her eyes, took a deep inhale of the fresh arid air, and blew it out slowly. Soon, they would be relegated to their quarters, away from such pleasantness.

As the crew orchestrated the *Eagle* into motion, Captain Smythe welcomed the family back aboard.

"Ah, George, Mary, I trust Lt. Allain provided you an appropriate experience?"

"Yesh... Yes, your man resplendidently, resplendedidly..." George hiccupped, "Yes, sir. Lt. Allain was very gracious in his graciousness of our excurshion."

Glad that the man was well lubricated, Captain Smythe genuinely smiled, first at him, then Mary. "I am pleased, sir, that my man has afforded you safe keeping while ashore, clearly to which you were able to enjoy yourselves in one of our dear friends' dens. It is not common for those like us to be welcomed in those places, but I have established rapport with a few, who grant us occasional entry, and participation of their customs."

"Yes," Mary entered unexpectantly, attempting to quell her husband's drunken prattle, "Mr. Addae was quite kind and generous to take us in, and treat us to the custom of their drink. I say, we are not accustomed to such potency, and you'll please forgive us if we are an impropriety."

"Not at all, madam. I am elated that Mr. Addae welcomed you in and allowed you inclusion. Upon our return, I shall see to it that I thank him myself for his hospitality and caretaking. Now, if you will excuse me, we are getting under way and shall need to attend to matters at hand. If it pleases you, I would have you join me for supper in my cabin?"

Captain Smythe, in an unusually good mood, and in speaking to Mary, didn't quite realize he'd just invited the drunken man to dine with him, but in an attempt to convey goodwill and pleasant relations, he proceeded with the charade.

"Yes, but of course." Mary replied gracefully, "We would be grateful to join you. Thank you."

"Fine then, I shall send for you when it is time. In the meantime, please do settle in once again. We will be asea in no time, and from here on to our next stop in Barbados."

At that, Captain Smythe dismissed himself and returned to his affairs.

Unbeknownst to the Darlings, Captain Smythe had taken on approximately four-dozen Africans. Though, because the ship was not a slave ship, he was only able to procure so many as he could stow aboard in secrecy. While the Darlings were ashore, distracted by the baubles and fares of the markets – and the exceptionally alcoholic ceremony – Captain Smythe and a few of his men attended the auction at the castle. He had selected a lot of the strongest, healthiest looking men he could acquire at his price, and shuttled them quickly back to the ship. Once the slaves were captive in the hold, caged among the livestock, Captain Smythe raised the signal flag for Lt. Allain's attention that they were finished in their dealings, and that the family could return.

Captain Smythe was hired as an agent to transport the family and their belongings across the Atlantic. He was not on a trading nor on a slaving mission, and it was in very poor taste for him to take on the men, while in Mr. Darling's employ. However, always looking for an opportunity to fatten his pocket, the captain was willing to risk a tirade from the pompous man, should he be found out. The slaves were worth more than George's fare alone, and therefore, Captain Smythe would still profit from the venture, two-fold as the case were. To him, it was worth the risk. He could offload the slaves in Barbados easily for a profit, sell off some other cargo, refit with cargo sellable in the colonies, and be off in no time at all. In the entire process, he would nearly triple his worth in this trip alone.

After taking leave of the Darlings, Captain Smythe retired to his quarters to itemize the ship's ledger, taking account of the purchases in port. Upon arrival in the Caribbean, he would be required to present this in order to sell the slaves off. He would have to report his inventory, or face a crippling fine, and possible restriction from the future business on the islands. However, if he did not find buyers or a price to his liking in the Caribbean, he would keep them caged in their stall and sell them in America, once they reached Virginia. Each African was a commodity, and the ledger needed to reflect this, so the landing taxes associated could be fairly assessed.

******

Lt. Allain called for the Darlings and escorted them to the captain's quarters. All gussied up, the Darlings entered and were greeted by Captain Smythe, who at the moment, sat behind his desk pining over nautical charts, calculating distance to their next destination. He peered over his over his spectacles, and properly stood, welcoming them. His jaw clenched instinctively at the sight of George but composed a smile at the sight of Mary and Wendy. He had an eye for the women, specifically the unmarried Wendy, and was delighted to see them in finer dining attire.

He gestured to the table, prepared with the ship's finery, laid out in a display of prestige. The family entered and took seats at the table. As they did, Captain Smythe ticked off a few more measurement on his charts and set the instruments down to join them. The Darlings had sobered up by now and were returned to their general selves. Still being in the vicinity of the coast, the ship steadily held, not rocking as it was apt to do on the open ocean. This made for a much more comfortable experience.

"Thank you for having us Captain," Mary opened primly.

"The pleasure is all mine," He returned grandly and out of character for his actual feelings toward George thus far. "I hope that this meal finds us well together and fills our bellies satisfactorily."

George shifted in his seat uncomfortably, under orders of his adoring wife to behave himself, and understand he was not the host of the evening, and that it would benefit him to act properly.

"Yes, I say, this arrangement is quite fancy for what I presumed and expected for dining accommodations." His statement was laced with snobbish undertones but was delivered well enough to pass as appropriate.

Sensing the loftiness, the captain remaining ever the firm jaw, would not fall victim to the man's quips, and replied also as appropriate as he could, "I'm sure the trappings are not necessarily what you might be accustomed to in the grandeur of domestic entertaining, but I do like to keep a particular level of higher comfort where I am afforded to do so."

"It is very nice," Mary charged, "And we thank you for sharing your table with us." She cut eyes to George signaling that was the end of the matter.

After the pleasantries were concluded the captain said a blessing over the food, and the group began to dine. A meal was spread before them, all fresh from the provisioning in Africa. Arguably, it was the best meal the Darling's had enjoyed since leaving London, with the exception of their time in the markets earlier that day. Today's experiences had renewed them in sustenance and exercise, allowing their bodies to reawaken to a more normal usage of their faculties. Having been cooped up for weeks prior had taken its toll.

Once the meal was finished, the settings were cleared away, and Captain Smythe invited the family to join in a digestif of madeira, also fresh from today's supply. Graciously, they accepted, all but Wendy. She was growing tired after having spent enough of her day regaling with her parents in the markets and Addae's den. She wanted to stretch her legs and catch what fresh air she still could, before being relegated below deck again for weeks on end. Politely, she asked if she could take leave of the party and enjoy the open air outside on deck. Generally taboo, Captain Smythe acquiesced, and asked Lt. Allain to accompany her, in the event any of the crew got the wrong idea. He nodded in compliance and escorted the girl from the room.

As they walked topside, the air bristled through her hair giving her a bit of a chill, as the night was devoid of the day's heat. She was wearing a lovely gown, cinched up and beautiful, but her dressings were not suited for the night's climate. Lt. Allain, a proper gentleman, offered her his coat, to which she demurely accepted. Her cheeks reddened at the gesture as she found it to be very sweet of the man to take notice of her in such a way.

"I'd like to thank you, Lt. Allain, for attending to us today. You proved yourself a proper gentleman in the company of my parents." Wendy said, as she paused to look over the railing into the endless night.

"Of course, m'lady. Doing my duty as the captain requested."

"Do you enjoy your station, Lt. Allain? Doing as the captain bids, I mean?"

"Yes, ma'am. I intend to be a captain myself one day, skilled like Captain Smythe himself. I've sailed under his command for some time now and have learned quite an amount with his tutelage."

"That seems quite fitting, then. How will you advance to your own captaincy? Surely there's no examination of sorts?

"No. However, each voyage is in and of itself an examination of proficiency. I do as the captain bids me to do, and I maintain order about the ship, so that the captain needs not trifle in affairs beneath his command. As I continue to prove myself independently worthy, the captain will perhaps allow me to take control in smaller ventures he has no interest in. Perhaps he will speak kindly of me should I take employ under an owner in need of a captain. It really comes down to being granted a ship, and that ship's company trusting that I am a man fit for the helm."

"That seems very dedicated and entrusting to rely on the reference of a man whose employ you already serve, is it not?"

"Aye, it is. That is the jeopardy I am subject to presently. I have to trust that when my time comes, those of whom I rely upon will be honest and true."

"What is to stop you from doing so now?"

"It would be deemed mutinous, and therefore no proper company would hire such a man to captain their ship. As well, I am admittedly still learning the advanced responsibilities on these longer, cross-Atlantic endeavors. There are many dangers out here in the open water, and very few means to enforce law and order. We have our own accords upon our ship, but there are others who don't, and seize the opportunity to revolt, mutiny or go rogue. It is those who have succeeded in such acts that are a threat to honest, god-fearing sailors."

"Pirates you mean?"

"Yes," he replied caught off guard by her forward candor and knowledge of the subject. "It is pirates to be feared, as they act by their own devious and vulgar behaviors. But that is no concern for a lady as you, madam."

"Lt. Allain, you take me for some whimsical fool, that I do not hear stories and tales of these scoundrels? The gossip is all the buzz for the endlessly droll sittings a 'lady' such as me is meant to endure. All manner of talks are floated around like a child's bedtime story. I assure you I have been privy to more tales of swindlers, thieves, and murderous villains, than you might believe."

Shocked at the forwardness, Lt. Allain adjusted himself, knowing now that he was speaking to someone free of tongue, and with no issue with such uncouth subject matters.

"Oh, don't be so rigid Lt. Allain. You needn't discuss the specifics with me or provide me any testament to your experiences. But you mustn't mistake me for a little girl who needs to be sheltered from the likes of the very world we share."

"Of course, m'lady, it's just that you surprise me with your cavalier manner on the subject. If you'll forgive me, I do not mistake you for a child. I suppose though that I misunderstood what ladies of your status discussed when gathered…"

"Of my status, Lt. Allain? You speak of me as some fanciful object not permitted to enjoy conversation beyond the etiquette befitting some prude in a nunnery? We discuss many subjects in private that men of *your status* might blush at."

"I meant no discourtesy, m'lady. The admission of indelicate discussions among the circles of ladies is of some bewilderment. I knew not of this gossip, and you'll please forgive me of my ignorance."

Lt. Allain was flustered because he had no actual comprehension what ladies discussed in private or at parties – nor would he – and he was now embarrassed that he had insulted Wendy.

"I forgive you, Lt. Allain," she said with a coquettish smirk.

"Right. Good then…" He responded, straightening himself in narrow recovery of the situation. "If the lady would, please call me Theodore."

"Lt. Allain, Theodore, I have enjoyed our repartee, however, I feel it is time for me to retire. I wouldn't want anyone thinking us indecent."

"Of course. If it would please the lady, I too have enjoyed our exchange, and I thank her for broadening my understanding of the social circles. If the lady wishes future intermission from her confinement, I would be pleased to accompany her."

"Lt. Allain, I thank you. You have remained a gentleman, and I am gratified by your offer. It would bring me joy to escape the confines of our berth and my parents on occasion. Though do not mistake my jubilation for anything less than the freedom to move about. I am still a lady, and do not conduct myself mischievously or improperly." Wendy smiled again teasing her escort once more.

"Yes'm," he replied, bowing slightly. "Allow me to escort you back to the others."

When the two returned to the captain's quarters, they found the two men pouring over the charts in his desk, and Mary sitting primly to the side. The raucousness of the two men bickering was not of argument, but of consternation on George's part. He was dismayed that the next leg of the journey could take as much as three months to complete! Having reeled in seasickness for only a few weeks to start, he was less than excited to be boxed up for exponentially longer.

"Hello dear," Mary groaned in boredom of the two men's discourse. "Did you enjoy your escape?"

"Yes, mother. Lt. Allain was an exemplar of courtesy and cordiality."

"Thank you, Lt. Allain. Your grace is cherished. I only wish I had joined you instead."

Wendy laughed as her father and the captain argued senselessly about the course ahead. "Perhaps you can join us next time."

"Next time?" Mary inquired quickly. George's attention turned.

"Yes, I have asked if Lt. Allain would be so kind as to chaperone me on other breaks during our time at sea, and he has politely obliged."

"Has he now?" Captain Smythe and George both chimed in, now a part of the conversation. Lt. Allain stood nervously at attention by the door.

"Yes, though I understand his duties to the captain and the ship are priority…"

"Yes, Ms. Darling, they are," the captain interrupted. "Lt. Allain, what is the meaning of this, and what have you to say about the matter?"

"Captain, sir, I only meant that if Ms. Darling sought the need for accompaniment topside, I would be obliged to ensure her safety, sir."

"Lt. Allain, I will remind you; you are under my command on this ship, and I will not permit you to fraternize with Ms. Darling. There should be no consorting of the officers with these people unless I say so."

"Aye, sir."

"Pardon me, Captain Smythe," Mary wedged in, "I should hope that during this passage, we might be granted recess to improve our weariness, when permissible to do so. We shall not impede the running of the ship, but I also believe that having a watchful eye with *any* of us, would be an appropriate measure while doing so. And if the captain will allow us this privilege, I trust my daughter's choice in character and confer based upon our time with Lt. Allain in port. I too should like to have him accompany us during our recess to ensure neither of us are cast overboard or harmed in any sense."

"Now see here, Mary…" George said sharply for his wife to recognize who, and how, she was addressing. However, Mary cut her eyes from the captain to him with a glare of warning that he should not press the issue any further.

"Mrs. Darling, it is dangerous and highly irregular for women to be parading about on the deck of the ship while we are at sea. We are headed on a path that could be very tempestuous, and I should not like to risk your safety for frivolity. As well, my men are not babysitters for passengers."

"But it is not illegal? It is not illicit? If the captain permits it, then it shall be accepted, shall it not? I understand you hold the power over all of us while in your charge, and you may rule with dominance. Or you may have mercy, and allow us to breathe fresh air on occasion?" Mary manipulated her inflection to strike at the core of his masculinity, a trick to which she was no amateur.

"Mrs. Darling, it is not illegal, however it is bad luck to have women aboard a ship at all, let alone a centerpiece on display."

"Yes captain, but we are already aboard the ship as passengers, are we not? This is nothing hidden from your crew. We are not omens to be locked away because of a mariner's superstition. We simply ask for periodic reprieve to stretch our legs, fill our lungs with clean air, and bask in the sun's radiance. We will not be in the way in the least."

Captain Smythe realized he was losing ground in the argument, and instead of becoming defeated, opted to exert his control over the situation, and ruled that the Darlings could be permitted to come out for a short time, when the conditions permitted. Should they meet swell or storm, they should not be outside. It was a bargain to which they all agreed. Mary had won, exacting a result to her and Wendy's benefit by way of the captain believing it was his idea and decision. Mary patted Wendy on the leg subtly in victory.

"Thank you, Captain. We are appreciative of your concession and will abide by your allowance. In that we do not overstep our boundaries, would it be acceptable for Lt. Allain to call on us when the time is appropriate that we may take our exercise?

"I shall see that he does, when, and only when his duties are satisfactorily replete."

"Thank you, captain. You are most gracious. Wendy, do you have anything to say to the captain?"

"Thank you, Captain Smythe. Forgive me my trespass. It was inappropriate of me to not seek your counsel on the matter prior." Wendy bashfully apologized, knowing all too well her mother's tact in getting her what she sought from the start.

"Yes, yes. You're forgiven. Let us move on from this vexing conversation."

"Thank you again, captain. I believe we have taken up more of your attention than intended, and we should take our leave for the evening. George, would you be so kind as to deliver us to our quarters?" Mary directed her inquiry at her husband once again laced with intent, that he would not be wise to ignore. They had spent an amiable evening with the captain, and she did not wish to spoil. She knew George's temperament could easily shift and condemn all progress they had made with Captain Smythe in thawing the relationship between all of them.

It was true. George had not acted obnoxiously the entire day and had allowed for a very pleasant experience. The time spent ashore, he had not grumbled, nor had he been cross with any of the locals, especially Addae, who shared a special, foreign encounter. Even with Captain Smythe, a man seen as an unnecessary rival, he had comported himself as a gentleman like he would at any dinner invitation back home. Perhaps it was the feeling of inclusion or equitability that George sought, which tempered his unlikable nature. Maybe that was just it, indeed.

III

Over the next week, the sailing went without disturbance, allowing Mary and Wendy to take periodic strolls along the deck as they had negotiated. Lt. Allain accompanied them and provided casual conversation. George either remained in the cabin or attempted to gain audience with Captain Smythe. To the best of his ability, Captain Smythe strategically occupied himself to divert or limit interactions with the man. They had shared a decent enough time during the meal, but the captain did not care to foster relations beyond their current business arrangement, nor did he wish to provide the man an opportunity to involve himself in the captain's affairs. His business was his business, and he did not need George sticking his nose in any of it.

On one of the walks, Mary was discussing Wendy's necessity for finding a husband as quickly as possible upon arrival and settling. Once in Virginia, they must waste no time in searching for suitors, so that she could be married, and not left subject to gossip rendering her undesirable. This conversation irked Wendy because she was in no personal hurry to wed some colonial stranger. She felt it decent to reside for some time in their new home and get to know the people and surroundings. Surely this would not set her up as an undesirable prospect. However, Mary urgently disagreed, citing that she would, in fact, be a prime candidate for marriage, being new – and beautiful.

"Your father has partners and connections in Virginia and Philadelphia. I'm sure he will match you nicely with a gentleman of repute."

"I'm sure he can mother, but I am not ready to be married so soon upon our arrival. I think that this is happening all too soon, and I should be afforded the ability to settle into our new home first. Not into an unknown husband's estate when I will not know him, nor his affairs, nor the land for which he lives."

"You're a beautiful woman, my dear, but we risked your distinction in London by not marrying you off, because of this relocation. There is no time to dawdle in this matter, lest you bring about undesirable position."

"I know I am to be married mother, despite my wish to go about it my own way. I only wish you would provide me opportunity to establish ourselves, myself, in this new place."

During the discourse, Lt. Allain stood afar trying not to eavesdrop on their conversation. However, due to proximity, he could not help but hear most of their tête-à-tête. During the short time together, he had taken a fancy to Wendy. She was striking, quite desirous, and as her mother had made the case, available. This made him awkwardly intrigued, as he secretly wished to ask for her hand himself but had no place presenting himself as a suitor. His mind searched for a means to make himself noticed beyond their steward.

As the women continued to fuss, Wendy became impatient at her mother's pressing and unwillingness to budge on the matter. Wendy knew this was expected of girls her age and had conceded to being married despite her preferences to remain untethered for the time being. Only that during this particular conversation, her mother was very domineering, and this off-put Wendy from the onset. Typically, she could navigate and divert the subject temporarily until it was broached again. But Mary seemed uncharacteristically firm in her viewpoint this time.

Seeing there was no escape from the commandment, Wendy made a final outburst of protest and stormed off back toward the aft. Lt. Allain made motion to go after her, unsure if he should, but Mary stopped him.

"Leave her be. She will be fine once she cools off, and she has nowhere to go aboard this ship, regardless if the captain thinks she is in any danger."

"But m'lady, should she not be looked after for that very reason?"

"No, she will go back to her bunk and sulk. She will either brush her hair in a frenzy or read her books until she passes this emotion. I know my daughter. Trust me, you need not chase after her. I fear you will not be well received even if you did."

"Yes, mum. As you wish. I shall stay with you then until you are ready to retire."

"Thank you, but I will be just fine on my own as well, Mr. Allain. After all of our walks, I feel quite safe, thanks to your accompaniment."

"Yes, mum. However, it is my duty to see that the lady is accompanied at all times; the captain has made his position clear on this. And if the lady will forgive my saying, despite these orders, I have grown to enjoy the company of you both during these times as well."

Mary was pleased that he held to his convictions and did welcome his presence regardless of feeling she didn't need him there. "Thank you. You are a good and kind man."

And so there they stood, as Mary peered out over the railing into the endless horizon.

*****

When Wendy stamped off, her only intention was to be rid of the tiresome conversation of her future unknown husband, some banker or farmer in all likelihood. How dull. She wished for a gentleman of favor one she was familiar with in the court she knew back in London. But she was not in London anymore, and this suddenly saddened her. She grew instantly homesick and forlornly wished to return to her comforts. She was daunted by the new world, and all the stories she'd heard of its foundling days under the Virginia Company, and the Jamestown experiment. Was it not possible such horrors still existed, lying in wait for the right opportunity? Would native savages come and kill her or her family – or worse? Her mind raced through scenarios, all dreamed up from grandiose tales from years ago.

Knowing her father was still in their cabin, she wished to avoid his persecution also. Instead, she just wanted to be alone. She wanted to put her mind at ease, free from any counterargument. So, she fled below into the hold. She figured she could disappear among the beasts and stores for a bit, and no one would bother her.

When she ventured below, she was instantly met by horrid smells, such that offended her senses to the extent of causing her to nearly retch. Fecal pungency hung thick in the stale cell. A dissonance of misery emanated from the animals, and they seemed agitated. Wendy made to retreat up to fresher air when she caught a glimpse of something not quite right in the pen. She covered her nose and ventured inward to see what it was.

In horror, she tried to scream but no sound escaped her. What she had seen was the mangled remains of a body, trampled by the animals. Broken bones, torn skin, blood, and entrails were strewn about as the animals jockeyed for space. As she looked in utter disbelief, she noticed the body was cuffed and chained to one of the support beams toward the rear of the stall. When her eyes followed the lead to the bolt, she saw more chains leading against the back wall. It was then her eyes met other eyes fearfully staring back at her.

The dark faces, black as night in the shadows, huddled together as far back as they could muster to avoid further assault from the livestock. Equally in terror of Wendy's presence, they shied away for fear of potential torment from her. They averted their eyes and cowered in the pen. Wendy, in shock, couldn't manage to speak, think, or make any other motion upon her discovery. Aghast, she just stood there staring, taking in the atrocity before her.

Negroes were not unfamiliar to Wendy, as many of the servants and scullery maids back in Kensington were of African origin. She had been raised with them in her life and was not at all discomforted by their presence. Those she had the privilege of interacting with throughout her life, particularly Liza, were nothing short of cordial and doting. The staff in her home were waged servants with liberties and freedoms not afforded to those in other parts of the world, or even England itself. She had adored these people and never saw them as anything less than parts of her daily interaction. Seeing these people chained to a wall amid beasts was nothing short of monstrous, particularly with one of their own splayed out like discarded rubbish. The awe sunk in and broke her heart instantly, tears welling in her eyes. Her only instinct was to run.

That night, Wendy lay in bed sleepless, thinking of those poor souls somewhere beneath her. Their sad eyes haunting her mind as they so desperately tried to avoid being stamped to death like the one unfortunate member. Staring into the darkness of her bunk, she wondered if she should say anything to her father. But what would he do? There was no way to set them free, was there? These were slaves, never would Captain Smythe think of letting them loose! But what if she could parley them some sort of freedom? Her mind raced unrelenting.

The next morning, having not slept, Wendy crawled out of bed weary and distracted. Their breakfast was provided, yet she was unable to eat, nor did she have the desire to taste anything. Guilt riddled her to the point of depression and discomfort. Mary noticed her daughter was not herself and urged her to eat,

"Wendy dear, you haven't touched your breakfast. You must eat."

Wendy snapped from her trance, "I'm not hungry today, I didn't sleep well last night."

George ignorantly interjected, "What's the matter with you? Eat, Eat!"

25

"I'd like to be excused, please. I'm not feeling well. I think I'll go for some air."

"But you cannot go by yourself, you know that." Mary protested.
"Please mother, I must. I need to... I just can't be here right now."

"Then I will come with you. I won't have you tripping into any of the crew's business."

George, still oblivious to the situation continued to shovel his meal down his gullet.

"Mother, I really don't..."

"I will accompany you, or you can stay here and eat your breakfast and wait for Lt. Allain to call for our daily walk."

"Fine!" Wendy exclaimed.

Mary and Wendy excused themselves from their breakfast, leaving George to himself to finish eating. Having learned not to concern himself in the matters of women, he stood from the table to dismiss them.

Wendy forged ahead of her mother in an attempt to gain distance from her, but Mary was quick to keep pace, grabbing her by the arm in the corridor outside their quarters.

"Wendy Darling! Stop this unbecoming behavior at once! This marriage arrangement is of no surprise, and for you to act in such a spoiled manner is unladylike!"

"Mother, this has nothing to do with the arrangements of my husband-to-be! How dare you assume I am so juvenile to still be so upset at that!"

Mary, now caught off-guard, was confused as to what plagued her daughter's countenance, "What bothers you so if it is not relative to our last conversation?"

Wendy stood facing her mother, fuming at the inquisition, not knowing the appropriate thing do to...

"Come with me," she said emphatically. Turning her mother, Wendy led her down the dank access to the hold she happened upon yesterday evening.

"Wendy, we are not permitted to…" Mary pleaded, but Wendy interrupted her, "I know. I came down here after I left you yesterday. I didn't want to stew around father, so I fled to the recesses where no one might discover me for some time. But in my escape, I came upon the most frightful of circumstances. I know not what to do, but I must warn you, Mother, what I am about to show you is the most revolting of sights."

Bewildered, Mary couldn't imagine what her daughter had in store for her but was led onward in sheer curiosity.

When they entered the space, the smell had worsened since Wendy's discovery the day before. The body of the dead slave had bloated and been picked at by the animals. Maggots crawled over the decomposing flesh appearing as though the corpse now writhed. Feculence intermixed with intestines in a repulsive disarray. Fractured bones protruded amid the blood-stained hay. A pig greedily snuffled into the carcass without care. Nearby, the remaining slaves wept, covered in their own excrement and vomit.

Aghast, Mary stood clutching her face in dismay at what Wendy brought her to behold. Wendy's eyes once again sorrowfully connected with a few of the captives. Still afraid, they averted their eyes for fear of hapless abuse.

"I didn't know what to do Mother…" Wendy spoke mournfully.

Mary, still in shock, couldn't make words at the moment. Wendy shook her to regain her attention.

"Mother, I didn't know what to do. I found them yesterday. I couldn't sleep for knowing the plight of these poor souls."

"I'm afraid there is nothing we can do, my child…" Mary whispered despondently. "We cannot save these men, I'm afraid. They are destined to their fate now… All we can do is comfort them in their suffering."

"NO!" Wendy cried pleadingly. "We must tell Captain Smythe to release them at once! We can tell father to make him…"

"Your father has no authority over the captain to force him to release them."

"But he is under our employ, is he not? We have paid him for our transport; Father is his superintendent…"

"Yes, we paid our fare, but your father has no jurisdiction over the captain at sea, on the captain's ship…"

"Then we will buy them. We will purchase these men for our own. We shall take them as ours on our arrival in Virginia."

"We have no present means to pay for them Wendy. And if we did, Captain Smythe would never free them while they are on his ship. They would remain locked down here away from everyone. All we can do is ease their misery. And we must not tell anyone, not a soul, that we know they are here. This will be our secret. I fear that we will be punished if we make known of this, and I fear they will be harmed worse. We will find the right times to visit them. Bring them food if we can."

Wendy couldn't protest her mother's thought because she knew she was right. In no scenario would they be allowed to roam about freely for fear of some risk of danger to the crew – or themselves. These were slaves, and their unfortunate destiny had been sealed. Wendy's heart sank now knowing the conditions of which these people suffered and thought of all the people she had known back in England. Had they endured the same plight before reaching their destinations and employ? Wendy felt less like a person and more like a monster contributing to their doom.

"I'm sorry…" she choked the words out softly as tears welled in her eyes.

The Africans didn't know what she was saying but could tell in her face she meant no harm to them. This understanding eased their fear, but only marginally because they still knew the men on the ship would torment them. As well, they were still subject to trampling by the animals, just as their lost brother had succumbed. This gruesomeness still terrified them because the corpse lay before them, fodder for the pigs and flies. There was nothing stopping one of them from becoming the next victim of this fate, and it was a pure chance when a 2,000-pound hoof crushed their body.

Upon this resolution, the women departed the abhorrent keep before they were discovered by any of the crew. The chains banged as the Africans cried out, desperate for salvation. Their wailing echoed deep into the cavity of Wendy's chest, burdening her with sorrow and helplessness. She wept silently as she trudged up the ladder. The memory would hound her until she could find a way to free those men.

Days passed with no change in the scenery above or below decks. Topside, the endless panorama of the ocean remained the same. Within, the slaves remained shackled to the wall, fearful of a horrible death. Being chained and vulnerable became a miserable norm, as they huddled amid the sickening stench and rot. Mary and Wendy had been unsuccessful in accessing them as frequently as they'd hoped but had still managed to check on them briefly a couple times. The charade bedeviled them, unable to express any feeling or concern to anyone. Their walks with Lt. Allain were uncomfortable, as they felt he was man with scruples and might rally to their aid; they just weren't willing to risk their access. The interactions became a falsehood; Lt. Allain oblivious to their secret.

Nearly a month had passed in their successful withholding of any knowledge of the slaves. By now the *Eagle* had tracked significant distance toward the Caribbean. They were almost half-way between either destination, and the monotony of the journey was weighing on many of the crew, as well as the Darlings. George had become irritable again, and pestered Captain Smythe regularly. He had often been banished to places away from the captain and did not take kindly to those directives either. However, in his relentlessness, he had preoccupied himself and as a result paid little attention to Mary or Wendy. In this case, they were afforded relatively unquestioned freedom from him. The crew, however, were a different situation.

It was during one of these nights, a handful of younger crewmen set to unauthorized drinking and let go to a bit of excess. The elder crewmen warned the junior sailors to knock it off, because if the officers or even the captain caught them regaling in such a way, they would find themselves at the mast in the morning.

With liquor in their veins, they boasted bravado in the face of this warning. Pressed again to settle down, the men quit the room with bottle in hand. The older sailors made no effort to stop them, for they wanted no association with the deviants.

The carousers found their way into the belly of the ship so they could continue their amusement uninhibited by killjoy salts. They found themselves in the stalls where they could revel without being heard by anyone else aboard the ship. Ill-behaved as they were, they figured tormenting the animals would be a bit of fun. In doing so, they unintentionally also found themselves among the captive slaves. By now they were fully drunk without control of any inhibitions, then took such atrocious advantage of the bound negroes. Without care, the sailors freely urinated on the slaves, whipped them with straps for laughs, and made such a commotion to startle the animals with intent to squash the slaves in such discomfort. After the childish antics no longer held their interest, one sailor took up a younger slave, smaller than he, and beat the slave so terribly, he lay limp, bloodied, and swollen to unrecognizable limit: an act of deliberate supremacy. The other slaves wept in such sadness, and averted their eyes, lest the white devils muster the energy to go another round. However, the alcohol had begun to subside, and the sailors had had their fun and made their way back to their hammocks for the night.

Two days passed before there was an opportunity for Mary and Wendy to check on the slaves. When they reached them, they were mortified to see the state the people were in. Deep cuts on their skin oozed as dried blood crusted on their dark skin. The young one who had been the victim of the beating lay naked and battered. His breathing was so labored, through a broken face, and his eyes swelled shut with violaceous bruises. Unable to care for the wounds and laying helpless in the filth, infection was setting in, and he had become febrile. He now lay dying amid the others.

Mary and Wendy burst into a fury at the sight. Immediately they sprang to his aid, lifting him up to give his limp body relief from the binding gravity in which he lay suspended. The manacles dug into his wrists as his weight pulled against the crude metal edges. Unresponsive, the body was heavy and spiritless, so much so, it took both women's efforts to prop him up. Sweat, blood and dirt stained their fine dresses. The sallow faces of the others looked on in shame as the women inspected their lacerations. Having no medical accessories, the best they could do was blot the wounds with their already ruined ruffled sleeves and skirts.

"We cannot go on like this, Mother; leaving them to the abuse they are subject to."

"I know Wendy, my heart is in pieces, but again, we are powerless to save them beyond attending to them."

After they had nursed the injuries, and eased the unconscious one's position, the two women knew they needed to get out of their dresses immediately. With sad eyes everyone understood the women must now leave, though they promised to return as soon as they could, despite the words meaning nothing to their patients. They cautiously made their way back to their quarters, desperately attempting to remain undiscovered by anyone. It was then that Lt. Allain found them, as he was leaving their place after calling on them for the day's outing. The women stood in shock and panic being trapped and motioned to retreat in hopes Lt. Allain would not notice their dishevelment. He did.

"My word!" He cried out. "Are you hurt? What has happened? Who did this? Tell me at once!"

"Ahhh, no... we are fine. Thank you, sir." Mary stammered unconvincingly.

"M'ladies, you are not fine! Your gowns are blighted with... blood! I ask again, what has become of you and at whose doing?"

"We know!" Wendy blurted out, tearing up. "We know about the slaves below," now in full sob.

Lt. Allain pulled back confused, alarmed, and afraid of what this meant.

"Did you know?" Wendy pleaded. "Did you know they are there? Did you know they are lying in the death of their own?"

"I know. Captain Smythe brought them on during our stop in Africa. They were to be secreted away from anyone, except for a trusted few of the officers."

"You are a good man, leftenant." Mary spoke firmly. "I cannot fathom someone with your supposed character would be so callous as to the treatment of these people."

"It is not my business, but that of the captain. I obey the orders given to me and ensure the operations of the ship run without issue, so the captain may conduct his business accordingly while in command. That is my position. If the captain of this ship chooses to take on human cargo, that is out of my control and shall not be a place for me to hold any emotion toward. I am sorry if this is not to your liking, but I am not sorry for my every attempt to get you and every other item – person or thing – safely to its destination."

"I understand your position, and I am in no place to tell you how to conduct yourself. What I cannot conceive is that you allow your men to take such liberties with those poor souls to the point of abject savagery."

"What do you mean?" Lt. Allain quickly countered. "Is that... Have you been down there with them just now? Is that their blood upon you? What did they do to you? Have they broken free?"

"Yes. We discovered them weeks ago and have been visiting them in secret. Just now we discovered them beaten, bloody and near death. Be it as it may to keep them chained up, but to abuse them in such ways while they are, is repugnant. One has already been killed by the animals, but the others have received a thrashing so detestable, we were compelled to provide what little aid we could."

"M'ladies, go to your cabin at once, and attend to yourselves. Do not come out until I call for you later. I will inspect the slaves myself upon this notice."

Nothing more was said, and they parted ways. Mary and Wendy retreated to their quarters to change out of their soiled garb and re-primp themselves to ladylike measure. Lt. Allain quickly made for the hold to assess the situation they had just described. When he stormed in, he startled the animals and slaves alike. The animals shuffled around cramping the slaves against the wall. The remaining slaves retracted in fear of another white devil approaching them so hastily. Here he stopped. The sight of the mangled corpse, nothing more than ragged flesh and broken bone strewn about by the animals was a shock. His eyes then shifted to the bunch whose wounds the women had attended, and the unconscious one, who sat in pooled blood and offal. He carefully approached to get a closer look.

What he discovered enraged him. The unconscious one was not breathing strongly, could not open his eyes for the swelling, and was bleeding out on account of the violent pummeling. The wounds of the others were becoming infected and would kill them all if not dressed. Lt. Allain was furious for the fact that his men had done this, and that Captain Smythe stood to lose much of his inventory in these men as a result. This would not sit well with the captain, but he had to tell him immediately. At this point there was nothing more for him to do, so he left to find the captain.

Captain Smythe was at his desk calculating distance and times with his maps when Lt. Allain rapped on his door ardently. "Enter..." he spoke annoyed at the alarm.

"Lieutenant, to what do I owe this urgency?"

"Captain, your 'secret cargo' has been compromised." At this, Captain Smythe looked up meet Lt. Allain's face.

"What do you mean, compromised?"

"Sir, it appears the captives have been subject to amusement and used as conquest by the some of the crew. One has been mauled by the animals, one lies near death, and the others sit with infected wounds. I fear your investment may be in jeopardy."

"They are savages, Lt. Allain. I care not of their condition, but of their value upon arrival to the auction block. I suggest you take less care over their accommodation and attend to the matters to which you are responsible."

"Aye sir. However, you should know that their current and continued state will not provide you profits at sale, for they will be deathly at best. Worse, you could stand to lose nearly half of your stock. Moreover, the crew now know these slaves are aboard, and without putting a stop to this behavior, the captain's property will quickly become target for further abuse."

The captain mulled over the objection presented.

"Root out the culprits and make an example of them. Forty lashes upon the mast each. Make sure the rest of them take note that they will receive my wrath so fervently, they will wish they were coddled upon their mother's tit, should I be apprised of any further contact with those macacoes. Take the surgeon and have him inspect them. Tell him to spare them from death however he may."

"Aye Captain."

Lt. Allain sought out the surgeon and escorted him to the keep. They were met with such a salutation to their nostrils, the surgeon covered his face with a dirty rag from his crude bag of tools. The pillaged slave had expired, and the release of his bowels spilled across the planks of the ship. Lifeless, he hung from the rusty chains, shoulders dislocated from the dead weight. The surgeon was unphased, as he was no stranger to the grisliness. Lt. Allain retched at the sight and smell.

"Not much I can do for this lot..." Mr. Sawyer said flatly.

"Clean the wounds of the living, Mr. Sawyer. That is the captain's instruction. Keep them alive. When you are done, you will help me carry the dead one above for disposal."

Mr. Sawyer made quick work of cleaning the gashes with stained rags. There was little else he could do for them. When he was finished, he packed his kit, wiped his face, and told Lt. Allain to monitor them. If the cuts turned colors and worsened, he would typically amputate. However, a slave without full dexterity was worthless at market. If any required this measure of attention, they would likely need to take other action. Lt. Allain acknowledged the surgeon's instruction with frustration, as this was not a task he desired to take on above his other duties. They then unshackled the dead one and lumbered the body topside. The presence of captive Africans at this point, would no longer be a secret. They dropped the body haplessly and gathered the crew.

"One or a few of you have exploited your position aboard this ship." Lt. Allain called out sharply, as the crew looked on confused.

"Your conduct has cost the captain directly and will not be tolerated. You who are responsible took it upon yourself to have your way with this thing, at the cost of its life. Come forward now, and face your punishment like a man, and it shall be fair and just."

The men all stood murmuring, looking at each other for the culprits to present themselves. Most of them were unaware the slaves were even onboard. All of them were afraid of the repercussions, as they knew just how bad the punishment could be. The five responsible shied away, aping the nescience of the others.

"No? None of you has courage to come forward? I give you this last opportunity to do so. Should you not, and I discover you later, I pledge to you in front of God and man, you will wish you had taken this offer. As well, all of you shall be docked your rations until we reach our destination. You will be granted a quarter ration of tack for the duration until this matter is resolved."

This angered the innocent, as punishment in the way of sustenance was dire let alone the only nicety they were afforded. They were halfway to the Caribbean islands at best by now, and the squalls that whipped up took every bit of strength to combat. Yet still, the guilty did not come forward, putting the others in deprivation.

"Mark my words, I shall ferret you out. You had your chance and squandered it. Those of you not responsible are condemned for the actions of your fellow shipmates."

The finality of this statement sent the men into an uproar, as Lt. Allain and Mr. Sawyer tossed the heap overboard unceremoniously. Pushing and shoving ensued as the men blamed each other. The guilty retreated from the squabble in hopes of being undetected. Doing so caught the eye of a the few who had taken their drams that night along with them. Drunkenness was a punishable offense itself, and now these men were guilty of another crime, for which everyone was now subject of.

"Them! It was them!" one of the men shouted as he espied them sauntering away from the group. Lt. Allain turned sharply to see the five crewmen apart from the others.

"Take them!" He ordered. They were quickly apprehended and set before him.

"What have you to say for yourselves?"

"T'was not our doing sir."

"Oy, t'was them. They took off the other night after gettin' inta the rum. They's disapear'd that night an' we din't see no more of 'em after we's turnt in."

Lt. Allain stood above them irascible. The undermining of his authority exacerbated his ire, and he breathed heavily.

"Mr. Sims, these men stand accused of unauthorized possession of liquor, drunkenness, and impropriety of the captain's personal property. They are to receive forty stripes apiece and will remain lashed to the mast for three-days' time."

The men were then bound around the mast, and the Bo'sun fetched the cat.

"Let this serve as warning to the rest of ye. You're now aware of the slaves on board belonging to the captain. If one or any of you are discovered disturbing them, you will be hung from the yard arm post haste. You shall be hung by your arms like the Lord our God, so you shall know the same misery, and be a public reminder for any others who care to tempt their fate. Mr. Sims, please deliver the lashings."

The bosun was a viciously skilled master at the whip. His punishments were notoriously brutal when doled out. The crack of the first snap in the humid sea air was like a shot. Blood and flesh exploded like macabre confetti. The boy's body writhed with no room to move as the others beside him bore witness to what they could expect. The young man struggled to maintain himself as the stripes counted seventeen, eighteen. By twenty his cries were voiceless and sweat drenched him, stinging the raw pulp of his back. By twenty-three, he had expired from the pain, and went limp, soiling himself. One of the onlooking crew splashed him with a bucket of seawater, waking him for the remaining belts.

The remaining four prayed as they awaited theirs. They each suffered similarly through what took more than an hour's time to complete. Mr. Sims made sure to prolong the exercise not only to belabor the sentence, but to maintain his own stamina. Typically, these instances involved only a couple men at most; it was rare to have five at once. Two hundred licks was an exorbitant amount and exhausting for the punisher.

When all was said and done, the crowd dispersed, and the offenders were left tied together to finish out the remainder of the three days' sentence. Destroyed, they languished in the unrelenting sun; their scars searing in the salty air.

While this was happening, Lt. Allain had reported back to Captain Smythe, informing him the derelicts had been discovered, and the punishment was currently being administered. Still the captain, seemed to care little, but thanked him for following through and just as quickly dismissed him, all without even meeting his line of sight. Once removed from the captain's chambers and the responsibility of the ensuing beating, Lt. Allain returned to Mary and Wendy.

The women had cleaned themselves up by this point, redressed, and were sitting in their room awaiting Lt. Allain's arrival. When he knocked on their door, their hearts skipped a beat at the surprising rap. Lt. Allain was agitated over the entire ordeal and was not in the most becoming mood when he greeted them.

"The situation has been resolved, the guilty parties found, and the property below attended to. The ladies shall not be escorted outside presently on account of the delivery of punishment to those parties. The surgeon has inspected the negroes and has thus instructed me to keep an eye on their injuries, so they do not worsen. I have no time nor the interest to attend to this matter, and as I am certain it shall be impossible to keep you from sneaking to their aid, I charge you with this responsibility. The rest of the crew have been strictly forbidden to approach them, so you should have no issue doing so. If you find they are failing, you may report this to me, and I shall deal with it as necessary. That is all. Good day."

IV

Roughly a week more had passed since the incident with the junior sailors, and they had returned to their labor. Mary and Wendy had continued to check in on the slaves, none of which succumbed to any worsened conditions on account of infection or injury. Lt. Allain recontinued the allowance of the women having their daily walks, and they respected the distancing of the conversation after establishing the knowledge he only cared if things were dire. And so, the days rolled into the next with little deviation from the previous.

One morning, dawn broke with a burning red sun and a dark blanket of clouds marring the distant horizon sky. The superstitious crew were uneasy as they trimmed sail in anticipation of a coming storm. The red sky was an ominous warning, and this put them all on edge. The helmsman surveyed the expanse ahead, watching for any disturbance in the wind, current, or ocean's surface. Thus far, there were no indications of change, and with cautious readiness they stayed their course. In hopes the storm would pass afar, they set a line alee to run hard from the threatening clouds.

By the afternoon, grayness ensconced skies and curtained the warming sun. With the barometer dropping, they were still trying to outpace the storm, but it was closing in faster than they could make for. The sea roughened with increasing chop and white caps. Snapping gusts of wind bit at the sails, and the temperature was dropping. They were not going to be able to outrun the squall, and so the crew prepared for hard going with an effort to at least skirt the worst of it. Lt. Allain instructed the Darlings to take safety in their quarters in anticipation of unpleasant conditions.

By evening, no stars were visible above and the winds began to howl. In the cold distance, the chop now roiled and turbulent waves caused the *Eagle* to jar in contest to the afront. With no escape, they were now committed to facing the tempest head on, providing any hope of besting it. Relentlessly they steered the ship into the crashing waves. The bow pierced the incoming wave before being thrust violently upward, then slamming down again and again.

The storm was in full force by the middle of the night, and the sustained jolting was taking its toll on everyone and everything. The Darlings held on for dear life in their cabin, desperately preparing for the next strike. Outside, the wind shrieked like a banshee and the sea gnashed vengefully. The crew who hadn't lashed themselves down, perilously attended to the combat forging onward with vigilant directive, navigating the riotous sea. The *Eagle* was under bare poles now, save for the fore, which was helping keep some semblance of speed against the roaring waves. The effort to keep her steady was nothing short of exhausting, as she battered through the waves for hours on end, never ceasing in the slightest. The hull groaned each time it lifted toward the heavens and bellowed woefully every time it smashed down. The ribs flexed in expansion and contraction at the weight of both her and the ocean respectively. Captain Smythe spurned the weather with a madman's passion, screaming into nothing, cursing Neptune's fury.

Throughout the night, the storm dogged the ship as it fought mightily against the onslaught. Progress continued, albeit negligible. More than anything the ship unsteadily rode out the storm in attempts to keep the heavy stern from fracturing. With each plunge she shuddered, and the rudder wrenched fiercely in protest. The winds continued to wail, and the cloud cover in the sky swirled apocalyptically. Wave after wave tossed the ship around like a bath toy.

In the early hours of morning, just before what should have been sunrise, a rogue wave sideswiped the *Eagle*'s prow. As it was punching through an oncoming wave, a cross current ran unexpectedly through and landed on the vulnerably exposed hull torquing the ship, the aft bulk of her still set in the passing wave. As the *Eagle* came down, she was pushed askew, perilously near rolling over. Had she been any further along in trajectory, she may have broached entirely sending everyone into the deep.

As the ship was thrown, it landed contortedly in the valley of the waves. Ensuing crests immediately twisted the ship in contrasting degrees. The immense pressure on the hull created such strain, it pushed the limits of its structural integrity. The twist threw the helmsman violently, ratcheting the rudder hard, shattering the connecting mechanisms beneath. At the same time, because of its height, the main was thrown against the force and collapsed in splintered response. Yard arms were torn from their attachments as they dragged in the passing waves. The cacophony of shattering timber, snapping lines, and ripping destruction was deafening, even above the din of the cyclone.

As the ship rolled precariously crewmen unlashed themselves and scrambled to cut the remaining lines of the mast, so it could be pulled freely away, otherwise it was certain to seal their briny doom. The mast tore away wildly once cut free, ripping the railings to pieces as it was sucked into the hungry sea. Others rushed below to see if any immediate repair could be made to the tiller. They were now fighting for their lives and salvation from the misery still yet to come.

Below, the Darlings, had been so ferociously tossed about, they agonized from the onslaught. Nauseated, bruised, and miserable, they clung to life in unbridled fear, having no visualization of the conditions outside. It is impossible to prepare for that which cannot be seen, and all they could do was brace themselves in suspension of the unknown. When the *Eagle* took its finishing blow, they were thrown from their bunks into a familial tangle of disarray. Pained and sick from the turbulence, their misery was their living nightmare.

Meanwhile, through tenured seamanship, the ragged crew had managed to fashion a temporary fix for the steering and were muscling the rudder against the tide. The ship was able to hold a course enough to avoid imminent danger but was not yet free of threat. In testament of determination, the exhausted men carried on through the morning, fighting against nature.

Toward the afternoon, the winds began to taper off from the full gale they had been. Flecks of light mottled the cloud cover above. The sea was still at unrest, and this was the most important time to remain vigilant, strong, and careful. They could not take for granted the decreasing conditions, because any negligence could still spell disaster. Until the seas were once again calm, and the winds easy, they were in no safer place now than when the storm was at its worst, particularly with a damaged ship.

By evening, the seas quelled to a disorganized mess, and the *Eagle* floated along at the mercy of the current. No canvas adorned the remaining rigging. The crew was now expired and took a long overdue rest. Like drowned rats, they lay where they fell. Captain Smythe and Lt. Allain surveyed the damage, taking report for the repairs necessary to get them to port. The Darlings emerged cautiously, desperate for fresh air.

As Captain Smythe tallied the toll, he paid little mind to the Darlings, unconcerned with their presence amid the wreckage. Ignorant to the cost of being caught in such a storm at sea, the carnage was astounding in their eyes. Their stomachs dropped at the thought of being stranded in the middle of the ocean after all they had endured. Lt. Allain shepherded them out of the way of any lingering danger and assured them they would soon be under way again.

"Worry not, Darlings! Though it looks dire presently, these men are fully capable of getting this ship back to working order."

"Lieutenant," George winced. "The ship is in utter disrepair. You've no mast to hang sail and carry us onward."

"This is not catastrophe, despite what it may seem. Considering what we've just survived, no men were lost, and we are not at the bottom of the sea. We took a blow at the loss of the mast, but had we attempted to save it, it would have spelt our demise. We've still the fore and aft upon which we will still fly canvas. We will not make such time as we would fully rigged, but we are still within our threshold to capably sail. The men will make quick work of the repairs necessary to get us under way once again."

George could only stand by, taking in the scene before them. Captain Smythe approached, still assessing the damage sustained to his ship, but also knowing it was better to address the family now, instead of being pestered later when his attention would be required elsewhere.

"Greetings, Darlings. I trust Lt. Allain has informed you of our situation?"

"Y…yes, Captain. He was just explaining everything, assuring us we are still seaworthy?"

"Thank the almighty, yes. That was one hell of a storm we've just weathered, but by my take, we are all accounted for, and the working order of my ship is manageable overall. We shall soon be back on our course, and upon our arrival, I will have a mast refitted. This will delay our departure for America of course, but from there we will make excellent time with full sail and the northerly current. I'm confident we will still make our arrival in good time."

Instead of finding fortune in the news that they could still progress, George instinctively resorted to perturbance and clapped back, "Yes, I hope so, Captain. This setback concerns me as we sit here lamely. You assured me we wouldn't encounter such storms along the way, and now here we are, adrift following a calamitous event."

Unable to bite his tongue, given the charged circumstances and expense to be incurred, the captain erupted at George, "You vile, contemptuous man! I am not God! I do not control the heavens and most certainly I do not control the weather produced by them. Asea, storms are as commonplace as any passing fancy you might have sitting highly on your throne. I need not explain to you this is *my* ship and my means of livelihood! Damn you and your impatience and inconsolable personage."

The rashness of the captain's retort was not unjustified, though social decorum might have dictated a less brusque exchange. Then again, societal convention didn't exactly apply to the etiquette aboard a ship, though the captain had managed as best he could, given present company. At this point, his temper was uncontrollable, and George had provoked him.

Not one to be diminished, George puffed up ready to counter with some inconsequential threat, but the captain, silenced him before he could get the first word out.

"No, sir. You will say nothing. Not one word have you about my business and our lot cast. My men have just endured a mighty soaking hell and will make quick work of righting our course. You will stay out of their way and provide nothing in the way of criticism, or as the lord as my witness, I will remove you from this ship here and present."

Mary pulled her husband back. Abashed, he flung free of her and scrambled to assault the captain. It happened all so quickly, that Lt. Allain naturally leapt at him to shield the captain from the attack. This collision sent George toppling to the deck in a discordant melee. The yelling had already garnered the attention of some of the crew, but now, they were all eyes. The commotion was so disruptive, they began to gather curiously. Had anyone of them dared lunge for the captain, they would be killed on spot. But George wasn't a subordinate sailor, he was the reason they were on this venture, and statutorily an equal by class. How the captain responded would determine his position, not only in the eyes of the crew, but his reputation as a commander.

Flailing to regain footing, a formidable silhouette appeared over top of him. It was the captain, and he stood with absolute ire welling inside. He held a pistol at the offender lying prone beneath him. Mary and Wendy clutched each other at the sight of the weapon aimed at the disgraced patriarch. Fear gagged them at the thought they might witness the death of their husband and father right before their eyes. The world had gone silent, and every soul looked on. George held up a pleaful hand as terror gripped him.

"I have provided you more than ample opportunity to comport yourself as a gentleman and guest should aboard my ship. Yet, from the onset, you have chosen to challenge my authority as though you believe I should answer to you. Until this moment, I have extended my courtesy permitting you the benefit of existing in a capacity which you might find familiar and comfortable. I see now, this was my folly. I say this, and you will hear me: You have no sovereignty over me, and you will no longer regale in my grace.

Nay, you shall no longer know the comforts I have provided unto now. You will no longer be permitted to speak to my crew, my officers, or myself. You, and your family will henceforth remain secured in your quarters for the duration of this crossing. Should I, or anyone witnessing this transgression, find you outside of your confines, I shall, without hesitation, make usage of this pistol of which it so hungrily yearns."

Defeated, George bowed his head, nodding in understanding. Lt. Allain assisted him up off the ground. Without further instruction, George tidied himself and turned with his head held high, falsely maintaining his pride. Mary and Wendy relieved and equally humiliated, also turned, holding each other, and retreated. Lt. Allain followed behind them. It bothered him that he would no longer have interactions with Wendy, but his allegiance was to the captain, and this was how it must be.

As they departed, Captain Smythe holstered his pistol, finally noticing the audience.

"Get to work, the lot of you!" he yelled angrily, and they all disbursed to begin salvage.

Lt. Allain ushered the Darlings in to their confines, doing his best not to make prolonged eye contact. Though, as Wendy passed, their eyes met, and between them, unspoken disappointment was conveyed. Behind them, he closed the door. With his key, the bolt dramatically clanked into place, locking them inside. He could hear the women weeping. Not a word came from George.

Back on deck, the crew had begun the process of repairs, first clearing the splintered wood, busted tackle, shorn lines, and other flotsam strewn about. The jagged stump of the mast seemed so unnatural now, without the towering pole filling the gap. On the starboard, the railing and deck edging were completely gone so men were fashioning stanchions from the scraps to provide structural integrity. Seasoned hands scurried the ratlines reworking the rigging so the remaining sails could be unfurled.

Under deck, the jostled cargo and food stores were inspected. The more able carpenters of the company were fast at work rebuilding the steering connections. Pulleys had been ripped from their homes and the tiller ropes hung slack. Comparatively, the task of reassembling the linkages was the most difficult and most important challenge of the entire undertaking. Without steering there was no purpose to any other repairs or sail, therefore wrestling the blocks back into place, tensing the lines, and connecting the rudder stock all required abled know-how.

Throughout the cold night, they labored to bring the *Eagle* back to life. Captain Smythe drove them hard to complete the work by morning, so they could make way quickly before dawn. An idle ship was easy prey, and he had no designs of sitting dead for any extended period. Under the cover of night, they would not be so easily espied as they would in daylight. Torchlight was only permitted below deck in steerage, and no light was permitted topside.

By midnight, the rudder and wheel were reconnected and operational. The lines and pulleys had been reset, but only to the extent that they served their purpose. The whole system needed to be properly attended in port, but barring any stress or rough seas, they could manage to limp along the rest of the way. Theoretically the conditions should be fairly smooth from this point, so they stood reasonable chance to make it to their next stop without incident; it would just be slow going given their plight.

Once the ship was deemed sea-worthy, a skeleton crew was selected to maintain course through the night, and the others found a place to lie for the remaining night hours. Come dawn, they would all be rested enough to dig in on the daylight sailing, and test limits of the *Eagle,* and the others would take their much-deserved respite.

Throughout the night, the winds were mildly scattered, and the sea was still calming following the storm. The midnight watch crept onward, fearing any jolt or jar might loose the repairs made. Every creak, groan, and splash was met with utmost apprehension. Tensely they kept on making up what time and distance they could.

In their current state, they needed to make Barbados as quickly as possible. There they would be protected and could make proper repairs to finish their remaining run to America. Being a Dutch-English outpost, they would find favor on the island and could attend to their total needs while they were landed. It was also a perfect stopover without having to navigate Spanish waters, or the interior of the Caribbean, known for troublesome passage. From there, they could proceed north with newly rigged sails could make quick transit with the help of the Gulf Stream.

That morning, the skies were still greyed but gave way to a gradient of warming orange streaks. Clouds still peppered the distant horizon as a reminder of what had passed. By the afternoon the sun burned off the remnant clouds, giving way clear skies and warmth. As lovely as the weather had turned, so too had the seas. However, this was the result of a void in the winds. The ship, with only limited sail, crawled along, unable to reach. There was not enough energy to propel the cumbersome vessel along at any high rate of speed. And so, they crept trying to inch along to their destination, making the most of their predicament.

Curious dorados bulled the hull of the ship, inspecting the giant mass. The banging against the hull echoed in the bowels of the ship, terrifying those unfamiliar with the phenomena. Their brilliant colors refracted in the sunlight beautifully. And though more a nuisance than anything, they were an exotic change of scenery, even if they were below the waterline. The men hurled harpoons at them in attempt to score a delicious meal, but the deftness was that of lightning, and they would dive deep in avoidance of the haphazard spears. Eventually they landed seven sizeable catches and hauled them aboard. The dorado was such a delicacy, so delicious, that they were cleaned and prepared for eating that night.

The fresh catch was such a welcomed meal for the crew, and because of surviving the storm, the crew celebrated with a feast to the joy of forward progress; despite the crawling pace. Captain Smythe permitted the fete to the extent the revelry did not devolve into disorder, mostly because he was as gleeful of having fresh catch to eat himself.

The next morning, everything and everyone was back to rote process, and the men were busy at their tasks. The majority had begun scrubbing the decks following the cleanup from the storm. The lines were recoiled, and the cargo re-balanced. The helmsman carefully navigating the winds to keep the *Eagle* running true. Atop the aft mast, as best as could be managed, the lookout kept watch on the horizon. The day was warm, the sun was bright, and the seas were moderately calm, a perfect day for sailing. After everything they'd endured, all was feeling proper again.

By midafternoon, the sun was overhead and burning hot. On the horizon a figure could now be seen trailing off to port. The lookout espied it after the sun was no longer low on the horizon. Calling for a monocular, he trained his eye on the object.

"SAIL Mr. Lewis! Port tail, full sheets!"

Mr. Lewis, the helmsman, spun around to put his eyes on the trailing vessel, but he could only make out a faint shadow. Hardy, the lookout, climbed down, and handed him the spy glass to take a look. Holding course, Mr. Lewis put the instrument to his eye and sighted the ship. From this far, he couldn't make out a signal, but they needed to prepare, regardless. In these waters, it could be anyone, and with the storm, they too could be seeking deliverance from weather. But it could also be foe, and they could not be too careful in that regard. They were handicapped and could not fend off a predator if they needed to.

"Alert Mr. Allain and the Captain." Mr. Lewis said impatiently.

"Aye, sir" and Hardy leapt off to find them.

When he returned, both Captain Smythe and Mr. Allain accompanied him. Mr. Lewis was fixed ahead, attempting to gain speed as best he could manage. Captain Smythe peered aft to make out the figure or signet. It was still a fair distance off, perhaps a few hours' time, but it was closing in on them. No colors flew from the mast, so he still could not make out who they might be. This vexed him, and he directed Lt. Allain to ready the men. And so, he turned and mustered the crew to stations.

"All sail, full on! Ready the guns!"

The crew sprang into action, including those below off duty. Bare feet pounded the planks, as the few cannons they had were wheeled out and made ready for purpose. The sails and lines were tended to maximum allowance. The armory was unloaded, and weapons stored inconspicuously accessible. Men readied to run the ship in countermeasure setting the guns and waiting in formation as a second wave of protection, should the railings be breached. They were the last defense against full capture.

The following ship was still closing in on them. Mr. Lewis tracked the wind to fill the sails and felt the helm arguing in response. It was all or nothing at this point. They had to push to keep distance between the ships in hopes of making it to safety. Unfortunately, the ensuing ship was faster, lighter, and had all sail at its disposal. It was an arduous race.

"Fly the colors on my command…" Captain Smythe ordered.

The men responded by preparing the flag to be hoisted on the aft mast, as a signal of their nationality. This was their hope that the trailing ship seeing they were English, would in turn recognize, and come along peaceably. Or, if they were of a less friendly nationality, they might second think approaching an English ship and steer off. Under a full outfit, they could have held the chase and kept a good lead ahead of the pursuer. Flying their flag at the wrong time could spell disaster. There was only one way to find out, and they had to play their hand.

"Hoist!"

The ship had closed in on them enough that the *Eagle* could still run ahead, but they still couldn't make out any familiar markings, and it was as though the ship itself had just flown in from nowhere. Like a jockey at the end of a race, Mr. Lewis beat the sheets in a frenzy, praying for more speed. Captain Smythe kept an eye on them, calculating possible maneuvers and watching for their guns. No colors had been raised by the company, and this made him worry that he had played his hand too soon. If it were an English ship, they would have flown their flag in response, and everyone could have eased off. Yet, no flag had been raised, not even an enemy's colors. They were closing in fast.

"Prepare...! Hold steady for attack. She shows no colors and still encroaches. Soon she'll be in shot range, make ready for fire."

"Captain,"

"Yes, Mr. Lewis?"

"We are as full of sail as we can be. I can't get us any more ahead of them sir."

"I know Mr. Lewis; you're doing a fine job. Keep the wheel full ahead."

"Aye sir. But I see the tale ahead, in a moment, we could come about hard to port and possibly break loose of the imminency. We'll come across 'em, and unless they intend to run us through, they should counter. It's not much sir, but we could give ourselves a gap before they can come around, sir."

Lt. Allain's head was on a swivel as he previewed the conditions ahead, and the incoming aggressor. He knew that if they did peel off, the other ship would quickly counter and be in better position to broadside them. But, if they could gain more time and wind to power on, they could at least delay the meeting. They were in no position to fight, though they would if it came to it. But, if the intruder was not a violent party, they could just wish to converse or carry on. But they hadn't shown colors. Captain Smythe needed to decide quickly. He watched. He waited.

"All hands, make ready to come about on Mr. Lewis' command."

The men scrambled to stations, ready for the tack, and called down below to ready those otherwise unaware of what was happening topside.

"Ready…." He called.

"Aye!" they yelled in response as the waited for the command.

"PULL!" Mr. Lewis finally cried out and sent the ship's wheel spinning.

The men wrenched for all they were worth, and the sails whipped, heeling the *Eagle* hard around. With a precision unspoken, when the men saw the sails luff and catch, again they hauled the lines to set against the wind's breath. Sea spray splashed up, atomizing in the air, and dousing the men forward. The *Eagle*, still weakened from the storm, held strong and righted into the changed path. The men tied off and watched aft for what their pursuer reply. They needed to be ready for anything, especially shots fired.

The pursuing ship, continued on its forward path, with enough distance between them to not even flinch. In turn, they being skilled sailors themselves, came easily to port, now positioned alongside on the *Eagle's* stern. The gunports raised and out rolled the cannon. From the bow, the chase gun was loaded and aimed at its intended target.

From the *Eagle*, the entirety of the crew could now see the men challenging them. Swarthy faces lined the rails, eager to catch their prey. A more villainous-looking bunch never hung from the gallows on Execution dock. Dread consumed them, and they stood frozen in time, awaiting their next command. Captain Smythe stood, knowing they'd made a grave mistake with their maneuver. It was a risk he took in hopes of shaking the other ship, but it only proved to give them a prime position against them. Mr. Lewis, raving mad was still focused ahead desperate to beat them on the line.

The cannon shot shattered the silence.

The shot was a warning shot. It was not meant to strike the *Eagle*, but to signal there would be further volley if they did not heed and surrender the pursuit. The pealing thunder of it echoed in the emptiness as the ball splashed explosively ahead of the prow. Captain Smythe feared the worst, as he should. He'd miscalculated their opportunity for escape, condemning his ship and crew to the mercy of these pirates. It had happened. It was real. He knew they could not win in a fight, and must now think about the crew, cargo, and his ship. Oh, and the Darlings… my god… the Darlings!

"Mr. Lewis, we've been bested. Drop sail. Leftenant, go immediately below and guard the Darlings. I will do all in my power to disguise the purpose and contents of our voyage, but in the happenstance, I am unable to belay them, I will need you standing as guard. Go."

At once, Lt. Allain fled below deck to serve as protector to the Darlings armed with a brace of pistols. The crew, dejected in their captaincy to flee or fight, disappointedly dropped sails, sending the *Eagle* to a slowing halt. Anger welled in the men knowing they might be killed for no reason upon boarding and thus denounced any loyalty to Captain Smythe at this point. His relinquishment was not their idea of salvation. It was subterfuge to protect his interests. His capital. His ship.

When the pirates came alongside the *Eagle*, the grappling hooks were thrown across, biting mercilessly, grabbing hold like a fly trapped in a spider's web. The men had not even weaponized themselves and collected dolefully along the opposing rail afraid of being murdered, tortured, or captured.

V

When he stepped aboard the *Eagle*, a darkness veiled the atmosphere and trepidation enraptured the crew. He was lumberingly tall, dressed as fancily as one could have ever imagined. Hair, black as the darkest night curled to his broad muscular shoulders, tied with an opposingly delicate bow. A beard equally as sable cascaded from his face. His eyes, piercing blue like the blooms of scorpion grass, and a scar than ran across his left brow to his cheek. His polished black boots thundered under his cadaverous stature upon the planks. He was handsome yet fearsome all at once. Charismatic and domineering. Good and evil. And the hook... All eyes were on that hook adorning his right arm where a hand should have been. Their worst fears were realized.

No marauder on the open waters was as nefarious as James Bartholomew, otherwise now known as "Captain Hook," save for his predecessor, the infamous Edward Teach - Blackbeard. Hook had served under Blackbeard and still revered him to this day. He had served as bo'sun but ascended into second-in-command once Blackbeard had ostracized then first mate, Israel Hands. James was one of the few men in the cabin that fateful night Israel was shot in the knee. As he recalled it, the room went black as Teach blew out the candle. The sudden flash of the pistol lit the space between them, and Blackbeard's face could be seen resembling the horns of Hell.

However, in his ever-yearning desire to assimilate into high society, Teach "retired" to North Carolina. He had made a bargain with the governor and attempted to live out his days off the account. However, if anyone knows the deep-rooted nature of Blackbeard, this was never going to last. A man so famous cannot just wane into history so blithely. But it was during this time, the crew were left to their own devices. Teach kept a skeleton crew on the ready, but most had either disbanded, been captured, and killed, marooned on the Queen Anne's Revenge, or signed on to other crews. Israel Hands, now maimed an unable to serve in the capacity he had prior, had signed with Captain Flint. This is where James Bartholomew's opportunity prevailed.

Hungry to carve out a future for himself and not sit idly by, the enterprising James Bartholomew gathered a crew and set off in a brig captured as a prize. Teach blessed the ship to him and wished him fair winds and following seas as the new captain, carrying on his demonic legacy. And so, the new captain and crew set sail for Jamaica in the newly christened *Jolly Roger*.

During all of this, Captain James Bartholomew, built a lustrous career, parlaying everything he had learned from Teach, adapted through his own rakish mind. He made a name for himself, but no moniker ever stuck, as he was not yet known by his present title; so, he was able to skirt purview of authorities, because no one could pinpoint "Captain James." Ultimately, this non sequitur afforded him a thin margin to capitalize on the burgeoning Caribbean trade routes.

Captain James was the most feared pirate to ever sail under the black flag during his time. He was an ogre of a man, and as skilled a sailor or buccaneer could ever aspire to be. He was diabolical in his methods and actions. His crew never questioned him, pledging undying loyalty, mostly out of fear for themselves, but also because the spoils were so rich. Nearly every prize they captured issued reward, making them royalty among the brethren.

"Greetings and Salutations, my dear men. I do applaud you for foregoing the formalities of battle. I gleefully appreciate the opportunity to keep you afloat, as I do say that you are quite the more valuable above the water line." He said, his voice velvetly scathing. "And to whom do I owe the courtesy of providing me with such a catch?"

The crew parted, revealing a very agitated man, blistering with rage at his own blunder, but also at such a charade of pomp.

"'Tis I" Captain Smythe spoke up.

"Very good then, Mr...?"

"*Captain* Thomas Smythe. Captain Hook, I understand, you are called?"

Hook cooed, specifically ignoring titles. "You may call me James."

"I will do no such thing you cur. Just who do you think you are?"

"Devil to some, savior to others. But let us not concern ourselves with such insubord'natries, shall we?"

"We are but God-fearing men aboard this ship, and we intend to make our way..."

"Tut, tut, tut. We shall all be on our merry way soon enough."

Hook, surveyed the ship, casting his glance over a multitude of men who dared not look him in the eye, nor muster behind their captain for solidarity. It was about this time, Hook's bo'sun climbed aboard the *Eagle*. He was wiry, calculated, stern, and intent. He wore pantaloons of a wine-red color with a hemp tunic that hung loosely off his shoulders, and a kerchief around his sinewy neck. His lean figure was an offset to Hook's coifed cadre, making them both together, an intimidating pair. He was balding, with white stubble along the sides of his head and rosy cheeks. He wore ill-fitting spectacles to help him read, which he peered over most times.

"Smee, do take inventory with Mr. Teynte. I shall like to know of what our prize consists."

"Aye Cap'n" Smee replied, pushing his glasses back upon the bridge of his nose.

"If Mr. Smythe would be so kind as to provide us the ledger of his ship's contents, we shan't make a mess of things."

"I'll do no such thing. We are but ord'nry seamen on our way to the Carib, set to take up employ to a plantation owner in need of shipping crops."

"Yes. You see, I'd like to believe you, sir. However, I have been tracking you for some time now, and I do find it unlikely that you are not presently laden with precious cargo. You see, your ship lies heavily below the water line. And, why else would you attempt to run against me and my ship while you are so obviously in disrepair?"

"You bore no colors, you bastard! We flew ours, yet you responded naught! Of course we should run!"

"Oh, you're right. If you'll please forgive me, where are my manners. Men, do hoist our flag?"

At this late juncture, Hook's crew raised their black flag, adorned with the death's head, a crossed bone and sword, and a hook piercing a heart. In a time where God was very much a part of a sailor's daily life, seeing the death's head flying in the breeze was a haunting symbol of what terror awaited anyone captured by a murderous lot who brandished it. It was an icon designed to instill fear, and any man who had the misfortune of sighting it, would wish for expedient delivery. But, the crew of the *Eagle* already knew what fate potentially awaited them, so the flag only drove home the point.

Smee began to go to work on taking record of their prize, but Captain Smythe obstructed him, prohibiting him from advancing.

"I say again, you'll make no collection of value from this ship, and I won't have you ransacking my provisions. Damn you for dogs and be gone with your lecherous wont, lest I cast you off to the hell you deserve!" With hostile opposition, Captain Smythe spat on the ground at Hook's feet.

Hook, calmly turned and stood before the captain. The hook shimmered in the light as he scratched his lip with it. Smee turned, stepping abreast of Captain Smythe, seeing the red fire in Hook's eyes. Captain Smythe jostled for his pistol to take a stand against the ruffian.

In the blink of an eye, Captain Smythe lay dead on the deck of his ship. Black Caesar had been guarding the whole time, watching for any spurious action. He had a brace of pistols loaded, and when he saw Captain Smythe go for his, he fired one shot, striking the opponent in the jaw. Gruesomely, his head exploded, and he dropped dully to the ground. Blood and bone splattered Smee, only inches away. It was over before anyone could conceive what transpired. Hook stood unfazed. Smee, removed his glasses and wiped them clean of the matter.

"Tis a shame" Hook spoke irritated. "I try, and I try, and yet death always follows me. Now you have no captain to speak for your account. And I have grown weary of this charade. Mr. Teynte, Smee, if you would, please now take inventory of my ship."

"The rest of you, should you stand in my way, you will not be afforded such swift delivery from your living status. While we are attending to our affairs, I encourage you to consider your future. I offer you one opportunity to join ranks with me. Otherwise... well, you know how this works, don't you lads?

"Mr. Starkey, will you and the others please take care of our guests?"

At his request - more accurately command – the Gentleman Starkey and the heavily tattooed Bill Jukes corralled the bystanding crew, forced them to their knees and bound them.

Below deck, Lt. Allain had been guarding the Darlings awaiting safe call. He heard the shot, and the thud of something falling to the planks above him. Armed with a blunderbuss, he had prepared it and had it on the ready. He had no comprehension of what was happening topside, but he had sworn to protect the family. His palms began to sweat, and his nerves were on the highest of alert.

Down the ladder came Hook's men, led by Skylights, followed by Cecco, Whibbles, Black Caesar, Smee and Ed Teynte. Assuming all crew were topside, they foolishly proceeded without caution below. Lt. Allain was unwittingly prepared for battle, and when he saw the pirates come below so freely, he positioned himself on the ready. As soon as he had a clear view, he fired.

Skylights took the shot in the gut, sending him tumbling down the remainder of the steps below. Cecco, a fearless behemoth continued down, cutlass drawn. He was a muscular giant, one that any opponent would be hard pressed to overtake. Unaware of how many opponents he faced, nor from whence the shot came, he charged on to discover the corridor where Lt. Allain stood attempting to reload. Without ample time, he had to quickly abandon the gun to pull his saber in defense.

Cecco's blade landed with all his weight behind it just as Lt. Allain's came to meet it protecting him from a deathly strike. However, he was now pinned against the wall by an olive-skinned minotaur of a man and no room to parry. He struggled to push Cecco off him but strained at the overpowering might. With his dominant position, Cecco was able to hold Lt. Allain at bay, and tire him by strength. He then landed a knee to the abdomen, buckling Lt. Allain. It was like a medieval battering ram against his body, brute and crushing. He fell with the wind knocked from him, and unable to avoid the attack that came next. Yet still, he threw his counter, only to receive a sanguineous slash to his arm and thigh.

Regaining his footing, he advanced at Cecco but was deflected and caught by his throat in Cecco's burly hand. Choking for air as his windpipe crushed under the powerful squeeze, his face purpled and his eyes bulged. He flailed in attempt to land any sort of hack, but Cecco controlled his foe easily. He gagged for air, as consciousness faded. Cecco pulled him close, to look him in the eye as he dug his sword into his belly. Lt. Allain screamed in pain, but nothing short of a gurgle escaped him. Cecco jostled the blade deep before jamming hard downward. If it weren't for the pelvic bone, he would have been rent clean apart, entrails spilling out. However, Lt. Allain was grossly perforated, with crucial organs torn asunder inside the cavity. This wasn't enough to kill him in instantly, but he would quickly bleed out agonizingly.

Cecco let go of his throat, breath refilling his lungs, blood coughing from his mouth. Still no sound but gurgles emanated. The blood spattering at each labored breath. Tears streamed from his eyes from pain and sorrow. He collapsed to the floor grappling at the spilling gape. He had lost, in a most cruel and punishing way. Life slipped from him, as his mind raced across multitudes of thoughts: how he hated Captain Smythe for this; how he had failed Wendy and Mary; how he would never be able to ask for Wendy's hand; how he had tried; why? Cecco wiped the blood from his sword on the Lieutenant's coat and sheathed it in his belt.

During this escapade, Smee and Ed had gone about their business and were sacking the captain's quarters for the ship's ledger. Black Caesar sought to flush out any remaining crew attempting to hide. Whibbles aided Skylights topside to be attended to. He was bleeding out profusely and clutching his abdomen.

"Skylights was ambushed by down below, Cap'n. Cecc's made quick works of 'im. Th'ship's secure. Smee and Ed are tallying the prize now."

After Cecco's duel, he felt compelled to discover what the sentry was guarding. The door was locked, but inside he could hear people, people in fear. With a solid kick, he broke open the door to discover the Darlings holed up in terror. George stood ahead of the women as a protector, but not knowing what he could possibly do at this point. He would hope wit and instinct might prevail, but again, he was dumbfounded in the moment. All he could do was shield the women.

"Bendecimi!" He uttered at the sight of the family.

To George and Mary, he was a frightful man. He donned a freshly blood-stained shirt, a sword tucked in his waistline, billowing pantaloons hanging below his knees revealing bare shins and feet. He had a handsomely chiseled face with age lines, stubble, and a dark pencil moustache. Dark tanned olive skin, and sinewy muscles behind the costume; his chest taut and sweaty. He was a pirate, and this was the stuff of nightmares. To Wendy, he was romanticized fiction in the flesh.

"Salve!" he descanted with a smile and a slight bow, "Buon Giorno, amici! Good day, my friends. Don' be frightened. I'm not going to hurt you, and you don't hurt me. Please, come with me, so you aren't in any more danger."

"We'll do no such thing, you barbarian!" George howled in return, still standing ground ahead of the women.

"Tsk, Tsk. Please, ami, I do not want to hurt you or your beautiful women. And you have nowhere else to go. Come with me, and you won't end up like this one." Cecco, side stepped to show Lt. Allain bleeding out on the floor behind him. George's face went white, Mary gasped, Wendy shrieked and attempted to run to him, but Mary and George held her back.

"I tell you, he defended your honor nobly, but I had to put him down. You see, he shot my mate, and I can't have that, now."

Tears streamed down Wendy's cheeks, and the Darlings collectively motioned out of the cabin. Cecco followed, checking the recesses for any more surprises or people. As they stepped past him, Wendy knelt in a fit, trying to care for her sea faring beau. His eyes glazed, and stared through her, not at her. Wendy brushed the matted hair from his brow and cried. She kissed his forehead, as she sobbed, and was pulled away by her father.

"Come now child. You can't help him now." He said sullenly.
Wendy had heard many tales of the rogues of the sea, but the death that actually followed them was never *real*, until now. Hatred boiled inside her like an impregnated seed. She would cut *his* throat for this if she got the chance. But for now, they climbed the planks topside, only to find a band of imps scurrying about at various tasks. As they came through the companionway, her eyes met with his, and her heart sank. A glint of red fire burned in his pupils, and she knew right away it was the devil himself.

"Well, hello...." He cooed genteelly offering a slight bow. "And who might we have here, my good man." Seeing Wendy then with blood smeared upon her face and fine dress, he took a half step forward and asked, "Are you hurt my dear?"

"I's can't say, cap'n." Cecco replied. "The lady is fine, cap'n. Didn't harm a hair on their pretty heads. That's the blood of the mate that off and blasted Skys. Found 'em locked up down below. He was guardin 'em."

Hook speculated, now twisting the onyx moustache with interest. "Aren't you fetching, m'ladies. And you my good sir, quite the proper gentleman. To whom do I make my acquaintance? I do find it brusque not to know my fairer company."

Amazed at his eloquence for such a villain, Wendy was taken aback, though still rich with rage. George straightened his coat and addressed the captain. "I am George Darling, of Kensington. My business is with Captain Smythe, and we are due in the new world post-haste."

"Yes. George, from Kensington, I am no longer – nor may you be - concerned with your captain at present. What is it you do, my good man?"

"I don't see that as any of your business."

"Oh, but this is all my business. You see, sir, you belong to me now, and I must see that you fit my company's purpose."

"I am no such thing! Where is Captain Smythe? I am his employer and will not be deterred otherwise!"

George was getting hot under the collar again, as he was apt to do, but he was also forgetting the caliber of man he was bickering with. It was then that Captain Hook directed his attention to where the captain lay, unrecognizable, the innards of what remained of his head fodder for gulls. The morbid hump of the body, and the gelatinous pool of crimson, made George realize he was not in a position to hedge his way out of the situation.

"As you can see, Captain Smythe, shan't be joining us any further. Now, I ask again. What is it your purpose?"

George aghast and desperate, stammered, grasping at a plan or a thought to gain an upper hand. "I'm a man of power in Kensington. I see to the monies of commodities. I hired Captain Smythe to carry us to the colonies to arrange for new employ in the tobacco trade. It would serve you well to consider the value I can provide you with crop."

Hook contemplated George's statement. Would it serve him well? Could this man provide him benefit in the trade of tobacco from the colonies? No. Of course he couldn't. To a pirate, tobacco was nothing more than a vice. The value in the 'cash crop' was only worth it's share to England, or other places unable to harvest and dry it themselves. But the load it took to secure a return wasn't worth the effort to the pirates, especially since they weren't exactly on friendly terms with the depots in England.

It was also at this point, Smee returned from below making an awful racket. He called to Hook gleefully, as his prize was unveiled from behind him. Hook's eyes widened, and a teethy smile spanned his face. There, trapsing behind the mate, were the most precious prize of them all. A little over three dozen ebony slaves made their way into the blinding sun, shackled in a row to be presented to the captain.

"Sakes alive, Smee! You have once again proved your worth to me. Unbind these beautiful heathens and let them be free!"

"Aye, Captain. As soon as I find the key, Captain."

"Smee…"

"Yes, Cap'n?"

"You mean to tell me you don't have the key to these shackles?"

"Not yet sir. Didn't think I'd find such a prize as this. I'll check the ol' captain's pockets."

"Smee…"

"Yeah, cap'n?"

"Find those keys, or I shall feed you to the sharks next!" Hook shouted, spittle exploding from his emphatic frustrations.

Smee, ran off to the captain's bloated carcass. His hands made quick work to access the captain's pockets to no avail.

"No keys on the cap'n Captain."

Hook, thin on patience now, grappled Smee with his hook by the collar, and drilled a stare through his soul.

"By Hades' horns. Go to his cabin NOW and search for those damned keys!"

Smee hurried off to the captain's quarters post haste. Hook embarrassed by such ineptitude, felt a bit demeaned in front of his company. However, with the very real threat of death and his hook, he still controlled them by fear.

"You were saying?" He directed angrily back at George. "Ah yes, a man of monies and such… You see, sir, in my business, you are of no use to me. You serve me no purpose, and frankly, a man of your condition is no more than a risk or burden to me. And I trust this lovely woman is your wife? Such a grace, and seemingly too good for the likes of you! Count your blessings, sir. Alas, I will not be attending to your needs aboard my ship. And I regret that you have made a woeful deal with your late captain."

The Darlings were ushered away to await the outcome with the other sailors.

Smee came bungling back, carting the keys in hand, "Keys cap'n! I got 'em!"

"Very good Smee. Unchain them at once and escort them to our ship."

As Smee began unlocking the shackles, Hook addressed them, "My dear men, today you are free! I grant you clemency and the opportunity to participate in the functions of my crew. You are free men. I will not bind you to the wall, but you will work. If you do not, there are punishments befitting. Remember this day, that I saved you from your present hell."

"Now, gentlemen!" He then said, turning to the captive crew. "You have had your peace, and I give you this only opportunity. Any of ye who wish to go on the account, I welcome ye aboard. Stand now and make your mark."

Most of the crew stood at this point, ready to turn hand for the pirate life, but more for the chance at surviving this ordeal. Whether the decision was of genuine desire, lack of better options, or realization that whatever awaited them if they didn't surely wasn't an appealing alternative. Only the officers remained. The defectors were unbound, ungagged, and sent aboard the Hook's ship with the slaves. Here they signed their names upon the code and awaited further instruction. The officers who refused to sign aboard took their chances, because they were ranking sailors, and to go a'pirating would forever damn them. However, the defecting crew knew their opportunity to endure the pirate's life was as uncertain as anything that awaited them otherwise. The way they saw it, they could die adrift on the *Eagle,* or they could carry on to freedom and fabled riches. The choice wasn't a difficult one to make.

As Hook and his crew proceeded with their pilfering, the orchestra was nothing short of finesse. Smee directed, Ed tabulated, and Hook supervised like a tarrytown schoolmaster. Throughout the entire ordeal, he was calm and calculated, leaving nothing to question. His order was truly a polished process, from which he had clearly honed his craft. Despite the criminality of it all, it was actually quite a sight to behold.

By evening, the *Eagle* had been pared of anything and everything worth pillaging. Every haveable element of the ship had been transferred to Hook's. Beast, barrel, and battery were confiscated for their own use, leaving little but scraps behind. Since the *Eagle* was in such disrepair, the pirates did not bother to strip the sails for their own because they were in such tatters. By their reckoning, with only two masts, tattered canvas, and hardly a week's worth of food remaining, those left behind were now all at sea.

The time had now come for the pirates to heave off and be on their way. Hook's crew were now all aboard his ship preparing for their departure. Before taking his leave, he offered one last appeal to the men refusing to sign away. All of them, curbed along the railing were resolute, including the Darlings. George was beside himself, and for once, wisely did not challenge Hook. Albeit low, the body count was evident, and these men had no qualm in taking a life of anyone presenting obstruction, he sat dejected among the remaining few at a complete loss. However, one of the crew did voice up, knowing the outcome was bleak at best. If Hook didn't kill him now, the days adrift might very well.

"Come the devils what prey on the malevolence of your sort, and may it be strange and unusual, the punishment befitting you and your lot. Be off, you bastards. I curse your soul, and may you meet the purgatorious hell you deserve, you swine!" At this he spat at Hook's feet.

Unwavering, Hook replied smoothly, while twiddling the point of his hook, "I myself, am strange and unusual. I have afforded you the gift of life, and yet your ingracious inclination is meant to offend. My good man, you see, I *am* the devil what preys on what I please. So, to your ineptitude, and that of your former Captain, you have chosen your fate. Or, in your words, a *'purgatorious hell.'*"

"Smee, if you will please bind them in the chains of the slaves, and let's be off."

One by one they were clapped in the steely fetters linked around the rail posts. They were stripped naked to bear the worst of the unobstructed conditions, both night and day. When it came to the Darlings, the same was imposed upon George, to which he complied as he wept defeatedly. Mary was also stripped of her gown and left among the men; she too wept at the gravity and embarrassment, fearing for her daughter. However, a different treatment was accorded to Wendy, who came last. With ironical politeness Hook raised his hat to her, and, offering her his arm, escorted her to the side. He did it with such an air, he was so frightfully distingué, that she was too fascinated to cry out.[i] She was captivated by his dashing eloquence yet riddled with fear all the same. She had been selected by the fiend, separated from her parents, and made to essentially parade across the deck on show for all to see.

Everything was final. The direness of the situation was locked in at this point. Smee and the others stepped back inspecting their work with pride. They collectively agreed in silent accord they had done a proper job, then awaited their captain's approval for dismissal. Knowing they expected this, he smiled and signaled with a slight genuflection of his head. They then wiped their dirty hands on their trousers and hopped back onto their ship where casks of madeira awaited in celebration.

"Dear gentleman, and m'lady, I bid you adieu. Our time together has expired, and I must take my leave. I thank you for your company in the time we had together. Au revoir, and good day."

Wendy, was then led by Hook toward his ship, still attached on his arm. She was terrified but knew she could not break free from his grasp. Mary screamed so virulently, her voice broke, and tears cascaded from her eyes. George, ashamed of his inability to protect his family and his only daughter, tried to assuage his wife. There was no consoling her, so he redoubled his guilt at the hurt she suffered. He was beside himself so, that he could crawl into a cage, and spend the remainder of his days as nothing more than a dog.

Wendy glanced behind over her shoulder to let her mother know she would be fine. With her eyes, she wished to impart *"Do not worry for me, dear mother. You have taught me well. I love you. I must be strong now, and you must also."*

VI

Wendy watched forlornly as the *Eagle* slid further and further out of sight. An unrepairable hole was carved into her heart, so much that she was numb. She couldn't cry, she couldn't protest, she couldn't move. Her parents were stranded, left to die a slow miserable death among those few left aboard. Her guardian had been slain protecting her, whom she held in her arms with those empty eyes. All around her the pirates scurried about while Ed Teynte tallied the spoils and divvied the rewards accordingly. Lost and alone she stood as everything she knew and loved faded on the void horizon.

The setting sun was a backdrop of angry reds, oranges and purples accentuating the revelrous men. Night was creeping in ominously faster than normal it seemed. Wendy's dejection turned into apprehension as reality gripped her. She was a prisoner among pirates; men who were notorious for debauchery and destruction. What would become of her now? Where would she end up? Was there any possible outcome of this situation that didn't end in death? What would these tossed men do to her? Her breath began to heave, and her heart pounded. Anxiety consumed her, and she began to look around in a panic.

Smee eventually approached her and offered her dispatch from her despair. He was an empath of sorts, if one like him could be, and had the clarity to recognize her discomfort from across the deck. A gentle fellow, Smee always looked after others, particularly the captain. It seemed he was always attending to Hook's whims or what-have-yous.

"They're not such a bad lot, ya know…" Smee spoke out beside her. She wasn't fully aware he had come up. "A lit'l rough around the edges, but good through and through once you get to know them."

Aghast, Wendy snapped back, "I don't want to get to know them. I've been stolen, and you stand here as though I'm interested in delighting with these thugs?! You are an uncouth band of rogues and have killed men in front of me! No good man kills another for naught!"

Smee calmly let her vent. Obviously, this wasn't an easy predicament for a young woman such as she was. He sucked on a back tooth, and when she had finished, he offered a counter point. "Aye, tis not a bountiful way, killin' others for sport. But do you not applaud your countrymen when they go off to battle enemies of some selfish king? Are they not regaled when they return as heroes of the crown?"

"What you do is hardly the same! We were not in battle; there was no war being fought. You chased us down, captured us, and killed innocent men! And you are certainly in no grace of the King."

"You can't see it now, but we's don't aim to kill when we take a prize. But we shan't be taken for dandelions either. Your captain attempted to murder ours. It was either ours or yours, merely defense you see. And the gentleman below, guarding you? Fired upon my mate. All but killed him with that shot, he did. We had to end him for savin' 'im of his own miserable sufferin'. Your man might've then killed me or Cecco next? You think it not fair we protect ourselves?"

"You're brutes! You took our ship as marauders and deserved to be cut down. You're a far cry from the Royal Navy and should never be held as heroes!" Wendy lost the irony for which she had, until today, held pirates in favor from the tales she had heard in whispers while sipping tea in her sitting room socials. With tables turned, it was quite different being actually held captive by them.

"Nah, you're right, m'lady. We're in no grace of the king, nor do we please to be. Some who wear the crown aren't so noble as they seem. Power corrupts, and greed abounds. I'm sure you've no concept, sitting on high back in merry ol' England, and all, but we '*brutes*' took up the oath in rebellion of the false king, and the self-interest he pursues. He sends his Royal Navy to pinch men like us on the sea and in the colonies. We're just roamers, living a life of brotherhood and duty to what's right as we see it."

"What's right? What's right?! You think stealing and pillaging, and killing is doing what's right?"

"Against the tyrant King and the pettifogging papists, aye."

"But we were not agents of the king, and clearly not the Spanish, yet you sacked us no different!"

"All at the decisions of your captain. Each of his actions resulted in our reaction. If he hadn't given chase, attempted to murder Cap'n, and your beau hadn't followed his orders to the death, I wager it might've been an entirely different outcome."

With her father's temperament and mother's wisdom, Wendy pined for a counter argument but found herself coming up short as the conversation progressed. In no way was she conceded to the circumstances. His replies were calculated and calming, and this chided her even more so amid the frolic.

"So, what is to become of me? Am I to be a plaything for the men to be used at their disposal then? Does your captain expect me to obey his commands and take up a life of lawlessness?"

"Nay, I don't suspect he does. The captain is a wise man, educated finely, trained in battle, skilled as ever a sailor was. But he must see something in you he treasures. He only wanted you, and no other spoils. Granted, having a woman aboard the ship is bad luck, but they fear him more than to protest."

"So, am I at risk of these men ridding me of my presence?"

"I can't say entirely what the captain has in store for you, but I can assure you that you are safe in the presence of these men. Safer here than on the ship from whence you came, I'd wager. They would never cross him and risk their lives by accosting you in any fashion. I imagine you will find yourself freer upon our ship than you were prior."

"I am free to come and go as I please, then?" Wendy questioned, now softening in intrigue.

"That is for the captain to decide. But yes, my dear, you won't find such restrictions in our company as you did among those men. We haven't the time nor interest in keeping tabs on you."

In a short matter of time, all of Wendy's bristling ire had subsided into a mottled manner of disgruntled acceptance of her circumstances. She was not capitulated by any means, because she had shut off her emotions and built a wall to protect herself. The loss of her parents less than a few hours ago still hung heavy upon her heart and soul, but as she had signaled to her mother, she would be strong. She would carry on. She would not break. She had somehow quelled the urge to rampage and accept her new station. Though, the apprehension of what Hook wanted with her also shrouded her like a cloak. He was a villain, a scourge in the highest form, however prim he might be.

"I shall take my leave now, Miss. Should you need anything, trust anyone will aid you."

A stir of emotions, Wendy nodded, tears forming in the corner of her eyes again. On tenterhooks, the gravity of it all was too much to take in. She was put at ease by him for his words and that was comforting, but she was still raw from the day's events. She wasn't clear on how to feel, but she knew deep down it would be alright, somehow; she had to believe that. This was both reassuring and unsettling together. She was trepidatious about the expectations between her and Hook, and his intentions for her. It didn't make sense why he would choose her (it did, but she didn't want to think about that if it were true). She could never have feelings of any kind for a monster such as he; one who could so order to kill and to steal her from her family so easily.

At this point she didn't quite know what to do, where to go, or how to act. There was no one attending to her, overseeing her safety or comings and goings. She was in fact, free. Another wave of uneasiness washed over her. Was she really so able to move about the ship as one of them? Without fear of personal danger? She tried to take a step in any direction, but she seemed to be pinned to the planks beneath her feet. She looked down not knowing what she expected to see – perhaps a tack between her toes – but saw nothing. This made her feel better, because she was worried something had happened and she hadn't felt it in all the numbness she was feeling. Though as she looked down and around, the burl of the wood seemed so sublimely intricate and pristine. Then she noticed the ship almost shined, even in the growing darkness of night. It seemed to sparkle ever so slightly, almost like an apparition.

She ran her finger along the railing, not a splinter about it raked her delicate fingertip. The ship was impeccably clean, much more than the *Eagle*, which boggled her mind. Captain Smythe always seemed to have his crew cleaning the decks, but now in comparison, the *Eagle* was quite an inferior ship; it was no wonder they were caught so easily. This thought then led her to ruminate on Smee's statement about Captain Smythe's decisions and judgment. No, she would not allow Smee to be right about this. But what if he was? Captain Smythe wasn't the most noble of men and was rather shady about stealing away the slaves without anyone's knowing. And the constant arguments with her father? Her Father… she remembered him, and that she had stopped thinking about him and her mother, and this made her sad again. Alas, from a different perspective, she could see that what had transgressed could entirely be plausible at the fault of Captain Smythe. However, she could not excuse the murder of Lt. Allain, and her heart hardened, angry that Captain Smythe was the one at fault for all of this, and in her spiral of emotions, she was glad he was dead now! But she was a lady, and ladies shouldn't feel that way. Oh, and Lieutenant Allain, she was sad again at seeing his empty eyes, and the gore of his disemboweled body. At this she felt ill and nearly wretched. She sat down and cried, alone in the dark. The feminine parade now closed off and protected by visceral intuition.

She heard the heavy footsteps approach, and she jostled herself up; her gown, still stained of blood and grime, her face filthy except where the tears streaked down her cheeks – only making it more evident how dirty her face actually was. She composed herself as quickly and properly as she could in the moment, before knowing who or what approached, but she was a façade of a proper lady by this point; she was a hostage, bedraggled and disheveled. She got to her feet ready to defend herself, though hardly equipped to do so. Her only retreat was overboard, which in the inky black night was not an option. She was trapped.

Hook stood before her, debonaire and enchanting in the early moonlight. She instinctively panicked for fear of his reputation and the glimmering hook, but something about him now seemed less dangerous. She wiped the tears from her eyes, embarrassed by her appearance, despite her attempts to ameliorate herself. She tucked her arms behind her back and intertwined her fingers nervously. Hook stood looking out over the men below relishing in their triumph, hardly paying any attention to Wendy. He espied the newly freed slaves, collected in the shadows, apprehensive and closed off from the rest of the crew, which was to be expected, but Hook took note of it. Hopefully they would assimilate soon, and pull their weight, otherwise he'd have to press them into service – which was the antithesis of the purpose of freeing them from servitude in the first place. Nervously, Wendy took her eyes from Hook to the scene below which he surveyed.

"I hope you find respite this evening. The frivolity will last some time, but they will remain preoccupied. You should find comfort below while they sprawl about up here. Tomorrow, we can refit you more comfortably and be rid of the frippery adorning you at present. Sleep well."

Turning away from her, never catching her eyes, he took his leave of her and retired to his quarters. Wendy was quite taken aback at the interaction, or lack thereof. In her worst thoughts, he would torment her or harass her in some uncomely fashion. Her chest heaved at the relief, and her hand pressed against herself to try to calm herself. Dizzy, she gripped the railing and looked out on the milieu below. Smee had watched the affair from below, and smirked a satisfied chuckle, before returning to his dice game. After slapping his cup on the barrel, he looked back to see Wendy slowly withdraw and disappear into the night.

Once in the interior of the ship, she fumbled around unfamiliar with the layout and location of everything. She knew she wouldn't be afforded such a luxury as having her own berth like on the *Eagle*, but she was still trying to find some sort of comfortable quarters. In the hold, she found a few hammocks rocking with the tossing of the ship. She was not enticed by the discomfort this appeared to provide, and she certainly did not want to be wrapped up in one of the pirates', unable to move or escape if the need arose. So, she continued in the subdued darkness, hoping to find a quiet secluded place to lay down. Eventually, after navigating a labyrinthian maze, she found sacks stacked in a corner behind some casks. Firm, but malleable, she made herself comfortable enough and laid down. Desperately she tried to fall asleep, but the loneliness was creeping in again, and the thoughts of her parents, stranded aboard the *Eagle*. Tears welled in her eyes, and the convulsions followed in an all-out sob. She had been strong all day, but now, in the darkness of a strange and dangerous pirate ship, she gave out. She bawled until she expired and fell into slumber without knowing.

While most of the Africans opted to stay out in the open on the deck, or at least in a defensible position for themselves against the pirates, two slaves saw Wendy retire for the evening. They were two of the surviving slaves she and Mary had nursed back to health, and they felt a kinship toward her. Unaware of what risks or danger she faced on her own as a beautiful young lady, they left their larger group, cautiously into the dark. Really, they had no idea what to expect, but their sense of tribal protection for her usurped any doubt or fear of what they needed to do. Quietly they followed her inward, keeping safe distance, so as not to spook her or get themselves hurt. In all fairness, this was all new to them, and the very real possibility of them being beaten or killed did give them appropriate pause. Without incident though, they had kept up with her until she disappeared behind the casks, but they could hear her. They waited. Then they heard her woe emanate in coughy bursts. In the shadows they sat, keeping watch for her. When the sobbing slowed, and eventually went quiet, they crept over to find her asleep on the sacks, so they both sat guarding their paragon.

The next morning, Wendy woke, stiff from the contorted night's sleep. She stretched, to no real relief, and sat up. She climbed out of her hiding spot and attempted to straighten herself out by flushing her stained and tattered gown. When she looked up, she was surprised to find the two slaves on the hard deck just in front of the casks. Under any other circumstances, she might have been fearfully alarmed, but the manner in which they lay quickly gave indication they meant no harm, and that they were there *for* her. She smiled empathetically, and knelt down to wake them gently, trying not to startle them just as they had been so careful not to do with her.

"Good morning..." She said softly.

They woke with a startle, despite her attempts, but the alarm was fleeting once they cognitively recognized who was waking them, and where they were. They were all three still alone in the recesses of the ship, as almost all the crew and others had spent the night topside in the open air. It was a luxury not afforded to the newly freed slaves, but for the pirates, not uncommon on calm nights. It made for quick action, should anything arise, and it wasn't squalid like the belly of the ship. Fresh sea air was always a better option, when afforded.

The young men weren't aware of what Wendy was saying, but her gentle demeanor conveyed her appreciation and civility. Not forgotten was her care when they were abused, and because of that, the two were resolute in being her protectors in return. She smiled at them and said thank you. They smiled back and nodded with their dark faces giving way to bright eyes and pearly teeth. It occurred to her, she had not taken the time to introduce herself before, but given the prior circumstances, it hadn't really mattered.

"My name is Wendy," she said. They looked back at her somewhat confused, but intent on trying to understand. She patted her chest and repeated her name a few more times. Eventually they started to emulate the sounds and were able to replicate her name.

"Wendy"

"Yes, Wendy. I am Wendy."

They now understood, and returned with the same mannerism of patting their bare chests,

"Danso"

"Osei"

Danso was the taller of the two by a half head. His skin was a deep rich ebony, and his eyes were almost as equally dark, save for the whites surrounding them. He had wily unkempt hair and a spotty bristly beard growing in. Not having any grooming, he looked quite wild at this point. He was also quite lanky now from malnourishment, but his frame depicted he was muscular before. If one had come across him in this state on his native territory, he might very well fit the "savage" depiction told over and over from explorers and traders. Unquestionably the witless Europeans seeing people like him would easily label him a black devil.

Osei was not much different in description and condition, except that he was, as mentioned, slightly shorter than his partner, and had a more oblong face. His too had sprouted a beard but was growing in more fully and evenly. His skin wasn't as deeply hued as Danso's but was a beautiful rusty chocolate color. His complexion was striking, though he had also diminished in stature. Like Danso, you could see he once had a fit physique and his face was strong, even though it had sallowed. When he smiled, it was a genuine and warming face, one that made you feel good and welcome.

"It is a pleasure to meet you Danso and Osei. Do you speak English?"

They repeated their names again with smiles. Clearly, she could tell they didn't speak her language. And now she had a purpose it seemed, to occupy her time on this ship. She would teach them to speak and possibly to read if they were able to comprehend. She wasn't sure how long they might be at sea, but this would certainly prove a distraction from the ruffian surroundings.

Wendy, now acutely aware that she was hungry and needed to find food. She smiled at them and turned to leave and figure out what to do about this need. Danso and Osei followed behind almost shoulder to shoulder, two sentinels at her heels. She heard them behind her and peeked over her shoulder to take account of them. This gave her a small spark of reassurance, and she felt stronger in that moment going forward. Her entourage offered relative protection, though very little given their current malnourished state. Despite that, though, she believed that they would at least intend to look after her from the possibility of danger among the other men.

When they reached topside, all the pirates and other slaves were moving about at various business. To her surprise, the slaves had been divvied up among the pirates and were being taught the rote tasks they would furthermore be expected to manage. Wendy was taken aback at this impartiality and shared tutelage. Her experience had taught her that Africans were most often condemned to unequal servitude, and that aboard a ship such as this, or more accurately, the *Eagle*, they would be chained up inhumanely and left for relative dead in some corner. But this wasn't the case at all! The pirates were working alongside them, guiding them, providing them responsibilities and a working part of the mission.

Danso and Osei remained by her side, two pillars to her docility. None of the pirates paid them any mind, for they were too busy about their orders. Danso and Osei also felt a relieved sense of joy seeing their brothers toiling away, seemingly interested in the work they were learning. They looked at each other with toothy grins, feeling a sense of safety instead of instinctive fear. When they had snuck away last night amid the amusements, they had been cowering in the shadows, unsure of what would become of them. This was all new and frightening for them, so it was not an unwarranted reflex. Smee had seen them emerge and came to intercept them.

"Good morrow, Miss Wendy. How does the day find you?" he said, wiping his spectacles on his shirt, then looking up to the sky to inspect them.

"Good morrow to you, Mr. Smee." She replied, again disarmed by his unexpected eloquence. "We are well, though a bit puckish."

"Aye, I can imagine, ye didn't have anything last night, and heaven knows when ye ate last at all for that matter. The captain has a table prepared for you and hopes he might have the grace of your company."

"Only if my two friends may join me. They have not eaten either and shall offer me escort. As you can see, they have already established themselves as my chaperones."

"Apologies, Miss Wendy. They can get their ration from the galley. Still some left and should still be warm. After that, they can fall in with the others. I can appreciate they're looking after you, and I've no quarrel with that, but they'll still be needin'ta pull weight. Captain lets no man go idle on his ship."

Keeping in mind their conversation from the previous night, Wendy mulled over the reason for her audience with Hook and was reluctant to oblige alone. Unfortunately, she had little choice. She could refuse and risk repercussions unthinkable, or she could concede and enjoy a meal. She was still quite famished after the past however many hours since she last ate. She looked and Danso and Osei and nodded for them to take leave of her. She signaled to eat, and then realized she didn't know where to direct them. Smee pointed across the deck toward the fo'c'sle. They looked at each other uneasily but did as instructed.

Smee then escorted Wendy to the Captain's quarters. He rapped on the door and announced their presence. A gravelly reply came from inside, granting them permission to enter. Smee opened the door for Wendy, and ushered her in. Once inside, he closed the door behind her, leaving her alone in the dim room. Daylight tried to creep through what few dirty windows adorned the aft space, providing a tenebrous setting within. Heavy curtains hung about, swaying in time with the rocking of the ship. Toward the rear, Hook sat at his desk with a plume wiggling from his good hand in a heavy journal. He was so focused on his work, he didn't so much as look up, but invited her to sit at the table, where a modest spread of eggs and salted pork sat ready for her. She took her seat and reservedly picked at a meager portion, attempting to maintain her lady-like grooming in Hook's presence.

"You need not put on airs. I've seen the likes of which would haunt your days. Eat. You surely have not had a meal in some time now, and I won't have you turning a waif."

"I am a lady, and a true lady is a lady that shall ever be and ever was."

"A lady you surely were, and no doubt as ever a lady as ever there was. But in my company, I am not concerned with your mannerliness. Eat."

"If I discharge my etiquette, then I am no less a mongrel as the likes of your company."

Growing impatient, Hook jabbed his quill into his inkpot and looked up at her now.

"In case you've not been made aware, you are my company. Eat!"

At this curtness, she could see the fire growing in him. She would forever dig in her heels on being the well-groomed high society woman she had been raised to be – she inherited this stubborn trait from her father but curated finesse by her mother. However, in her current environment, she absolved herself to relax. She heaped a plateful and unrefinedly devoured the meal. Sustenance filled her belly, renewing her with nourishment. She could feel her mind and body coming alive again. Hook continued on in his journal, being sure not to visibly pay attention, specifically after scolding her in the manner he had.

When she had finished, she sat primly, wiped the corners of her mouth, but wanted nothing more at this point than to recline and digest. Hook took nonapparent notice she had finished and ceased his scribing. He closed the journal and stuffed it into the escritoire, producing a key to lock it, which he then tucked away on a chain around his neck. He stood to address his guest in a more congenial manner than before. It was when he turned, she noticed he did not have the terrifying hook adorning his arm.

In his private morning attire, he still presented as a gallant gentleman. Instead of a coat, he wore a regal robe, gilded with intricate golden lace and threading. The sleeve was tied to obscure the stump where the hand – or hook – would have been otherwise. Though, the dark robe, raven beard and hair, and the muted light begat an even more sinister aura. Shadows cast across his face made his eyes like dark chasms, with only two smoldering embers glowing in the depths. He approached slowly and offered her his hand. Instinctively she accepted it, as she was trained to do, before realizing what she was doing. She stood, and he stepped back, still cloaked in eerie tenebrosity. She focused hard on not staring at the missing appendage, but it was obvious. He slowly paced around her in a circle, sparse light accentuating his strong jawline as he passed the salt-stained glass panes.

She could make out his features as her eyes had adjusted, and in the mystery and exhibition, he… was rather handsome in his own way. No, this wasn't right, he was monster! She couldn't help but feel strangely drawn to him. He was a strong, educated gentleman and this appealed to her, except that for all of that, he was still a pirate. It was a dichotomy she which vexed her. She studied him just as he with her. Sizing each other up, learning persona in silent observation.

"You present yourself tenacious, yet I feel you are conflicted with your purpose. You would no sooner leap at the chance to strike me down, given the opportunity, as you would investigate the life led by my men for interest of adventure only read in your tabloids."

His eloquence and observation surprised her. He continued.

"You are tormented, understandably, as to why you are here. Allow me to explain. But first, these rags you wear will not do. Though, you must forgive me. It appears we did not confiscate your belongings in the transfer of goods from your former ship. Alas, a gown as to which you are accustomed, will not be the couture. Then again, those are not fitting for duty, either. For now, you will suffice in what I have at my disposal to offer you, and that is of my personal raiment. On the chiffonier, you will find an appropriate change of attire while on my ship."

He directed her to the other side of the cabin, where a change of clothes awaited. Here she discovered a blouse top, pantaloons, and a sash. She was saddened by the ill-fitting selection. She was, as he had mentioned, accustomed to fine dresses, and this offering was unflattering to say the least.

"Surely you jest? These are not suitable dressings for a woman!"

"It is that, or only what you came into this cruel word with. Taking into account the men out there, I wager the former is your most optimal choosing."

"Then surely, the gentleman will allow me proper privacy?"

"As the lady wishes."

This was not advisable, and he knew it. He dared not leave her alone in his quarters, lest she rummage through his belongings, arm herself against him, or any other number of possible deviations in his absence. But the play here, was to gain her trust, even if it was to his own vulnerability. Despite any malfeasance, he would grant her an appropriate moment to change, since it was his insistence anyway. He collected his pistols and stepped outside, closing the door behind him.

She began to untie her dress and loosened the stays. It had been over a full day in which she had been constricted in her dress, and as soon as it was loosed, it was an overwhelming release. Her lungs filled with ease, full of breath. Her gown fell to her feet, and she pried the corset from her torso. She stood now in her chemise and felt the humid air more acutely. Shedding this layer, the air warmed her skin as she inspected the attire Hook had left her. Donning the pantaloons and the blouse, they were a bit oversized for her, and quite unflattering. She tied the sash around her waist as a belt, in an attempt to keep everything together. She was bare footed still but desired some form of cover for them. Beside his desk, she saw his boots, so she attempted to put them on, but they were far too big for her. She looked like a silly schoolboy who was trying on father's clothes and was discomforted by the clumsy manner she felt wearing them.

Before calling back to him to return, she looked around, seeing all kinds of artifacts decorating the space. He had amassed an eclectic collection of items from what seemed an extensive pirating career. Maps covered his desk, but what caught her eye especially were his books. Oh, how she loved books! Tattered copies of Perrault, Browne, Locke, Cervantes, Homer, Bradstreet, and Shakespeare adorned a shelf near the desk. She sat down, and pulled one after the other out, and thumbed through the weather-worn pages. The smell of them, though damp and musty, transported her. So much so, she didn't hear Hook re-enter.

She was out of sight behind his desk, and this gave him pause. He could see her garments were in a pile on the floor, but she was nowhere to be seen. He tiptoed in cautiously half awaiting an ambush but soon found her behind the desk. His first instinct was to thrash her for going through his things, but he saw she was only inspecting his literary collection. This instead, pleased him. She had interests beyond social affairs and galas. Perhaps he might be able to hold a conversation with someone with a comparable education, or at least one above a primary level. He quietly observed her as she poured over the pages, devouring the exquisite works of the authors.

He rasply spoke "All the world is but a stage, and all of us, merely the players.[ii]"

Not knowing he was there, this startled her, and she scrambled to her feet. Bumping into the corner, knocking things about, she uncoordinatedly attempted to collect the trinkets from falling about. He took a step back, so she would not feel so threatened. He was never more sinister than when he was most polite, which is probably the truest test of breeding.[iii] He enjoyed her discomfort. This gave him power, which was his position overall. But bringing her aboard posed a complicated risk, especially in the eyes of the crew. Women did not belong on a pirate ship and were bad luck.

When she had regained herself, she looked him dead in the eyes, and replied "You cannot, sir, take from me anything that I will not more willingly part withal - except my life."[iv]

This choice of quote puzzled him, "You are a defiant child…"

"I defy you because I am strong and know my worth."

"I sense that about you, thus why you are on my ship, presently."

"I am here, not on my own volition, but by detention. I am the subject to your whim, which I fancy is to fulfill some dubious intent."

"Dubious? No. I am far more perceptive than you comprehend, though I am not capricious. I observe. I wait. I take what serves me in means of fulfilling an objective, and for you, that is parlay upon our arrival in Port Royal. You see, there is dereliction in our little haven, and I quite believe you are capable enough to contribute to the path to great reconciliation among those seeking to destroy the utopia we have established."

"You think I am an instrument to dissuade the authority of the crown to permit you and your kind to thrive in a sanctum of depravity?"

"Not quite. It is evident I am not one to wave the banner of the false king, and I certainly am not in agreement with the delegates he sends to regulate our affairs, however, I do believe there is a manner in which we can subsist, appellate to each other's interests. But, if they were to surrender to our authority alternatively, what would be so poor in that?"

"And what, pray tell, do you see my role being in that congress? I don't believe I have established myself as an advocate of your kind, and I happen to be loyal to my king and country."

"Patience, and strategy are my intention. You see, there are those – of my kind, as you say – who seek to dissolve our mission with mischief and mayhem. That is not in our best interest, for longevity's sake. There are also those, those cursed natives, who make it nigh impossible to exist and grow peaceably."

"Natives?"

"Yes, we are constantly at war with them, and they are a clever bunch. Their chief is not to be trusted. He is mendacious. But his daughter, she is also a defiant child, much like you. It is my hope, that you two will strike common ground to diffuse the hostility between their people and our own."

"So, to be clear, having never spoken a godly word with me ever before, you expect that I am one willing to mitigate your mis-dealings to the crown's authorities *and* those who have been forced out of their land for that of which you pirates have since disgraced and made a heathen's cove?"

"Crudely, yes."

"What makes you think I have interest or ability to speak with this native girl and convince her or her father, steeped in rite surely, to allow you and all the others to exist freely in their land, while you wage war against all others in the world?"

"It is not we, who conquered and drove them out. Nay, it was the Spaniards who tortured and decimated them upon their arrival some two-hundred years ago. In taking the island from the Spaniards, the natives still believe us to be one in the same. In my design I would rather afford the natives the opportunity to exist among us, yet they choose hostility, and further the divide in which I aim to close. It is not in my interest, or that of my companions, that we battle with them endlessly. Lives are lost on both sides, to which I find counterproductive."

"I see. You aim to set me up as a pawn in your chessman's conquest."

"You cannot fathom my predicament in your current circumstance. But I can tell you, should you succeed in this mission, you would be regarded as that of a regent in our realm. You see us as monsters, but we are merely men of our custom, tried by the tribulations of ill-repute to that of a monarch only seeking to squeeze our very livelihood for his own self-interest."

"The king is our sovereign, and it is right that we shall obey him!"

Hook took great umbrage to this blind allegiance, and while he had remained even keeled to this point, fumed at Wendy's ignorant statement.

"You damnable little shrew! You know nothing, *nothing* of the world outside your safe confines of prominence! That bastard is a false king and does not belong on the throne. He's nothing more than a pimp of those who uphold him and deserves not the respect of anyone paying the least bit of attention to the world outside of the palace! Damn them for crafty rascals! He is the villain, and all his bloody tariffs are destroying what is good and right for the common man! They vilify us, the scoundrels, but they rob us under cover of their laws. I am a no less a king, compelled to rob the rich under protection of brotherhood!"

She had struck a nerve. He wanted to lunge at her, throttle her, but decorum prevailed. He collected himself, turned and stepped away. She was startled by his heated outburst and took note of it. On one hand, she knew she could get under his skin, whether this was good or bad was still undetermined in her mind; she could play both sides. Secondly, she was now starting to understand why he had abducted her, and to what purpose she served him.

"You are but a child, sheltered from that of the real world. You have not experienced the hardships of those beneath you, nor do you comprehend the struggles the less-than-mighty are burdened with. However, your world changed in an instant, and you are now thrust into the tragedy we call life. Whether or not you choose to aid me in my mission, you now play a part in it. Your role is now tantamount to mine, even if you turn tide. But should you choose to oppose me, rest assured I will not tire in putting you beneath the dirt."

The matter-of-fact way he concluded this statement sent a chill down her spine. She could masquerade as though she were above him in all things, but this was his realm now. He had the upper hand, and she would have to play by the rules to some extent if she wanted to get out of this alive. She had no doubt he would stop at nothing to succeed; or take her life if he didn't.

"It seems as though I have no choice. So, if I am to play your game, I have a few demands of my own."

"Do you now? I was not aware you were positioned to make demands. Pray, tell."

"First, I want liberty to teach the Africans how to speak and read. You may not know, but two of them have bestowed upon themselves to be my guardians, and I shall like to address them in a comprehensible manner."

"The Africans will learn what they need from my men, as they need to know it. Nor will I permit them to follow you around as some entourage."

"You may try, but they are resolute in seeing that I am safeguarded. You see, I spared their lives under the care of Captain Smythe. They were beaten and dying. It is no doubt their indebted service to my saving them from death."

"They're slaves. Product. That is how they are treated among his kind. They are lucky to be alive at all, and that should be enough. You have some affinity for them then?

"I do not have affinity as you think. They were despoiled and left to die. My mother and I were charged with caring for them, so Captain Smythe would not lose his profits in them. If anything, they have affinity for me, as their Samaritan."

"Fine, you may teach them the English language. But you will do it at mess, so as it will not interfere with their duties, or my men's. You have more?"

"I wish to learn to defend myself. If I am to go into this place to stand against rebellion, I should know how to wield a sword. Teach me how."

"A woman does not wield a sword. If battle will be waged, it will be by shot, not blade."

"Surely, the great Captain Hook is not threatened by a *shrew* such as me in brandishing a saber?"

"I am not threatened by you, my dear. I am astute, and do not see the worth in skilling you in combat. The cutlass is a heavy, and superbly crafted weapon, the likes of which requires durable strength to handle."

"I am just as capable as you, or any of these men, in my strength and will. Have you not been paying attention all this time?"

Piqued by intrigue, and the lambent efforts she was countering his every objection, he stroked his beard and reflected on the matter.

"Smee!" he called loudly over his shoulder.

Smee entered, as though he were waiting just outside the door (which of course he was).

"Yes, Cap'n?"

"Miss Wendy here wishes to learn swordplay. Take her with you and begin her lessons."

Smee's jaw slackened in surprise, as he looked from him to her, then back to him.

"Bu..but, Cap'n, ladies don't participate in such activities, do they?"

"No, Smee, they don't. However, I believe, that she has agreed to terms in her own way, and if that is to be the case, she has made a good point, that she should be as equipped as we, to defend herself against foe. We need her alive, and this shall give her a *fighting* chance."

Hook waited for the pun to land on Smee, but he completely missed it in his confusion. Hook was disappointed at the loss and sighed.

"She has also volunteered herself to educate the daft in speaking our language. I have made it explicitly clear, that she is not to disrupt operations, but that she may do so at supper time. Any who wish to participate, may do so at that time, assuming there are no tasks that supersede."

"Aye, Cap'n. Will be nice to have a sort teaching thems how to understand what we're saying when we tells 'em what to do."

Wendy, still cornered behind the desk, held her head a little higher than earlier, feeling as though she'd won something big in this.

"There you have it, girl. If there is nothing else, I kindly ask you to withdraw from my quarters."

Wendy came from around the desk, still holding two books in her hands, and as she passed by him in his towering magnitude, she said simply, "I will be taking these with me. Good day."

Hook sat behind his desk once more, unlocked the drawer, and pulled out his journal. Inking the quill, he set back to the work he was focused on earlier, only now his mind was preoccupied with Wendy, and her befuddling behavior. He was perturbed with her pluck to stand up to him. Maybe, just maybe, he could escape the oppressive rule with her embedded into the Port Royal society. It was a gamble all along, and only now was he formulating his strategy effectually. He now believed he had the final piece he needed for it all to come together. Only time would tell.

Over the course of the next few days, business went about as it should on the ship, apart from their guest holding school at night, for any of the crew wishing to learn. It was specifically arranged for the now freed slaves to learn how to speak English and participate more productively in their duties, however, it quickly morphed into a story-time of sorts, where Wendy would read from the books she'd lifted from the captain. For as gruff as the pirates were, they enjoyed the interruption of her reading like a mother at bedtime.

Mostly she read from Shakespeare with a periodic deviation by way of Chaucer. The stories weren't always easily understood, and so many questions peppered the narrations. Initially this disturbed her, but as she noticed more and more of them paid attention, she appreciated the participation. A side effect of the inquisitory listeners was that educational conversation actually aided in the learning for the originally intended audience. The more dialogue occurred at a digestible pace, the better they were able to learn the language, words, and constructs of conversation.

To Hook's verbalized disapproval of his men participating, they still gravitated to the gatherings. He would watch from the railing above, but knew he couldn't, and wouldn't do a thing about it. As the captain, he ruled by terror, but also by influence and conviviality. He knew the Juvenalian ideology of keeping them happy, to which then they wouldn't revolt. As well, it showed him that Wendy was charming and could settle even the despicable of men.

In contrast, her lessons of swordplay were slow going. They were not nearly as productive or consistent. The men were either regularly busy or didn't see the value (or benefit) of teaching a woman to fight. It was a foreign concept, and they routinely passed responsibility to anyone they could; often, it ended up Smee's charge. The issue here though, was that he was not the strongest or ablest swordsman in the bunch anymore. He could defend himself sure, but he was not the one you'd find leading the charge to board a prize. He was more reserved at his age now, and was more particular in attending to the captain, while the others handled the dirty work.

Be that as it was, he still had the wherewithal to instruct her in the basics. He taught her simple things, like posture and stance, how to hold the sword properly with a good grip, how to advance, slip, and most importantly how to parry. Once she seemed to understand these maneuvers, he began dueling with her at slow speeds so she could transfer the learned fundamentals into action. Patiently, he would dance in circles over and over with her, while she blocked, cut, and countered amateurly. It came as no surprise to him that she was a quick study. Though, what did surprise him was the level of endurance she had. Though they weren't practicing at a full speed, she was able to continue for longer periods than Smee anticipated. Often, he would tire, and she would still be eager to keep going.

During resting periods, Wendy would ask Smee various questions to learn about him and the others. In the days spent among them, she had witnessed all manner of personalities, some to which surprised her were not as menacing as she was prepared for. They treated her kindly to an extent, never once causing her to feel endangered. But it was one afternoon, she mustered up the courage to ask about *the hook*.

"The Cap'n doesn't talk about it. And if you ask him, he might well cut you down for the inquiry, so I suggest ye not." He replied. "You see, none of us really know what happened, but I was there when it did. That night was the last time the injuns attacked us, set off by some brat of a farmer in the hills. That's why the Cap'n wants to squash the discord, because it was unprovoked, but we lost a lot of lives that night. It was a nasty event."

"I don't understand," she retorted. "A boy sacked the town with the natives, and he lost his hand because of it?"

"Aye." And to this, Smee recounted the details he knew, telling the tale of the fateful night as best he could.

"The accuracy of that night is still somewhat shrouded in mystery because there is no witnessed account of what really happened. As James has told it time and time again, some of the details have fallen away, changed, or contradict the version told previously. However, what is known (or remembered) amongst the crew, is that while in port some years ago, the village was ambushed by the natives led by some mainland farmer's boy. Quite a row erupted in the streets, ending in significant destruction and bloodshed. It was during this skirmish James caught sight of the pecunious rabble-rouser and took after him. The two clashed in bursts of fighting as they dashed out of the city into the bog.

"...So, they chased each other into the marshy bank, where the boy had previously landed his canoe. He was fleeing to escape James, almost setting off, but Cap'n brandished his pistol, and took aim. The shot blasted, causing the boy to flounder and fall into the muddy water. The canoa half-capsized drowning his escape. Cap'n splashed into the water, where they reengaged in duel, Cap with a cutlass and the child with only a dagger. Slogging in the muck, they battled for an exhausting time, tiring quickly. What they were unaware of, is that their raucous fighting had alerted the crocs nearby, and feeling threatened, they encroached.

"At this point, the story gets a bit foggy as to what actually happened, and each maintain a different side of the story. The imp's viewpoint is that he was the victor by winning the fight, slashing Cap'n's wrist, severing the hand clean off. Cap'n's is that he lost footing, falling backward where the croc latched on to his hand, ripping it off while attempting to drag him into the water. Left now to die in the jowls of the beast, Cap'n's fight became one for survival, and the boy flew off into the night, naught to be seen again in our time shoreward. We've heard tale though, he's still about, and mark my word, Cap'n will get his revenge."

As Smee described, the crocodile had latched on to his arm, dragging him into the murky quagmire, preparing for its death roll. As it wrenched its prey into the shallow fen, James' hand was gruesomely detached, rendering him loosed from the jaws of the monster. Now freed, he clambered up the bank, bleeding profusely from his arm. He staggered back into town, white as a ghost from the loss of blood and near shallow drowning. He collapsed just inside the street where his ilk were reeling from the melee. It was Smee that happened to catch James stumbling back into the village before falling out. Though they were not yet an allied pair at the time, Smee is credited for being the one who saved the current, most infamous active pirate alive from an uncelebrated death.

Smee assisted James back to the tavern, where the limb was cauterized, saving him from bleeding out. Feverish, he laid in a bed in, for days. The stump was a nightmarish sight and required constant attention to keep from festering. The pain was unyielding, leaving James to delve hard into dust and drink to mollify the misery. Nearing debilitating addiction and outright self-destruction, he became an uncontrollable, violent, and vengeful man during this healing time.

Dust is a hell of a drug, and when taken gives the user an unparalleled high, with the feeling of flying. A user feels out-of-body – consciously unconscious; functionally unfunctional. It is very popular among the pirates of Port Royal, but very expensive, hard to obtain, and questionably concocted. After you sober up, it's like waking from a dream you can't remember. But in the case of James Bartholomew, he had been given a medicinal dose to quell the pain of his wound, but again, the pain was miserable, so he spiraled quickly into abuse. Now quasi-sober, he had no memory of the days that followed the ambush. Due to the combination of the trauma and drugs, he didn't even fully remember the fateful fight, only bits and pieces. Hence, the details of the account are spotty at best in his retelling.

When he finally emerged, everyone joyously welcomed him back. Curious what had happened, and what was next. When asked, he would snarl, and offer a simple reply,

"I have been plotting how to rid us of that pestilent lot of scoundrels. And mark my words, the one what did this to me, I shall one day have his head upon a pike!"

To this, he would always receive jubilant cheers and agreeable support. What followed, was the beginning of the legacy of *Captain Hook*, and the hellish feud that wouldn't end until that contemptible ponce's head was cleft from his shoulders.

VII

Piet Banning came from a pastoral Dutch family who emigrated to Jamaica years ago along with a network of families who had done the same in a form of exodus from Europe. Though removed from the parishes in the lowlands, Piet's family used their wealth and established themselves further inland in the foothills. Here they built a plantation with vast acreage where they could raise goats, crops, and more. Piet was educated at home, learning to read and write, as well as schooled in cultured subjects like the arts, music, and mathematics. He even learned to fence in the elitist fashion from some remaining Spanish defectors. Piet was a very cultured boy, and so too as boys are, he was very mischievous even at this young age.

His father would often chide him when he would get out of line, or if he had not attended to his chores. He was a very dour man, taking no humor in the pranks or silliness Piet was prone to. This created a rift between them, and Piet would often disappear for days at a time, exploring and adventuring. At the time, this was dangerous, but Piet had no comprehension of that, as he was arrogant and rebellious. He would sneak off with his dagger, his flute, and a pocket full of bread, and when he had grown tired or hungry, he would come home, only for his father to beat him for all the aforementioned reasons, creating a disruptive cycle.

Piet loved to adventure off into the wild, tracking rivers, following the coast, climbing trees, and chasing wild animals. If he grew tired, or complacent he would find a large tree, and either curl up underneath it, or climb into the bough, and rest. To entertain himself in these times, he could often be found playing his flute to some classical melody or using it to imitate bird calls. In his schooling, Piet was learned in the Greek arts, and musically, he had been taught to play Pan's flute. In Jamaica, it was exceptionally easy to acquire, as bamboo shoots grew like weeds, so one could be fashioned with simplicity. His mother loved to hear the chimes from her favorite boy, whistling idly by. She loved it so, she'd given him the moniker, *Piet der Pan*. Not having many toys to play with, his flute was most often in his pocket.

As he grew older, his adventuring took him farther and farther, where he could be gone for weeks at a time. He'd learned to hunt by now and explored most of the surrounding areas. Unbeknownst to his parents, he'd been apprehended by the Tainos, and taken to their chief for punishment. With little hope of living to see the sunrise, Piet was in a bind this time, but he had caught the attention of the chief's daughter, Tiger Lily. After some convincing from her, her father eventually released him under conditional terms: he could return to hunt with them, but he would not antagonize their way of life, upon penalty of death. To this, he happily agreed.

Piet had grown estranged from his family, taking much more pleasure in the fascinations he'd experienced than the caretaking of the family farm. His father had all but disowned him, and his mother yearned to have her sweet boy back in her arms. Austere as her husband was, Piet rarely found joy when he would return home, as his mother could not disobey her husband. Her love for him became a chasm, to which neither could ford. This only led him to venture farther still, occasionally accompanying the natives on scouting missions, or hunting forays. He learned their ways and became privy to locales only accessible by dugouts; specifically, the cays and atolls in and around the peninsula that was Port Royal.

When Colòn had established the island under the Spanish flag, they ruthlessly eradicated the natives, razed the land, and destroyed everything in their path to build. Ever since, the Tainos detested and distrusted intruders, from the oppressive and dangerous whites in the lowlands, to the multi-cultural heathens in Port Royal. What numbers the natives consisted of in the thousands, now only consisted of a few hundred. As well, they had lost all their precious land, so they retreated into the trees, hiding among the wilderness. They could survive where they couldn't be found. Piet learned this in his time with them and created a system all his own. He'd learned that the Tainos used the land – the trees – to camouflage them from any enemies in an attack. He'd also learned how to make a dugout canoe, and so similarly, for added strategy, he began carving out the trees and hiding within them.

While he was off playing, the family farm was sliding into ruin, and his parents were growing unable to sufficiently maintain the land, crops, and animals. They were getting older, and the Caribbean heat did not fair them well. Unrelenting humidity choked their fair genetics, causing them to exhaust quickly. Heat stroke and dehydration were common maladies for the transplants, and without proper assistance, could be fatal among the elders. Many of the other farmers had taken to putting slaves in the fields.

Such was the case with the Bannings. As they grew older, and Piet was absent more oft than present, the slave count increased to continue the maintenance of the land. This was their legacy, and if it collapsed, they would be destitute, so the only option was to purchase abled bodies to tend to the chores required. Unlike their kin in the lowlands, the Bannings were prudent and proud to get their own hands dirty – they did not desire to spend what little money they had on slaves unless need required. This was a costly investment both up front, and long term. The Bannings did not have a taste for owning slaves, so only when they needed to, would they pay the price at auction.

By now, Piet would only occasionally return to the farm, and would mingle with the hands, developing relationships in assumed secret. This infuriated his father, because as far as he was concerned, Piet was no longer a part of this and would cast him off. His mother though, would hide her sad eyes behind her husband. Selfishly, he wished she would stand up for him – go against the patriarch and save him, allow him to be here and gone freely. He wasn't deserving of this salvation, but only a mother will love unwaveringly for her children. And so, he began to detach from them both, driven away by his father, but abandoned by his mother (or so he believed).

It was on one of these occasions that Piet returned late at night and stirred up the servants with his wild antics, looking for company in his merriment and desire to jubilate. Of course, this awoke Piet's parents and when they discovered the culprit behind the revelry, his father burned with ire. He stormed out of the main house to the bonfire to catch his son dressed up like a redskin, painted for war, aping their dances childishly as the field hands pounded drums. When he saw his father before him, he stopped dead in his tracks. The others, realizing their master was displeased, grabbed their things, and scattered quickly. The party was over, and before he knew it, Piet and his father stood face-to-face by themselves. Piet's father's chest heaved with heavy breath and furious anger. He minced no words that night and banished his son from the property forever. Should he ever show his face again, he would be shot on sight.

The entitled, spoiled child pleaded that he was just having fun, and begged his father to reconsider, but he would not. He was unshakable in his decision. Piet was exiled and was never allowed to return. A father's scorn, borne of frustration is a folly both in decision and execution – only to be realized upon the final days spent in sad, lonely regret. But the hammer had fallen, and no plea would convince him to waver. Chest heaving with animus, he stood firm in his decision.

Piet threw his plea and boyish eyes to his mother, in hopes she would – *could* – convince her husband to reconsider. Tears welled in her eyes, and she turned her back to him. She could not bear witness to this resolution and the ousting of her baby boy. Message received, with no hope of yield, he would forever visualize that he had been abandoned by his parents, and for this he could never forgive them. To him, he was now an orphan, even though he was old enough to fend for himself. Into the darkness of the night, he disappeared from their lives forever.

Exiled, Piet bounced from living among the Tainos, teasingly courting Tiger Lily, to exploring the island and the beauty it offered. He watched as more and more travelers arrived, pillaging the land, and establishing a foothold for passing ships, traders, slavers, merchants, and thieves. While his familiarity of the island encompassed the mainland, he would venture out into the peninsula that was Port Royal on occasion. This happened more and more as he gained skill and experience. As a naïve boy, he was not versed to the impudence and cutthroat mannerisms. Slowly he became more and more acculturated, blending in as part of the fabric of the town. He became a familiar face inelaborately mixing in among them; just another body moving along the rutty streets.

He hadn't yet developed his rebellious nature toward the populace because at this stage he was fascinated by the wildness on display unceasingly. He would duck in and out of alleys catching glimpses of lasciviousness, which made him curious. Because of this grand parade, Piet began spending more and more time there, for increasingly longer durations. This proved tiresome for him to traverse from the inland hills so constantly. Along his navigation, he regularly skirted an isolated islet, wrapped in twisting mangroves and trees. This cay wasn't habitable and was mostly just a biome for birds and other insignificant creatures, save for the intermittent crocodile passing through in search of a snack, like the birds. Piet landed his dugout one trip, and with difficulty, wound through the labyrinthian roots, vines, and branches. It was so dense, that it provided such perfection for a hiding place. Given his learned ability to carve trees for secret shelters, he created a network of secluded burrows and tunnels. The place transformed into his own treehouse of sorts, and as it took shape, he all but claimed it for his own, using it as his present residence. He could see Port Royal in the distance from the waterline, and it was a quick jaunt to the shore, where he could easily pilfer food and supplies to bring back to his enclave.

By this time, Piet was completely surviving on his own from the little island he called home. On few occasions, he would sneak back to the farm, to visit with the hands, only to find that his parents had closed off the main house, locking the doors and windows, rarely to be seen anymore. Little did he know, his parents had broken hearts between them, living a shell of a life now, without their son, the heir to their bucolic throne; the one they had tried to provide a better life for by fleeing oppressive Europe. The farm was only now subsisting at the efforts of the servants, and falling into disrepair, despite their efforts. Without proactive investment, tools, animals, and crops were dwindling to a minimum at best. This also put the farm at risk from being usurped by other neighboring landowners.

It was during one fateful visit Piet learned his parents had passed away. Sad, alone, and malnourished, their health rapidly declined in the tropical climate. The Caribbean islands were rampant with disease for those unacclimatised – especially European settlers. Malaria, originating from the plague of mosquitos, had taken hold of his parents, and in their weakened state, defeated them. They died and were buried on a knoll behind the main house. Two small makeshift crosses marked the shallow graves, dug by the hands. He blamed his father for how things turned out and took no responsibility of his own. This was the pretentious immaturity that would define Piet going forward. He would never see things as his fault, and became a rather conceited, pompous man-child. His way of coping with their loss, and not being able to reconcile, was to cast off any acceptance on his part, because as far as he saw it, his father was too obsolescent and forbidding for not allowing a child to play indiscriminately, and his mother was too cowardly to rebuke her husband's dominance. At no point, did it occur to him he was being conditioned to become a real grown up, and take over the family's business, which for a short time was one of the most prosperous on the island. Piet was educated to the finest available ability to empower him over others and set him up for greater things. Piet squandered this entirely by choosing the path he took.

Now that his parents were gone, he inherited the plantation and a sum of money at an early age, with no real understanding of how to be an adult, or what it took to run the plantation. The servants had maintained everything, and so Piet's solution was to continue the status quo. He owned the property and the money and essentially gave the servants their freedom to live and work as they saw fit. His life revolved around being the free spirit he'd grown to become and still spent a large amount of time away from the plantation, whether on his bungalow island or intermingling in Port Royal.

Now that he was unceremoniously in charge of the estate, and everything that came with it, he began to realize the care given to his servants was not the norm among others – especially when shipments of slaves arrived in port. They had always been spirited and playful with him, and so he viewed them as friends in a manner of speaking. He'd never paid attention to the treatment of these people before being responsible for them himself. This did not sit well with him, so his ignorant solution was to protest to the landowners buying them, and the auctioneers to take compassion on them. To this they would scoff and shoo him away like a stray cat. Realizing he was getting nowhere with this approach, he turned then to competing at auctions. He had money (he had no idea how much, how quickly it could be spent buying a lot of slaves, or that it required making more to replenish spend), so he wrestled his way to the front of the pack one day and raised his hand eagerly and constantly in attempts to win the bid on human life. For the wealthy, and experienced slave owners, this incensed them, as Piet unwittingly drove up the price for the slaves. Though not to be bested by a stripling, they responded by muscling him out both physically and financially. The auctioneers also quickly learned not to acknowledge his bids. Piet's attempts failed once again, but he would not be swayed. If he couldn't save them by playing the game, he would make his own rules and change the game (something he was also well known to do if he didn't like the outcome).

In the coming months, Piet began tormenting the establishment of Port Royal with juvenile nuisances that were irksome in the beginning. These annoyances gave way to bigger transgressions as he either didn't receive the response he'd hope to receive, or as he became craftier and more devious. It was also during these times, he would visit with the Tainos and convince them into teaming up with him to raid the town. This escalated the offense far more quickly than anyone expected. Upon the attack, the natives descended on the village with warlike intent, which in turn incited an equal, if not grander response from the pirates and business owners. To a significantly fatal result, the Tainos fled almost as quickly as they appeared. They were not prepared to meet the unbridled volley of gunfire, and many of them were killed. Piet found this onslaught callously entertaining, never considering he had led them to slaughter. To him it was theater, a performance at his making, and he remained untouched. The value of their lives meant nothing more than his amusement, for his petty persecution.

It was during this incident that Piet engaged with one of the pirates, who pursued him out of the town into the blackness of the marshy shore. This pirate was a hulking giant with surprising speed and agility for his size. Pocked by sporadic clashes, the pirate attempted to end the boy's life, but through deftness (and luck), Piet was able to escape to his canoe. Just when he thought he was in the clear, an explosion shattered the safeness, splintering the gunwale, toppling him into the water. With a lightning quickness, the pirate descended on him, where they fought awkwardly in the shallows. With the lightness of his dagger, Piet was able to outpace the pirate as they battled hand-to-hand. Water filled the pirate's boots, weighting him down, whereas Piet was barefoot, able to step more easily in the silty bank. Piet dodged a heavy thrust, landing a detrimental slash to the pirate's wrist. Blood poured from the gash, staining the water below. The pirate recoiled, unable to land sure footing, and fell backward into the reeds. Piet scrambled for his overturned canoe to escape, only to hear a mad thrashing and guttural screams behind him. Looking back, he saw the pirate clamped in the jaws of an angry crocodile. Piet fled the scene, lest he end up in the belly of the beast next. Assuming the pirate was left for dead, he hastily paddled for his refuge, terrified of how close he'd come to meeting his death.

Following the calamity, his relationship soured with the Taino tribe for some time, and they shunned him for what he had brought upon them. This he discovered when visiting with them shortly after the raid, expecting a warmer welcome. Again, taking no responsibility for his actions, he was upset by their outward treatment toward him. He sulked off to his island that night, climbed a tree and played his flute for the moon, cradled in the bough. The next morning, he went to work constructing an even more elaborate network of tunnels, hollows, and aquifers for fresh water. For the entirety of his disappearance, he labored away at the infrastructure within the camouflaged web of winding roots and reeds. None were the wiser because no one ever cared to investigate this little speck of land since it was inhabitable and impenetrable. So, Piet existed in secrecy building his own little playground of hidey-holes, chutes, and canoes.

Ostracized, it would be many moons before anyone ever saw Piet again. He had vanished, leaving many on edge that he would pop up again unexpectedly with another war party, or some other formidable foray. Others were glad to not have him around any longer, hoping the fates had dealt with him. But in this equatorial den of sin, there was no divine intervention. It was a place where righteousness, karma, and morality passed over, suffocated by sordidness. And so, the hopes that any form of cosmic retribution befell Piet were simply laughable. No, Piet was dispirited that everyone was against him, when all he was trying to do was free the slaves and have some fun in the process. Having never been held punishably accountable for anything in his life, the disasters he caused never landed on his conscience. But he was sad, and he did miss Tiger Lily, this he did have actual feelings about. She was very pretty and loved to play games with him – because she was intrigued by him and his childish demeanor.

Long about when things had returned to normal in Port Royal, and anyone who hadn't set sail by now had all but forgotten about the thorn in their rib, strange occurrences began happening. Non-descript things. Things out of the ordinary, like barrels, crates and supplies, or arms and ammunition whisked away into thin air. Piet was the culprit, but the incidents were so inconsequential and inconsistent that no one really gave much thought as to who, or why these things were happening. They just seemed to either be misplaced things, or petty crimes which no one could pin on anyone in particular. But what Piet was doing, was fortifying his refuge with the trappings of the town. Hidden within the encapsulated shield of the trees had evolved a booby-trapped sanctuary which would make any children's fort pale in comparison. It truly had become a wonderland of juvenile playthings, meets strategic outpost, meets armed anchorage. He had made a harborage replete with a fleet of canoes, moored among the trees, disguised so that to the untrained eye, looked like the trees they hung from.

What Piet had learned in his time under cover, was how to navigate the town, without being detected. He had stolen away so many things, it was a mystery how he got them all back to the fortress. Many items which he pilfered, were significant, yet he managed to get them away unnoticed and undeterred. Throughout this guileful process, he took note of schedules, timings, comings and goings, locked doors, open windows, shadows, and more. He had become pedantic, a master of midnight, preying on those who preyed on the world. He took no shame in this practice, and quite truthfully, it inspired him. Such was the result, that he was finally poised to phase his master plan into action.

Still motivated by the mistreatment of the slaves, he aimed to free as many as skill and craft would allow. Since he was incapable of competing effectively among the plantation owners, he would best them preemptively. On many the plantations, the slaves were kept in miserable quarters guarded by overseers to ensure they stayed put. Piet's plan was to jailbreak them. He studied the overseers' routines and schedules. Surprisingly for most, they were quite simple and laxed for such a responsibility. Complacency and an illusion of security allowed the wardens to act as they did, which allowed Piet to easily case the keeps. A jailbreak under the nose of an armed boss still posed high risk, and could only be executed with irregularity, but it could be done. Each plantation required a different manner of infiltration, and so if a pattern emerged, his methods would be figured out and thwarted. The best he could do was strike once, and reassess the changes to any comings and goings, and strike again at a later time, and so forth.

Now that he had established this aspect of his plan, he needed to integrate the second, and possibly most significant facet: integrating into the populace as a common character. This was going to prove more difficult than he anticipated. Given the havoc he had caused, he was still likely execrated by those who might remember him. But by his thinking, that was some time ago now, and many had come and gone in that time. Those he needed to be cautious with were the ones from whom he had been stealing from – the shopkeepers, inn keeps, smiths, and other non-transient people trying to eke out a living.

In his insouciant thinking, he had merely been playing games before, and he should have no reason not to stroll back into town. He reckoned he had laid low long enough, but these day-to-day folk were the ones he'd caused the most destruction to, and they had good reason to harbor ill-will toward him if they recognized him. He'd cost them significant money in restoration and reestablishing business as normal. When his hijinks cost them life and wage, there was no abatement as though nothing had happened.

Ever the schemer though, he returned to his family farm to rummage through his father's wardrobe. He would charade as a plantation man, to blend in. The costumes were another game for him, so he took glee in playing dress up. He donned the clothing and stamped around aping his late father's stark demeanor, but this, as it turned out, wasn't fun, so he took off the excess and kept it simple. Standing in front of the looking glass, he looked normal; exactly as he intended. Packing some additional outfits in a satchel, he prepared to infiltrate Kingstown and Port Royal.

Being back on the farm, he suddenly realized the opportunity before him. The hands had been sustaining the property and took pride in doing so. They were able to defend the property lines under the Banning name, though encroachers attempted to confiscate them and the land while Piet had been off galivanting. Regardless, as much as he loved his little cay, the farm provided much more in the way of living with the bodies he planned to steal away through this endeavor. Realistically, he wouldn't be able to *live* in his little refuge with all of them, but it could serve as a waypoint once he'd helped the imprisoned slaves escape. And so, his plan evolved. He would get them to the island temporarily before escorting them the long trip back to the plantation at a later, more opportune time. While the hunt was on for the missing captives, the salty bay would cover their tracks and lose the scent from the tracking dogs set loose. Here they could lay low for as long as they needed and use it as an outpost. In the process, he would make them conspirators, giving them roles in the future operations. If he could show them how to defend themselves, they could aid others in the future while he hid in plain sight, while also selfishly not risking himself getting caught.

After he considered all possible outcomes, requirements, steps, and logistics, he approached Nibs, one of the servants who had essentially assumed the leadership role of the farm. He liked Nibs because he was one of the hands that Piet had grown up playing with all those years ago. So, he conspired with him as to his plan, which required his help in integrating the newcomers, and potentially providing them hiding places. Nibs was troubled at first by the idea and wanted nothing to do with the plan, nor the risk of punishment that would follow if he were caught aiding and abetting the stolen slaves. However, Piet assured him he was in no danger (but really Piet couldn't promise that). With Nibs on board, Piet felt readied and set off for Port Royal.

With seething parvenus, he arrived, strutting into town like a proud cock, chest puffed and sure. False bravado and ignorant immaturity fueled him. He was wholly arriviste, strolling through the congested streets. He had gilded the lily with his costume, making him stick out a little more than he'd intended. He received a few glances, dressed in his father's clothing, though he also received glances out of odd curiosity. He had appeared out of nowhere, clad in somewhat ill-fitting habiliments, but exuded a confidence as though he were someone of worth. This was an easy charade for him because he always had a holier-than-thou ego about him.

It was no exaggeration that the nearly one hundred taverns and houses of entertainment made up most of the town's depraved reputation. It was lawless. There were no restraints, no police, and the soldiers who happened to be stationed there, were merely self-serving at the hand of the equally corrupt governor. They were arguably just as damnable as the pirates and thieves who rowed ashore in droves.

Among the shopkeepers in the market, exotic fruits, fish, and beef teased the palate after long months at sea with little variety at all, besides tack and stale ales. When ships arrived, casks of wine were rolled ashore and cracked open, flowing into the bellies of all. Local brews and rums were opportunely available as well, and so there was rarely, if ever, a shortage of drink.

More accessible and sought than drink and food though, were the countless women who flooded the establishments and streets, addicted to the men as much as the men were fiendishly in need of them. They came from all over the Caribbean, Europe, and Americas, so the menu was a cornucopia of colors and creeds. They fueled and contributed to the riotous living, and never let a moment go unattended.

The streets were bustling, so ultimately, no one paid much attention in the end. There was so much happening, Piet blended in easily. He had aged into a young man now with longer hair, so he resembled many of the younger mates taking advantage of liberty and readily available trouble. He followed some into the tavern where bawdy wassailing was on full display. Music tolled from a poorly tuned piano, while equally crocked choruses accompanied unharmoniously. Tankards teemed with ales and spirits while they regaled, sloshing across crude cedar tables, soaking the floor. In all his sneaking around in the years prior, he'd never dared to venture into the taverns, he only pilfered around them late at night when the festivities were a bit more subdued or expired. The sights before him were possibly the most enticing and exciting spectacle he had ever witnessed. But what left him slack jawed, were the beautiful women parading around among them, flaunting themselves in any manner of dress – or more acutely, undress.

Standing frozen, a couple men bumped into Piet, jostling him from his awkward paralysis. Pulling him into their little group, they shoved a beer in his hand and swayed along to the tune. Piet had never had a beer before, and was a bit offput by the bitter drink, but dared not expose himself as a cub among bruins, so he drank, and he danced, and sang. Of all the adventures he had lived, this was now his favorite. The extravagant merrymaking fit him to an unparalleled level. Everything he had experienced prior to this paled in comparison to the freedom of living so wildly. For hours, he played and danced with the men and women of the tavern; and he drank excessively. Unknowing of the physical effects of alcohol, Piet became inebriated, which confused him, being unable to capably control his body and mind. Things became blurry, but the fun persisted, until everything went black.

The next day, he woke stiffly in a corner of the tavern, his head pounded like a tack nail had been hammered into his skull. Still dizzy, daylight seemed blinding, sounds reverberated like thunderclaps, and the stale smell of the squalor singed his nose. As all the senses collided, Piet's maiden experience with drunkenness pirouetted inside his body, and he wretched. Toe curling, full body heaving bombarded him violently as the feeling that all his insides were turning out. Never in his life had he felt so miserable, cramped up in the stall, covered in bile and the liquified contents of his stomach. The purging eventually gave way to guttural dry heaving in which every convulsion wracked his weakening body. He couldn't move, and all attempts to do so pained him. The room spun uncontrollably. Piet did not care for this feeling, nor the inability to function. After what seemed like an eternity in purgatory, he looked up to the blurry vision of a seraph. She was the most beautiful creature he had seen. A halo of light ringed her figure, resembling wings, translucent and angelic. She reached out for his hand, pulling him up.

Her seductively raspy voice warned, "You're going to have to take better care of yourself, if you plan to last any time here. You were quite the entertainment last night. Out you go. Go sleep it off. Come back and find me when you're yourself again."

"What? How will I find you?"

"Name's Belle. Won't be hard to find me here."

She pushed him out the door into the dusty streets. He looked back at the beautiful figure, still hazy from his delirium, and a strange new feeling coursed through his body. She closed the door unceremoniously and was gone from his sight. Lost, confused, and dreadfully uncomfortable, he staggered to his canoe and shoved off to his little refuge cay to recuperate. Paddling was agony. Each oar stroke felt like barbs raking his muscles as he pulled one by one until he reached his inlet. When he had made it to his oasis, he climbed into the cool cleft of a tree and fell back to sleep.

Piet had made a spectacle of himself that night in the tavern. His first swig of ale was the gateway to an entirely new sphere of gaiety. All night long, they sang, danced, yelled, laughed, and told stories of adventures far and wide. He was enamored by the party, with all the behavior befitting him as though he had been preparing his entire life for such puerility. His personality, his immaturity, his wanton disregard, it all suited him keenly, and so he fell in sync with the actors to his play without pause. And they too welcomed such a lively soul so willing to participate, instigate, and celebrate. Though, as the night wore on, his cockiness and pompousness bubbled out, causing some on the fringes to take note of this vaudevillian stranger. He was attracting attention he should be careful of receiving, but it wasn't long before the novice boy was incapacitated by his drink, and so his loudness was quelled soon enough.

When he finally woke again, it was dark, and he had no immediate recollection of where he was – or how he got there. On the tiny slip of the shore, his canoe pulsed rhythmically in time with the lapping water, the oar accentuating the timing with a gentle thump.... thump.... thump. Slowly things began to come back to him, but only in bits. He inspected himself, and realized he was filthy; his clothing stained by the dirt and crusted with dried vomit. He doffed his clothing and tossed them in the water to rinse them clean. As he was redressing himself, a memory flashed across his brain like a lightning strike – gone as quick as it had come. A face, delicate and cherubic, shadowed from the light behind only revealing faint features, eyes entrancing in the obscurity. He paused, desperate to reassemble the memory. He forced the vision to return, but the pieces were too scattered. Her indistinguishable face, a hand reaching out. A door. The door shutting behind her. He was... where was he? In his tangled mind, he remembered the tavern from the night before. The tavern! He'd woken up there... This apparition had ushered him out. He flushed with odd feelings urging him to return. Quickly he threw on a new set of clothing, and shoved off in his canoe, entirely uncertain as to what – or who – he was paddling toward.

When he landed, he scurried back into the village, desperate to find this mysterious mistress. Careful not to arrive breathless and rash, he slowed his pace and composed himself a few doors down from the inn. Taking a deep breath, he walked in the door to a feeling of déjà vu. This was the place. The raucousness was once again in full swing. Though this time, he was more careful not to get roped in with the likes of the rowdy; not yet at least. He needed to find this girl, and he stood no chance of finding her subdued by drink and parade. He scanned the hazy room, poorly lit by the oil lamp chandeliers hanging from above. Throngs of bodies moved about in chaotic cadence with the music and manner to which the tavern provided. A staircase in the corner led to a balcony above where women in little more than robes, bodices, and bustiers flirted with the patrons below. Piet had no recollection of this from the previous night. But seeing the display now made his pants suddenly ill-fitting, the unfamiliar feeling returning from before.

He sided up to the bar, and asked the keep awkwardly, "I'm looking for a girl."

"Ain't all'a ya's?" came the reply.

The bar keep was a husky woman, dressed keenly enough to be both knavish and refined in a strange way. Piet found this amusing.

"No, you don't understand. I saw a girl before. I don't know her name. She told me to come back and ask for her."

"Must've been a good night with'er then, ey boy?" she jeered. "But a gentleman such as you surely are, would've asked for a name and treated her all nicely like, no? You not a gentleman?"

Piet was getting uncomfortable. He was out of his element, and as much fun as he could have, he didn't know how to play this game. He was unaware just what he was inferring when he was asking for a girl, as much as misunderstanding the barkeep's cynical replies. There were also, no gentlemen in all of Port Royal.

"I am, I think, yes? Of course, yes. I was in last night, but she ushered me out onto the street this morning."

"Oh, did she now? She make a man out'a ya, now ye back fer another visit?" She tittered.

"No, you see, I was still here this morning, and she put me out on the street. I was ill, but she was kind to me, and I want to see her again."

"I got lotsa girls, boy, an' no way'a tellin' which one tickled yer fancy. I got lotsa drinks to get served up too. So if'n ya wish'n to have a pint and look around, be my guest. The name's Nena. You let me know if you find your lost love now, alright dear?" And with that she shoved a tankard at him, its foamy amber contents splashing onto the bar top.

Piet looked at the drink, then at Nena, then back around the room. He was on his own, and he'd have to step up his confidence if he was ever going to last any time in this place under disguise. He took the ale, kicked it back, and wandered off to a corner where he could scout the place more fully.

After a short amount of time though, Piet's idleness turned to boredom, given that he was perpetually mischievous. He'd drained the drink in his hand and wished for another. He returned to the bar and flagged Nena for a refill. She obliged asking, "Ya gon' 'ave'ta start payin love, this ain't a charity."

Piet pulled out a pouch of coins and plopped it on the bar top. This was yet another amateur mistake, displaying the wealth he was pocketing on his person. Luckily enough, no nearby eyes caught sight of the purse, but Nena was quick to correct his mistake by cupping the pouch and his hand in an assertive slap. This startled Piet leaving him to think she was taking it from him, so he attempted to reproach, but her grip was strong. Their eyes met in a seriousness that gave Piet pause.

"Boy, you're not in a place you ought'n ta be slinging that kinda coin around. I don't know why, but I like you, and I'll's give you this bit of advice for free: Keep yer money to ya'self, keep it tight, and pay only when your debts come due."

"Yes ma'am," Piet eeked out.

"Put this away and pray none of these bastards pegged you for a fish!"

Piet shoved the money back into his pants and looked around awkwardly. Nena eyed him suspiciously, but *had* pegged him for a fish, as she said, and then laid on the charm.

"You seem rather lost to be in here aimin's to fit in with this bunch. What can Nena do to make it easier for you to be at ease?"

"I'm still looking for the girl I inquired on previously. I wish I could see her again."

"Sugar, I got a lotta girls upstairs. But to find the one you're lookin' for, with no detail or memory? That's not likely a outcome ya hopin for."

"She said her name…"

"Yeah? Out with it then. If you had her name, we coulda saved ourselves a heap'a hassle, now."

"See, I don't remember. My memory is cloudy, but I think she said Ella?"

"No Ella here boy. Maybe you meant Belle?" Nena chirped surprised and exasperated.

"Belle! Yes, that's it!"

"Lord seize me!" Nena snorted in hysterics, her tightly drawn bosom bouncing at every chortle. "You're looking for Belle! Have mercy! She's here, my boy, but allow me to let you in on the ground floor. That girl is a piece of work. She won't waste her time for just anyone, so whatever you got goin on down there, you better have the top of the crop to pull her attention."

"I just wanted to see her again… I want to know who she is…"

"She's a combination of sensitive and savage, that's who she is. You take this 'ere drink, and one for her, and I'll send her your way once'n I catch her."

Looking like a lost puppy, Piet took the two drinks and turned to find a place to sit until Belle found him. As he was walking cautiously with the two drinks, a gruff salt approached him, stopping him. Piet looked up at the man, standing a full head above him. He had long thinning hair, weather worn skin, and maybe five teeth total in his mouth. A gold ring hung from his lobe, and his left eye was marbled gray, blind. With his good eye, he sized up Piet forbiddingly, and scratched out a warning,

"Belle ain't a girl for the likes of you, pipsqueak. She's a hellcat and needs a man to hold her down. I'm that man, and don't think for a minute you've got the goods over me in this here district. Maybe you'll find better luck down by the docks."

The man then took Piet's beer, slugged it back, shoved it back in his hand, and then dumped the other over Piet's head, soaking him. The group around them, roared at the show. Piet, not one to be bested lunged at the formidable opponent, knocking him back a step, but unsuccessful in toppling him. The contrast was like a fly to a horse, but Piet was quite spry. When the man lunged to clobber Piet, he was able to dodge the giant, and trip him up as the strong arm passed. Using the inertia against him, Piet sent him hurtling to the ground. The laughter ceased in amazement, and then roared once again at their fallen pal, embarrassed by a pup. He stood, wiped himself off in equal parts rage and shock ready to obliterate Piet. Just before he could however, Belle intervened suspending the squabble.

"That's enough out of the two of you. Ben, what've I told you about actin' up? You know I ain't yours and no one else's. I'm my own, and I keep company with whomever I please, whenever I please. And right about now, I'm not pleased with the likes of you. No go on, get back to whatever it was you were doin' before. And you owe me a drink. Go fetch it, and I might reconsider later."

Ben, testing the situation stepped forward once more, motioning to come at Piet, but Belle stood between them, and snapped at him once again, "what'd I just say. Try it again, and I'll have you out on your ass. Now get me that drink!"

Ben scowled and turned away shirking off the jeers by the others.

"Now, as for you," Belle turned to face Piet. "What's your name?"

"Piet," he replied.

"Piet, you look familiar, have we met?"

"We sure have, miss. Last night, er, this morning, rather. You told me to come back and ask for you."

She laughed at this pathetic creature in front of her, and said, "Right, I remember. You're the poor thing I had to clear out. You covered the place in your sick."

This diminished Piet a bit. It was not the memory he hoped to have been recalled by. Ben returned with a mug for Belle, still glaring at Piet.

"Come find me when you're done babysitting," he growled.

"We'll see. I told you, I'm not keen on you actin' a fool, Ben. That'll be the last time I say it."

He grunted displeased and left the two of them. He'd asserted his dominance, though, not with any real outcome.

"Come with me, let's get you out of these clothes. They're no sort for the likes of a man that stands up to Benny Guns."

This made Piet stand a little taller again. Whispers began circling, following the scuffle with Ben, though he had no idea who he had picked a fight with. All eyes were on the newcomer being led to aloft with the top girl of the house. So aloof, Piet had no idea what he was involved with, nor the inadvertent credibility he'd just assumed by standing up to one of the most tested men in all the Caribbean.

Belle led Piet upstairs by the hand and showed him to a room at the end of a slipshod corridor. When they reached the doorway, she unlocked the door and let him in, following behind. Piet was mystified by the room, and the heavy scent of burning incense. Belle locked the door behind them.

"Well, Piet, what's your story then? Why so hard pressed to find me of all the pretty girls around here?"

"Like I said downstairs, you told me to come back and ask for you and so, I did. I couldn't stop thinking about you all day."

This made Belle giggle. He was adorable in this moment. He had a way about him that was so uncannily brazen, while at the same time so innocently ignorant.

"I did, yes. And I'm glad you did. I'm pleased to meet you in better health than before. But what is it you're looking for?" She replied with practiced dalliance.

"I needed to see you again. I needed to remember who you were. You're very pretty, and I couldn't get you off my mind. I just needed to come find you."

Indeed, she was pretty. She was slightly shorter than average, not much over five feet tall, with exotically tanned olive skin, able to withstand the sun's intensity. Her eyes were wildly captivating, glittering in the candlelight like a rare chrysoberyl gemstone. Her pert little nose turned up ever so slight at the end, giving her face a cuteness in stark contrast to everything around her. Her indefectible face framed by two perfect cheek bones pulled it all together for an unmistakable cherubic charm. She had a soft raspy voice, piqued with an accent that placed her origins from among likes of French creole. It was exotic, alluring, and able to melt the hardest of souls, much like a siren's song.

"But what do you really want? What does your little heart desire from a girl like me?"

Belle was starting to realize he really didn't have a plan. He didn't know what he was doing, that he really only wanted to see her again; that was it. She was so used to this being a straightforward transaction, the small talk never took so much prying. She decided to switch tactics.

"Come, let's get you out of those clothes, like we said. You shouldn't have to stand around in soaked rags such as these. Take them off, I'll find you something more suitable. You wait right here."

Belle reapproached the door, unlocked it, and closed it behind her once more locking it, with Piet inside. He looked around, looking at the bed, vanity, wash basin, and a chair. He sat down on the chair taking in the bedchamber with all senses. Visually, it accommodable – though by the standards of someone who sleeps in trees is concerned, it was frilly. He didn't know the scent, but it burned his nose pleasantly. He'd had no experience with incense before and was unaware it was masking the grotesque smells of the barroom below as well as the emanant odor of sweaty bodies. The sounds were very confusing, and seemed to issue from below, but also the other rooms. There was a strange amount of screaming and banging. This didn't make sense to Piet, so he took another drink after he'd finished undressing. Now naked, the chair was uncomfortably hard, so he stood again, inspecting the baubles and trinkets on the vanity.

The lock snapped back, and Belle remerged with a handful of fancy clothing. It didn't occur odd to him to be standing nude in a room. He'd run naked many times with the natives, that being *free* was just as normal as anything else. Fortunately for him, he was in a place that condoned this, and Belle was none-the-least offended; truthfully, she was impressed by his nonchalance, another attribute that pulled her toward him. He spun around to see her in such a way that she caught all there was to see of him, causing her to uncharacteristically blush.

"Here," she said as she locked the door once again. "I found these. I think you'll find them much finer than those you had before."

"Thank you," he replied, still as naked as the day he was born, and so oddly at ease.

"I'd like to show you something," she said quizzically. "Come, sit here. Lie back, make yourself comfortable." She guided him to the bed, and sat him down, standing in front of him.

"Sure, what is it?" He asked almost comically childish at this point. "I like surprises."

"You're just too much! Yes, I have a strong feeling you'll like this surprise, and it's not something you've received before. But don't worry, I know just what to do with that. Now just lie back and let me show you."

VIII

Late afternoon hailed an alert from the crow's nest, that the island of Jamaica was in sight. The men aboard scrambled to the rails to view the majestic blue-green mountains on the hazy horizon, barely visible without a spyglass. Cheers erupted from the men, happy to be so close to land – and liberty! The commotion brought the captain from his chamber to see for himself. The warmth and humidity felt resplendent and anew with the sighting of land – and home.

Wendy ventured out on the deck as well, curious, and excited to finally see land again after all the time at sea. The monotonous panorama she had experienced for so long now had grown tiresome. As she approached the railing too, she bore witness to a spectacle beyond her wildest comprehensions. There are few visions so beguiling as the Caribbean, and this scene was nothing shy of breathtaking. She could never in her life imagine the brilliance on parade before her. The spectacle was as if it were a fable; an over-extravagant depiction of the scenery added to a story which otherwise lacked color.

Looking out, dolphin raced along the prow of the ship, gliding with the carving undercurrent from the draft of the ship. Sea turtles floated in the rippled expanse in such quantity, they proved as much of an obstacle as the reef and shoals; their giant carapaces a tapestry of earthen magnificence, reflecting in the sun. All these excitements were too much for her to take in. She was awe struck, frozen in complete bewilderment. Jamaica ahead of her was an illustration of majestic colors. The dark mountains a blanket behind the bustling dusty city of Port Royal, browns and tans and other spatterings of muted tones.

The crew bustled with fervor, pulling lines, trimming sail, yelling commands, barking orders. Hook and Smee stood stalwart upon the helm deck, keeping an eye out ahead. For all the seamlessness in the open ocean, everything ran as organized chaos in this moment. As they approached their entry, each maneuver and task were executed precisely following the order it necessitated. Still in the crow's nest, Mr. Turley called out waypoints as they now cautiously dodged deadly reef heads and shoals below. But what struck Wendy most odd, was as they neared, all the men plugged their ears with cannon wick. They even handed wick to the Africans and instructed them to plug their ears as well. None of them however, offered her the same.

As the ship cut through the idyllic water, the men were on high alert, deafened by the plugs. Yet, they all orchestrated a seamless execution of duties toward their mooring. On the port side, a bizarre island approached, and as it did, Wendy noticed all the men moved to the starboard side. Bewildered by what was happening, she too followed, looking around for any clue as to what was happening. Nothing presented itself obvious, and this perplexed her even more. None of them would look her in the eye and deflected any attempt to explain. They were all as silent as they could be, not speaking a word, not mumbling a sound, communicating only by gestures. Wendy grew irritably impatient, wanting to know what was happening. In a huff, she stormed off, stamping along the deck. One of the men nearest wrapped her up, sacking her to the floor. She began to shriek in protest and fight off her apprehender, but the pirate looked her true in the eye and sternly hushed her. The look on his face was as somber as could possibly be emphasized, and this quickly quelled her commotion. They lay there, silently unmoving.

A moment or so following this ruckus, as the vessel slipped through the running tide, a thump was felt against the hull. Then another, and eventually another. Wendy, worried now because she hadn't been given any wick, didn't know what was happening. Still, she laid on the deck pinned by the subduer, with fear in his eyes. Seeing the men in such alarm was unsettling and was enough for her to grasp the severity of the situation and keep dead still like the others. Above them, Hook and Smee had also disappeared. Everyone had taken cover against this unseen peril. Her subduer mouthed silently *"merrrrmaaaaaids!"*

Wendy's curiosity piqued to an all-new height, but she was still held down. Mermaids weren't real? Yet all the men were hiding silently from the supposed reality. Sirens were something she had only heard of in tales, and never to any logical description. They were yarns, fictional legends. She desperately wanted to see for herself, but she was pulled back down. He shook his head 'no,' with an imploring look. She eyed the railing above her, then him, then the railing again, then the teak deck planks. The ship crept on ahead, easily as could be managed. Thump. Thump, thump. Then a strange sound followed, a song of eerie beauty, so harmonious and pure. Wendy heard it plain as day and yearned to see for herself. But what she couldn't understand, was that she wasn't being drawn to her demise as the stories foretold.

After what seemed like hours, the siren song ceased, as did the banging of the hull, a cry came again from the crow's nest, "All's clear! Helm, pull to starboard, sheets free save the jib, carry on to stand!"

The men all clambered back to their respective positions, and began the final approach to drop anchor, safely within the refuge of Port Royal. They thrummed in unison calling to each other as they hauled the lines, struck the sails, and readied to come to a heel to drop anchor. Smee reappeared on the main deck to ensure everything was in order, and found Wendy standing about, looking back at the island. Crystalline blue water lapped sublimely against the ship, translucently showcasing the treacherous crags of the reef deep below.

"Mermaids, lass. Certain death for menfolk, as you might know from yer stories. Well, they ain't stories, they's true."

"But why all the silliness of hiding? I'm quite aware of the luring songs from all I've heard, but…"

"A sailor can't be too careful by the likes of a mermaid deary. They plugs their ears so's not to hear the song. They hides behind the rails, so's not to catch an eye with the she-devils."

"But why didn't I get any wick? Was I bait?"

"Because'n you's a woman, Miss Wendy. Their songs don't have no effect on the fairer kind, but if they'd seen you, well, they'd've been right spiteful, and likely sunk us sure as day. Wraiths they are, if'n a woman's seen on a ship of men, and for that they'll kill you and us all in one."

This gave her pause, and Smee excused himself to finish attending to his business. She looked back toward the island once more. It was a fair distance behind them now and they were close to port. The mermaids stayed far enough off, so they weren't in shot range of the man's world, but she swore she saw three mysterious floating heads just at the water line. She didn't want to feel hated, so she raised her arm to wave, but no sooner did she, the heads disappeared below followed by large splashing tails. This was such a strange encounter; how could she not take the chance at seeing (or even befriending) a real-life mermaid? The memory would stay with her forever.

When the ship came to a halt, everything was prepared for disembarking. All around them, ships sat fatly in the road, their masts rocking hypnotically to and fro. The men were eager to get on shore and take their leave for a spell. They had been at sea for nearly a year now. Most of the time had been in search of prizes returning to Europe, therefore the hold had decent supply of wares to be bartered off. This would be an undertaking to relieve themselves of, and not all of it would change hands here in Jamaica. Hook was anxious to make his deals and arrangements in town and be compensated for his efforts. As well, the crew were also since they would be paid out on any exchange.

On the Jolly Roger, it was customary that the captain and Smee would shuttle over first, establishing their presence and intentions with any authorities who might have arrived in their absence. Nothing would be advertised or displayed under the black flag until it was clear they were in safe company. If the crown had sent any cronies to establish law and order in their land, the story would need to fit the appropriate inspection for fear of seizure and capture. As this was taking place, the crew remained aboard the ship finishing the breakdown and tidying of the ship. When their captain returned with report, they would receive their instructions or permissions for what came next. Either of three things could come of it, they would be allowed shore leave, they would need to flee quickly, or they would be clapped in chains and sent to the gallows. Keeping busy until he returned was the only way to keep their minds off the latter and keeping sail and guns on the ready was response to the former. It could take hours before he would return, and this left them in a precarious situation until he did.

Wendy and the Africans were the most anxious, not understanding the gravity of the situation they were in, though the Africans had chores to keep them occupied, but this only allayed their fears to minimal extent. For them, they knew, nothing was guaranteed. Wendy paced, rattling her saber with every heavy step. She had no chores to preoccupy her, and so she was left to simply wait out the process, pacing. This made her impatient, and her impatience made the men weary of her idleness.

Cecco eventually approached Wendy to distract her and keep her at bay while the others were toiling away. She had become a gadfly to the others, and they were in powerless to squash the incessant biting of her pacing and rattling sword.

"Ascolta Ragazza, you're makin' us a bit crazy with the back and forth. Why don' you have a seat somewhere. It's gon' be a while 'afore any us gets ashore, so give it a rest, huh?

"Mr. Cecco, I have not been brought all this way to be held captive on this ship. I should be accompanying the captain in town if he's honest about his purpose for me!"

The men all laughed at her self-importance. This upset her, and to further her insistence, she pulled her sword, an act of hostility among her company. Time stopped as they all paused to watch what happened next. Cecco was not a man to muss with, and she was in no position to challenge him. Fortunately, he had a level head about him and was willing to play along with the little lady with the big ovaries. He playfully put his hands up in surrender, and looked back again at his mates, all enjoying the show.

"Miss Wendy, I don' think this gon' end like you wan it to. You see, I cut you down, you dead. You dead, I dead too. Not gon' happen. So jus put your blade away, and les go about our way. You let us get our work done, we get to go ashore. We don' get our work done, we don' get to go ashore at all."

"I'm not going to sit around like some dilettante, awaiting permission to be paraded about."

"Lass, we all gotta get the ship ready, an' ye makin' it right difficult. You wan'go ashore? We needs t'be finishin' our works. But if'n ye feelin itchy, let's see what you got on that skewer of yours."

Cecco whistled to the men, reaching his arm out, signaling for one of them to toss him a blade. When he was ready, he stretched, flexed, rolled his big square head, and took his position as well. Unbeknownst to Wendy though, he wasn't setting up for a kill, he was testing her in an effort to preoccupy her. The only pitfall to this, was now no work was going to get done, because everyone was tuned in for the show. With the captain and Smee off-ship, wagers started peppering the air, along with some ribbing, goading and insults. The men also didn't know their man was only toying with her.

"Well alright, let's have it then. I'll make it easy for you this time." He said with a smile.

Wendy huffed and made the first advance. It was a novice mistake letting her opponent taunt her and affect her mental acuity. He, in reply, simply took a step to the side easily avoiding her jab. She reset, eyed him more surely, knowing she was being watched by everyone. The pressure to not define her as just another tart mounted with every second she faced him. Again, she stepped at him, swiping quickly, then jabbing again. She was quick for her skill level, and so Cecco had to deflect with his blade, metal clashing against metal with a frenetic clang. Again, she pursued her offensive position, making Cecco now engage defensively. He stepped back with intent, now on guard. However, like a chess master he had already defeated her in his head. She was too eager, uncalm, and severely unskilled to match his capabilities. This did not mean he could assume she wasn't dangerous, quite the contrary. She could easily kill him if he wasn't careful. He had seen plenty of men so sure of themselves, only to be bested by their own ego and arrogance.

For some time, they engaged. Cecco patiently on the defense, allowing her to get her work in, but also to tire herself. This wouldn't take long, he thought, but oddly she had improved stamina, and continued to keep him on the move. That's not to say he didn't give her a challenge. He made a few lunges at her, allowing her defense to gain equal practice. He was making her work for it, and impressively she met the match he was serving her. The men all agog, still yelled and jeered, antagonizing them to finish the other. After some time, Cecco knew this needed to end, because if any of them were caught in this engagement by the captain, he'd have their heads. So, he provided her a few more opportunities, but finally set up a feint, to which she fell victim. He had bested her, but in such a way that she was not decimated. She had fought considerably well against one of the strongest men on the ship.

"You've done well, m'lady. You should be proud of the progress you've made. Master Smee would be quite tickled, were he here."

"So, a lady can wield a sword then, eh?"

"Not any lady, m'lady, but you're not a ord'n'ry lady are ye?" He winked and offered her his hand to pull her up. She obliged, and blushed.

"Maybe next time, you won't go so easy on me then?"

"Ahh, Miss Wendy, I ain't gonna let you get it easy. Where's the fun in that?"

Wendy was exhausted. She had displayed an incredible level of competence and was now willing to rest quietly out of the way of the men. She hadn't intended this avenue but wasn't displeased by it either. She (more accurately her mouth and entitlement) had gotten the better of her, and she was grateful her challenger was wise enough not to let her imperil either of them in the duel. He gave her a real go, at least more than she'd been able to square out of Smee in their practices. He had trained her as well as he was able, but she hadn't applied any of the lessons in any sort of test until now. All the practicing she had done on her own in addition to her lessons had burned in the techniques and increased her durability. For this she was proud. Her father had always reminded her as a child in anything she undertook:

Always align yourself with someone better than you. You'll never advance if your skill is above that of your partner's. But, when you have advanced your skill, allow others to learn from you just the same. For this, she appreciated Cecco being the better opponent and giving her the chance.

****

As evening approached, Captain Hook and Smee returned with report. When back on the ship, he called the company together to give them the details they should heed.

"Since our departure last, little has changed in the way of liberation from the crown, and the agents of his governance still abide in our homestead. It appears though, they are still very much self-interested, and for our landing to be granted we must satisfy their wants from that of our coffers. I have provided them with my *public* ledger, and they have agreed to a tax to the crown, though, they will be confiscating a few items in lieu of a larger tax. We have met on agreeable terms, as to what is fair — as far as they know, mind you — and Smee will adjust the earnings with Mr. Teynte accordingly. To recompense the losses, I will be making arrangements in the coming days. You will all receive your adjusted dividends after we have collected payment for the remaining merchandise. This reward will be distributed among those who remain crewed to our little faction at such time we take our leave of Port Royal. Mr. Teynte will also make record of this sum, due upon sail. Have you any questions, men?"

Everyone on the ship had been through this shakedown before, and nothing came as a surprise. No one seemed to have any questions or concerns since this arrangement was common and necessary to remain in port — *their* port. So, despite some general grumbling, everyone was agreeable to the terms, and this allowed them to proceed with offloading the salable items they had captured. Spices, casks, seeds, bolts of fabrics, cotton, and tea were hauled out to shore and made available for sale. Ten bricks of tea, four carpets, and two slaves were due to the governor - the acting agent of the crown. An additional two percent of expected sold goods would be due to the crown. Though, the crown would never see that tax since the governor and soldiers were merely masquerading as officials in Jamaica. This was a frustrating arrangement, because at any time, if they found the gusto, they could strangle the comings and goings of the pirates through force, particularly in the forts positioned along the banks. But all the agents on this lost lump of land were no more interested in waging war against the pirates, because it was bad for their business and self-interests.

107

At Hook's cunning, Danso and Osei were to be relinquished to the governor. He had no personal qualms with the two men, except that they would not advance his plans by following Wendy around like protective dogs. Wendy was incensed by this and of course protested to the utmost extent. Smee would not allow her any court with Hook throughout the tallying process. What was done was done, and there was nothing she could do about it. Yet, they held their heads high, knowing their fates were at risk all along. Wendy promised them she would see them again and thanked them profusely for their stalwart watch over her throughout their voyage together. As they loaded into the skiffs, and chains clamped upon them, she wept. They had come so far for freedom, to learn to read and speak, only to wind up captive property again. The familiarity with them was beyond endearing. They had devoted themselves to her and watching them ship off into servitude gutted her.

When the sun faded behind the towering blue mountains, shadows cast upon the island and the city darkening deeper and deeper into the night. Fire lights flickered in the town illustrating a devilish den of vulgarity and ribaldry. The humid air smelled smoky now, suppressing the seaside saltiness and floral bouquet. The din of the town could be heard in muffled waves upon the ship. The men were chomping at the bit to gain their opportunity for lasciviousness. Smee was appointed with finding Wendy and preparing her to be escorted into town.

"Cap'n would like a word with you, Miss Wendy. The time has come for you to go ashore, and he will be taking you with him forthwith. He expects you to be ready when he departs, as he has an appointment to keep."

Wendy was eager to have words with the captain about the loss of her two friends, and as much to get off the woeful ship. Smee received no protest from her, and she followed him back to the captain's quarters. With a rap on the door to announce their presence, he opened the door and ushered her in. Smee closed the door behind her. When she entered, Hook was leaning against his escritoire, polishing his hook, awaiting her company. Seeing her ready for a fight, he pre-empted her with his silver tongue.

"You're angry I sent your guardians into servitude. That is understandable, and for your displeasure, I hope you will eventually forgive me. Until then, they have been placed in servitude to the governor, the very seat of power I – we – aim to depose. See now though, that with your conspirators in the house of the governor, you will have inside access to that vile man, and how best to navigate controlling his bidding.

My dear, this could not have played out better if I had scripted it. Your men are the precise instruments of intelligence for this endeavor. How they are so dutiful to you is sublime! You will find avenue to confide with them and report those details back to me. It is so perfectly genius!"

"You have cast those poor, innocent men into the worst construct imaginable, all to be pawns in your quest for depravity!"

"I could not guarantee their life to be any better elsewhere. Especially here, among the sugar plantations. I do not condone slavery as a model for human life; it is contrary to our decree. If they, or any other man on this ship for that matter, is caught in the act of what we do, there is no alternative. The only end is death. A gruesome, public, death. And those two men, they would have it worse. A swift death would be the lord's blessing upon them. Nay, they wouldn't be hanged but instead butchered for the rest of their days on some other man's cane field, who would have it in for them as being pirates aforetime. No, I cannot promise they will not have a hard life ahead of them any more than I can guarantee I myself won't be swinging from the gallows on the morrow. But what I can promise, is that they are in a house of fancy, and will be expected to abide by proper decorum, insulating them from the oppressive landowner who would otherwise break them."

Wendy was taken aback at the straightforward, logical response, and was humbled by the reply. Her mannerisms shifted from confrontational to resolve. He was right. Damn him, he was right. By sending Danso and Osei into the governor's employ, they would survive better than on the streets, or elsewhere for that matter. They didn't have papers, so it could easily turn into an oppressive problem with no one to speak for them. She hated that he was so devious to know this was a wise play. In the moment her mind raced through thoughts and emotions, he had given her the pause to process it all before he spoke again.

"Child, you continue to oppose me as a soundrel, because why? You're taught that I am a villain, killing and plundering on the high seas? That I am a character in some horror, to be despised? At every turn, you are quick to rebuke my efforts to set the world right as we see it – free from tyranny and oppression. Not all criminals take to the sea with gangs of swarthy men, seeking carnage. I believe you will find, quite quickly here in fact, that the actual criminals are those with power unbefitting their station. Have I not attended to you as an equal in our time together? Have I made any efforts to be rid of you in this journey? I think your worldly view is not so grand as you might believe it.

Take a look around. See for yourself. Those men out there, they have protected you and will do so in the days ahead. Cecco? He sparred with you willingly, when he could have cut your head off before you had drawn your sword from your belt. It would suit you well to consider, you are one of us now, like it or not. And that comes with a great amount of power. Because not only are you one of us, you are also born into class, allowing you audience with the elite. They do not know you are one of us yet, therefore you are a chameleon, able to blend into your environment. You are to be the pirate queen of this god-forsaken spit of land."

Her brain twisted in revelation, digesting everything he had just said. He knew about the duel. He called her a pirate like them – was that really true? *A queen?* As she processed all this information, she slowly began to see things from a different lens. Whether it was all accurate or not, there was no denying that Hook was conniving and clever.

"Now, if the lady pleases, we shall make our way to shore. I have an appointment to keep, and I am not one to be tardy. As well, I have made arrangements for you to be kept with a very dear partner and caretaker in town. I trust you will be comfortable there, and I will call upon you as necessary. But before we go, you should not make an entrance in those rags. First impressions are everything, you know."

At this, presented a gorgeous dark purple gown, glittering with lace and trappings. The fabric was soft; unlike the heavy brocade she had been so used to wearing before. She was speechless at the beauty and surprise of it.

"Where did this come from? Where did you get it? It's beautiful!"

"I obtained it upon my venture into town earlier today. I was not deceiving you before when I apologized for not commandeering your belongings. A beautiful woman belongs in a gown of equal design. I shall give you a moment to redress and then we shall be off."

As she felt the sateen fabric in her coarse fingertips, she was elated to don such fineness once again. She slipped out of her pirate's rags without hesitation, and into the dress. How wonderful it felt on her skin, and breathable. The corset built into the dress was made from whalebone and conformed to her perfectly. Unlike her old dresses, requiring a maid to cinch the ties in the back, she tied off the laces on the front, making it exceptionally easy to dress herself.

Hook finally reemerged in the dusky evening light. He was finely dressed in his best coat, ruffled blouse, and boots. The hook gleamed in the breaking moonlight, polished to mirror-like shine. Wendy followed him, glittering like a gem. She was radiant, and the dress accentuated her embonpoint figure. His heavy steps on the deck made his presence known above the fracas across the water. All eyes turned to witness the two making their appearance before them.

The eager men gathered before them, hopeful their leave would now be granted, and it would be, however, he was to be rowed ashore first with Wendy, and the rest of them were to follow once he was on land with her. Without haste, Smee readied the skiff to take them ashore and the crew all watched the beauty depart with their captain.

The rowboat bumped alongside the low dock and slid slowly to a stop. Hook stepped up on the slip and then offered up his arm for Wendy to aid herself in doing the same. He looked at her with steady eyes, expecting that she should now be unphased by this. Awkwardly, she reached out, gripping his hand, and climbed out onto the embarkment beside him.

Together, they walked into town from the North Docks, right down the middle of Lime Street, past the customs house where he had negotiated earlier in the day. The dirt road was mottled with sandy patches and ruts from carts. The village town was a maze of buildings in various stage of dilapidation or repair, as the case may be. Wild townsfolk hung from balconies, ripped madly through the avenues, fired shots into the air, and fought ruthlessly as drink burned in their bellies. As they processed, the rowdy crowd parted as the infamous Captain Hook had returned, and on his arm was the most spectacular woman they had seen in some time. Awestruck, the crowd filled in behind them as they passed, murmurs, gasps and whispers floating in the wind behind them. Hook was relishing this. Wendy was also. Turning the corner onto Canon, they came to a shiplap building with two stories, and a carnival of noise piercing the night. Above, a sign hung demarking the establishment: *Pixies*.

Hook, chivalrous as any gentleman ought to be (despite being a pirate), opened the heavy wood door allowing Wendy to enter ahead of him. When she stepped into the establishment, she was affronted by such unexpected depravity on parade within. Her head reeled as she absorbed a saturnalia of senses. The stench of the place was sour, reeking of stale ale and mildew, coupled with effervescence of old wood. Aurally, her ears rang at the cacophony of song, piano, violin, yelling, swearing, whistling, and more.

Visually, the place was smoky, both from pipe and lamps, but it was luminous enough to see what – to her – looked like perdition's playhouse.

Hook entered behind and beside her, gripping his coat lapels, he drew in the same senses, in contrastingly nostalgic fondness. This was his stomping ground, and he was quite merry at being back. He ushered Wendy over to the bar to introduce her to the keep as his guest.

"Nena, my love, this is the woman I spoke of earlier. This is Wendy" Hook rasped as she served him a frothing pint.

"Nice t'meet you deary. Jasper 'ere speaks very highly of ye. Says you're a spitfire, you are. I'll take good care of her for ye, Hooky!"

"I know you will, and you know where to find me in the meantime. Wendy, I am to take leave of you for my prearrangement now. Nena here will look after you from here on out. I will seek you out in the coming days to further our affairs." Hook explained as he toasted Nena with a raise of his mug. He walked away and ascended the staircase to the last door at the end of the hallway.

"What a curious name for such a place…" Wendy opined.

"Yeah, Pixies are a devil of a sort. They be mischievous things who dances in the moonlight. Their favorite pastimes are leading travelers astray and frightening young maidens, if you get my drift darlin!" Nena replied with a toothy wink.

"But this is a wicked place, as a girl, I was told of stories that pixies were such gentle creatures…"

"Aye, I've got a fine lot of nice creatures in 'ere'll make a cock crow, but make no mistake, there are plenty of evil sprites who enjoy causing chaos for unlucky sots. The scary stories usually start with the little ones being disrespected in some way or other. And the punishment rarely fits the crime, but who's gonna say otherwise in this den of thieves?"

"My word," Wendy gasped in horror.

"What'll ye have then darlin'?"

"I shouldn't. I feel it best to keep my wits about me in this place."

"Don't be a prude! Trust me, it'll take the edge off, and it seems you could take a few edges off. Ain't nary a soul in here gon' trifle with you tonight darlin'. I got my eyes on you, and I'll get ye accommodated shortly. Got a nice room upstairs waitin' for ye. Go on then." Nena slid her a chalice of wine and instructed her to make herself at home.

Across the tavern, a figure sat skulking in the shadowed corner. He had seen her come in and she instantly caught his attention. She was radiant, the regalness of her aubergine dress exuded distinction. In contrast, her obvious naïveté gave her a relatable innocent charm in a place such as this. He then watched as the man appeared behind her and his heart dropped into his stomach. It couldn't be… but here he was, plain as the nose on his own face – the man with hook for a hand. The legend who survived the crocodile. The man he had dueled with years before in the fen. He watched from the recesses, so very intrigued, as Hook escorted her and handed her off to Nena at the bar. From his post, he could see when Hook took his leave, he made straight for the room at the end of hall, upstairs. That was his flop; more accurately, it belonged to his girl. The notion of this brute calling on Belle was unwelcome. Piet, always the one to play with fire, made straight for the girl.

"Good evening, miss. I see you have been abandoned by your suitor in the most unfortunate of places."

Wendy blushed unexpectedly at the young man's advance. His hair pulled back neatly, his clothes a bit more refined than the filthiness she was accustomed to seeing the men in. He was cute, and she was instantly smitten, without any forewarning.

"He is not my suitor, but how kind of you to be concerned for my well-being."

"Not your suitor? Goodness, you mean to tell me you are joining us on your own this evening so coincidentally?"

"Hardly. He is but an associate of sorts if you will."

"I see. Allow me to introduce myself, I am Piet. I would love to have you join me if you would be so willing?"

"Wendy. Charmed. You are kind, Piet, and I thank you for your offer, but I shall wait here for him to return, so we can be on our way."

Piet laughed, irritably. "He will not be back for some time I can assure you. He has gone aloft and called upon the most bewitching lady of the house. They will be otherwise occupied for what I believe to be the remainder of the night. Come, join me."

"Not so fast boy!" Nena barked out, rejoining the conversation having retrieved the empty drinkware. "She's to stay with me until I get her sorted. Keep it in your pants. You've got yours."

"Tsk, tsk, Nena. I mean no harm to the lady. I merely wish to get to know her. She clearly has a mind worth discovering, improved over general average around here?"

"No. She's not on the market, and she belongs to me and the very man'll gaff your figs clean off!"

Piet laughed, knowing his secret regarding Hook. "Nena, charge me if you must, but I am going to entertain Miss Wendy, and when that scoundrel is finished with *'mine,'* he may have *her* back, and I shall then take the rest up with Belle."

"To be clear, I belong to no one. Do not speak of me as property, either of you. I am an agent of Captain Hook, and we have business to attend to."

"No deary, you misunderstand. You belong to me now. You're my charge. He'll come for you when he needs you. And when he does, ye best be nearby to answer his call."

Wendy's world began to spin once again. So unceremoniously she had been dumped into the ward of another stranger. So callously the man she had (foolishly) begun to trust duped her and handed her off like scraps. How could he do this, after all the confiding and planning? Her expectations of their partnership were clearly misjudged, though truthfully, she wasn't quite sure what that would look like now that she considered it. She was though, sure that it did not look like this. She took the chalice in front of her and downed it. She handed it back to Nena to refill and told her to put it on Hook's tab.

"Nena, when you have secured my arrangements, I will take my leave. Until then, you can find me with the gentleman. Come Piet, I wish to learn more about you and this place."

Before Nena could protest, Wendy led Piet from the bar. She was going to have to break her if that behavior continued. The gall of the girl, so new and foreign, to act so privileged. Nena had seen it before in younger girls who were ignorantly so sure and full of themselves. But with Wendy, she was sure of herself, and she was not a gutter girl like so many others before her. She was of status and class, though here, that would tender very little and might just be reason for concern among her general clientele.

As the evening wore on, Wendy and Piet engaged in idle conversation while the madness broiled around them. They talked about their family lives, their struggles, and their perspectives of various subjects, including pirates. One thing they found common ground on was their general distaste for the reprobates, yet here they were, both among them in the lion's den.

One thing that struck Wendy was how Piet was ostracized from his family, and how much he missed his mother. He harbored a great undercurrent of resentment having not been able to reconnect with her after she was forced to turn her back on him, and so, he spent most of his time in the company of Belle, who he explained, is whom Hook was with presently. Piet also boasted of his family farm in the hills and how he would return every so often to play games with his lost boys.

"Lost boys? What are those?"

"Freed slaves, who I keep on my farm. They take care of it for me while I'm away."

"Let me get this straight," she interjected, "You have 'free' slaves on your family farm, taking care of it for you. Do you pay them? Do they earn a wage?"

"No, but they have everything they need, and no reason to leave. I take care of them. I'm like their leader."

Wendy deduced Piet did not see the irony in his statements about this arrangement.

"I can take you there someday, and you can see. I rescue them and give them a place to live. They're grateful, so they're my friends."

It sounded a little less ironic at this explanation, but Wendy was still unsure what Piet's angle was. On the surface, he was a deluded landowner seeking adventure and filling a maternal void with the company of a bangtail.

He also loved to talk about himself, and controlled most of their conversation, even to the extent of speaking over Wendy at times, just to make a point about something inane. Despite these cautionary aspects, she did enjoy his company and felt comfortable with him. He was the first person she had been around in ages, whom she felt she could let down her guard a little. Maybe though, it was the alcohol.

Piet got up to get another round of drinks for the two of them, leaving Wendy at the table. When she was unattended, others began to eye her mischievously. Her senses were dulled, but she still had her wits about her. She had been pacing herself, and as a lady, had been taught when it comes to alcohol, *not less than two, not more than three*. A lady could be social and maintain decorum in most instances with an edge taken off, but beyond that, a fool you could easily make of yourself while inebriated. Men began to maneuver in, like sharks to blood in the water.

Taken by surprise, another woman sat down in front of her. She was short, wearing an ivory shift, lacking the appropriate accoutrements to pull it together primly. Her brown curly hair was a mess but pulled back to make it neater. Her cheeks were rosy, and her skin glistened from a lightness of sweat. She had a scowl marring an otherwise adorable face, and Wendy was immediately on defense by her abrupt appearance.

"You're the new girl, yeah?" she inquired.

"Excuse me?" Wendy replied, off-guard.

"You're the new girl. The one the Cap'n dropped off. Nena told me about you. Told me to get you situated."

"Oh, yes, I suppose that's me. I'm Wendy. And you are?"

"Working. I haven't the time to coddle you, so you're going to have to learn quick."

Wendy, now very perturbed, sat up more straight, ready to snap back. But before she could, Piet came back to the table with two cups of wine.

"Belle! You're back! I'd like you to meet Wendy!"

"I'm not back, I'm still on. The ol' cap'n's takin a breather, so I ducked out to get some more rum. I'm hopin' he'll black out soon enough after this though."

Piet was displeased once again at sharing Belle in this way, but she was a parlor girl, and this was her work. It was one thing when she would bag a quick John or two and come back to him just as swiftly, and they would share the rest of the night with each other; but this was different. Hook, the man he'd quarreled with so near to death, was giving it to his girl, all night. Piet's selfishness began to bubble up. Of all the men to re-appear in this shit-pot place, it was him. He was not inclined to share a bed after tonight's coition, and so he became fractious with her.

"Take your rum then and have your fun. I shan't be here when you expire, so don't come looking for me after."

Belle, attuned to his usual manner of pouting and false sense of exclusivity, simply rolled her eyes, and sighed. She didn't have time to placate him again over this. She cared for Piet, and he was the nicest of the men she'd shared herself with, but she was not his alone, and he never seemed to completely understand that. In fact, he had spent so much time with her, that her business had begun to suffer for it. Regulars began to assume they were partners, and so they slowly ceased soliciting her. Only on occasion would she advertise herself to them, and that coincided with Piet being away for a few days, but mostly, she was only courted by newcomers and, of course, long-time status-holding familiars. Ultimately this was bad for business, and she had to remind herself (and Piet), that she was the top girl here, and if she was going to stay that way, she needed to produce for Nena. If she didn't, she wouldn't have a doss for them to share at all, and their comforts would cease to exist.

"Piet, you forget my place, and yours. I am not yours alone, and at times you must share. Perhaps it is best you return to your farm for a few days, and when you have come to your senses again, I will be here."

Wendy, witnessing their interaction, felt awkward to be included, and shifted in her seat, looking for any ability to exit politely. As she did, Belle returned her glance, as if to signal she needed to stay put.

"As for you, Nena has had me prepare the grand boudoir for you. I don't know who you think you are, but that type of finery ain't going to sit well with the other girls deservin' upgrades. Watch yourself. Yours is the top of the stairs, second door to the right. And you stay put until morning; you hear me?"

Wendy nodded, secretly gleeful at the mention of a 'grand room' that she would have a fine bed to sleep in once again. Her mind began to race with all the niceties she might find, and that she might return to the caliber of woman she'd once been.

"Now, both of you say your good evenings, and clear out."

On that, Belle took the bottle of rum and returned to her room. Wendy and Piet lingered a bit longer, Wendy massaging Piet's fragile ego. She didn't intend to, but it came almost as second nature to care for the weak.

"Would you like to come to the farm with me?"

"Tonight? No, you heard her. I need to settle in here. I imagine Nena and Belle will be expectant of me in the morning, and if I am not about, I could very well lose my accommodations."

"Can I stay with you instead then?"

"Piet, that is an impropriety. I am not such a woman as Belle and will not have my reputation sullied in such a way."

"I don't want to be alone tonight."

Wendy, knowing the situation could devolve if she didn't stand firm, stood up to leave. Piet grabbed her hand before she could go and looked at her plaintively.

"I'm sorry, Piet, but it will do you well to take time for yourself as Belle said. I too will be here when you return, and we might share another conversation. Have a good night."

She left him there and made her way to her room. She was exhausted after all the excitement, confusion, and seafaring she had just been through. She very much looked forward to a proper bath and a posh bed. Many of the remaining clientele took pause and watched her ascend. The perse dress was seducing, a beacon, contrasting the drab surroundings as she climbed the stairs. There was a new girl in town, and she had been seen in the company of James Hook and the local ordinary. Who is she, and what is her place, they wondered.

Entering her room, she was alarmed to see it paled to the descriptive feeling she imagined, when Belle said she was receiving a suite of envy. Inside, there was marginally ample space, certainly more than she had been accustomed to of late, but nothing '*grand*'. There was a changing screen in the corner, a small armoire with a basin, a water urn, and a bourdaloue. In the other corner was the bed. Once again, a more acceptable furnishing than she'd been privy to prior, but it was not the downy pad she'd envisioned. It would suffice, but she reckoned Belle's interpretation of finery was a bit adjacent. If this room was that of envy, she was chagrined to believe what the others resembled.

She laid down on the bed, taking it all in. In the solitude, she could hear the disorder around her. The beguilement downstairs muddled into an indiscernible warble. Upstairs now, she heard the thrum of rhythmic pounding and wailing from the other rooms. Cackles and moans both feminine and masculine vociferated in an orgy of indecorousness. She closed her eyes, attempting to block out the commotion, meditating, finding peace among the sadness creeping in on her. As her mind wandered, visions of everything she had experienced in the recent months, flashed in a montage of memories. Her parents lost at sea, Lieutenant Allain, Danso and Osei, Smee, Captain Hook, Piet. Varying waves of emotions rippled through her, a tear rolling down her cheek. For all the madness, she was alive, and for that she was grateful, despite the circumstances. She remembered she was product of two doting and intelligent parents. Everything she had endured made her stronger. She would use all of it to her advantage to become the most tenacious woman she could. She would survive. She would prevail.

She hadn't realized she'd fallen asleep and was awoken by such a commotion. It sounded as though a brawl had erupted in the hallway. She sprung from her bed to see what was happening. Opening the door, she witnessed Captain Hook, roaring wildly and screaming incoherently down the hallway and stairs. No one dared stand in his way either. When he was this far marinated, he was his most dangerous. Ever since losing his hand, he would roam the streets like a lunatic, searching for the boy or the crocodile that had separated him from his appendage. The first person he came across might expect he would mistake them for his target and chop off an arm or a leg without anyone daring to intervene. It wasn't that anyone didn't care; it was that they accepted the terror for spectacle. The fabled fury of Captain James Hook.

Belle appeared naked in her doorway, behind her a proper mess displayed as though a tornado had ripped through her room alone. Wendy instinctively averted her eyes, but Belle walked out and approached her.

"He's on the dust..." she said standing nonchalant in the corridor.

"Dust?" Wendy asked, shyly trying to maintain propriety by avoiding direct eye contact.

"Yeah, it's a drug you can only find here, and it's ain't for the weak. The Indians make it and use it in their ceremonies, but they trade us a type mixed with something else, so it's not holy like theirs. You gotta have real money to get it too. Makes you feel like you're flying. But when he gets on a rip, lock your door, and hope he really doesn't want in. Come on then, let's get you back in there, eh?" Belle pushed Wendy back in her room.

"Here, let me get you out of that fancy dress. Bettin' you don't wanna wear that out?"

"No, it's fine, I can manage."

"Hush and hold still."

Wendy was uneasy. She had had plenty of maids help her in and out of dresses before, but they were all clothed. Here, now, Belle was as free as a bird; her spritely physique and retrousse tear drop breasts could not be ignored. It was no wonder why she was a favorite among the men – and Piet. Wendy continued to try to maintain decency, but it was clear – and awkward – at this point, that she was uncomfortable. After Belle had helped her out of her gown, she took Wendy's hands and put them on her chest, so that she was squeezing the fleshy pair. Embarrassed and horrified, Wendy blushed and tried to jerk her hands back, but Belle held them tight, staring at her with a challenging gaze.

"Let go!" she cried.

"They're just tits, love. You got'm just like me, just like any other woman got'm. Ain't nothin' to be afraid of." Belle replied as she loosened her grip. She gave Wendy a smirk.

"I know you're not so dull as you lead on to be. Surely, you're a girl who's used her wiles to attract the suitors? No woman your age is so hoary that she hasn't imagined the feeling of a nice hard... embrace?"

"I am not a whore!"

"Hoary, love. Means stale, tedious, boring."

"Right, I knew that. And no, I was raised with an understanding that men and women should be matched and married before anything should occur betwixt them."

"You're all the same, you are. That's the problem. That primness is bygone, ancient history. Things aren't so '*may I please sir, thank you sir*' any longer. Us women, we run the world, the menfolk just don't know it yet. Why do you think they all lose their sense when they get 'round a woman, eh?"

You see me and these other girls as dregs to your high society. You look down on us for that, but I tell you this, it's just fine to live a life that others don't understand. Don't make you any less a person. It makes you able to live your life free of trying to live for everyone else. I live my life for me, love, an' there's no man can take that away from me. Even if I make'm beg!"

Always one to know when to make an exit, Belle once again approached Wendy, held her hands in her own, and looked her in the eyes.

"The harder you resist, love, the harder it will be to get on in this new life of yours. And if I was wagerin', I'd venture you're not the kind to sit around hoping it'll come to you." And with that, Belle returned to her room, closing the door behind her.

Wendy was dumbstruck... *women run the world?* In her mind, it called to her, and she liked the thought, yet it was so unexpected coming from a girl such as Belle. Here *she* was, so properly educated back home, and being learned by a prurient prophet; so unexpectedly enlightened. Maybe she wasn't such an ill-bred person after all?

She was so puzzled by the interaction and didn't know what to make of it. Earlier, Belle was rigid and uncomely toward her, but now, it seemed the opposite. Her head swam in all the feelings she was experiencing, and just how to process them. Yet, at every turn, she was still. Why was she so still? Was it that Belle was right about opening up and leading her own way? Was it, that she was her own woman already, and hadn't realized it until now?

She *was* free... Belle was right. After all the resisting, nothing changed, except her role in it. It was so natural to take offense or rebuke, but that constantly exerted wasted energy in all the cases leading up to now. There was no turning back, there was no '*what used to be*' anymore. Strangely, Wendy was comforted, pushed forward by this promiscuous encounter. She *would* become the empress of this hellscape. Wendy looked at her door, as if trying to peer through it, dazed, and sat back down on her bed. Finally resolved, she slipped back into slumber, spent by the past few months of trials.

IX

When the day broke next, Wendy arose, bleary, hoping to find some form of breakfast. She was unphased that nothing of the sort was to be found anywhere in the place. Nena was retired for the morning, having tended to business throughout the night. Belle and the other girls were still sleeping off their night's exploits. No one was stirring, so she was on her own.

Stepping out into the muddy rut, the town was ceaselessly alive as merchants, smiths, bakers, and fishermen scuttled at their tasks. The heat was already creeping up and the tropical humidity was still prevalent having not reprieved overnight. The fortress on the point glowed in the tangerine light, reflecting the sun off the bricked walls. The briny sea air aided in masking the otherwise noxious odors of refuse, excrement, and fish. She carefully made her way deeper into town, taking in all the colonialism, and how she never could have conceived it if someone had explained it. Men slugged away barbarously against a background of palm trees swaying lazily in the morning breeze.

Her stomach lurched, reminding her she needed to eat, so she returned to the reality that was in front of her. She had no money, and no idea how to go about feeding herself here presently. She eventually caught sight of a kitchen and stepped in to see about some sort of barter for a quick bite. The keep greeted her, surprised to see such a fine woman gracing his doorway. He tipped his hat to her and asked what he could do for her.

"Good morning, sir, I've only just arrived, and am still getting sorted. My company has left me for other pressing matters with the governor, and I'm afraid I've been left unescorted to find a bite to eat. I'm only getting my bearings, presently. I wonder if you might have a little something what to tide me over, until my court returns?"

The shop keep eyed her up and down, sizing her up, debating if he should believe her. She presented herself accordingly, was dressed fine enough to be believed, and was far more courteous to him than most who came in looking for handout. Though, he knew no ships had come in of any caliber to have consult with the governor, but supposed perhaps, they could have come from Kingston or Spanish Town.

"Aye, I got some pickin's, I can give ye, but you make sure to tell those rascals that left you unattended in this place, they better keep a better watch over a dame such as yourself. Lots'a wicked intent 'round here, ye likely find yourself tangled up with some uncouth treatment not befitting a lass such as you are."

"You are too kind, sir, I thank you. And yes, I will of course ensure they are made aware at the soonest urgency, that they are so aloof as to leave a woman in such a vulnerable position."

The baker handed her a wooden bowl with a strange mixture inside. He also handed her a mug of an odd black liquid.

"Plantains and coffee. Welcome to the Port Royal!"

"Plantains and coffee?" Wendy inquired.

"Aye, you take the plantain – it's like a banana – and ye cut'm up into bits, and cook'm with sugar."

"And coffee?"

"Yeah, it's a plant grows here on the island, up in the hills. Them crazy injuns figgerd out you can roast the nut, then you get this. Careful though, too much'll give ye the jitters, somethin' wild."

Wendy tried a bite of the plantains, and was instantly amazed at the rich, sweet, gooey texture. It was like having pudding for breakfast. She loved it and audibly validated that with an approving moan. The coffee, she wasn't too keen on. It was bitter and unnatural, and her face soured, giving note that she wasn't a fan. The baker gave a chuckle and told her it takes some getting used to.

"Sir, you have been most gracious. I can never repay my gratitude for taking sympathy on me in this state of affairs. I am embarrassed to beg in such a way, but as I said before, my consort was quick to take audience with the governor. A matter most pressing. Something about the Spanish, but I shouldn't spread rumors, as I am a lady, and should not have been privy to those conversations from the outset. I apologize. I should take my leave now, and get back to my lodging before, as you say, I attract such uncouth treatment. Good day"

"I can escort you to your…"

"No," she interrupted. "No, I will be sure to get back toot sweet. Thank you. Again, you are most gracious."

Before any further interaction could transpire, she exited back out into the beaming sun and bustle. The pulse had quickened since she ducked in to score her meal – to which she was quite pleased with how successful she was at obtaining. Carts rattled down the alleyways, Men were barking oddities from corner to corner, and coquettes cawed for attention. Pirates groggy from the night's activities sought to ease their conditions by getting right back at it.

She had walked a few blocks when she came upon a mob. Many stood circled around as a few other men bickered and fussed with each other, but not exactly at each other. When she pushed through, she could see these men were all of some status, as they were dressed finer than the others sniping along periodically. It seemed quite a row, and it was drawing more and more curious onlookers to the scene.

"What's going on?" she asked the man next to her.

"Seems someone broke into ol' man Coombs' last night and set all the slaves free."

"Set all the slaves free?"

"'at's what I understand. They've been cussin up a storm 'bout it fer ever now. Guessin the warder caught his forty winks sometime in the night. Come back to find all of 'em, escaped clean away."

Knowing the supposed details, Wendy had no further interest and kept on about her business. When she'd reached the end of the road, she looked out across the bay taking in the island before her. It was magnificent. After a few moments surveying the grandeur, she turned and headed back in the direction of Pixies.

The crowd was still there as she approached again, though it had attracted more attention by this point. Many of the men were still steaming, screaming threats for lost money or that someone should be out there looking for them instead of standing around. On the skirts of the crowd, she noticed Piet, watching with an odd glee about his face. He was in the mix, and every now and then would join in the jeering, but it seemed entertaining to him, as he looked at the people around him when he did. Wendy sidestepped the crowd and snuck around the back to where she could grab him.

"Piet, what are you doing?"

Piet giggled boyishly, trying to contain himself. He led Wendy away from prying ears, and admitted to her, "It was me! I did it! I let all those fellers free!"

To say Wendy was shocked, is not a sufficient description. She was stupefied if that can encapsulate the sheer amazement and bewilderment.

"What do you mean it was you? Piet, these men are blood-thirsty, and if they find out it was you, they won't hesitate nary a moment before they cut you open!"

"Shhh!" He hushed her quickly, "It's okay, they'll never find out! This isn't my first time! Every few months, I sneak in with the help of my lost boys, and we get the trapped ones out!"

Obviously, Wendy was confused, and the look on her face was a clear sign, so Piet pulled her further away from the crowd – and prying ears – to explain.

"Remember, the other night, I told you about the lost boys on my farm?"

"Yes... You mean to tell me..."

"Most of them come from these capers!"

He was beside himself now, as he admitted to his crimes to her. He thought it the funniest thing.

"Please stop paltering with me. What are you saying?"

"There are an original few who were slave slaves when my parents ran the farm. But like I told you, when they died, I let them go, and they could stay on the farm if they kept it running. They were my friends growing up, and since then, I've hated seeing them bought and mistreated. I tried to save them the right way, but I couldn't against the richer men who come to buy them in lots. The wealthy owners with power and bigger plantations always get priority, and scoop up dozens at a time, and so on until they're all sold. So, I hatched the best plan!"

Piet hooted now. This was pure comedy to him. Wendy was perplexed, and didn't know what to say or ask next, so she stood there, mouth agape, taking it all in.

"So, where are they now?" She asked, finally advancing the conversation.

"I have a hideaway on one of the cays. I take them there for the commotion to settle. Then when it's clear, I move them to my farm upland."

The twists of this story just kept unfurling like a rose bud. This adolescent fool was either a maniacal genius, or a suicidal dimwit. And why was he confessing all of this to her? It seemed that should be something you take to the grave with you, so you're not implicated in any case against you... but, here he was sparing no detail about it. She deemed he was both the maniacal genius *and* dimwit. They had only had one conversation together the night before; he had no business trusting her so prematurely by admitting his involvement. His plan was deviously admirable; all the same, it was so daringly risky, that if he were ever caught, he would be killed without haste.

"I can take you there," he said, interrupting her thoughts. "We can go tonight when the sun is gone so no one sees us."

"No, not tonight," she replied. "I would very much enjoy seeing your arrangement, and meeting the lost boys, but it is too soon for me to disappear for such a time as it would take.

You should leave, now. You need to be away from this before you find yourself ensnared. Go. You know where to find me when you return. We can talk then. Until then, stay away, and keep to yourself." She gave him a kiss on the cheek and left him standing there, entranced.

"I know what I'm doing he said. I'll be back for you!" He called out to her, but she didn't turn back to acknowledge him. She just kept on.

Continuing up High Street, she came upon the Governor's mansion, and she slowed her pace. This was the fortress she was to ingress. The task suddenly seemed a grander challenge than she had imagined conversationally before. The house was a grand façade of white brick, lording over the grounds upon which it sat. A large three-story building boasted opulence in contrast to an otherwise comparative wasteland. She stood at the hedgerow, wondering how Danso and Osei were getting on, and if they were being treated as well as Hook had promised they would be.

Eventually, she found her way back to Pixies to discover some of the girls tidying up from the night before, preparing for the night ahead. Some of them cut eyes at her, knowing she was the new trick who received favor from Nena and Belle. Others hadn't seen her the night before, asked who she was and when they found out, also soured at her presence. Wendy could sense the mood, but kept her head high, chest out, and stride steady; until she heard a murmured barb.

"Look'it 'er. Struttin' in all fancied up, like she owns the place. Must be nice to wake up all fresh and stroll about town, instead'o moppin' up sick. Can't imagine what it's like to be the cunny o' ol' Cap'n Hook."

Wendy stopped. The others stopped. What was going to happen next? Normally, decorum would dictate Wendy keep moving and ignore such insults; rise above the filth. But this wasn't a normal circumstance. She took a deep breath of confidence in defiance of the petty jealousy.

"If you kept your own as fresh as your mouth, you might not be cleaning up sick or crossing the one that consorts with the maddest pirate to walk these streets."

As amazed as she was that she had the gall to snap back, she internalized it, keeping it stern on her face. Delivery and total confidence were crucial to establish herself among the ranks.

"What you say?" came the reply. Wendy was expecting it. She turned to see a disheveled sprite stamping toward her, her hair a mess and sloppily dressed.

"Perhaps you should spend a bit more time tending to your own honeypot, than worrying about mine, and where it's been?"

"I'll wreck you, you pretentious two-bit…"

Wendy brandished a small stiletto she kept hidden on her since leaving the ship, holding it steadily aimed at her assailant. The girl stopped short of her reach. Wendy had a fire in her eye, ready and burning.

"We are going to be in close quarters, do you understand me? You leave me be, I'll leave you be. I've got nothing to take from any of you, but you come for me again – or any of you, for that matter – I will turn you inside out and leave you for the rats. Do you hear me?"

The girl scowled in acknowledgement and backed off. As she did, the other girls got back to their business, not wanting to look Wendy in the eye. From the staircase, Belle had been watching and stepped in to intercede before anything else happened. She gently pushed Wendy's arm down, lowering the threatening blade and stood between the two. With a voice loud enough for the other girls to hear, she said,

"Rosetta, hear me now. If I so much as catch wind of you starting shit again with Wendy here, you'll be on your ass in the gutter without a pot to piss in. She ain't got nothin' to do with where she's put. That's up to Nena and her business. You wanna bicker, you take it up with her. Now go on and get back to cleaning up the shit stalls out back."

Rosetta... Wendy made sure to remember her name. Belle then turned to Wendy, and in a quieted voice intended only for Wendy, looked her dead in the eye and told her,

"Nena catch you with that blade to one of her girls' throats, she'll have you on your little ass quicker'n you can fathom; Hook be damned. These girls pay her bills.

Now, I can say separately, you're proper scrappy. Rosetta, she's a salty wench, and likely would'a knocked out your teeth had you not sprung your blade. Put it away now and go upstairs. Wait for me in your room."

Wendy's heart was racing, beating visibly in her chest. Taking the cue from Belle, she dismissed herself. The other girls awkwardly got back to work, so not to incur the wrath of Belle – or Nena for that matter. Rosetta, fuming and humiliated, stormed off to throw more hay and sand on the latrine out back. Belle stood watching for a moment to make sure everything was indeed quelled. Feeling satisfied that it was, she left on the errands she had been tasked with. Wendy, upstairs in her room, door locked behind her, fluttered at her bravado and tried to catch her breath.

A few hours later, Belle arrived back with two of Hook's men carting two chests with them. The clamor of them drew a bit of attention when they came in and carried them upstairs. Belle rapped on Wendy's door, asking to be let in.

"Louvri, kite m'antre tanpri." She sang from outside the door.

Wendy had no idea what she was saying, but could tell it was Belle from her voice, and obliged. To her surprise, Foggerty and Scourie barged in behind her, banging the trunks recklessly.

"What is the meaning of all this?"

"Your benefactor has arranged for your things to be delivered from the ship so you can settle in here more easy like."

"But these aren't mine. I don't have this much stuff… I don't have any stuff!"

"Aye, he also made some arrangements to get you some replacements and what-have youse."

Wendy looked at Belle, who shrugged none-the-wiser when their eyes met.

"Well, just put them anywhere, I suppose."

At that, they dropped the trunks where they stood. They made an awful thud, heavier than Wendy had anticipated.

"Thank you. And tell the captain *thank you* for me, when you see him next."

"Tell'm yourself," Scourie barked. Foggerty elbowed him sharply. "M'lady," he quickly added, post jab.

"Well, thank you again, fellas. I know this wasn't the type of duty you signed on for. It is most appreciated, nonetheless. If you'd like, allow me to repay you for your troubles?"

"We can't take your money, Miss Wendy. Strictly forbidden."

"Well, if I can't pay you in coin, perhaps I can repay you another way? I have a friend downstairs, goes by the name of Rosetta."

The pirates grinned at each other, clearly interested in the *free ride*.

"Belle, would you be a dear and see if Rosie is available? Tell her, no hard feelings."

"Highly out of the ordin'ry, but what the hell. Let's go boys."

Belle shoved them out and directed them down the hall. Wendy attempted to reposition the trunks, but they were definitively as heavy as they sounded, crashing to the floor. She opened them to discover a full wardrobe array. One trunk contained dresses for varying occasions, while the other contained what appeared to be general garb, boots, and other miscellaneous accessories; as well a sealed letter marked to her attention lay atop the appurtenances. She was equipped now with anything she could possibly need to blend into any situation. She started sorting the items, inspecting each one with a renewed pleasure of material objects. It had been so long, it seemed since she had access to anything at all. Belle returned shortly to find Wendy unpacking; all the contents spread about in neat piles. Envious, she closed the door behind her again, to prohibit any other prying eyes.

"Rosie thanks you for your referrals. How you gon' pay her for them two? You know she's gon' come lookin' for coin, and last I checked you a little short in that area?"

Wendy turned out a pocket, producing a small palm full of patinaed doubloons. Among the items Hook had gathered for her, he had left a pouch of coins inside one of the boots. Before Belle had returned, she made certain to re-hide it, so there was no evidence there was more to be found.

"Will this take care of it?" Uncertain as to how much a double turn cost, she played it safe only revealing a few. What she did know well enough, was not to show it all.

"He left me these few to get on my feet, I suppose. I don't know what she expects, but some of this should cover it, no?"

Cursing under her breath, Belle replied, "This much will almost cover it normally. But what we're going to do, is give her four-piece, and you put the rest with Nena for her troubles, and so you can treat yourself to drink later. That will put you in plenty good standing for the time being. And don't go showing this around anymore, you hear me?"

"Yes," Wendy replied diffidently.

"Don't nobody need to know what you got hangin' around in here. You keep your things tucked away. Lock 'em up in these fine chests, and the door locked behind you all the while. They'll be safe, trust."

"Of course, heavens no, I hadn't intended on keeping it all strewn about. It's just, it's like Christmas morning! I just had to see what was in here!"

Here was a divide between the two. Belle had never experienced a Christmas morning and couldn't relate. She could understand to a lesser extent, the feeling anytime Piet brought her some trinket or bauble, but never anything so privileged. She just politely smiled, trying to maintain patience with Wendy, patted her hand, and left the girl to her sorting.

As Wendy finished inventorying and situating her new things, putting them all in places, she locked the door behind her, sat on the bed and opened the letter. It was from Hook, and it read:

Wende,

You will have by now accounted you are amply furnished with everything you should need to get on in this place. Ignorant to couture you are in need of precisely, I trust the panoply here within will suffice. At the guidance of my agents, you should find what they have deemed appropriate for the various engagements you will find yourself. Additionally, you should find apparel befitting general day utility, such as we are accustomed. This will no doubt decry the spoils to which you may enjoy, however, you will find those vestments will turn to tatters expeditiously in this purlieu. If any item has been overlooked, yet required, you will find a stipend for such expenses.

From here, you and I will have little to no interpersonal interactions, as I shall not be seen associating with you under the guise of our concord. Should we see the other in passing, ye shall not acknowledge, and continue about your affairs. Unless a scheduled meeting has been organized, we shall only communicate through trusted accomplices, whom of which will be stealth in their conveyance. You will know it is one of mine, and there shall only be three, by the introduction: 'Church on Sunday.' If anyone gives you inquisition, and they have not made themselfs known, you will be sufferd deth.

Last, the Governor will be hosting a ball for the aristos three days hence. Assuming you receive this on schedule, that will be Wednesday fore. Tho, the expediency is sooner than expected, there is no time to dally. You will be escorted as a guest by one, Norval Marlin. He is amassed a large plantation and well connected from the sugar trade. You are to meet him at the Governor's, as he will not be seen collecting you from the brothel. He will see to it that you are chaperoned as social necessity dictates. He is ignorant to our contrivance, though his ignorance cost a sum; therefore, you shall not discuss the topic with him or anyone otherwise. You shall present yourself eligible, newly arrived. Gain audience with the Governor. Ensure you are seen and desirable. I need remind you not, the success of your incorporating dictates your future, be it with the Governor according to plan, or else the failure I wish not consider.

I will send correspondence in the days following the affair, establishing a rendezvous that I may learn of your exploits. Continue about your ways until you receive further word.

Yours in confidence,
-J

P.S. It would behoove you to commit your duties to memory and burn this correspondence, that it not incriminate you or I in cahoots.

She put the letter down on her bed and rummaged through the trunks once more to see that she had some semblance of vestments appropriate for the Governor's soiree. The paucity was not what she was accustomed to, when attending a ball of this expected grandeur, but she could make do. One of the gowns was a brilliant bone ivory decorated with floral stitching, perfect for an evening of opulence.

By now, activity was beginning to rumble downstairs, and Wendy had little interest in participating. Knowing that she would not see Hook again any time soon, she wondered what Piet was up to, and if he was still in town. Truthfully, she wondered if she could accompany him to his little island while she bided her time. Since there was nothing else for her at this time, she decided she would go in search for him to see if he was still about.

She freshened herself, locked away her things and descended the stairs. Some of the girls were already hard at work soliciting themselves. Belle was behind the bar, tending, so Wendy approached her to tell her she was going out, and she wasn't sure when she'd be back. She intentionally omitted that she was going off in search of Piet, because as far as Belle knew, she'd sent him off. She didn't want to let on that she had seen him just this morning, hanging around watching the fallout from his exploits. She reckoned this wouldn't benefit any of them, so she kept it her little secret.

She hoped, in the short time since their meeting, she might find him along the water's edge or along the road out of town. She had no idea where to look… it was preposterous to think she'd find him at this point. On she hurried though, keeping her eyes peeled for any sign of him – good or bad!

As she passed the Governor's mansion again, she slowed her pace, taking it in once more. When she'd seen it earlier, it was just a gaudy effigy among the rabble of the town. Though that hadn't changed in her mind, it was now a landmark she needed to heed, know, and enter. Her mind flashed back to all the balls and galas she'd attended in England with her parents when she was younger. She had the experience under her belt for the event, but this would be different. This, she would need to prevaricate from the very beginning and never breaking character. She realized, she might need to collect her thoughts, prepare her story, commit it to memory, and act it out in three days. It was hardly enough time, but what choice did she have. If she failed to establish herself, it wasn't just a bad impression with an elite, it was the threat of being viciously murdered by a barbarous scallywag with a hook for a hand. She shuddered at the thought and set her mind to work. Onward she strolled, now preoccupied with who she was going to become.

Passing the square where the morning fracas had occurred, she continued talking to herself with her inner monologue, preparing for her showcase with the Governor. To the unsuspecting passerby, she likely seemed a loon mumbling, twiddling her fingers, and eyes that seemed to look through things – not at them. Still, she walked on her path out of town.

She was in a world all her own before she realized she'd once again strolled out of town down the dusty, sandy road leading to the mainland. She was also unaware someone was trailing her at a distance behind her. Every so often, she'd look off into the bay, taking in the view of the mountains and the water colliding in a colossal contradiction of nature. The summer swelter was thick, and dark clouds were forming in the distance. It would storm soon, yet she wasn't versed in the weather patterns here, and how you could almost time the squall upon the first breath of that cool wisping breeze across the water. Clouds roiled afar, menacing and fat with precipitation. Behind her the voice called out...

"Wendy... WENDY!"

It was Piet. Still lurking in the shadows of Port Royal, he was as stubborn as ever he could be, refusing to leave when told to do so. He made his decisions and did them on his own accord. As Wendy had passed by through the market, he had seen her while he was hiding in plain sight. She oblivious, he had followed her curious what possible adventure she might be off on. He'd been behind her for some time, but she had never so much as taken record of her surroundings, a dangerous mistake in such a sewer as Port Royal was. In all account, she was lucky it was only Piet – both, because he was whom she was in search of, but also because he was not a marauder.

His calling broke her trance, and she wheeled around to see his boyish face displaying concern and urgency. She had been walking so long without recognizing the in-between parts that she was surprised when she realized she'd come so far. She was relieved and glad to see him.

"Oh, Piet, I am glad to see you! I have been out looking for you, curious if you had gone off to your hideaway."

"Wendy, you must be more careful! You've been in a strange trance for some time; I've been calling you. Is everything alright?"

"Oh, yes, I'm sorry. I was deep in thought. I would like to see your little refuge if you are still going? I received word that my presence is not required until three days from now. I must return though, in time to attend the Governor's banquet. I have an invitation and must be in attendance."

"Well, isn't that just delightful! How is it you are already so connected to be invited to the party?" Piet was delighted, it sounded quite fun – and he was jealous, because it sounded so fun.

"It is not I that is connected, and I am unaware of just how I gained invitation so quickly. However, I do know that my attendance has been requested and is required. Perhaps I will know more after."

"You will tell me all about it, won't you?"

"I will tell you what I am able." She said allowing for omission of specific details. "Now, if you are still leaving, I think it would be fun to see this place of yours you've told me about. Shall we?"

"Yes, yes! Of course, we can. Come, my canoe is just beyond the reach there. It's not quite dark enough though, that I would depart undetected. But those clouds foretell a storm is coming our way. It might raise suspicion if we shoved off right now…" Piet was deliberating between his routines and his excitement to show off his utopia to Wendy.

"Do men not come and go regularly in canoes and skiffs throughout the day to ferry to ships, or go fishing, or some other manner of errand?"

"Yes, but they all typically steer in the other direction to leave the harbor. We will be going into it."

"I think that if the storm is coming, none will pay much attention to our affairs. And the longer we stand here, discussing in the open road, are we not raising suspicion?"

Piet liked her reasoning and impulse, and once again, was excited about sharing his island with her. It made him feel accomplished and proud, but he had never shared it with anyone before – not even Belle – but only the absconded slaves. And presently there were a quite a few on the island from the earlier heist. Surely, they were hiding out scared and confused, and alone. And so, they launched out, Piet pulling the oar hard, making quick pace, but careful not to make a spectacle of themselves.

What neither of them were aware of, (and why should they be?) was that Wendy was being watched the whole time. Hook, not one to be so carelessly cavalier with his chattels had eyes everywhere, some of which were indistinguishably keeping tabs on her. From the point, the weather-worn face scowled at the canoe heading out with her in it. Sternly, he watched through an eyeglass for where they headed. Thunder rumbled in the distance behind him. This would not please his superintendent in the least, but he would have to report back. He was equally concerned that it would mean punishment due to him for allowing her to depart. But his, as well as the others' instructions were simple. *Watch. Do not make yourself known. Do not interfere unless imminent danger is presented to her as related to her duties to him.* He snapped the spyglass shut and turned to find the captain to provide the concerning update.

X

Grouchy darkness was ensconcing the late afternoon sun as the storm rolled in from the East. Thunder barked angrily following the explosive white flashes from within the gray clouds. Incoming sheets of rain could be seen wiping across the horizon. The temperature cooled as the rain approached. This was no more than a periodic storm; nothing to be concerned about. The rain was always welcome. It provided sustenance for the dense jungle, crops, and other vegetation, and it provided a cleansing refreshment to an otherwise filthy place.

Piet and Wendy landed in the little inlet of his cay in time to tie off and watch the clouds roll over and dump fat, heavy rain like a curtain sweeping across a stage. Piet made to seek shelter in one of the trees, but Wendy stood still as the heavy drops began to pelt her face and smacked the broad leaves of the plants around her. The noise became clamorous as the heft spattered frenetically. Wendy was drenched now; her hair matted in ribbons on her forehead and down her shoulders. With eyes closed, she smiled, outstretched her arms, and let the rain wash away the heaviness in her heart. Here, now, in the wild rain, she began to feel refreshed and renewed.

As she stood at the shoreline, Piet watched from cover, expecting that she would have done the same. But seeing her so resolved to be bathed in the deluge, he stepped back out to stand beside her. Awkwardly staring at her and the sky interchangeably, he too gave in and let the rain wash over him as well. In all his wild years, he'd been caught in storms before, but had always instinctively sought shelter, even when he ran free with the natives. They couldn't hunt effectively in the rain, so they would find places to keep dry until they could resume. It was just a normal response that he couldn't recall a time that he'd just let the rain take him like Wendy was doing now. He finally broke the silence after growing bored of being quiet.

"Why do you stand here in the rain like this?" he asked.

"It reminds me that even nature needs to cry when it's sad." she replied.

"Are you sad?" Piet asked.

"I am. I was. I don't know. My world was shattered in an instant, and now I'm under the employ of the most devilish pirate on the open sea. I should count my blessings, what few there are, and there are, but I'm forced to find

137

myself anew here, and until very recently, I didn't know that I could. But I must heal. I must carry on. And since I must, I have to be willing to let go of the old me and be the new me I have to be."

Piet felt her words going around in circles, and this caused his interest to wane yet again, but he held on just enough to the tidbit about her reference to Hook, that he decided to confess yet another absurdity to her, "Hook isn't what he makes himself out to be. He's still a man and can be defeated. I beat him once. And now that I've seen him back with that hook for a hand, it is a gay reminder that he is mortal. He can be bested. And I will best him again now that he is back and taking my Belle — and you down with him!"

Wendy snapped from her cleansing and looked Piet in the face confused. "You did what?"

"Yes, I'm the one that did that to him! He tried to shoot me while I was in my canoe, so we fought, and I defeated him. I cut off his hand and fed it to that crocodile. He was so scared of his own blood that he ran off afraid the crocodile was chasing him! That was the last I saw of him for what seems like ages. When I saw him come into Pixies with you the other night, there was no mistaking it was him!"

As he told it, he did intentionally leave out a significant number of details before, during, and after the affair. Piet only recollected the variation of the story that he was the hero in the epic.

"Wait! You mean to tell me, *you're* the one who they talk about in those stories?"

"You've heard them?" he puffed up proudly.

"Yes, I've heard them. I heard it on the ship as we made our way here. Though, I must tell you, I heard quite a different version by their account."

"Of course you did! They are on *his* side, so surely, they'll make it so he is the better one in the end."

"I don't know that he's the better one in either version, but you seem to have omitted a significant lot in your telling. But what I do know, is if he ever finds out you're the one, and you're right under his nose, he *will* kill you."

"I'm not afraid of him, Wendy. And you shouldn't be either."

"I am in a far more dire situation and have little to protect me against his malevolence. I am no match for him at the sword, and I've never held a gun in my life."

"I can teach you! I can teach you how to fight, and we can take him down together! And then all the pirates will leave!"

"I have learned to wield a blade, but his skill is far superior. I fear it wouldn't be enough."

"I beat him once; I can beat him again. And if I can do that, I can teach you how to match skills against him too."

Wendy was enticed by the offer but reasoned that she could never hone the skills needed. Hook no doubt, had decades of swordsmanship behind him which gave credence to him being the nastiest pirate alive. If his own men feared him in this regard, it should heed her caution all the same. Piet could dream in his delusions of grandeur, though, if he was being truthful, she could continue learning from him enough to improve her skills beyond current stagnation.

"I would delight in learning how to improve and will take you up on the offer to do so. However, let us take one challenge at a time with regard to challenging him. I am not in the capacity to do so, nor would it be prudent at this time. I must play this game at present and incorporate myself into the life of Port Royal. I cannot say how long it will be a burden I bear, but I should say that it is equally strategic to blend in among them. Surely *you* understand?"

"Sure I do! We should make a pact!" Piet's brain was excited at the prospect so, that he had already begun scheming. And in this dizzying train of thoughts, he remembered his lost boys. He turned and signaled with a whistle, almost like a bird call.

"Come! I almost forgot! You need to meet the slaves I rescued; the ones I must get to the other lost boys on the farm!"

The rain was still coming down, though the force had abated. The slaves had sought refuge in the dugouts from both the elements and any wayward persons who might stumble across the island. But in hearing Piet's call, a few heads cautiously poked out of hiding. Piet dragged Wendy interior and called "all ye, all ye, outs and free!"

What a silly thing, Wendy thought, as she was being pulled along. He acts as though this is a child's game, and the jig is up. But there, in the bemired grove, stood the terrified would-have-been slaves. Their dark skin and white eyes portrayed a frightful vision as they emerged from within the trees in the rainy night. But as she began to inspect the faces staring back at her, she recognized a few of them. Some (not all) had been the captives Captain Smythe had procured, and that Hook had 'freed.' She was confused by this since she thought they were of his crew now.

"These men... I know some of them. They were on the ship with me... they were free before?" Wendy thought to herself, aghast as she saw them. How awful that they were so close to their freedom, and to trust the crew – and Hook – to be duped back into auction for a life most dreadful.

When the few recognized Wendy, they regained confidence and came further out of the shadows, happy to see a familiar face. Understandably, not knowing Piet, they had little reason to trust him, and so they were cautious until now. The other unfamiliar boys followed the older men as they embraced Wendy in relief.

"I don't understand," she said, happy they came to her. "You were free before! What happened?"

The three men attempted to explain, in the broken English they'd learned from her, but didn't have the words to convey – or understand – what happened. Piet intervened, dazzled by the familiarity.

"The pirates run free crews while on ship. But on land, they will trade these people for any number of favor, payment, or service if they're so inclined. I've seen it time and time again; they're just a commodity. If they can spare them for some sort of payout, they will and think nothing more of it. Those who aren't traded or sold, stay with the crew, maybe only until the next port when they need another advance. But, if they prove worth to the crew and learn fast, they could very well stay on. But they're too stupid to know how it works."

"They're not stupid! How dare you, Piet. How horrible of you to say such a thing. Especially when you are saving them and befriending them!" Wendy was disappointed by Piet's statement, and made it known quite curtly. She'd spent so much time educating them on the ship, she knew firsthand, what they were capable of, if given the opportunity to thrive.

"I didn't mean..."

It was too late. Piet's poor choice of words had passed out into the world, and he couldn't take them back. He didn't mean it disparagingly, but he'd said it. What he had meant to infer, was that they were unable to understand the dangers they faced. This wasn't their fault. Every day in the world was a risk for a black at the hands of the white. So many elements worked against them, there was no way to conceive, or to know what future awaited them, even if they managed to remain protected.

Wendy welcomed in the other unfamiliar faces and tried to explain what was happening through the broken interpretation of the ones she knew. She could see the fear in their faces ease, slightly, still a bit skeptical. Though, to their credit, the experiences they'd endured to be standing in a strange copse in the rain, hiding in trees was beyond comprehension. It was all make-believe, a strange tale scripting itself at every turn. Turning to Piet, she asked,

"When will you get these poor souls to your farm? How long will it take?"

"We can leave tonight, or tomorrow night. It has to be under cover of darkness, but with no moon, this is a perfect opportunity, so they're not so easily seen."

"Take them then. Return me to town and take them tonight. I won't have been missed. You take them to your farm. When you return, come find me, and we can figure out what to do next. I will have had time to contemplate and have played my part at the governor's dinner."

"Won't you come with me? I can show you the farm…"

"No," she interrupted. "I cannot be gone that long. It is risky enough that I left with you here. Perhaps I may find excuse to accompany you later, but not now. You must do this while you have the chance. Take me back to town at once and get them safely away."

She turned back to the crowd beside her and again tried to explain what was going to happen next. She told them to trust her, and that Piet had a safe place for them. She explained it is not without danger along the way, but to listen and follow what he says. The three that could speak shook their heads to let her know they followed what she was saying. She told them to be safe, and that they would meet again some time from now.

"Come, let us go now," She insisted.

Without haste, she climbed back into the dugout, urging Piet to get moving. She would founder along on her own if she needed to but far preferred to make it back to the other side alive. She'd never actually rowed a boat before, something she now considered a task she ought to learn. Piet quickly told the pack to wait for him to return. They would ready the other canoes, and they would need to work quickly before the clouds gave way. It was a waxing moon, so it still wouldn't be so bright as a fuller moon, but these ferries worked best under the veil of none. The two then shoved off back to Port Royal in the slackening rain. The bay was still textured from the blowing winds, but not a tumult that couldn't be navigated. While it wasn't ideal conditionally, it was fortuitous in that they should not expect to encounter any wayward company for whom would wonder what they were about. As well as for Piet relocating his packages to safety.

Having Piet in the stern of the canoe, she grabbed the extra oar and mimicked his strokes. They propelled forward noticeably faster, unsteady. Piet slowed and guided her to match her strokes with his on the opposite side of him. Stroke. Stroke. Stroke. Hold. Stroke. Stroke. The unsteadiness evened out and soon they were cruising keenly through the marbled bay toward shore. She was pleased with how easy this was and felt proud that she had taken the initiative to learn.

The canoe skidded into the bank outside of town, and Wendy hopped out quickly shoving Piet off again before any allowance for deviation could occur. Knowing the gravity of the operation, he didn't protest or stall and began his paddle back to his hidden camp. Wendy watched to make sure he got off well enough and turned to head into town. She was soaked through, like a... like a mermaid coming on land, she thought. This amused her in a wonderment kind of way as she clomped back toward Pixies. The cloud cover and rain were still eking out the last bits of their mission, leaving Wendy to still enjoy the washing away of the past. Cool night air still comforted the usual sticky humidity. Again, she passed by gallows point, the graveyard, the church, the mansion, the market, finally arriving back at the lively establishment. The distortion rumbled into the otherwise easy night.

When she entered, a few heads turned to witness the sodden girl walking through, curious as to she had gotten herself into. Wendy paid no mind to any of them and made for her room without worry. Nena also took note from the bar, but Belle got to her first.

"What in heaven's name happened to you?"

"I've just been on a lovely venture with Piet. He showed me the cays, and…"

"Piet?" she reproached. "He was supposed to have been gone! And what are you doing galivanting off with him?"

"Oh. It was nothing…" Wendy tried to reason to make her less offended. "I saw him in the square earlier, I thought he'd already gone and come back. When I was about earlier, I saw him milling around." She was lying to save Belle's feelings. "He offered to show me around and then the storm came in, and we took shelter…" Wendy realized she was beginning to spiral and stopped herself before saying anything more. "I'm sorry, Belle, I didn't think it would mean anything. I just thought…"

"You just thought… In all these years, he's never taken me around! But all of a sudden, you show up, and he's taking you about?" she sulked.

"I'm sorry Belle, but he offered to show me around the island. You were occupied with the bar and your… trade. You also told him to leave for the time. I don't think it fair to impugn either of us for befriending the other and finding entertainment elsewhere in our idleness."

Wendy wasn't wrong. She didn't think anything about Belle's attachment to him, based on her interactions, but Belle wasn't one to share either, ironically. She was jealous and upset by their escape. She was clearly hurt that he hadn't showed her the same attention and was envious that Wendy had been the recipient. She had only just arrived and was now the center of his attention it seemed.

"You just mind your own business." She said offputtingly and stormed off.

Wendy was uncertain how to feel about this interaction but was still dripping wet. Belle had gone her way in a huff, so Wendy made for her room to dry off and change.

In the following days, very little of anything occurred, outside of the usual comings and goings of rowdy pirates. Nena filled them with drink and the girls turned them over one after the other, as was the process. No new faces appeared, just the same ones spending all their prize for hedonism on a platter. Wendy made almost no appearance outside of her room but instead made herself comfortable within. She had books to keep her entertained, as well as her increasing anxiety as the governor's dinner, which was approaching quickly. It was now only a few hours away, and her stomach was going to knots. She read and reread the same paragraphs again and again, not taking any of it in because of her errant mind. She finally gave up reading and began getting ready. It was inevitable, but in that, she could at least prepare and focus on what was, until now, a distraction.

She had pulled out her ebony gown earlier and hung it, so it could air out and be crisp and presentable. She dressed herself with intention, so that the final product was something that resembled a debutante worth more than she was at present. In her observances of the girls at Pixies, she'd picked up on a few alluring tricks she could use to her advantage. She cinched the corset top, drawing her waist in and her breasts up. They rested finely in the taught cradle, with an inescapable cleft of cleavage between them. Draping a glittering choker necklace on her chest, the sparkling gems accentuated and drew attention to her porcelain skin.

Inspecting the final product, she was very pleased with the results. Hook had supplied her with an exquisite trousseau for the occasion and was rather astonished he had the wherewithal and means to procure such a perfect gown, both in fitting and finery. She smiled, twisted to each side to get a good look, and took a deep breath. The time had finally come to put on the show for the most seducing villain she could imagine. Locking up her things, she proceeded down the stairs like a bride to her groom. She was a bewitching beacon of radiance amid the grime of the tavern, making it impossible not to be noticed. Hoots, whistles, and caws chirped from every corner of the room, and time seemed to stand still. She had made her presence known without intention, and every eye in the house was on her. Jealous, snide whispers from the girls hushed across their lips, indiscernibly. If she could have this effect on this crowd, she hoped the same for the intended coterie, most hopefully, the governor.

Nena too was awed at Wendy's grandeur and gave her a great big smile. She cleaned up quite keenly and couldn't help but feel some semblance of pride for the girl. It was next to never that anyone so fine graced her establishment, so it was beautiful to witness. She had also had a small hand in ensuring Hook delivered her the good she would need to exist, in the sizes she would need, and the styles that were current. These came at no small cost to him, but he knew what he stood to gain if it all went according to plan, so he complied with the investment.

"Lookin, right fine, Miss Wendy. Fine like a crown jewel." She said as Wendy approached.

"Thank you, Nena. I feel so splendid in this, it's as though I'm in a fairy tale. I never had such a dress back home."

"Well, it fits you divinely. I'm sure Hook would be plum tickled, were he to see you all gussied up, such as you are."

"I'm sure he would be. If you happen to speak with him, please do give my appreciation to him for this."

"I be certain to do just that. Now, you be careful this evenin.' This here bunch may be the castaways of what's good and proper, but those you goin' to hobnob with is just as dangerous, if not more. They're jackals, they is. Wolfs in sheep's wool."

"I am plenty familiar with the sort but thank you for your concern."

"A'haps you do back merry ol' England, love, but this ain't the prim halls you might'n be expectin'. These here folk don't have no one keepin'm honest. No one tellin'm they's can't do this'n or that. They's do as they please w'out penalty. Not all criminals wear tattoos and sail the seas, love. You'll be best to mind that little truth."

Naturally, Wendy started to protest that she knew what she was doing, and the people she was going to be among this evening, but the truth was, she didn't. So instead of placating Nena, she thought about it in retrospect that back home, there were certain means of keeping things felicitous, but this was bedlam, and laws weren't even suggestions here. She digested this thought, and appreciatively thanked Nena.

Stepping out into the denim night, she headed toward the Governors estate, nervous. Low burning fire pots were coming to life, casting odd shadows along the street. Umbral faces watched her pass by, catching veiled glances at her splendor. Word had spread to some extent of who she was by now, more who she confederated with, so her risk of being beset by the cruel nature of these men was tempered for now. From the fringes they watched as the nubile chatelaine floated through the streets toward the detested argent manor.

When she arrived, torches and candles flickered a warm sepia glow. The blanched plaster walls seemed to dance in response to the firelights' unsteady dance. Its architecture was colonial, from the original Spanish establishment, and as fine as any manor which might have been found in rural Sevilla. The home displayed a dignity suited to that of a viceroy, and so it was fitting that this was held as the capital estate.

Fearing they would be rudely unpunctual, Norval impatiently awaited her arrival on the portico. Though she had never met him, she could tell it was he who was to accompany her for the evening. He was fidgeting, thumbing his pocket watch, irritably trying to keep his prominence from being jeopardized while he waited for her. His face betrayed him with rosacea from heavy drinking, and his left leg pained him from gout. His dark hair was streaked with silver flashes and matted down with thick beeswax pomade. He stood roughly six-foot tall but hunched slightly. His build was average, but a potbelly protruded from behind his slightly sweaty waistcoat, a sign that he was not going hungry in his home. He was, in fact, a very undesirable man from what she gleaned upon her first impression.

When he saw her, he let out an overly noticeable sigh, ensuring she was aware of his displeasure at having to wait for her, not the other way around. She didn't care, and felt that men should wait on women, *not the other way around*. With grace though, she approached with a belying smile as he met her discontentedly. She gave a slight curtsey, offering her hand out to him to take as an escort. He hobbled to her, grabbed her by the arm, and forced her insistently toward the main door. She rejected his stronghold, shaking him off, and with all the class she could mask her disgust with, made very plain statement regarding his uncomely manners.

"Mr. Norval, if this is how you treat a woman, a lady like myself, then you are no match for a chaperone this evening, and I dare say, I am better to attend on my own, than in the grip of someone so misaligned to the ways of etiquette."

"A lady like yourself? Don't be fooled; you're no less a whore underneath all this pageantry. I have been here waiting too long, and we are now late. I am the one escorting you this evening, not the other way around and you ought to know your place."

"I beg your pardon!" she exclaimed, repelling him. Who was this nasty creature of a man, so unattractive and vain? "A whore, sir, I am not, and how dare you treat me as if I were. I am a woman of worth. I come from stock and fortune, and you should be careful how you go about attending to me this evening. My sponsor would be most displeased to find you have treated me with such ill repute."

"Bah, piss on your sponsor! You mean the hag of that harlotorium from whence you come? The lot of you are a pustulant sore to this place, and I will not be wantonly threatened by the likes of you. You will not address me in such a way, and you will watch your mouth, lest I smack the taste out of it."

Wendy could not believe the vulgar conduct from this bitter malcontent. This was not going to fair well between them if they were to get on with each other this evening. She refused to be disrespected so, but knew this man wasn't going to pull back in any way.

"Mr. Marlin, let's get a few things straight..."

Just as he had warned, Norval slapped her across the cheek, knocking her off kilter. Tears instantly welled in her eyes, flesh searing from the impact. His heavy, callused, gorilla-like hand made such contact that she was dazed momentarily. It was a stark reminder that men of power acted unchecked toward anyone they believed to be beneath them, particularly women. He glared at her, wiping sweat from his brow with a kerchief.

"Will that be all, then?" he asked, knowing the answer. A woman was best kept in check, and to him, she was no different. She collected herself, straightened her dress, choked back the hurt, looked him dead in the eye, and succumbed to his control simply because, in this situation, she had no other choice. If she retreated, she was as good as dead. The order must proceed, and she now more clearly understood the stakes to with which she was dealing. Vehement hatred burned deep inside her like a caldera. One foot stepped, the other in front of that. Incommensurately they joined the pageantry inside.

Entering the house, it was a showcase of luxury. The interior was just as well constructed as the outside, with floors made of polished hard wood and Spanish tile. She hadn't seen anything like it and was impressed by the intricate magnificence of it. She held her head high, so not to let on to any of the guests that she was in any way repressed, despite the swollen, bruising cheek. Despite the assault, she was compartmentalizing her association with Norval, who constantly fidgeted with his pocket watch, as though time was his sole concern. She was here simply to make company with the governor, and that she would do. Her constituent would be managed elsewise later.

"Don't be a huss, ya hear me girl?" He growled beneath his breath to her. "These folk ain't interested in the likes you gutter sluts." His crude remarks cut through the gaiety like a red-hot knife. She couldn't believe he was still on in this manner, and with every word, it became harder and harder to control herself.

"Trust that I will conduct myself with the utmost decorum." She replied, biting her tongue. He grunted, and walked off, leaving her to herself amid the strangers.

Mingling on the patio, regal finesse oozed among powdered wigs, flashy suits and gowns, and jewelry. Quickly, Wendy felt out of place, but she gritted her teeth and forged ahead. With a theatrical smile, she made efforts to ingratiate herself among those immersed in pompous conversation. Eventually, she landed upon a small group somewhat willing to allow her entry into the conversation.

"I am Wendy Darling, newly arrived from Kensington. I have been sent by way of my father to rendezvous with an uncle in the Colonies. There I am to be married to a lawyer, who liaises with Governor's court."

The reception was generally welcoming and pleasant among them. She had portrayed herself well enough to be of vague status, but without so much detail as to get trapped in a web of lies she couldn't untangle. And yet strangely, none of them seemed to care beyond what had been said. She had an eloquence about the way she carried herself and her speaking was educated, so it was not unbelievable. As she had come to find out, this wasn't uncommon, though most didn't stop over in Jamaica without some connection or reason. Only few asked the question making her squirm, "And how do you know Mr. Marlin?"

Wendy tried to keep the answer as simple as possible, without raising any other concerns or questions, "He is liaised with my family back in London from the Sugar Trust and chaperone while I am here, before finishing the journey north."

To her surprise, the few that asked divulged that he was not a favorable man among them; that he was a foul-tempered landowner. He was known for establishing poor conditions in the parish, and kept his slaves in squalor, beat them severely, often killing them, but had yet to be accused of such. Rumors also circulated that he had sired bastard children from a few of the women slaves. While this was wasn't uncommon among slave owners, it was still an atrocity, and the wealthy elite swept it under the carpet while regarding those persons as hypocritically disgraceful.

Learning this (and based on the very short time spent with him) she could see that in him, and she was further perturbed by him. She was now more embarrassed by being associated with him, and begged that they not judge her on part of his character. This was merely a temporary arrangement, and that she was in no relation to him personally. Of course, they understood and took pity on her, warning her to be careful. This, she already recognized, and so any time he neared, she would make it a point to keep distance between him among other conversations.

Eventually, the governor made his grand entrance, and everyone pretended to fawn over him. Sir Tomas Lewis was one that could control a room, whether by status or boisterousness, which was a shame, because if he weren't so self-inflated, he held the capacity to be a respectable official. Instead, he was consumed by unchecked power, and so he carried himself as such. He was in his late thirties, still healthy looking and young enough to have the energy to match his demeanor. His powdered wig sat heavily upon his head, and in the late summer heat made him sweat. His uniform was impeccably fitted with what neared excessive brocade. He was averagely attractive in a non-descript way – one that could be the object of desire, or not just the same.

These affairs were typically an exposition of his ego, money, power, and clout. He loved to surround himself with those who seemingly adored him and lifted him up on high. He also loved to flout his authority over the people, because as he saw it, he viewed himself as an extension of the crown, therefore in a roundabout way, a king himself. Of course, this was not the case, but there was no one to challenge his behavior, so long as he provided report and riches back to the actual king in England. And so, ruling in the pirate's covey, he was favored back in home for the wealth and trade he was able to send back.

However, recent developments had created a pinch in that process because other pirates were sacking his ships and taking his prizes back to other islands for their own. This displeased him, and so his favor had begun to turn sour toward the pirates. At present he was now scheming how to be rid of the plague. The pirates however, outnumbered the governor and the small naval fleet at his disposal, making it exceedingly difficult to gain any advantage over them forcefully. Instead, he hoped levying entry taxes on them would quell their mischief, but this only proved them to broaden their distaste for him and the crown. Now, here stood Wendy, their puppet for this last attempt at cooperation and harmony.

After some hapless mingling, everyone was invited into the grand dining room, where a bountiful spread was prepared for the guests. A long heavy wood table occupied the center of the room with hand crafted chairs lined on each side, a large commanding chair placed at the head, almost throne-like. The room was decorated sparsely, so that the table took the attention. Windows opened up the space, with a view overlooking the bay. All the guests filed in and took their seats, Wendy now reunited with Norval, who at this point reeked of liquor and was breathing heavily with an annoying nasal whine. Without so much as a chivalrous effort at pulling out her chair for her, he sat himself, popped his napkin open, and sat ready to feast. Uncomfortable around him, she attempted to scoot her chair further way but had little space to do so. The knowledge and pain of all the eyes on her (and him) increased her anxiety and discomfort. Every whisper felt like a damning judgment against her.

Finally, the meal was called, and the servants brought in the meal, plating each guest. The table and food were a grand display of wealth and privilege. It was highly unlikely that anyone in Jamaica was eating that well at any point, even on their best days. Wild roasted pig, jerk chicken, corn, beans, plantains, dasheen, and even fresh cut fruits like mango and papaya. The tender meats and succulent fruits were an explosion of flavor together, using old Taino recipes, modified with for English palates. The guests were wildly impressed lavishness of it all and devoured the courses as they came. Not quite what they would have been in England, proper manners gave a bit more in the way of crudeness as everyone poked and stabbed at their plates.

Wendy awkwardly sat and ate meagerly as she had been raised, while the guest all gnashed at the food cloyingly. Her training was hard to break in this setting, and she conducted herself noticeably more proper than those surrounding her. Carafes of wine and liquor were splashed into glasses with such rapidity; decorum slid further away from custom. Most of the guests had now had many drinks and were getting louder and more boisterous; Norval especially. He offensively consumed the space beside her, and as she pecked at her plate, he stole the food straight off it for himself, without pause or shame. Not being one of gluttony, Wendy began to feel quite alone.

Inconsequential conversations bounced around the table, ranging from racist rhetoric to policy and law frustrations, to wealth and abundance, and the utter abhorrence of pirates. Each mind-numbing anecdote was a definitive divide of the rich, in a world of classist, entitled supremacy. Wendy continued to sit quietly, biting her tongue at many places she felt she could interject. She was outnumbered and out of place here with her forward thinking and recent finding of her new self among the prostitutes and pirates.

Any deviation of opinion would exile her, killing her ability to blandish herself with them. Though, she was pinned to offer reply or opinion, she would answer with some form of deflection or lady-like dismissal, such as, "that has not been a conversation I have been privy to and have no place to offer response." This crushed her internally because she truly wished to bite back with what would surely be unfavorable or unpopular riposte.

After what felt like hours, the meal was eventually finished, much to her appreciation. It was becoming unbearable to palate the poor manners and distasteful conversations. All the while though, Governor Lewis had been taking note on her posture and position. Though there was next to no interchange between them, he was curious about her and had asked under breath to those closest to him, who she was. In slurred whispers, they gave report to the best of their knowledge, which of course was very little. This only intrigued him further, having so few details. He would take the opportunity to get a moment with her when they reconvened for aperitifs.

Following dinner, most everyone gathered in the drawing room to finish off the evening. While she sat struggling to conform, she was offered more drink along with everyone else. Conversation became a discordant battery of talking over each other, while gross laughter pummeled the empty spaces. For how prim everyone appeared at the beginning of the evening, the opposite was now the display. Wendy watched as the decline of social mores unraveled. It became evident to her that these people were no better behaved than the pirates and merchants they themselves detested; the only thing that separated them was position, money, and favor.

After some time, Wendy felt her body begin to tingle and her vision aberrate into bokeh flashes. Shapes and faces of the guests became caricatures of their original form. Everything around her was spiraling into decadent degradation at the expense (and cause) of their host. Lazing and reclining about, the gentlemen turned to groping the ladies in an orgy of open promiscuity. Panic set in, but euphoric numbing quelled what would have normally been the response. She felt light, almost as though she was floating. Her body was disconnected from her mind. Sounds echoed cerebrally. Consciousness faded to black.

XI

"I don't know, love, she's been in there for days now. Hasn't come out since she got back the other night. Doesn't answer the door, doesn't take food."

"Is she still alive?"

"Far as I reckon… ain't no foul stench comin' outta there."

"Haven't you a key?"

"Aye, but it ain't my custom to intrude if I ain't got reason, and I ain't got reason yet."

"Send word when she emerges."

XII

For days she kept herself locked away for fear, anger, but most of all, shame. She had heard the knocks on the door at different times, but she couldn't garner the courage to answer. With each rap her stomach dropped, and her heart raced. She didn't know what to do. She couldn't talk to anyone. She couldn't trust anyone. She had no one.

Lying in bed, trails of dried tears streaked her dirty cheeks while fresh streams replaced those before. The once beautiful dress now lay on the floor torn, filthy, bloodstained and haunting her. The shift she wore was in no better condition. She forced her mind to recall what happened, but she couldn't piece anything together. Exhausted by the effort, she would fall back into effete slumber. As soon as she slipped below the veil, scattered pictures of carnivalesque faces mocked her, and she was thrust awake again fumbling at the anamnesis. The pain would well up, and she would double over clutching herself and squeezing her legs together trying to make it stop to no avail.

She was so naïve. She had entered a situation she had experienced countless times back home under the safety of people she knew. But here, the depravity and lawlessness knew no bounds, even among the most elite. Nena had warned her, but she had been so sure and dismissive. The most ironic aspect of all, was that she had been safest among the most hated and feared. In all her time with the pirates, not once – even as a tenant of Pixies – had any of them made unsolicited advances at her. Yet, in one evening cohorting with those she deemed socially equal, she had been stripped of all dignity and innocence.

Eventually the feelings subsided enough into a defeated assent. This would forever remain a stark reminder that even the high class were disreputable and vile. Though, in no way did this reason to be acceptable, but she had to move forward. She collected herself and her courage to egress from her sanctum. She wiped the evidence from her face and stepped out into the hallway. One foot, then the other. But she paused, unable to proceed, something stopping her. She turned to retreat, but in doing so she saw the dress in a pile on the floor. She scooped it up in a bunch and walked downstairs.

Having been hidden away, she looked sallow, and her eyes stared through, not at anything. She proceeded like an apparition out the back without word or acknowledgment of anyone she passed. She was a shell of her former self, a void within. Belle happened to catch a glance of her from across the tavern and quickly followed after her.

Wendy had gone to the beach and stood at the shoreline, the light Caribbean breeze blowing her hair and bed dress softly. The rhythmic tide splashed at her feet with each breaking rush. A gang of pirates were down shore cavorting around a massive bonfire. The flames licked the mid-evening sky, and embers floated into the heavens like fireflies. The songs joyously filled the silent night as the sleepy moon hung in dusky space. Belle secretly watched from the tree line.

Wendy dropped the dress in the sand and walked into the warm ebbing water until she could no longer stand and was submerged. Beneath she floated, suspended in the visceral womb of the sea renewing herself in the embrace the ocean's warmth. Instinctively, Belle rushed out, worried she was going to drown herself, but stopped when she reached the dress and saw the grisly crimson smears. She looked back up to the water line sympathetically and sat down in the sand beside the gown, waiting for Wendy to resurface.

Wendy cleansed herself, removing any trace of the incident upon her body, as though it were a baptism. She hadn't yet seen Belle waiting for her on the beach, and for some time, floated in moonlit sea, peacefully meditating in natal embrace, staring into the starry sky above. Recognizing she was safe, Belle quietly slipped back into the shadows and headed back to Pixies. Wendy clearly needed to be alone right now, and she would respect that. She would offer herself when she returned.

When Wendy felt well enough, she crawled out of the sea reborn to the life she knew now laid before her. In all the cruel episodes she had faced prior, constructing resolve within her, nothing compared to this. As she stepped back onto the beach, dripping, she was no longer the child Wendy who had come from England with her dear mum and dad. Instead, she reemerged as Wendy borne of Port Royal, the most hedonistic, God forsaken swill pot on earth.

Soaking wet, she picked up the dress and walked down the beach to the fire raging. Pirates danced around like devils, swinging jugs of rum, engaged in merry making of their own interest. They had made an encampment on the beach as comfortable as any place to lie your head, content to be as they were (anything was better than being aboard a ship in port). As she approached, they couldn't help but notice the oddity of her appearance, her hair matted by the salt water and her soaked smock clinging to her, translucently exposing her feminine body beneath. The men of course, found this seductive as though a mermaid herself had climbed from the seabed and transformed into the vision before them.

She stood unphased in front of the fire, warming her cool wet skin. She stared into the flames dancing erratically among the burning timbers. She heard none of voices around her making lewd comments toward her. Instead, she gazed ahead still into the fire. She then threw the dress into the pyre and watched the expensive material melt into a smoldering cloud of smoke and cinder. The pirates, confused by this, stopped their cattle calling, and too watched as the flames leapt higher.

"Play." She spoke, breaking her silence.

Confused, one pirate questioned the request with a grunted, "eh?"

"Play. Sing me a song and give me drink."

"And who are you, lass, that comes strangely to join our party, such as you are?"

Without breaking her gaze from the fire, she replied "I am a woman, born in the wrong time, and that is my lot cast. I don't know if shall live to be remembered, or that I deserve to be, but if I am, may I be seen as a phoenix, born of the ashes of this hell. That I am one who forged ahead courageously paying my price to be paid[v]. I am like Portencia. I have been tortured by the duplicity of those who see me as a moppet in some selfish game. But here, now, I stand among you, the firebrand of this scoundrelry."

They all looked at each other perplexed by her big words, ready to laugh her off like the drowned rat she exemplified, but before they could, she cut her eyes to the fiddler, and barked, "Strike up a song, I said!"

Surprised by her outburst and gall, he put the fiddle to his chin and raked the bow across the strings. A melodic hiss from the chord reverberated above the crackle of the campfire. Another of the tribe reached out handing her a pot of rum, and she knocked it back still transfixed to the orange blaze before her. Both the rum and the fire burned her inside and out as the music quickened tempo, and the pirates returned to their jollity. She closed her eyes taking in the heat and the song:

There once was a crew that put to sea
On a ship so fine, the finest there be

The Last King of the Neverland

The sails set tight, the lines were drawn
To the second star and on til dawn

Yo Ho and anchors aweigh
On to the shores of that hidden bay
Heave, Ho, in the galleon's hold
We'll find the Spanish gold

Through sun and moon, we sailed our way
A prize was spied the following day
Thirteen men on a dead man's chest
Plunder the few and pillage the rest

Way ho! The devil may play
Up to his tricks as some may say
Pull hard bully boys til the storm is past
He's looking for one more

Down in the depth lies Davy Jones
A beating heart and a heap of bones
The winds whipped up and the waves did rage
To take us all to a watery grave

Way ho! the ghost ship comes
Through crashing waves and hammering drum
Beware you see the death's head flown
The ferryman take your soul

Forty days we sailed on back to port
For a flagon of rum and an upturned skirt
Once on shore, we'll spend our score
On the next high tide we'll sail once more

Blow Blow the coconut tree
A pirate's life is the life for me
We bid farewell to the girlies on shore
And hoist the colors high

Yo Ho and anchors aweigh
On to the shores of that hidden bay
Heave, Ho, in the galleon's hold
We look for Spanish gold

"Again. Play it again." She spoke when the shanty ended.

"We've got others…"

"I like that one. Play it again, and then I shall take my leave of you, and you may play to your heart's content whatever you damn well please."

When the song was concluded, she thanked them for entertaining her request and for the drink, and as promised departed. She continued down the beach and heard the group behind her play on. Darkness deepened as she distanced herself from the light of the fire.

With no intended destination, she walked to the docks and saw all the ships moored in the bay, floating almost like toys in a bath. As the current shifted them slackly this way or that, there she saw the behemoth *Jolly Roger* sitting squatly on the tide. In a wakening she realized that by being in public put her at risk of being seen by Hook's spies. She scowled at the drifting ship, wishing to burn it to the waterline. She turned to head back to Pixies.

When she arrived, she found Belle sitting at the bar in a thin satin robe, her shapely curves half exposed without any care. The evening was still stagnantly hot, so Belle was quite comfortable as she sat airing out. As Wendy approached, she turned to greet her in pleasant surprise,

"Look who we have here! Are you an apparition, or are you real?" Belle snickered.

"I am the ghost of Wendy Darling! I have returned to terrorize you and your sinful ways! Repent… Repent!" Wendy playfully moaned, somewhat instigated by the rum.

"Then do your worst, for I have nothing to repent, I am but a saintess among sinners!" Belle laughed back at her.

"Come, follow me, I have something for you," Wendy said, and led her up to her room.

She opened the trunks, the lids banging heavily against the wall.

"I want you to have these. Take whatever you want, and whatever you don't, share with the others."

Belle was speechless and dug through feeling the delicate fabrics against her skin, the colors, a rainbow of fancy. She'd never been gifted such a haul and was so joyous at the offer. But she then realized what they were, who they were from, and *who* they were for.

"I cannot take these, Wendy. These were a gift to you from Hook himself. These are yours, I can't."

"I have no need for these any longer. They are a dour reminder, and I would wish to wear rags rather than parade around in these for show. The intent of them was wrought with deception. If you do not take them, I can certainly guarantee the others will have no qualm. I wish for you to have the first take, for all you have shown me these past weeks, and the lessons you have taught me in my short time here."

Belle stood, concerned at what Wendy was divulging. Just a week before, Wendy was agog at the contents she now cast away. It didn't seem right. Her innocent aloofness was missing. Her ignorant optimism wasn't an undercurrent to her demeanor. She was dispirited, dry.

"Why do you say such things?"

"It is nothing. I have just been further enlightened to the realities here, that I wish to make myself my own person sooner than expected. Not at the whim and fancy of a despot manipulator."

"Don't lie to me. This isn't the way of '*nothing.*' You've been holed up for days after you were sent off to the palace, locked up like Rapunzel in the tower. And now you offer me everything to your name… What happened? Why were you withdrawn for such a time?"

"I shan't say. Please, just take your pick."

Hoping she would've come out with it, Belle had to own up to following her at this point, "I followed you to the shore. I saw the dress, Wendy. I saw you wash yourself and burn it in the fire. Tell me what happened."

Wendy felt betrayed at her sneaking behind her, and grew angry, "You are spying on me too? Why, you're no better than he, or the rest of them! How dare you!"

"What? Who? No, it's not like that, Wendy! I saw you leave after days of hiding, carrying your dress, wearing nothing but what you have on now! I found it queer, so I followed you to make sure you were okay. By the time I got to you, you were in the water. I was coming to save you, but then you just floated. I thought maybe you needed time, so I left when I saw you were alright."

"No, you are an accomplice to him, and you are keeping him apprised of my whereabouts. You are buggered by him, and he keeps you around as an accessory to his plans."

"Be careful Wendy, I am not a servant to him. But he protects us, and he gets what he wants. Tell me what happened." Belle snapped back on the defensive.

"I don't know, Belle. I don't know! I awoke in my bed from agonizing pain, covered in mine own blood and the dress sullied on the floor beside me. But what do you care? This manner of life is the life you live."

She was yelling now, and Belle closed the door for privacy. She tried to take Wendy by the arm, but she cast her away. Belle calmed herself, and replied, hoping to draw more out of her.

"Wendy, what I do wasn't a choice for me, but how I do it is. I never had the option to aspire into anything else. My mother was a slave, and I was sold off into the houses as a girl. But now, I control what I do, and I survive by knowing these things. You are not in that position, and if I understand it all, you had no control either. Is that right?"

Wendy began to cry. She was so ashamed of herself. "I don't know. I cannot, for the life of me recall. I have no memory of the night. When I sleep – what little there is anymore – I am plagued by visions to which I cannot reform a single connection between them."

"These visions, what are they?"

Sobbing now, she continued, "Oh, Belle, they are a fog. Clouded pictures of maniacal faces. Loud and indiscernible noises, shrill laughter. It is all my fault. I shouldn't have been there."

"No! It is not your fault! Don't you dare! I know you well enough that you wouldn't put yourself out there like that. Not willingly. Think hard, what is the last thing you remember? Tell me where it all started."

"I don't know. I remember getting there and meeting my escort. He was a nasty man. Before we even entered, he gave me this," she pointed to the still puffy cheekbone Norval had struck. "I followed him in, and we mingled with the guests. Drinks were passed around freely in excess until the governor appeared, and we filed in for dinner. After sitting down, I cannot, retrace anything else until waking here in my condition."

"This man, your escort, he hit you? For what reason?"

"Because I did not arrive afore him, and that he must be so inconvenienced to wait for me to arrive. He was a horrible man, but he left me be most of the night. He had no interest in associating with me, thinking me a shined-up whore. He knew I came from here, and inferred I was..."

"Like me, and the others..." Belle finishing Wendy's thought.

"Yes. Yes, forgive me."

"I am not offended, Wendy, so there is nothing to forgive. I know what I am, and there are plenty who knock on my bustle for the services I fulfill, some of who'd not be so pleased if I were to reveal them. Go on."

"That's all I can say. The governor did not speak with me hardly at all, but I knew he was learning about me, watching me throughout the evening. Like I said, we all sat for dinner, and it was such an ugly affair. Oh, you wouldn't believe."

"What happened after that, do you know?"

"I don't. It's then that everything goes missing."

Skeptical, Belle asked, "Do you recall feeling anything? D'you get real dizzy? Feel like maybe you were floating?"

"I don't recall, maybe? Yes? In these sporadic flashes, I have this feeling about me, that I'm not in control of myself. Lifeless almost"

Belle sighed heavily, believing she had deduced the issue, "Sounds to me like you were dusted."

"*Dusted?* You mean... You mean, they drugged me?"

"I'm afraid that may be. Was anyone passing anything around, like a vial of glittery powder? Did you see anything suspicious like that?"

"No, but that doesn't mean it wasn't happening out of my purview. I only had drinks given to me, and given freely, I might add."

Wendy sat on the edge of the bed, her head in her hands, processing what she'd just been told.

"I'm sorry, Belle. I can't... I need to be alone, again. Please, take what you want. Or don't. You can take it later. Please, just leave me be."

"Wendy, you must know, I am no stranger to this. I hope you will let me be with you right now. You need someone... someone like me, a woman, to confide in. You're not alone. What happened isn't right, but we can make it right."

"Perhaps. In time. But right now, I need to take care of some things of my own."

Belle knelt down and lifted her chin with a finger. She looked deep into her eyes and leaned in to embrace her. The comfort was genuine. Wendy put her arms around her in return, and thanked her, promising she would come find her later. Belle let go and left her sitting on the bed processing all her thoughts and emotions. It didn't feel right, but she had to respect her wishes. Forcing herself into the situation wasn't going to help anything.

Looking around, her room was stale and unkempt. She peeled off the damp clinging nightgown and tidied up a bit. In doing so, she rummaged through one of the trunks looking for the loose items she'd seen before, specifically among them a quill, inkpot, and a sheaf of paper for correspondence. She sat at her little table, the hard wood chair rough against her bare skin. She began to write, the words falling like a cascade:

Sir,

The information you seek from my confabbing with the governor, is that he and all those alike are scoundrels, the lot of them. None of them are of any repute above you or your ilk. I say with immeasurable disappointment, that they quite possibly rank worse, and that is to say very little of either of you.

Your ability to overturn this place is but a futile endeavor. Ridding yourself of the king's envoy is but one challenge of many, and yet the simplest part of all. That lies in plying the viceroy with the same of which you partake and then cause him to disappear.

The soldiers in the forts, and those upon the warships will carry out the king's orders, accordingly, should they be provoked. Strangle them against retaliation, and they will fall quickly, especially with no sovereign at the command. They are an embarrassment to the Navy, and in no such form to muster to ranks effectively.

Alas, the landowners inland are whom you should focus your concern. They are the true stronghold and with collective effort, are within their means to seize control wholly. The governor is merely a jester to them, the embodiment of the seven sins of man. Their money and influence control everything. Should you threaten their pockets or station they will strike back with an economic force, I am confident in my telling you, you will be ill-prepared to withstand.

I have done as you asked, and I shall do no more. I retire myself from your indenture. Should you seek to strike me down for not upholding any further part, is of no concern to me now. You wittingly placed me in danger, the manner of which has caused irreparable damage to my self of which you could never conceive. I will no longer subject my self to the jeopardy you impose upon me at the hands of these oppressors and your selfish plans. Be it known, it is your folly which has brought us to this exigency.

Do not call for me henceforth, for I am now independent of you and shall survive on my own accord.

-Wendy

She folded the letter over, sealing it with a wax signet. She then laid down and closed her eyes, hoping for sleep. Unable to rest, she dressed herself in a common shirt and breeches and carried the letter down to Nena.

"Please deliver this to the captain at your soonest." She asked, handing it over the bar.

"You know he's been lookin far ya? I'll see he gets this, but bet hon, he'll be wantin' to speak with ya soon as he knows yer about."

"I have no interest in speaking with him, Nena. Everything he needs to know is in that letter. He may come for me, but I cannot say I will be present when he or his men come looking."

"That ain't gonna go over too well, you know. He'll be hotter than a spit if he finds you gone, girl."

"So he may. But, as I see it, I have done what was asked of me, and I now need to find space. A place away from the things of these men. I can't... I won't be exploited for his benefit."

Nena shifted her sternness to what passed for her version of concern, "You alright, girl? What happened t'other night? You's holed up so long, I had right mind to knock down your door to sees if you wasn't dead."

"I was an offering served up like a pudding for those atrocious people. A sacrifice to the depraved who pretend to hold themselves on high above all others. That is the simplicity of it. I will be fine. I am fine, but I will not play a part in his game any longer. I make the rules for me now. I am no longer his captive, his ward, or his servant. I have done as he asked, and that is all I owe him."

Nena, being a proprietor of flesh, was not surprised to hear this, but wasn't expecting it either. She clicked her tongue and shook her head. After handing over the letter, Wendy asked, "Have you seen Piet recently? Or Belle? Perhaps she knows where he is?"

"He was here not long ago, hanging around like his usual self, just over there in the corner. Haven't seen 'im in some time though. Maybe he went upstairs? I can't be sure."

Wendy looked around but didn't see him. "I'd like to speak with him if he comes around. Or Belle for that matter. I'll wait for them, but if you see them, please tell either of them to come find me? If I'm not about down here, they can find me in my room."

"Will do, darlin.', and I'll see that Jamesy gets your letter, soonest."

"Thank you. Oh, and Nena, please accept my gratitude for all you have done and provided for me. It is not without knowledge that you have gone out of your way to accommodate me. I do not take that for granted, and you need to know that."

"It ain't a thing to be worryin' about love, your debts are paid on time, and you ain't a headache for me to be fussin over, so I might say, you's the best girl I've had take board in my place in all the time I been at this."

Wendy made a circuit through the establishment but didn't see either of them. Pausing to consider what to do next, she went back upstairs. She opened the trunks once again and rifled through them for anything she might keep and set them aside in a pile. She opted to keep the writing implements, a few books, two shifts, common clothing, and a brush. The rest she discarded for the picking among the other girls. Not long after she had sorted her things, Piet knocked on the open door. He had seemingly just come from Belle's as he was fixing himself as he stood there in the doorway.

"Hi Wendy! It's wonderful to see you up and about again! I saw your door open. I hope I'm not interrupting. It looks like you're busy at... what are you doing?"

"Piet, I'm pleased to see you again as well. I hope you have taken good care of the matter we last encountered?"

"Oh, yes, of course. They have all been moved to the farm and are settled in with the others. We saw you leave earlier, but you didn't so much as notice us. Belle followed..."

"Yes, she followed me, I know. We spoke earlier." Wendy interrupted.

"Oh, right, I forgot."

"It's alright Piet. I wanted to see you because I have a favor to ask of you."

"Sure, anything for you, Wendy. Just name it! Want me to kill Hook for you? I heard he's the one behind all this."

Wendy, slightly miffed that he was in the know of her very personal affairs, scrunched her face, and asked, "And what is it you know?" Her tone was a little more aggravated now.

"Oh, nothing really. I just know he set you up at the Governor's place, but I knew that already. Belle told me she thinks you were dusted, and I..."

"I don't care for her telling all my business and spreading gossip!"

"Oh, no, it's not like that. She told me because we're all friendly, the three of us, and she was concerned about you. Told me to be careful about what I say or do around you, because..."

"Because what? I'm out of my head? Something's wrong with me?" Wendy was getting upset. She was still very emotionally frail and taking everything as a snipe against her and her character. Though she had every position to feel that way, Piet and Belle were genuinely bothered by what happened to her and wished they could get through, but Wendy had put up trenchant walls to protect her mindset against all things.

"Wendy don't be silly! Nothing's wrong with you! You're perfect just the way you are!" Piet's disarming ability with his inapt childish demeanor settled her slightly. The unexpected flattery was an added easement. He noticed this in her body language and capitalized on the momentum he was gaining back.

"Really, Wendy, you're such a breath of fresh air, it's just delightful to have you around. You said you had a favor to ask of me? What was it?"

After a deep, calming breath, she asked, "Will you take me to your farm? I need to escape this place post-haste, and I wish to take you up on your offer."

"Of course, you can! I have some things I must attend to, but we can leave later today! I'd offer to take you right now, but during daylight. I only go at night when I'm stealing away the lost boys."

"I cannot stay here. Once Hook gets word of me about town – if he hasn't already – he will call for me and take me to his ship, for what I wish not fathom. I must escape at once."

Piet contemplated the option. The truth was, he didn't have anything pressing to attend that couldn't wait until another time. The sun would rise in a few hours, so he would have to get her off soon.

"I can be ready to depart soon. I can meet you at your canoe. Where have you left it this time?"

"Just on the edge of town, near Marshallsea. Head toward Gallows Point and keep an eye out. I'll be waiting for you." He was very excited about her going to his farm he started to dash out.

"Piet, wait! Will you take my things, so it's not so evident what I am up to?"

"Of course!"

Wendy collected the things she'd separated and bundled them into a pile, tying it up for him to carry easily. While she did, Piet ran back to Belle's room to tell her he would be leaving for a short bit but would return in a few days' time. By the time he'd returned to Wendy's room, she had her things ready for him to take. She gave him a kiss on the cheek to keep him baited, knowing he responded to the attention. His heart skipped a beat, and he looked her in the eyes with adoring curiosity. She smiled and pushed him out the door on his way.

"I'll see you soon. And Piet, please keep this a secret. My safety depends on your discretion, please understand that."

Piet darted out the back into the pre-dawn shadows. The night's affairs were dwindling, and the place was quieting down. Little mind was paid to him as he shifted through the streets like a cloaked nomad.

Wendy, in the meantime sought Belle once more, and told her she would be gone for a while, but she would return. She thanked her for taking care of her and promised to come for her; that she would save her from this place in time. What Belle didn't know was that Piet had told Wendy he was taking her away again, though hadn't provided any actual details. Jealous for Piet's attention, she was standoffish toward Wendy, but feigned appreciation. She was mindful for Wendy's attempt but couldn't help resenting her. Belle wished her well with a biting reply. Piet was the factor of contempt, unwittingly creating divisiveness within.

After Belle, she thanked Nena again for her caretaking, to which Nena urged caution going forward. She was happy to have Wendy as a ward, and would welcome her back any time, but her choices would have repercussions. Knowing the man Hook was, she tried to convince Wendy once more that she would be better positioned to stay put and find out what happened next as opposed to disappearing without his allowance. Wendy was resolute in her decision, reasoning that anything he would put upon her here was no better than what he would put upon her elsewhere; at least she would be on ground she could defend herself more easily. In the end, it all meant death, and she preferred to control that end if she could.

With a heavy sigh, Nena blessed her and watched her leave into the languishing night. Once she'd gone, Foggerty approached the bar. Nena handed him the sealed letter and asked, "Tell him to go easy on her. She's just been through an awful ordeal. Give her time. She's not in her right mind and needs to come back to her senses."

Foggerty tucked the letter away, knocked back his cup, and replied, "You know he gon' do what he gon' do, no matter what anyone tell 'im."

"I know. I just hope he'll take that to mind when he does."

XIII

Taking it from Foggerty when he arrived back onboard the ship that morning, Smee delivered the message to the captain. This was a protective measure for the crew, so that the captain was unsure who the messenger was and did not react rashly toward any of them. Smee was Hook's right-hand man and did not fear wrath from him if it came. In all the years together, Smee had borne countless rages, only to clean up the pieces, and calm the captain down again from his furies, nightmares, or bothers. But all the same, Smee had also been witness to many unwarranted punishments to the crewmen, where he held little to no judicature over the captain, and those poor unfortunate souls were possibly closer to hell's damnation, than they'd ever imagined they might find themselves. It was for this reason, Smee was always the messenger de facto. And so, in the morning light of the captain's cabin, Smee stood picking at his fingernails with his blade while Hook stewed.

When he opened the letter, it came as no surprise by now, that Wendy had defected. This nettled him, but he knew this was a possible risk at having her doing his bidding. She was a novice, and for that he knew was his hasty choice, but he'd hoped her breeding would have sufficed for the interim until she became more accustomed to the standards of living in Port Royal. Her message to him was matter of fact in that she had done what he'd asked and would do no more. To a marginal point she was right, and she had provided him wise instruction in his quest, though, he wanted and expected this arrangement to last much longer than one engagement. In his plan, this had no deadline.

Hook sat behind his desk in his heavy robe, in the dusty morning light. Silently he deliberated. He stared through the stained aft panes. His breaths came heavy and coarse from his nose, so that you might think a wild mare were locked in the cabin. Smee never once looked up, knowing the news, whatever it was, obviously wasn't good.

"Damn this preposterousness!" he yelled finally, standing in a rage.

"What's next, Cap'n?" Smee asked coolly, while his commander paced frenetically.

"She's gone. GONE, Smee!"

"She's a little bird, Cap'n. Flown off away from danger, I reckon?

"Spare me your metaphoric sympathies, man!"

Smee put his knife away and looked at the captain now. "You knew she wasn't cut out for this. You told me this was a risky effort, the last effort at taking this place."

"So help me, if you say you told me so, I will cut off your balls."

"What I mean to say, is she wasn't cut for the job, and you knew that going into this. You'd only a brief time with her, unable to build any trust or rapport for her to become a suitable addition to the crew. Mayhaps with more time, you might've done so, but here we are. So, I ask again, what's next?

"Pissfiddles and shit sticks, Smee, I don't know what's next! She's still here somewhere. We go find her. Until then, I'll figure the rest out."

"Little birds who fly the cage, can still be trapped, cap'n. I'll call the men back to the *Roger* and assemble the search. We'll need a few hands to stay back and keep the ship, but I think we'll only be needin' a few to go scoutin'."

"You do that, Smee. While you're out there, inquire with Nena what she knows."

"Aye, Cap'n."

"And Smee, do be delicate in your methods with her. I need not remind you, that she is an element unreplaceable in our fold. Beyond that, whatever means necessary is at your discretion. This little nuisance has set us back detrimentally, I fear."

Smee nodded in understanding and set off to corral the crew in port. A few hands were already aboard, keeping the watch, but most had gone on liberty in town. He lowered a rowboat and scuttled away. Stepping onto the shore, he was greeted by a few familiar nods and made his way into the dirty streets to find Nena and the others. It was now mid-morning, and the village was bustling with activity, so he would need to locate the men sporadically to find them all. But he knew where he could find some, in all likelihood, and they would find the others while he sought out Nena.

Sure enough, in the market he found two of the men, yelling about some details of an account neither could appropriately recount. This was often the case, and how many stories and rumors spread, often inflated by narrative bravado.

"Oy, Cap'n wants erry'body back on ship. No time to waste. Find the others and get back to the *Roger* quick like." He interjected to the bunch. The discord was nipped instantly, because everyone knew that when Hook beckoned, you didn't leave him waiting. They scurried off in different directions at Smee's order.

Smee kept on his way to Pixies to find out what he could. Nena hadn't yet woken, sleeping off her graveyard schedule, but some of the girls were about, and attempted to swoon him when he entered. To their disappointment, he declined the offers but told them to tell their superintendent he was looking for her regarding an urgent matter. One of the girls ignorantly, chimed in, "You lookin' for that Wendy girl?"

"I am, but it is not of your concern. I wish to speak with Nena about the matter."

"She took off last night with that boy Belle's always cozy with."

Smee, turned, surprised at the gainful information, "Go on, what more do you know?"

"Nothin' much more than that. Seen 'em all makin' a fuss last night. Real damper to our fun, ya know?"

"And where is Belle now?"

"In her room, far as I know. Ain't seen her yet today."

Smee proceeded upstairs to the end of the hall and banged on her door. He called for her boisterously. Inside confusion could be heard as footsteps scrambled about. She opened the door to find him standing in her doorway, her night's last call putting on his pantaloons. Standing there in her natural state, she barked at him, "What's the meaning of this, Smee? You got no decency to call this afternoon once a girl is on her feet?"

Smee, not missing a beat, looked over her shoulder, "Dockson, how are ya now?" In turn, he replied with a half-awake grin, "Can't complain mate. If'n I did, she wouldn't have me back!" He chuckled. She scowled back at him over her shoulder.

"I say again, Mr. Smee, what's the meaning of all the fuss?"

"Hook wants to see you. I'm here to take you to the *Roger*. Get yourself together, an' meet me downstairs. You, me, and the crew all takin' company."

"He wants me, he knows where to find me," she clapped back.

"Not a choice, m'lady. I've got orders."

"Your orders don't mean shit in this place, an' you know it."

"I don't wanna have to force you, miss. You come along, and I'm sure it'll be the better for the lot of us."

At this point, Dockson had dressed, and was trying to excuse himself before he got caught in the middle of anything he wasn't a part of. He squeezed past her in the doorway, Smee stepped aside to allow him to pass. Once in the hallway, he looked back and gave warning, "Best you go Belle. He ain't no one to cross. I'd hate for you not t'be around next time on account of this, an' all."

"Mind your business!" she barked back.

"What's it gonna be, Belle? You comin' easy, or am I gonna have to take you kickin and screamin?"

Defeated, she exasperatingly huffed, "I'm coming Smee. Don't get your breeches in a knot. Gimme a minute to make myself ready unless he wants me like this?" The last inflection laced with seething sarcasm as she shook her body imitatingly.

Smee, never unappreciative of a free show, laughed off her attitude and told her, "I'll be downstairs when you're fit to go." And with that he proceeded back downstairs. Belle fumed and dressed herself.

When she came downstairs, Smee was waiting for her idly tapping his meaty fingers on the bar top.

"Jezza, tell Nena I've gone out. Business with the high and mighty cap'n. Not sure when I'll be back. Make sure the pots are tossed before she's up, ya hear?"

Stomping irritably across the place, her boot heels echoed with each impact against the hard floor. "Alright then, let's get on with it! If it's such a hurry, we shouldn't be sittin' here playin' tiddlywinks, now, should we?"

Smee stood from the barstool, hiked up his pants, adjusted his glasses on his sun worn face, looked at her over his glasses, and said, "Waitin' for the boys. We can wait here in comfort, or at the dock in less comfort. No matter t'me."

Belle sighed, clearly bothered (and rightfully so). She shifted the weight of her hips and rubbed her face. "What's this all about anyway? If he's lookin' for my treat, he ain't gotta send you all riled up, bangin' on my door. Better ways to get my favor."

"Nothin' like that, miss. Can't say he mightn't, but I ain't here to collect ya for that. I agree, better ways to get to you. Some things he's needin' answers to, and he's wantin' errybody on deck."

"Then get me there, and get me back, Smee. If you're waitin' for the boys to come out of all their holes, we might be here for days. I've got business to mind, an' the sooner we can get this out of the way, the better we all end."

"Suit yourself, miss. Let's get on our way. Got the dinghy at the docks. You're right enough. The boys'll make their way back when they get word. No question on that."

And so, they departed Pixies for the little boat Smee had rowed over from the hulking mass moored in the harbor bay. The *Jolly Roger* loomed like an angry parent over the other ships scattered about nearby, strewn about like pieces to a puzzle, not yet used. As they got closer, the mass of the ship became such a wonder to behold. Belle had never been on a ship, let alone one this big. It was intimidating, humbling, and spellbinding. She was without words as they neared. From shore, they were just pockmarks on the horizon, bobbing along, blending into the mountainous scenery behind them. It was something she'd grown used to seeing, and never thinking much beyond that, except sometimes there were more, sometimes less. But now, in the shadow of this colossal craft, she had an all-new appreciation for them. The masts towered above her, touching the sky like arms outstretched to their limits. The rigging waving in the air from blocks to pins to spars. She was mesmerized by the confusing webs of rope ladders leading to the crow's nest atop the masts, her stomach uneasy at the thought of spending any time up there – especially in rough seas.

"Up ya go," Smee called out, breaking her awe. She snapped to, realizing she was lost in time, and that she couldn't recount any of the last however long she'd been rowed toward the ship.

"What?"

"Up ya go, lass. Up the ladder now, here ya go." Smee held the Jacob's ladder for her and pointed upward. It hadn't occurred to her in this foreign experience, how they would get up. She looked up. She looked at Smee. She looked back up.

"Up this? Up there? Blimey Smee, how's about a little heads up, man? I gotta climb this to get up there? I'd'a put my knickers on, if I'd'a known that? You take any peeks, I'ma tell the cap'n you's a filthy ol' shit." Her nervousness was nearly paralyzing, and her defense mechanism was to attempt at jokes. They fell short in the delivery, but Smee understood well enough what she meant.

"Ain't so bad, miss. Just put one foot on top of the other and step up. Hold with the hands, and you'll be up in no time. Trust."

With that, she grabbed hold of the wobbly, weather-worn, knotted contraption that counted for a ladder, and ascended awkwardly to the railing where she was met by two of the crewmen who helped her get her feet steadily on the deck of the ship. She looked up again at the masts, then back down at Smee as he clambered up the ladder with such ability, it made her jealous. The juxtaposition was vertigo inducing, so she stuck to keeping her eyes trained on things before her. In a matter of seconds Smee was aboard right behind her. For his stature, he was incomprehensibly nimble to be able to scale those rungs, she thought.

"I'll let the captain know you're arrived. You wait here and I'll be back for you. Enjoy the view."

Belle was nervous and hugged her elbows in her hands as she looked around. Not only was her perception of size completely distorted, but she was also out of her element. She placed her hands on the painted railing and peered out toward the town. It was so foreign to look upon the place from the outside, she found it exciting. The grumpy moans and creaks of the timber beneath her was meditative and soothed her nerves. Listlessly afloat, she felt oddly calm now. No hustle, no madness, no noise competing for attention; just idleness.

In the distance she saw the other ferries approaching. A handful of men occupied them all, and they all came up in synchrony. With the same, if not better, agility than Smee displayed, the men scrambled up the ladder and hopped on deck. The rowboats below were tied off to each other knocking against each other with dull thuds. All the men were onboard now and scattered to various places about the ship. None of them paid any mind to her standing alone in the open air. They knew who she was and business she held with the captain. They all seemingly assumed as much as to why she was here, though, it was strange for him to have her on the ship, rather than in the inn. Bad luck to have women on ship… Still, they knew better than to meddle, so they left her be.

Smee eventually came back and let her know he would see her now. She took a deep breath of the saliferous air. He guided her to his quarters, and as with everyone else ever invited or requested, he knocked and waited for permissive response. He opened the door for her, and she stepped inside, bravely. Across the room he sat clearly agitated, pining away in the tenebrous shadows. She instantly recognized this was not a pleasure visit and grew apprehensive. He looked up at her, his eyes aflame,

"You're going to tell me everything."

"What have I to tell you on what matter?" she retorted before her mind had time to catch up.

"The little Wendy bird. The bitch who's gone missing right under our noses, with that silly imbecile you keep your bed warm with, when you don't have anyone else."

"Now listen to me Jas…"

"No!" he exploded, smashing the maps and instruments off his desk. "No! You listen to me, and you listen closely! That plaything of yours has cost me more than you can conceive, and you let it happen. You coddled them both, and led them to each other, and now they have gone off into who knows where… And you're going to tell me where they went."

Belle was truly terrified now. She had never seen him like this before. Even on a bender, he never took such asperity toward her, not in this manner at least. She hugged herself and cowered from him. The inferno in his eyes meant he was in no mood to take mercy.

"Believe me, Jas... I don't know. I really don't. They left in such a hurry, together. I didn't have hardly the time to..."

"To what?" He berated. "To dry the slick from betwixt your legs when you'd finished him off?"

His words stung. He was being malicious, though, it was his nature, naturally. However, for the times they'd shared together, he had never talked to her this way, and it was hurting her. She cared for Piet in a comfortable way. What she did with him was no one else's business. She attended to what she needed to when she needed to. She ran a tight operation, and though the oldest profession on record paid her way, she was ever the executor of a lucrative business for her and Nena. Yet, here in the cramped confines of his ship, her top client was spiraling madly into a fury that she was not equipped to defend. She stepped back putting her arms out to hold him off as she continued to mutter words.

"I don't know. He goes off into the night so often, I've stopped asking. He's not from down here. He comes from upland, inside. His family had a farm originally. I think he goes off there."

"I'm giving you more opportunity than I should, Belle. Tell me where they've gone."

"James. Please..." She begged, afraid. "She wasn't herself after what the governor did to her the other night. She said a lot of things, even tried to give me an' the girls her things. She needed to clear her head. I... I don't know where he took her. Maybe to his farm, but I don't know where it is... Maybe he didn't. Maybe they just disappeared and will come back tomorrow."

Seeing red with no sympathy or patience, Hook swung his husky arm, connecting to Belle's face. The hook lacerated her from her temple to her chin. Blood rushed out, and she was felled to the floor. A macabre display of a beautiful girl, dazed from the brutal impact to her head. She hadn't yet realized the damage done to her, except that the hot, viscous liquid from the gash blinded her in one eye. Outside, Smee heard the commotion and busted in to find him with a pistol now pointed at her as she lay at his feet.

"Cap'n, don't!" he interrupted. "She's the only one's got answers. Only one who's can get her back. Think about this... put the shot down."

Hook stood over her, towering like a goliath near ready to end her out of frustrated rage. She hadn't done anything to deserve this, but this is why Smee was always the messenger. He wouldn't do this to Smee, but now Belle lay maimed on the floorboards beneath him as he upbraided her for something she didn't have a part in. Slowly, after some contemplation, he lowered the pistol and stepped back. Belle crawled into a ball near Smee for protection. She all but hid behind him in fear, looking up like a whipped puppy.

Smee waved Hook down, saying, "I'm not speaking to the girl's intentions, cap', but I reckon she don't have the part in this you think she does. The men tell me this boy of hers takes a shine to any slit that'll give him the time of day. When he's not with Belle here, he's off harassing the others, and they find him an awful nuisance. Like a little bratty brother that pesters 'em all for attention. Seems as I understand, Wendy gave him consolation and they wound up stickin' together."

"He's right…" Belle squeaked pitifully. "He ain't had a mama to raise him right, so he's always botherin girls for the attention. Ask Nena. Anyway, that first night you came back for me, that's when they met, 'cause we was doin' our thing, they were stuck with each other."

"So this is my fault?" Hook roared back at her. She shrunk into further cower. Smee held him off still.

"Circumstances, I imagine Cap'n. Not a thing you, her, or them coulda missed, bein' as it were. No fingers pointed at anyone. But likes I asked a'fore. What next?"

Hook shifted his stance, pausing for a moment before walking back to his desk, and began picking up the items he'd thrown off. His inkpot and quill smashed against the wall, lay in a pool, oozing through along the veins of the plankboards. He studied his maps carefully, inspecting them for any ink blots or damage. They all appeared fine, so he placed them back on the desk. After some introspection, he turned back to his audience,

"We're going to pay this rascal a visit. And you're going to lead us to him."

"But… But I don't know where he went?"

"You're going to find out, and you're going to take us to him." He paused, thinking further on it, "No. Smee, *you're* going to find out where they've gone, and she is coming with us to watch me crush them. She will watch them both die, slowly."

"Aye cap'n. I'll set to it, then."

"Tie her up belowdecks. I don't need another little bird flying the roost."

"Aye, Cap'n." he replied once more. He turned to help Belle up, though she protested and shrieked for favor and plea from Hook. He, however, had concluded his attention to the matter, and continued cleaning up his mess. She flailed and kicked to no avail as Smee carried her out. Her wails drew the attention of the men nearby, and so Smee handed her off to them, giving them the instruction to lock her up below. Still, she squirmed, clawed, and kicked to break free. She was writhing and unruly, and this wouldn't do, so one of the men thumped her, knocking her cold. Limp, they took her to the brig below and locked her inside the cell.

Smee, rowed back ashore, taking Foggerty and Simcoe to do their work in finding out where Piet and Wendy had gone off to. When they landed, Simcoe brusquely started shaking down anyone who crossed their path. Foggerty had to reel him in before he made too much of a scene.

"Relax, mate. Don't none of these pissers know where those two got off to. We gotta start at the beginning, where they took out. The gals at Pixies is where we start. That Nena oughta know something. After that, and we still got nothing? Then we shake down the rest."

Simcoe was a bright character but had a bitterness to him. He had charm, but he was the one they brought in to make the recipe a little more gritty when it called for it. Hearing Foggerty's plan, he smoothed himself out and blended with the other two for a more balanced combination.

"When we get there, we'll do the talking," he said, referring to Smee and himself. "You can play nice with the other girls and see what you can find out. But don't go gettin' sidetracked, ya hear me?"

"Yeah, I hear ya…" he growled.

Arriving at Pixies, they found the place surprisingly quiet. By now, things would have normally started to see some life, but there wasn't the same energy as usual. It was noticeable, but not enough for the three to care since they weren't there on a pleasure visit. Nena was wiping tables and fussing at the girls to do one thing or another. She heard them enter, and looking over her shoulder saw who they were, and wheeled around.

"Look here, Smee!" she blurted out, face reddening. "Don't nobody wanna come in now, hearin' James is stealing folks up!"

"Nena, what're you on about?" Smee asked trying to placate.

"Word's out he snatched up my best girl, *his* girl, for carousing with the wrong people, and now not a soul trusts they're welcome here, for fear of his deemings. An' I want her back. I know he thinks he run the place 'ere, but she belongs to me at the end of the day. Can't go stealin' my girls whe'er he sees fit. I'll send her out, but he can't just go snatchin' girls up. Damn bad for business, it is!"

Smee took his spectacles off his nose, scrunched his face as he rubbed it in frustration. He readjusted them back on his face and looked around again, taking more account of the place.

"We'll get your flow back in here. But first, we need answers to questions we think only you or the girls might'n be knowin."

"You get me some thirsty pricks back in here, *then* I'll tell you what I know to whatever it is you're askin' 'bout."

Smee sighed heavily. "Sims, go out and collect whoever you can. Tell'm all a round on Hook for the misunderstanding, and it ain't what'n it seems."

Simcoe acknowledged and hurried out into the street to rustle up some patrons. Smee turned back to Nena and asked again with a little less patience now that it was going to cost them a sum.

"Now, if you would be so kind as to bless me with your wisdom of all things coming and going. Where has Wendy gone off to?"

"I ain't got a clue. She took outta here after I implored her to stay put. Wouldn't listen. She didn't seem good at listenin' to what was good for her anyway. Gave me that letter I gave to ol' Fog's over'ere, and that's the last of it."

"Belle tells us she thinks she went off with that puppy of hers. That scrap that's always hangin' around eyein' up the girls and what-have-ya."

"Well, I'll tell you again, I don't know where they got off to. Don't know much about him, other'n he pays 'is way. So, I never asked questions. Alls I know, he comes from up in the hills; old family. Mightn've gone that way. I can't say.... Now, I'll say again, I want my girl back, Smee. You, know this ain't right."

"You know I can't do that. He's got her held, an' ain't lettin' loose tils we find the other one. She is currently a guest aboard the Roger, with the cap'n. She has been interrogated at his request and will be set free in exchange for the Wendy girl."

"What in hell, Smee? You got my girl pinned up with him and hold'n her ransom?"

"I assure you we do not want her caged any longer than necessary. This is not enjoyable for any of us. Cap'n wants the girl back. We intend to root her out, and Belle is the closest thing we got to finding that thief. If he wants to see that she gets back here safe, he'll come out sooner than later. You see him? You tell him the stakes. You also put out word, if'n any a soul knows where he's capered off to, there's reward in it for 'em.

With that, Smee dropped a munificent amount of coin on the bar top and signaled to Foggerty it was time to clear out. As they were approaching the door, Simcoe barreled in with three scrubs and all but threw them into the establishment.

"She's gonna need more'n that, Sims. But we're done here. Come w' us."

Throughout the evening, they patrolled the streets asking questions and getting nowhere. No one cared about some nouveau riche squatter or any tart he may have scampered off with. That business wasn't of any concern to them. They did, however, take a care toward the open tab at Pixies. Most began to flock toward the place once the word spread. This made it more difficult to interrogate anybody. Free drinks were a gift and a priority, so the aid they provided Nena with reestablishing customers was a success. They just weren't succeeding in their mission. Foggerty finally threw up his hands, and said,

"If'n they alls runnin' back t' Pixies, why don' we just go back t'ere and let'm loosen up a bit? Then we start askin' questions."

Smee considered the logic, and shook his head diffidently, realizing this was a good idea.

"Damn me for all my efforts. Fog's that's a hell of a thought. I was too focused on the hard part to even see the easy part. Let's get back down there and shake a few bones, eh?"

When they arrived back at the inn, the place was crawling with all manner of habitués, rife for the picking. They slid their way through and cleared themselves out a table as a center point. Smee ordered Simcoe to take another fistful of coin to the bar to keep things flowing and bring back a few rounds for themselves.

As they sat drinking their own and watching the foray, they plotted and watched. Everyone in the place was getting looser by the minute. After they finished their first round, Foggerty and Simcoe mingled among the patrons asking questions. Still, no one knew much of anything about this Piet character. Some had seen him about, but mostly only on account of being a fixture of the place. He was beginning to truly rule out as a nobody. Smee wouldn't accept this as fact and mixed his way into the conversations. Bits and pieces of inconsequential information scattered about, but he too wasn't having any luck getting answers.

They had all reconvened at their table for another round among them, and to plot a new strategy. Rosetta arrived at their table with their drinks, setting them down as she scooched her way onto Foggerty's lap. She remembered him from her run in with Wendy a while back.

"Word is you're looking for that Wendy girl and Belle's boy?"

"Aye. What of it?" Simcoe snapped back, half mad she wasn't on his lap, half because the fruitless efforts were tiring him. He didn't sign on to crew to be a bloodhound for some trollop.

"I'm not one to kiss and tell..." she could barely keep a straight face saying this. "That girl tried to slit me up. Always better than all the other girls, she was. At least as far as she thought. I didn't never care for her, if's I'm bein' honest."

"If you're bein' honest, be a little quicker about it, would ya?" Simcoe snapped. Smee looked between them. He didn't feel any different, just that he had more reserve than his mate.

"Anyway, that lit'l bitch was always scheming 'bout how to get in with the gov'na. Get up in class. Spoils at her whims, and all..."

Smee grabbed Simcoes' leg to quiet him and gave Foggerty the slightest of glances to urge her on. She was running her mouth out of place and knew nothing of Wendy's placement. With all of this, there was hope she would divulge more than she realized.

179

"…Well, apparently, she got right tossed after that ball. Poor thing. So sad." She pandered. "So, she got it up her arse to get outta here with that simplin'. Heard'm talkin' 'bout goin' off to his farm in the hills."

"And what do you know of this place?" Smee asked smoothly. "What have you heard of this simplin's farm?"

"Oh, I don' know nothin' 'bout it. Just that it's up in the valley somewheres. I hear mutterin's of a place in the foothills of a farm with cimaroons holding out runnin' the place like their own. Bunch'a owners 'round in Spanish Town and Kingston raisin' cane on their slaves runnin' off in the night to this place. They hold up in this place inland and can't nobody get near 'em or find the missin' ones. And for all they try, they can't steal the ones there away neither."

The facts of what she was telling were becoming very misinformed or bordering on hearsay. However, for all the nonsense she was sharing, she had shared a crucial bit of information. This farm, that supposedly belonged to this mysterious beau existed in the hills. If any of the other info she was spouting had any merit, all they needed to do was head to Kingston or Spanish Town and ask around about this hidden refuge for escaped slaves.

"And so what would it benefit you from telling us this?" Smee asked, closing her off.

"She don' belong here. She ain't a Pixie, and that room 'o hers is rightfully mine by decree. So, she's out, naturally, well… I get a place to spread out…" As she said this, she did, in fact, spread herself out, showing herself and fawning over Foggerty. She felt his interest pique beneath her and giggled coquettishly. She wrapped one arm around his broad shoulders and slid the other one down between her legs to rub between his legs. She was playing her role again and was only interested in a payout for her time, one way or the other – or both.

Smee nodded to Foggerty that he was free to do as he pleased and dropped a couple more coins on the table for her time. She snatched them up and slid them into her cleavage. Foggerty scooped her up and carried her upstairs to handle the payout.

Smee slid back in his chair, raised his glass, and before taking a drink, said to Simcoe, "Go on an' find yourself a warm bed too, mate. Tomorrow, we head inlan' and it won't be so advantageous."

XIV

When Piet and Wendy landed across the bay, they quickly navigated the rutty parish streets until they were out of town. From there, they followed a dirt road Northwest into the dense green jungle ahead. The mountains towered in expansive tropical landscape; a variety of earthen colors spattered across nature's canvas. The terrain grew steeper and less tended as they put the coast further behind them. The humidity hounded them as they entered the forest, almost liquified air.

Wendy wasn't prepared for it to be such a journey but fared well enough. She still had an unassuming vigor, and Piet found this almost competitive. He thought for sure she would tire and delay their excursion, but she kept in lock step with him, even when he took to increasing pace. She was mildly irked that he seemed to be speeding up for no apparent reason other than to show off how fast he could go. She had no choice but to keep up – she didn't know where they were going. When they'd finally made it to the farm, Wendy was glad to not have to go on any further. She had wanted to take in more of the things around her as they traveled, but between their clip and the heat, she was exhausted.

Coming upon the farm, she could tell it once was a flourishing plantation. It still had great potential, if it could be tended like it needed to be. But, in the helter-skelter way Piet orchestrated his entire life, it was clear the hands were doing their best with what they had. The crops grew sparsely, the fencing and structures dilapidated, and the master house sat like a sleepy old man in a worn-out chair. This saddened Wendy. Piet had inherited it all –the land, the money, the everything – but he spent all his time in Port Royal, drinking and cavorting with Belle and the others. He could have brought her here all this time; taken her out of that hell and given her more of a life than that which she led night after night.

"Wait here," he called out as she surveyed everything.

He ran off down the hill, leaving her standing awkwardly in the lane. She explored within a small perimeter of where he'd left her, looking over the fields. She wasn't sure what to do since he'd abandoned her in the middle of nothing. She decided she'd walk up to the house and look around. As she neared, she could see it hadn't been used in ages and was in worse condition than she'd assumed from further out. This was unfortunate, such a waste, she thought. Why choose the life he had when this peaceful opportunity was wasting away? The steps creaked querulously as she stepped up onto the front porch. The banister, steps, decking, all of it needed repair. She cautiously stepped, hoping not to fall through a rotted board.

"Massuh's gone to town. Won't be back for a few days." She heard a deep raspy voice behind her say. She turned embarrassed, like she'd been caught doing something wrong. The voice had startled her, but when she saw the man, she tripped over her own words.

"He brought me here. I'm with him. He's here somewhere…" she offered back in response. "He just ran down the hill, I don't know why."

"And who are you?" he asked.

"I'm Wendy. I'm sorry, I didn't mean to…"

"Wendy? The Wendy?" He interrupted with perplexion.

"Yes… I'm sorry, how do you know me?"

"Massuh Piet's told us about you. Fancies you as I reckon."

Strangely flattered, she stepped back down off the porch, "and you are?"

"Ah, forgive me, miss. Name's Nibs. It's a pleasure to meet you."

"Nibs? Well, Mr. Nibs, it's a pleasure to meet you as well. Are you one of the Lost Boys he's always on about?"

Nibs laughed, "'Lost Boys!' He still callin' us that? He made that up when he was a boy, back when we was all youngins. Was a sort of game to him back then. Thought us slaves were *lost* because we weren't from here and all. Then he wanted to *find* and free all the others that come in. Means well, I guess. Managed to free a handful over the years. They here, but we gotta keep'm all hidden. Folk come up here lookin' so we gotta be careful. Them other owners know who's paid for, 'cause they all down there tryin'a buy'm up theyselves."

As Wendy was listening to this forward explanation, a lot of things began to make sense. Things she had talked with Piet about in conversations. She had no way of knowing what was accurate or not, but now, seeing a grown man in front of her, it was becoming evident Piet still held a jaded perspective in his mind.

"And so, you all just live here on your own, and care for the farm while he's gone?"

"Yes'm. Massuh Piet come back once in a while. Less now than he used to. He spen' all his time down d'ere in that place with all dem girls. We don' hardly see'm no more. An' we ain't got the freedom he do, or the money he do to keep this place up. It's the only place we can go, so long as he still the owner."

"Mr. Nibs, I'm sorry. All of this is so new, I'm not sure what you want from me, or what I can do, but I've come from that same place. I'm escaped too, hiding away like you. I expect I will be staying here for some time, and we will be seeing each other. I'd like to help however I can, though I don't know how."

"That's alright, Miss Wendy. I spoke out of line, and likely to get whipped if I'd said that to anyone else. I'm real sorry. We'd love some helpin' hands, but you don' have to get your hands dirty with the mess here. S'not your worry."

"It's fine. I'd like to. If you just..." Wendy was interrupted by Piet running back up the hill.

"It's ready! Come see!"

Wendy, confused, looked back at Nibs. Nibs shook his head disapprovingly, but only slightly so that if you weren't aware, it wouldn't have been obvious.

"Go on now. Don' keep the boy waitin'. He wanna show you what he's built. I'll see you later Miss Wendy."

She walked toward Piet, who was exuberantly waving her on to hurry up. Together they went back down the hill, Piet dragging her by the arm. It was uncomfortable, but she had to go with it, or might trip and fall. When they got to the end of the meadow, there was a line of trees leading into a denser copse. They stepped into the thicket for a few yards more before he revealed a tree house which looked very much to how a child might have built a tepee fort with boxes, blankets, and other knickknacks. Wendy was speechless.

"Whattaya think?" He asked, proudly. Wendy still trying to assess what she was looking at, tried to make words come out, but just nodded her head side to side. Growing a little impatient that she wasn't sharing his excitement and hadn't replied, he asked again, trying to maintain his jubilance.

"What is it?"

"What is it?" He giggled. "Wendy, you're a hoot. It's our house! Come on in and see. There's lots of room for us to share."

"Our house? Piet... what?"

"Come on, I'll show you..." She shirked him off, and firmly replied,

"No. No, Piet, I won't. This is not a place I'm going to spend my time and stay in. There is an actual house up the hill, and it needs to be lived in. It's falling apart."

"No, that's my dad's house. This is my house. We don't use that house."

"Piet. Listen to me. I am grateful you have brought me here. I hope to start my life over, so long as I can dodge anything coming my way from Captain Hook. I am glad we can be here, but I am not going to sleep with you in this plaything. We are adults. I am going to find Mr. Nibs again, and I'm going to get inside that house, like it or not. You can either come with me and help, or stay here in your fort, but I won't set foot inside."

Despondent, Piet looked at her with sad eyes. Her words hurt. He was so proud. He was excited to share it with her like kids. This response was not what he was expecting (though he really should have).

"We're only adults in body, Wendy. We can live young at heart and mind and never grow old like everyone else."

"That's not how it works, Piet. We are adults in body and mind. We have responsibilities as people. You have a farm full of slaves who are lucky to have not been stolen away, but also who are struggling to eke out a living here because you refuse to be accountable." With this she turned and left. She was frustrated and flabbergasted at his inanity. Pouting at her mean temper, Piet crawled into the fort while she trudged back up the hill to the main house.

When she reached the house, she called out for Nibs again, but he wasn't anywhere nearby. She called again. No reply. So, she attempted to enter the house. The door was swollen tightly shut and didn't want to budge. She put her shoulder into it a couple times as she jostled the knob. It grimaced each time she struck it but refused to give way. Her arm and shoulder were beginning to smart, so she figured she might need to go about it another way.

All the commotion she was creating did gather attention. Some of the other hands crept up to see what was happening. All of them confused by this foreign white woman attempting to break into the master's house. All the while, Wendy had her back to them and was unaware she had drawn spectators. She sized up the structure, felt its bones, and tried one of the windows. Those too had seized themselves shut from the humidity and lack of use. It seemed like it might be a lost cause, and she would *have* to go back down to that ridiculous camp of his. No… she refused. She couldn't tuck her tail between her legs on this one. She would figure it out.

Finally, she turned to come back down the steps, off the porch, to find a handful of black faces fixed on her every movement. She froze. Their sweat glistened, and their clothing dirty from toil. Experience had taught them not to speak, but they were so curious as to what was going on. After what seemed like years, Wendy nervously spoke,

"Hi… I'm Wendy. I'm a friend of Piet's. He's down the hill in his fort. I was trying to get in the house."

They all still stared back at her, unsure what their move was in this situation. They couldn't let a stranger access the master house, but they also knew what could happen if they disobeyed. She started to speak again, but before she did, a younger hand came running up with Nibs. He was focused and worried about what the boy had grabbed him for, until he saw Wendy standing, isolated and helpless.

"Miss Wendy, what is it?" He asked. Nibs was the unofficial leader of the bunch and was the one who regularly dealt with anyone who came snooping around, so it the others anxiously awaited her reply.

"Mr. Nibs…"

"Just Nibs, ma'am."

"Nibs, I was trying to get in. I wanted to make it a home again."

"Piet know you're up here doin' so?"

"Yes. I'm not going to live in that little bivouac of his."

Nibs laughed, knowing. He then also explained who she was to the others. When he did, the immediate joyful change of their faces and bodies altered the entire scene. They became welcoming and grateful to have someone with intention back on the property.

"Let's see what we can do, Miss Wendy."

"Just Wendy." She smiled back at him.

"Let's see what we can do Wendy." He replied with a warming smile; a bond between them forming.

With some effort, a couple of the men were able to dislodge the door from its saddled state. As it groaned open, the hinges nearly rusted to nothing, it was as though they had opened a sarcophagus, frozen in time. Dust covered everything in a blanket of decrying age. Spider webs sprawled across the moulding and fixtures. Roaches scurried noisily, having been discovered and disturbed after years of uninvaded privacy. It was disheartening to see the condition the house had fallen into. They all looked around, poking at artifacts, moving furniture, inspecting the structural integrity. The slaves were uneasy yet intrigued at being inside the head house. All the things gone to waste sitting locked away in this capsule.

Wendy stood with Nibs. The somber environment was eerie. It belonged to Piet's parents, and they had died years ago in these very rooms. It was as though they too remained, watching over them as they rifled through the place. The feeling was odd, not haunting, but almost like a presence was about, ambivalently glad that the seal had been broken and life was entering to continue the story.

Reviving the house was going to be a daunting exercise, but with the help of everyone, it shouldn't be so bad. They all had respective skills they could offer at bringing the life back into the home. *Home*. The feeling of the word settled in, and she became a little more at ease, despite the mess. She hadn't had this feeling in so long; not since leaving London so long ago now. She looked at Nibs, and said, "Tomorrow we begin. We bring this place back and shall share the table. So long as I am occupying this place, you are all welcome in."

The happiness from the slaves was endearing. They didn't know her. They didn't know what she was about. They lived in an incomprehensible fear as escaped slaves, even though they were "owned" by Piet. The fact of the matter was, Piet had only freed them from worse owners. He hadn't given them papers of release, so by convention, he in fact, still owned them. And though he never treated them as such, the landowners from surrounding farms and beyond were not above cruelty, stealing, or even killing them. This was the fear they ultimately lived with day in and day out. They lived out here alone as part of the farm, hiding in the trees like they had learned on the cay. Piet was the landowner, but he was never around to answer questions or substantiate the slaves' circumstance. So, they hung in the balance of safety, constantly making up lies about Piet to save their own skins. And so, with Wendy's arrival, it was a renewal of spirit, that they had someone to rely on. Someone to care and direct them. Someone to protect them.

It was late now, and the sun had given way to a perse sky, the moon glowing behind wisps of clouds as light faded to dark. Wendy's stomach growled angrily. She realized she hadn't eaten a thing all day, having journeyed. She looked to Nibs and asked if there was anything to be had. He gladly said,

"Come, we feed you. We make a fire, and you join us tonight. Tomorrow, we help shine this place up."

This delighted Wendy. She was glad to encounter such kindness from the group, and how willing they were to help. She was also very happy to get something to eat and hear the stories they had to share. And so, they closed up the house for the night, leaving the task for tomorrow.

As the meal was prepared and the fire roiled to life, they all sat eager to hear Wendy's story; though, she wondered if she should go find Piet. Nibs told her, he could see them from his fort, and if he wanted to join, we would; best to leave him be and let him decide for himself. He was never fun to be around when he was sulking. Those instances often led to some fatuous insult or harm. Wendy understood. She had seen that side of him in flecks and found his demeanor like that of a mean-spirited toddler.

It was also now, that those whom Piet had secreted away recently, those she knew, were joined in. She was elated to see them safely transplanted. So, she began to tell them all about where she came from, and her time in Port Royal. She also told them about her capture by Hook, and how she too had been stripped from her family and forced into indenture, in a manner of relatable speaking. They took no offense to the differences of their situation to hers, but appreciated she was not like the others because of it. Those she had previously known from Captain Smythe and Captain Hook looked on with understanding. The others were enthralled at the stories of how she was a pirate. They didn't know the full scale of Hook's persona, though they had heard stories of him, and that he was a larger-than-life character.

As things died down, the fire a low dancing glow, many of the assembly retired to their little shed. It was only Wendy, Nibs, and two others, who she had learned were called Lutalo and Pip. Lutalo seemed, for lack of better understanding, the second in command, next to Nibs. He was short and muscular with mocha skin, not as darkly complected as some of the others. In the fire light, shadows cast across his rounded face, making him appear stern, but he was really a teddy-bear of a young man. Pip was younger than the two, and youthfully fit. He was eager but calculated; traits he had learned from the others in caution. He was wise above his age, almost an old soul. His strong face was carved handsomely, the darkness of night also accentuating the stone-like features.

They had sat by the fire for a long time talking and getting to know the other. Some stories told by the others they didn't know prior. Bonds were formed in the openness of conversation. Wendy was filled with connection, eroding the nightmares she held within. But it was by this point, she realized there were no females among them. This she suddenly found curious, and asked,

"There are no women here. Why is it just you men here?"

Nibs replied, "That is true. We have no women here. None to join us and be with us. I am not sure the real reasons. Years ago, when the Bannings were still alive and running the farm, they had a woman, and she tended mostly to Mrs. Banning's needs. She died and w'n't never replaced. The Bannings weren't 'round much longer themselves and so no other women were ever brought in."

"But why not now? If Piet is freeing slaves from the cells, why isn't he freeing the women too?"

"Reasons I'm not sure of, Miss Wendy. But I know these two things: The women and children are separated from us before we even make it to the auction. They kept elsewhere, and so when Massuh Piet springs 'em, it is only the men who are there. But he has only succeeded twice in those attempts."

"But he has told me tales of all his breaks in freeing slaves and bringing them here?"

"All the same stories told differently each time."

"How deceitful," she murmured.

"We are the fortunate few. Massuh Piet has his ways, but for all we have to endure to live out here, not a one of us would trade our luck with any of the others who stay trapped. We get by, and are unrestrained here, but that is not without fear that one day someone will come and steal us to their farms or hunt us dead for going about as we do. We have learned from Massuh Piet how to hide in the trees like he does, or how to tell if someone is looking for mischief here."

"But when you saw me, how did you know I was not up to mischief or a threat?"

Nibs and the others laughed, "Miss Wendy, you not like the others. Them white men, the owners, they all have the same way about them, and would come with carts and whips. They know they way around a farm, and wouldn't poke around the massuh house, such as you was. You were just a lost girl looking for anything, kinda like them missionaries."

"A lost girl, you say?" She smirked at the ironic phrase. "I suppose you're right... I'll give you that. But if I am a *lost girl,* you will still be the *lost boys* to me."

They smiled at the witty connection. It was flattering coming from her, so they relented and accepted her terms. The fire had dwindled to glowing coals. They hadn't replenished the wood to keep it going, knowing it was nearing time to retire, and that time had now come. The men offered her a place in the shed with them, but she politely declined, not wanting to put them out of their own bunks, and said,

"I'm going to go check on Piet. I was brusque with him earlier, perhaps more than I should have been."

And so, they doused the fire and parted ways for the night. After sitting down, eating, and being able to let go, she realized she was utterly exhausted. It all caught up with her, and though the accommodations were silly and flimsy, she would make the exception just tonight to join him. Pet his ego a bit, as a *thank you* for bringing her here.

When she found the little fort again, she discovered he was not in it. She looked all around, but in the dark and among the weald she couldn't see far at all. She called out in a hushed yell, but all that answered back were the sounds of nature. She crawled into the fort, taking a seat. It was decorated inside with crude glyphs and drawings. She felt sad for him. He was so lonely and had no parental model to direct him in acting his age and taking responsibility. She laid down, listening still to the natural sounds outside, and fell fast asleep. The first real sleep she had had in many days.

The next morning, she woke, stiff from sleeping on the rough floor. The sun was up, and the air was already turning steamy. She emerged from the fort and ventured back out into the open. Surveying the land once again in the morning light, she could see all around her the staggering colors and the ocean far off on the distant horizon. She didn't realize they had climbed so high yesterday, but the air was clean in her lungs as she took a deep breath. The mephitic odor in Port Royal was all the more realized in the absence of filth. Up the small hill, she saw the lost boys toiling away at the house. She hurried up to see what was happening.

The men had woken early, naturally, and began cleaning out the house. They never dared before, but now that it was to be occupied by Wendy, and possibly Piet, they dug in and got to task. The furniture had been carefully carried out into the warming sun. A couple of the younger ones were meticulously wiping it all down, careful not to miss a speck. Some of the furniture was so dried out, it required oil to come back to life. The pieces that had been finished gleamed in the light, almost new. The others were busy sweeping, wiping, moving, and fixing all the miscellaneous other things inside the house. She said good morning to them all and found Nibs in the kitchen staring up at the ceiling, pointing.

"Good morning, Nibs! What a surprise this is! You should have woken me. I would have been more than happy to help. You and the boys didn't need to do this all on your own!"

"Ahhh, Miss Wendy, good morning! I hope you were able to rest after such an eventful day! 'Tis no thing. We're happy to get you settled. We got problems though... This here part of the roof gon' need be replaced. Rotted through – could collapse any second."

"Oh, dear..." Wendy replied. "What do we do?"

"We lookin at it now, figgur out what choices are. Shouldn't be much to fix it up. We make it safe for now, but we oughta fix it right when we's able."

"What can I do to help?"

"Not a thing, Miss Wendy, we got this. You go have some breakfast. We got maduros still warm in the skillet. Ham's still tending the fire. You go down an' see'm. We'll keep working.

"Thank you Nibs. By the way, have you seen Piet? He was gone when we turned in. I haven't seen him. I'm worried."

"Ahh, this is what he does. He disappears just as soon as he show up. Might come back. Might not. We just keep doing what we do. We learned a long time ago, if we waited around for him to be here, we be dead by now."

This was not comforting, but he was resolved in his reply, so much so, that she had no other option than to accept it all the same. She hoped nothing had befallen him. She still had concern but took Nibs' direction and went for food.

After finishing and thanking Ham for the victuals, she returned to the house, to see they were all still hard at work. Unable to gain any insight as to what she could do, she just leapt in, and helped orchestrate the furniture revitalization while she also cleaned and scrubbed the walls, counters, and floors. None of this restoration was an easy process, and what they were able to accomplish took the entirety of the day, and still there was much to do. At the end of the day, they had sorted the items worth keeping (per Wendy's preference) and the lot that was not. As well, they had scrubbed the heavy furniture, gutted the cabinets and pantry, and constructed a temporary roofing cover with palm fronds, palapa style. It was all coming together, and they were glad to see progress. Wendy though, was remiss that Piet was not here for direction and input. Everything she and the Lost Boys were doing felt a violation of his parents' existence. It all belonged to them, just as they'd left it, and here they were rummaging through it without any care or remorse. In the end, however, he had chosen to disappear, knowing this was imminent, and thereby abdicated his say to the refurbishment.

Once again, they all convened down by the fire after a long day's toil. Sore muscles, aching backs, and tired bodies littered the circle. Yet, they had accomplished so much in the day's work. They talked idly with some laughing at inconsequential anecdotes. They had all worked hard, and no focus was given to any one or the other. Wendy sat observing, relishing the connection among them. She felt like she belonged, even though she was an outsider brought in. She leaned in to talk to Lutalo, sitting near her.

"I am sorry you live in such conditions. You all deserve better, and I hope I may make good on that, some day. I can't thank you enough in the time we've spent together, that you have accepted me."

Lutalo, whose English was still a bit spotty, smiled and replied, "Izandla ziyagezana. You... good person... Wendy. Take care of good person."

Flattered by his comment and his humble nature, she thanked him for his kindness and excused herself. She went to find Nibs, who at the time was sitting now on the outskirts, alone, resting quietly in the dark.

"Nibs, what are you doing? Are you not interested in sitting with the others around the fire?"

"Ah, Miss Wendy... My bones are tired, and I enjoy my rest in quiet sometimes. No need to fret."

"I have seen you, in these past days, that you are burdened with much, and that is a heavy weight to carry. You must know, I see what you do, and I want to take that from you, so that you do not worry so. You are skilled in many ways, and I want you to feel able to do the things you do so well, but I wish to take over here, in what capacity I'm afforded. Allow me to be the one to carry that burden?"

"Aww, Miss Wendy, that's rightful sweet of you, but you don't want this? You're a spirit just as free as Piet. You have a life to live beyond this. Your story isn't finished. Don't settle for nothing."

"Nibs, I am humbled by your graciousness, and perhaps I am free, but I am not like Piet. I have risen from adversity with a purpose and ambition. I possess responsibility and the conviction to execute upon that. Consider it the pirate in me..." she winked at him.

"I don't wanna see you fall for his tricks. You a smart girl. Strong girl. One that can move mountains. I see that in you. This not the end for you."

Wendy reflected on his words as they sat together in silence, watching the others. The thought bounced inside her head as she contemplated her options apparent. She was at peace here, but he was right, she wasn't at her end yet. She was only just beginning her story, but that didn't mean it didn't include this, or that this was where it concluded after whatever else lie ahead? After some introspection, she quietly replied,

"Nibs, you're right. This is not the end for me. Not right now. I do have much left to do, but I want to believe the end is this. That this, when whatever I must do is concluded, is where I may lay my head and spend the rest of my days in the company of the Lost Boys, quietly fading from history."

Still, they sat watching the shadows of the others around the fire. Nibs did not immediately respond and too sat digesting her words. "That is a mighty thought, Miss Wendy. I know me and the boys would enjoy the company, if we still around. Be awful nice to have you take care of us like'n someone oughta. Tomorrow, we keep workin' on the house an' get you settled in proper."

"That would be nice Nibs. But please, do not carry on without me. I am capable of labor and would be glad of putting in my investment."

"Alright, Miss Wendy. We get you in line wit' us. You welcome to sleep with us tonight. That ridiculous fort can't be good for ya. Not for anyone other than a boy."

She laughed and conceded. However uncouth it may be by societal mores, she felt it rude of her not to accept and show unification with them. She had bonded with them today, working side by side with them, elbow to elbow. She could care less what those people thought of her at this point. She knew their secrets. As though they hadn't taken worse action upon themselves. Rage stirred up within her, but she shook it off, so not to ruin her moment here, the present.

"Yes, Nibs, I should like a better night's sleep than last. How ever does he do it?"

They laughed and bantered at his expense, light-heartedly. But it soon came time to turn in, so he showed her to their quarters, and offered her his space in the corner. She attempted to protest, but he shushed her and insisted. He told her he would take another cot tonight, as some of the others preferred to sleep under the stars when able.

The following morning, they woke again to the warming air and rising sun. Only a handful of them had sought comfort indoors. Nibs was right – most of them slumbered pleasantly outside in the trees, presumably as Piet had shown them in their hiding on the islet. Ham had already started the cooking fire and was preparing fresh eggs, plantains, and fruit. As the sky's fiery kaleidoscope marbled into blue skies, they all got back to the task at hand. The day's tasks would constitute mending the roof and structural decay, finishing the cleaning of ages, while replacing everything back into functional use and position.

For days they worked on the house and the fields, bringing life back to the dying property. Piet was still missing, but they had all moved on, occupying themselves with work as usual. Eventually it appeared the entire job was all but finished and most sat in the shade of the porch resting their weary bodies. All of them were spent. Refitting the house was no easy chore, and hewing the timber to refit the beams, roof, fences, and other spaces took constant muscle and effort. Wendy was amazed at the competencies they possessed, and the abilities they had to rebuild everything. Carpentry and management of this measure were notable skills, those that weren't oft found in peoples like them. She thought back to Piet's inadvertent teachings on the cay, showing them how to carve, build, hide, and operate. Maybe he had instilled in them some truly survivable lessons? They had managed to remain safe on the farm thus far, which itself was a mystery and a miracle.

Now essentially finished with the rehab, that evening they once again sat around the fire, proud in the improvements and repairs they had accomplished to their home not only for themselves, but for Wendy too. Piet had all but disappeared from thought and mind, but his presence still lingered like a specter. It was unpleasant that someone so vacant could still overshadow the environment so fully. Yet still they celebrated their success and hard work into the evening until they all essentially collapsed in total exhaustion.

In the darkness, Wendy stepped onto the porch slowly, her muscles aching and weary. She felt the house in her, connecting at her feet, rising up through her like a river after a heavy rain. She leaned against the banister, staring off into the misty night, trails of smoke from the fire wafting away into nothing. She wondered where Piet had gone off to, hoping he was alright, though, knowing he most likely was, given his nature. Had he gone back to Belle after she'd chastised him? Had he just run away into the night like a toddler? She couldn't even think of all the possible things he, of all people, could have done. She sighed sadly and entered the house.

It felt homely because she had put her own sweat equity into it. But it was dark, quiet, and still slightly off-putting that it hadn't been lived in for so long, and that the heir was stil so loomingly attached. It made her uncomfortable that she was now going to occupy his parents' home – his home – without his being there to permit it. But again, she reasoned, he had abandoned all interest or ownership by letting it fall into ruin and living in a hut out back. Lighting a candle, she made her way to the bedroom, shed her soiled clothing, and climbed into bed.

XV

"No. No, Piet, I won't. This is not a place I'm going to spend my time and stay in. There is an actual house up the hill, and it needs to be lived in. It's falling apart."

"No, that's my dad's house. This is my house. We don't use that house."

"Piet. Listen to me. I am grateful you have brought me here. I hope to start my life over, so long as I can dodge anything coming my way from Captain Hook. I am glad we can be here, but I am not going to sleep with you in this plaything. We are adults. I am going to find Mr. Nibs again, and I'm going to get inside that house, like it or not. You can either come with me and help, or stay here in your fort, but I won't set foot inside."

Despondent, Piet looked at her with sad eyes. Her words hurt. He was so proud. He was excited to share it with her like kids. This response was not what he was expecting (though he really should have).

"We're only adults in body, Wendy. We can live young at heart and mind and never grow old like everyone else."

"That's not how it works, Piet. We are adults in body and mind. We have responsibilities as people. You have a farm full of slaves who are lucky to have not been stolen away, but also who are struggling to eke out a living here because you refuse to be accountable." With this she turned and left. She was frustrated and flabbergasted at his inanity. Pouting at her mean temper, Piet crawled into the fort while she trudged back up the hill to the main house.

Inside he fumed at her egregious insult to him. He bickered with himself, mocking her in a replay of their interaction. Who was she to be so condescending? She had begged him to bring her here, and this was how she was going to treat him? He wasn't going to stand for it, he decided. He had brought her here, and that's what she wanted. She could stay here for all he cared, but he wasn't going to. He had done his part, and now being out here so far away from Belle and Port Royal, he'd go off on his own for a bit. Something he hadn't done in ages.

He gathered a few of his things, and stepped out into the open, looking for her. He couldn't see her now; she had gone off with Nibs, though he wasn't aware. This hurt him again. He had half a hope that she would have been just outside the fort, waiting for him to reemerge and everything would be alright. So, he slipped off into the trees behind him and picked up a trail he had cut some time ago. Though, it had become overgrown since his last flight. He pulled out his machete and began hacking away, clearing the path as he trudged along.

Eventually the terrain grew denser and more inclined as he neared the tall blue mountains. The jungle finally gave way to a stream running downhill toward the bay. Now he followed the running current south to where it would rumble into rapids at the rocky outcropping at the turn of the mountain's foot. The river kept running agitatedly as it fed into pools and still on beyond. The torrent met with the edge of the jungle and spewed heavily off the side into a cascading waterfall. This was his landmark to climb precariously down the side to get where he was going.

The waterfall roared mightily as it cascaded over the cliff. Wisps of spray wet the foliage as it was swept by the breeze. Piet scampered down the wall of the hill. He had to be careful though because the rocks were slick and muddy. For him though, this was nothing more than an obstacle to challenge his deftness. Like a nimble monkey, he skipped and hopped from spot to spot, making easy work of the descent into the valley.

Once at the bottom, the pool eddied from the impacting water and rippled out into a larger pool. Water, never an element to be contained, continued down a rocky creek bed toward the ocean. The jungle seemed as impenetrable as a castle wall with trees, monstera, curling vines and more. Piet though, knew precisely where and how to access the secret passage hidden behind the impenetrable portiere. He spread the hedged enclosure and popped in, feeling the warmth within the dense jungle. Cautiously, he proceeded down the artery ahead of him. It had been some time since he'd visited, so he proceeded slowly with careful intention, reminding himself of every nook and ridge of the pathway. He took his time also because he knew there always a lookout watching.

Of course, there was a scout present, standing guard, hooded by the folds of the enclosure. When Piet arrived at the inner village hidden away, he waited just on the edge and studied the comings and goings. When he saw his old accomplice, Tiger Lily, emerge from her father's hut, he was so involuntarily elated at the sight of her, that he was about to burst forth and make a grand spectacle, but something held him back. She was beautiful, grown into a real woman since he'd last seen her. He second guessed coming, but there was no turning back at this point. He felt about his beltline and pulled out his flute. Crouched among the bush, pressing into a firm wall of croton and poui, he blew.

The sound was melodic, harmonious, and nostalgically familiar. Tiger Lilly perked up looking for where the sound was coming from. She knew he was here, and this gave her great joy. She quavered at his announcement. It had been so long she couldn't contain herself. He was enjoying this more and more as it played out. He was crafty in his ability to bounce his tune about like a ventriloquist, so that it was sharper here, subdued there. It was as though he was teasing her.

Standing he poked his head up and blew an explosive finale, so that she could see him eye to eye. Her heart melted, she smiled shyly, then adoringly. She ran to him. He ran to her. They embraced like two lovers split across the world. For her, truly amorous, from the days of old when he would run with her wildly; her first exposure to the white man, whom her father strongly cautioned her about. He held her tight, flooded with memories of missing the days of freedom, running through the forest with her and the others. When they separated, they eyed each other up and down, each studying the other and the person they'd become after all these years.

She was radiant and grown into a very desirable woman, fully independent and strong. Her tan, brown skin curved around a taut, fit, bare frame. The tribe had yet to be subjugated by the missionaries and still existed in their natural existence. This was the way, and she, just like all the others milling around, lived free from the burdens of puritanic modesty. This is why Piet never felt out of place being naked at any point when he was younger, it just seemed normal, because to them, it was.

They didn't interact with the intruders and made it a point to keep to themselves for safety of what was left of their kind. They lived away from everything, subsisting on the world around them in the valley, tucked away. The Spanish had decimated the Tainos when they arrived so many years ago, that once they existed in the thousands, they were all but barely in the hundreds now. The Dutch, the English, and all others still didn't care for them, and it was best for all that they just keep apart. The last real interaction had been when Piet convinced them to wage war on Port Royal, and because of the outcome of that, there was still a simmering edge just waiting to boil over on anyone's instigation. It also did nothing to help the perception of them among the colonizers. Wisely though, the Tainos had cut Piet out and learned a hard lesson that they existed in frailty upon this island now. The best they could do to survive was disappear from memory, which is exactly what they were trying to do now, peacefully.

"Father is sick. Come, see him." She said to him and grabbed his hand to lead him back to her father's hut.

She entered first, telling him to wait for a moment. She reemerged and brought him in to see the heralded chief. He lay on a mat of woven reeds and was in the process of sitting himself up, painfully, when Piet entered to greet him. Seeing him in this state was not what he expected at all. The last time they were together, he was agile and commanding, and following the outcome of their attack, he was fiercely angry at Piet for dragging them into something that nearly cost him their existence. He was virile and spirited then. The pallid man before him was not the same man he'd admired in years past. Now he was sad and sickly. Piet was uncomfortable. This was not what he wanted out of this visit, and he wasn't capable of feelings of empathy, so he awkwardly fidgeted while Tiger Lily attended to her father.

The chief, now stable and upright, looked on at this old familiar face, and the recollection returned. In a strained and gravelly voice, he uttered, "The boy returns a man. How you have grown since last with us." He coughed and winced.

"Yes, your chiefness," Piet replied daftly. "It has been some time since I was with you, and I have grown into a man of my own now. I have been living in Port Royal, making myself a part of the fabric, so that one day I can finally take it down." Piet knew this wasn't entirely true, but it made him sound purposeful. The chief laid his chin down to his chest in disappointment. It was moments before he spoke again.

"A sheep in wolf's clothing, never makes change. Only set himself apart from others he needs." He said finally. Piet didn't understand at first, thinking he was mixed up in his sayings. But the chief was still wise in his dwindling state. What Piet failed to grasp in his message, was that he had dressed himself up as an enemy, but was not part of the flock, and would (had) alienated himself from those who could have been of use to him all along, or at least those of whom he better aligned.

"You were good hunter. Smart. Good to Tiger Lilly. Wanted good. Had wrong path. Almost cost the tribe everything. So sad…"

"Father…" Tiger interrupted, but he waved her to hush so he could keep speaking.

"I believed you. Believed we *could* take it back. I was wrong. I was fooled to think we had chance. No chance. Many perished. You did that to us. I cast you out. I hurt chance to heal and learn. But I hurt daughter more. She loved you and I hurt her from my anger at you. You must know. What you did not right. What I did not right. So, we sit here, fools to each other. Nothing better for it." He reached out for Piet's hand to wish him well in his future, and that he had absolved himself and Piet from their troubled past.

Tiger Lily bowed her head both in sadness and embarrassment for her father putting her heart out there. But she understood what he was saying, more what he was doing. She knew he didn't have long left with her, and one of the only regrets he still had in life was that incident. Magically, Piet had reappeared, as though it was an omen for her father to be able to clear his heart. A tear rolled down her cheek.

He had exhausted himself and needed to recline again to rest. Tiger guided him down as he wheezed heavy breath. She covered him with furs and kissed him on his forehead. She got up to leave him, and had Piet follow her out.

"He doesn't have much time. He will pass soon. I am glad he was able to see you one last time." She said, holding back tears as best she could.

"Tiger, did you love me? Like he said…" He asked selfishly.

"There was a time, yes. You were not like the others. You've been gone so long; I never thought you'd come back. I moved on like you moved on."

"You were my favorite." He replied. "We used to have so much fun together back then. You taught me so much. And I liked you too. I liked being with you."

"Where did you go?"

"I spend most of my time in Port Royal now. I've met some real nice people. I go back to the farm sometimes. I have my lost boys there, and because no one knows it's me, I still send rescues there when I can. Oh, and I've met these really great girls, I want you to meet them. Belle, who I spend most of my time with, and a new girl, Wendy who's on the farm now!"

The news of him splitting himself between two other women, after having her heart laid bare, was insulting and hurtful. She tried not to react out of jealousy and hurt, but it did cause her to shield herself and close off further to any emotion she felt for him. Unfortunately, as she had said, they had both moved on, but with his arrival, it had stirred up old feelings. Since there was never any closure back then, it still hung out there unanswered.

"I am happy for you. It sounds good for you. Better than here with me."

"No, you don't understand, you can join us too! The four of us and the lost boys would be such a team!"

"No Piet, I cannot. I must stay here with father."

He hadn't learned anything at all. She did love him, and that was sacred. She would not run off and abandon her people to compete for attention while there were other women in his life. It wasn't fair to ask. She had a responsibility to her tribe. If he had a heart, he should know that and not ask such things of her.

"It has been good to see you again, Piet. I am glad you saw father before he passed. I know his heart is free now. You are welcome here as a friend of our tribe, but now you should go back to your other girls."

Piet didn't understand why she was asking him to leave so soon. He had just arrived and wanted to stay with them like when he was younger. But things had changed. Everyone had changed and he had been gone far too long to recognize it. His new vigilante life had changed him, and Tiger knew that part of their lives had closed, and she must protect herself from him. She must protect the others from him. She turned to return to her father's side, trying to hide the tears from him.

"Tiger Lilly, wait..." he protested. "It's not like that. Wendy is a good girl, and she is escaped from the pirates – the one I fought with and took his hand. She's hiding on my farm from him. I really wish you would meet her. It would be grand if you both got along and helped each other and the lost boys while I'm away."

She'd stopped to listen, but when he was done speaking, she entered the hut fighting the urge to give him anything more. Taking the cue, he stood looking at his feet not sure how to shake off the rejection. He looked up at the village once more, taking it in seemingly for the last time. Everything had gone quiet, so he turned and left back the way he came. The scout watched Piet leave but still stood at attention, waiting for any provocation. Feeling that he posed no threat, then ventured back inward just behind curtain.

When he reemerged from the hidden entrance back into the open, he sat down and shrunk into a shriveled version of himself. He was spent; emotionally fragile from being cast out again. This was supposed to be different. It wasn't supposed to end so quickly. This visit was supposed to be a prolonged reunion. The stream flowed in front of him, running down the cleft out toward the open sea far below. He sat, head resting on the two mounds of his hands. He was still, lumped in sun as his brain pulsed with everything running through it. After a moment, he straightened up and threw a stone toward the little pool in front of him. It splashed in, sinking to the bottom, mixing in with the other rocks below the surface.

In the hot summer sun, he stared off pondering what had happened. Tiger Lily had sent him away... just like the others. Wendy had rebuked him. Belle hadn't shunned him formally, but she wasn't sweet on him, either given that he had run off with Wendy and left her behind. (Little did he know what she was enduring with him gone away with Wendy. Any feeling left within her, was likely carved out by a villain.) Gathering his energy and arrogant confidence, he stood erect and made for the entry once again. He wanted a second chance, and this time he wasn't going to let her send him out so prematurely.

The scout popped back to attention at the sight of him attempting to reenter, but instead of shadowing him, ran off to warn the village he was coming again. Tiger Lily came out of the hut to intercept Piet before he could do anything that might harm the village. Knowing him, she was aware his actions could be poorly thought. The scout gathered others and scattered off to protect both her and the village. When she approached him on the trail, she could see he wasn't his usual mirthful self, and so she stopped him.

"What are you doing? Why are you back?" she asked apprehensively.

"I want another chance, Tiger. We used to have so much fun together. Why can't we now?"

"You don't understand. Things are different now. Father is dying. We have lost many of our people. I have responsibilities for my people now. I can't be off playing your games anymore. And to want me to leave here now to go play your games with your other women is not what I hoped had brought you back here. Father was right, I did care about you. You were different than the others. But that was then. And when my father cast you out, I never saw you again, not even in secrecy. You left and started a new life. Without me. I had to move on, just like you did. This is my life now, and you cannot show up out of nowhere after all these years and think that I would just run away with you again." Her words cycled through a range of emotions, starting with compassionate pleading to frustrated realization.

"But Tiger, I'm not asking you to lead another attack like before. I wanted to see you again and invite you to meet Wendy. I think you would like her and could help each other out here. She's staying on my farm because she's hiding from Captain Hook. And, when I'm not around, she could really use the help and protection."

"Piet, look around. Really look around. We can't protect anyone from those invaders anymore. We have to protect ourselves. We are small in numbers because of them, their guns, and their willingness to kill for nothing."

Piet paused and looked around as she'd asked, and only now did he see that the village was a microcosm of what it once was, though the profundity didn't completely sink in. Only a few huts scattered about the forest housed the few remaining Taino people, and they all milled about nervously as a white man had found them so deeply hidden away. Most of them didn't remember him, but had heard the stories, and so they had reason for their apprehension of him reappearing.

"Piet, I'm sorry. I can't afford to send our people off to fight other peoples' fights. Your kind have killed us off with such force, we are in peril of surviving. We worry for our children, what few we have. When the time is right, I will go to your farm, and I will meet the Wendy. But I will not do so in alliance of war. I will offer myself in peace for her to know through you, but nothing more. I will do this when I am ready, not before."

Piet understood she wasn't going to budge and had to accept what she was offering. She had agreed to meet Wendy, just not on a frivolous escape at his whim. He had hoped for another adventure with all of them, and because he was denied this, he wasn't completely satisfied, but he had to concede to what she was saying, so he shook his head in assent.

"Now, you have come all this way, twice, to reestablish contact. If you truly understand all I have said, I invite you to stay. You are an old friend and are welcome here as a friend of old. Nothing more. Do you agree?"

"Yes, Tiger, I understand. And I would like to stay and revisit with you and the others."

XVI

Wendy stepped out of the house onto the porch, and took in the clean, relaxing air. Her lungs filled and she exhaled with resolved ease as she surveyed the property. Some of the Lost Boys were already tending to some chores, and so she stepped down onto the dry dirt path to go check on them. As she approached, she called to them, offering a good morning salutation. They looked up and waved back with genuine smiles at seeing her.

Life had settled into to a normal routine of simplicity now, and there was a collaborative unity among them. The slow pace of provinciality suited Wendy thus far. She wasn't afraid to get her hands dirty and dig in right beside her new crew. They too respected her, folding her into their tribe as one of their own. She had dedicated more time and effort into running the place than Piet ever had, and they appreciated that. She was kind to them, allowed them to teach *her* the ways, instead of the other way around. She was humble and hardworking; something the farm needed desperately. She was shrewd and tactical, and as she became more proficient and comfortable, she was off on her own tending to things before the others even realized it. The whole place was abuzz, and the efforts were showing in its coming back to life.

Piet had still yet to resurface and had all but been forgotten again. They didn't subscribe to his authority, and even less so now that Wendy was running the place. She wanted this. She wanted the farm. She would find a way to take it off his hands as a responsibility and truly make it her own. Outside of Port Royal below, she could see that Jamaica was a flourishing island, and quite important in the trade routes back to England and even the Colonies. Sugar was booming as a crop, and the amount of land they had at their disposal made them a serious competitor in space to sow. They just had to get a legitimate operation going, and Wendy was the key to that. No longer were they an outlier of fugitive slaves barracooned in the hills hiding in fear. She represented the white landowner to their establishment, and this brought protection.

As the farm and crops began prospering, other farms took notice. Through rumors word had filtered down to the other plantations that some unknown woman was now running a farm with vast amounts of land and hands, intended for cane – seemingly overnight. This didn't add up to those already established in the trade and wouldn't be welcomed or tolerated. It made even less sense that this bunch could think of growing such volumes and carting it all the way down to market without permission. The sugar barons were a very tightly knit group and conducted their affairs with an understanding of hierarchy reaching all the way back to the courts and parliament in London. Even competition on other islands was curtailed by indirect forces, so that the Jamaican cooperative controlled the trade. Islands like Saint Kitts and Dominque were abundant producers, but being of non-British establishment, they were often sacked and prohibited from trading with the colonies – the most voracious purchasers outside of Europe.

The speed in which they discovered this information was uncharacteristically quick. Since no crops had been harvested or brought to market yet, it was all only speculation and rumor. However, the overseers who had gone off looking for escaped slaves knew of the errant Dutch farm, and the sparse crops growing. Unable to find their missing slaves in the hills, they would return to their own farms with reports of poorly managed fields of various crops, most specifically sugar cane. Until now, it was never a threat to their operations, but with word of a new manager who appeared out of nowhere on the farm, it was an issue they felt needed attention before it became anything larger.

It was with this news, that meetings were held by the other sugar farmers about what they intended to do about this. Disruption to their control was not an option and share of their profits was unacceptable. Family dynasties were at stake. The conglomerate was cutthroat, and these men were despicable in their means to maintain supremacy. The instances with burning French and American ships were evidence of that, let alone the monopolistic laws passed to control the interests and prices of sugar shipped back to England.

Over the course of the deliberations, various possibilities were proposed ranging from profit sharing to outright elimination. The idea that a farm this large could produce more sugar was appealing to some, if they could throttle it and control the output for their gain. Others vehemently disagreed, and claimed the farm was unsubstantiated and had no business entering their market. Between them, they had as much as they could manage and by controlling that, kept the prices hostage back home. A surplus would undercut the value.

"What if we used that sugar, surely an inferior lot, to send to the colonies, and maintain our superior crops for return to home?" One offered as a consideration.

This caused another divisive argument among them, as the colonists were also unfavored for many reasons. However, this was an argument worth having, as they could price the sugar for the taxes due to the crown. And so back and forth the men bickered on how to solve the problem, which was yet to be a problem in actuality. All this uproar was pre-emptive and reactionary to their own interests, though, this is precisely how they managed to become the power they were, by getting ahead of any threats introduced.

After lengthy discussions, the group was inconclusive on how to address the issue. Since no harvest or transaction had occurred, and none of them had visited farm to verify its viability, they agreed to table the conversation until more information could be acquired. It was decided they would send a representative out to do some reconnaissance for them and reconvene after that report had been filed.

The next day, Abraham Willoughby, the second son of the second largest plantation in the interest was dispatched to inquire upon the status of this woman. Abraham was dutiful to the family business, while the eldest son was back in London representing the Sugar Trade Company. Abraham was prim, dry, and staunchly devout to God and country. He lived adjacent to the family farm with his wife of equal repute, both known to be very scrutinizing of anyone or anything deviant from what was proper; especially the heathens occupying Port Royal.

Uncertain of where, precisely, he was headed, he mounted his horse and headed north into to the hills. Those who had any information on the possible whereabouts pointed him that direction and wished him well. It was said that the escaped slaves hiding in the valley were armed and able to defend themselves against anyone attempting to steal them back. Abraham rode without any show of force, so that he might gain access without cause of danger or alarm. While he was trepidatious about not having protection against marauders, he knew that God would protect him and punish those who would do him harm.

The information he had been given turned out to be roughly accurate. Following the trails eventually led him up a hill to where a squat house-sat overlooking shoddy fields below. By the looks of the house, it needed demolition, and a rebuild strongly as he had been so accustomed with all his wealth and privilege. Seeing the state of this place, he couldn't believe what the rumors amounted to for their concerns. However, what he was seeing now did not mean it wouldn't one day prosper and present the challenge they felt now so prematurely.

Approaching the house, he dismounted his horse and walked slowly taking careful notes in his mind to report back on the conditions of everything. Just in looking, he could tell the fields weren't plowed as cleanly as his own, equipment for harvesting was lacking or deteriorated, and there was no organization to the property by his comprehension. What did surprise him though, was the quantity of slaves working the fields. This didn't make sense to him. There were far more than he would have thought, both from a cost factor and a management factor. There also seemed to be no field manager present. Were they all just working freely without an overseer? New questions on how a plantation should operate began filling his head.

Wendy had seen the stranger approaching the house and stepped out onto the porch to greet him. Nibs too had seen the rider crest the hillock and made his way up, as he'd done so many times before when people had come looking for what didn't belong to them. It was truly a wonder that they had survived out there, unscathed, as they had for so long. The reputation for the armed maroons wasn't untrue, for they had arms and abilities to defend themselves, but Nibs was always careful to keep situations from escalating to such extremes.

"Good afternoon, Mr?" Wendy spoke, catching him unaware of her presence.

"Good afternoon. Willoughby. Abraham Willoughby, of the Willoughby Plantation." He replied, as if she should know who he was.

"Good afternoon, Mr. Willoughby. What brings you all the way out here?"

"I'm here on business. Might I speak with the man of the farm, please?" He was scouting for information to verify if this was the right farm or not, since the concern centered around some unknown woman.

"The '*man*' of the farm you ask? What if I were to tell you, I'm the 'man' of this farm?"

"It would surprise me. Such lands shouldn't be managed by a woman such as yourself."

Wendy was finding him disagreeable in his ribald manner. By now Nibs had come within earshot and could sense this man wasn't going to be pleasant with his visit. It wasn't his first encounter with someone such as he was and had already prepared for the vulgar names he was about to be called. Still, he politely inserted himself into the conversation.

"Afternoon, sir. This here's Miss Wendy. Recently come into the operation of this here place. I'm Nibs, and I see to the others in the fields."

"A negro as an overseer?" Abraham was astounded. Never in his experience would such a thing be acceptable. They had always hired on Scotsmen for that role, and their reputation for being punishingly good at what they did to keep the slaves in line.

"Now, see here, Mr. Willoughby!" Wendy piped in, bitingly. "I'll run this place as I see fit, and I see it fit to have this capable man, a freed man, tend to the same work he's been at for years now. I'll treat my people the way I wish, and that'll be with fairness, and it ain't your place to tell me otherwise. Now, I'll ask you again, sir, what brings you out here?"

Not backing down to her gumption, he held himself vainly superior, and replied, "Rumor has it, this farm once belonged to a Dutchman and has apparently – very recently – changed ownership to – you – I can only assume."

"This land formally belongs to Piet Banning. As he has no vested interest, he has granted me the caretaking, and all that belongs to it. Including every one of these men you see."

"I see. So, you are not the actual owner, and therefore *not* the man of the farm as I requested previously."

This was intentionally meant to demean Wendy. It worked, and she began to get increasingly impatient. Abraham was getting the upper hand, as he hoped. This would lead her to admitting things inadvertently. A woman could be so easily distracted and irrational. It was easy to manipulate them.

"Missuh, perhaps I can answer any questions for ya?" Nibs chimed in, trying to keep Wendy from getting them all caught up in a bad spot. He knew how to talk to these types of men.

"I won't take answers from the likes of you. You oughta get yourself back to those fields before I show you how you ought to be treated. Now, get on, you black son of a bitch!"

Wendy lit up at the gall of this man coming onto her property, acting as he was. Nibs raised his hand to her, to calm her, signaling it was alright. He receded, not turning his back to the man, until he was well out of a whip's reach, just in case he had one hiding behind his back.

"Now, as for you…" he said turning back to face Wendy. "It has been brought to the attention of our cooperative, that you intend to raise cane on your lands for the sugar trade. Is there any merit to this nasty little rumor?"

Nibs' manner had given her enough pause to recalibrate her emotional intelligence and how she was going to further converse with Abraham. He was no different than any of the others, and she knew exactly what he was capable of – or more accurately what he, as a rich white man, could get away with. She would not play the dismissive to any extent, but she also wasn't going to allow him to speak to her so uncivilly.

"Mr. Willoughby, you are, no doubt, a powerful man, likely with a business you fear is threatened by my existence. I do not know you, and I do not care to know you in any capacity beyond this interaction. I find you uncouth, and you have overstepped your boundary in threatening my man and my land. This is unacceptable behavior, and any favor I might have granted previously, is forfeit on account of your presumptuous manner. I believe you are smarter than this, and that you know better than to expect business to be negotiated in any way favorable to you henceforth. You mistake me for a wit-less woman, unable to protect myself against your fortitude. This is where you have made your folly.

You see, my father was an exceptional businessman, my mother equally as intelligent and socially savvy. As well, I have lived through experiences, the likes of which would shatter the very sanctimoniousness you hold dear. You cannot and will not threaten me beyond anything I have not already survived.

As for my intentions? I will farm what I please as this land allows. I had not considered anything at such an early stage, nor do I believe it prudent to count until I know just what I might yield. So, until this little conversation, I was not a threat to you. You and the others were never a thought to me. You and your kind disgust me. But now, because of your unwelcomed approach, I might reconsider my intentions."

Abraham laughed at this. How dare she think so much of herself. The cooperative would decimate her and her ragtag outfit. There was so much they could do to prevent her from prospering. She knew this too but wasn't going to let him just have it without her own show of force. In all things she had been through in such a short time, some ungallant strong-arm wasn't going to scare her off. She didn't give hog's ass about him, or those that sent him. And really, this was the best they could muster to come all the way up here to press her? She laughed back at him.

Nibs reappeared, though this time he wasn't alone. The lot of Lost Boys she had spared on their crossing together followed him, each with a blade or gun. Wendy didn't flinch. She just stared down at her guest from the front banister railing. Abraham sneered and took two steps back. His horse whinnied and shook, uncomfortable with the tension in the air. Animals are not dumb, and this mare knew it didn't like what was coming. It clopped its heavy hooves impatiently. Abraham yanked on the reins to settle her down, but it was clear this visit had concluded, and he was no longer welcome. He looked back up at Wendy and warned,

"This will not soon be forgotten. Your inability to come to agreements will not be looked upon in your favor. I came to offer terms, but you have ruined any chance at equitable stake."

"No, Mr. Willoughby, you did not come to offer terms. At least not to me. You insulted me from the onset and threatened my men here. That is on you, and very ungentlemanly, if I do say. In all of this, you never once attempted to appeal to my function at the management of this land. Instead, you saw an opportunity to think yourself superior and showed us no decency. I bid you good day."

"This will not be the last you hear of us. Mark my words, woman."

"They are marked, sir. And so are you."

He mounted his horse in a huff, and spurred off down the hill in a trot, never looking back. Wendy wasn't wrong; his report would be nothing short of spurious and hateful. He would never allow the relative truth of her standing up to him and treating him as she had. A woman slave owner, with a backbone, education, and a will to fight? This was incomprehensible, and he would be certain to put a stop to it.

The Lost Boys settled down once the visitor had disappeared from sight and went back about their business. Nibs leaned against the railing at the bottom of the step still watching with Wendy, just to be sure.

"No good gon' come'a that, ya know."

"I know, Nibs. I know. There was no stopping it, and I wasn't going to let him think he could get away with it so easily. Hopefully we're more effort than they're interested in and only seek their revenge in market. I know I don't need to tell you but keep the boys close."

"Aye. You did right. That man there weren't lookin' for nothin' more'n what he got. He ain't had a weapon on 'im. He's just comin' out to see if the stories was true."

"What stories?"

"The world isn't a big place, Miss Wendy, 'specially 'round here. They know we's up here hidin' with no master to keep us in check. They always checkin, trying to get they 'scaped slaves back. But all a'sudden you here now. A woman, of all t'ings, watchin over us. That i'n't the way it works. Unless'n you's a widow, maybe."

Wendy understood what he was saying. She was vulnerable up here, all alone, at least from others' perceptions. She knew good and well that she was just fine on her own up here, and that none of the Lost Boys would revolt and cause her harm. They were a pack, and they looked after each other now. No small-minded tycoon down there could ever understand. She understood. She had been raised with privilege, and had things been different, and they'd made it to Virginia as intended, she would have wound up the wife of someone no different than Abraham. She knew better than anyone what this was about, and what their grievances were. But she had the added misfortune of living through a juxtaposed hell, giving her a very keen observance of just how to bite with venom.

"Well, Nibs, I appreciate you and the boys. I hope you know that. But if I may ask…, where did you get all those guns?"

Nibs laughed slightly. He hadn't told the whole story from the beginning, and knew he had to fess up now. Though, he was sure about Wendy now, that he felt he could open that Pandora's box.

"'Nibs' is, how you call it, a nickname? My Christian name is Nicolas. I was a slave in the Americas for the Spanish. I escaped and got aboard a pirate ship an' sailed under the crew for a bit before landing here in Jamaica, where I was left. The crew took off without me on the next tide, and I been here e'er since. I had nowhere's to go, so I just hung aroun' Port Royal until my coin ran out. Weren't no one wantin' to take me on, so I had to figure somethin' out.

Well, one day there was this ol' rosy cheeked man come down one day to fetch up some slaves for his farm. He didn't have much to pay from what I could tell, and he didn't get on very far on that account. He managed to score a coupl'a hands, but I think he was hopin' for a coupl'a more.

Anyhows, I catch up to him down the road, and told him I was a free man, that I was Spanish, but I needed work, an' if he was willin' to take me on kindly, I'd be willin' to go with him – he just hav'ta give me the necessities. Basically, I was askin' to be his field man.

Now I know I don't hav'ta explain to you that this was no ord'n'ry proposition. I sure didn't know what I was gettin' myself into, nor did he with my free-willed askin.' But he was in such a way, he looked at me right glad and told me we had a deal. So, I followed him up here, and here I been ever since. I've known Piet since he was a rascal of a boy and took to lookin' after him all those years. His dad, the one I hired on with, never understood him. Never cared to. It was hard to watch sometimes, but I had to keep my place all the same, and doggone if that boy didn't cause hell for me some days."

The complexity of his history unfurled like a dandelion. Wendy was captivated by his clandestine story, and so wildly taken by a common thread. She knew they had something that connected them, but now it was even more tangible. A shared history, kismet in the most strangest of places. She didn't want to diminish the moment, but replied,

"You are most fortunate, Nibs, to have landed here, of all the possible places you could have. That was incredibly risky but speaks volumes of your character. Now you have taken in all of these others, almost, well certainly as your crew, as you might consider. I know you know; those were the ones on the ship with me, same as you were. So… the guns…"

"Yes'm they come from those old days. Sneaked'm up here time after time. Piet often lift'm from town and brought'm from his little hideaway. Big supply on there too – just in case."

*****

When Abraham finally arrived back at his family farm, he was greeted by his father, Edmund, and his dutiful wife, Elzabet. They were eager to hear of his venture, but he was clearly in a stir. By habit, he greeted his wife and commanded his father to call the others at once. He poured himself a hard glass of rum made specifically on their farm and stared out the window overlooking their fields.

They were neatly tended, all things in a row. A dozen slaves worked the acre here, 10 the acre there. The family was exceedingly wealthy, and owned many more, but calculated to keep costs down, and work up. The Willoughbys weren't the worst owners on the island, but they did command a hard line. Their slaves executed their duties as expected. Rarely did they require harsh punishment, but the Willoughbys were not afraid to exact those punishments either. In contrast, other plantationers were barbarically brutal in how they operated. Many new laws had been passed allowing owners a very loose leash in how they punished any slaves who committed 'crimes.' Norval Marlin was one such owner.

"I have sent for the men. Tell me, Abraham, what did you find up there? Is it what we suspected?"

Abraham continued to pull on his glass of rum, watching still. Edmund poured himself a glass and sat down in the heavy chair.

"I do not wish to repeat myself, father. I will wait for the others to arrive and tell all at that time. However, I will tell you that we were right in our assumptions, and there is a woman running the farm with a nasty outfit of fugitive slaves."

Edmund was a pitiless man, rigid by his faith both to God and country. He was wise in the business; strategic and calculated, not one to pick up some new trend immediately. Many farmers had leapt onto some new method or crop, only to find it was too inefficient or outright ruinous. Those were costly mistakes, and he was patient enough to watch others succeed or fail and respond accordingly if it suited his needs. His money and position benefitted him in this practice. All that withstanding, he was unscrupulous and stopped at nothing to succeed. Their farm was the second largest producer in Jamaica, second only to the Appleton farm over in Kingston. They were however, the biggest in Spanish Town.

The coalition comprised of a handful of participants; however, Edmund Willoughby and Greyson Appleton had the most say and control over who produced what on the island. The remaining members included Norval Marlin, Joseph Myers, Seamus Livingston, and Jameson Scheffield, in respective order. There were other plantations scattered about, but none of them had the means to produce cane or had not been deemed worthwhile endeavors to be brought into the syndicate. This was also because, of the six majority landowners, they were perpetually scooping up land to increase their own property lines. Case in point, Norval had acquired twenty hectares just last year when Charles Moore had suddenly died. His widow was inconsolable and was making arrangements to return to England. Norval was entuned to this and bamboozled her out of the property she was leaving behind. Other stories similar to this were the recipe for questionable land grabs.

It was after this sporadic, and incongruousness had reached a fever pitch, that the two, Edmund and Greyson, stepped in to form the organized enterprise that existed presently. They had connection in parliament back in London, and had sent their sons to serve as members, lobbying for the sugar trade in their interests – meaning the price of sugar was at a premium, and in order to keep it so, they needed to control the votes for where the supply came from. Other islands, and even the Americas had sugar or molasses to offer, but it was argued that it was not of the same quality, nationality, etc. And so, for those ambitious men who sought to get a piece of this golden opportunity, nearly destroyed the entire island's control.

Now that things were agreed upon as a board, things worked much more equitably, at least for Edmund and Greyson. Norval had been granted permission to usurp the land because it bordered his property already. Each of the members contributed to the larger good of the cooperative and were paid out accordingly, and they all followed the agreements set forth. If any changes to crop size or production occurred without permission, it would be burned. There was no clemency on this. This was meant to keep supply in ultimate demand.

That night, they had all convened at the Willoughby estate to learn of what news Abraham had returned. In the dim library they sat as the fireplace crackled with warmth and glow. They all generously poured sweet dark rum, which was made from the inferior colony molasses. The molasses was not good enough for market, but they had figured out how to distill it into some of the finest rums in all the Caribbean. Norval, being the one to take most advantage of both the free rum and the distilling, arrived last, and gladly poured himself a heavy glass.

"Good, now that we're all here, tell us Abraham, what has come of your excursion?"

"Gentlemen, your suspicions are all true. The old Dutchman's farm in the Blue Mountains has been re-ordered by a most odious woman, by the name of Wendy. It seems the heir to the farm has no interest in keeping it and has passed it on to her. Under what terms, I cannot say."

"You mean to say, this woman, Wendy, has appeared from nowhere and swindled that land for her own?"

"It would appear so, Mr. Appleton."

"My word…"

"That is not all. As you can tell, my visitation was not as prolonged as I'd intended. I was unable to gain access to the entirety of the farm and inspect the magnitude or growth, but it would seem they do not have any amount qualifiable for trade supply. It would seem they have only just repaired what was falling to decay."

"So then, she is *not* a threat to our operations?"

"No, she is not a threat to us, *yet*. But this Wendy, she is brash, uncouth, and was so unpleasant in her speaking with me, I could not bear it. Though, she is educated, she is just not educated in the ways of her place and the necessities of keeping the farm operational."

"Then this meeting is of no consequence, it would seem…"

"Please let me finish. She consorts with her slaves; a quantity I cannot figure is economical or legal. There were many of them that I could see, and I am certain there were more; possibly hundreds of them. She allows them to just be free, no field manager or overseer. Just her, and them living together in heathenry. I met the one in charge, but he was dismissed as I spoke with her a while longer. It was then he returned with about twenty others, all armed with guns and swords, intent on killing me. She showed no concern against them in this matter, did not instruct them to stand down, but allowed them to show force, thereby threatening my life. I took out of there at once, lucky to have my skin on my back, I tell you. Savages, the lot of them. It is the makings of a rebellion."

At this news, the men nearly choked on their drinks. It was preposterous for an owner to allow slaves company, much less weaponize them. The boisterousness was incomprehensible, that no one could understand what anyone was saying, but they were all saying the same thing. This would not stand.

"Gentlemen, please, quiet down. Quiet down!" Edmund barked over them. "The issue is much more than what we thought. But yet what we already knew. It's true that our escaped slaves have lodged themselves in the mountains and are armed. We knew that to be possible, now it's confirmed. There's that. If anyone goes in there, they may not make it back alive, so we cannot easily go in with our own force, as we stand now. The issue with this girl, though, that is the perplexing part. How to rid ourselves of this anathema?"

"How, indeed?" Abraham answered. "On my ride back, I had plenty of time to consider our options based how despicably they treated me, but also plainly for the interest of our futures. While I believe these detestable people should be sent to their judgement, we cannot possibly succeed by force on their ground. But we cannot allow her to get away so freely, either. Her farm is not a threat at present, nor was it before she arrived. If she stays atop that hill, she will muster more attraction for our slaves to flee – or worse, revolt! The farm may grow and produce in time, but she has made it clear she will have no parts in consolidating to our ration. What we need, is to make them want to leave. We need to spoil their land, so that crops will not prosper. They will be forced to abandon and go elsewhere, to which we will recapture our slaves, rightfully ours, and punish them as the law allows."

The men grumbled in a semblance of possible agreement. It seemed like a good idea, but it would take a long-term commitment to reap the intended result. Of course, they had time, and could play the long game, but they all felt this should be nipped in the bud sooner, rather than later.

"That's not a bad idea, Abraham. But what if we just flush them out with fire? We send a party up there, burn the house, and set the fields ablaze?" Seamus asked.

"An option worth, entertaining, yes. So long as we can get to the places to set the fires. I tell you no lie, sir, there are many of them, and so few of us. It would be a risk, even if we took all our hands with us. But our slaves would never be trusted to attack their own, and we would march them straight to where there is apparent refuge. They cannot know where that place exists."

The conversations were spiraling around, as they all proposed some method of destruction to Wendy, the farm, and the Lost Boys. But they were all too concerned with how they would enact this, based on such little information, they couldn't quite land on an agreeable solution. Throughout the back and forth, Norval finally had an epiphany as the rum helped ease his mind.

"This girl, you say her name is Winnifred?"

"Wendy, Mr. Marlin."

"Wendy... yes... And she just came from nowhere... Is she about yea tall, dark hair, eyes like the winter's devil?"

"Yes! Yes, that's her! But how...?" Abraham questioned emphatically.

"That conniving, filthy moll..." Norval spit fitfully in revelation. "That woman is the same trollop I accompanied to that damned Governor's dinner you had me attend when you wanted me to grease his palms for our ships in port! Damn me! She is a nasty little bitch. Got a mouth on her. I right had to put her in her place afore we even went into that stupid house. What a miserable little shit. Now she's causin' this ruckus? Hell find me if we don't see this to a quick end."

"So, you know her, Norval?"

"I know of her. Couldn't stand her company from the minute she arrived. Entitled little priss. Tried tellin' me she was somebody, but she weren't nothin' but a whore from that bordello down in Port Royal. Pixies, I think it is?"

"You know... I just recently saw some of those pirates nosing around town, askin' questions of folks." Jameson piped in. "Seemed out of sorts to have them comin' into our stretch. You know we have agreements that they stay out there. I refused them company, the filth. I don't wonder now if they weren't lookin' for her?"

They all looked at each other, one after the other, as if they'd all come to the same conclusion with Jameson's information.

Greyson looked sternly and said, "Find these pirates. Find out what they want. If this is the tip they seek, you give it to them. Let them sort this out for us. Keeps our hands clean, and we don't know a damned thing else."

"...and when they've sorted it. We burn the place to ash."

XVII

For what Port Royal was a pothered encampment of derelicts, Kingston was becoming a flourishing colonial settlement on the rise. Following the great earthquake years before, when all was sucked into the sea in God's damnation of the original establishment of Port Royal, many had begun parceling out land on the firmer earth in Kingston. Port Royal was condemned to ruin, but slowly it was rebuilt and reinhabited by the denizens who refused to let go of their debaucherous sanctuary.

Any respectable person had moved inland and were amassing land across the entire eastern corner of the island. The gridded town of Kingston began as a fledgling relocated hub with every attempt to free itself from the spit of land to the south. To the rich landowners inland, the peninsula of Port Royal served only as a barricade against a direct assault and as a sewer for those pirates still lingering. With the little port tucked away in the bay and all the pirate ships at rest, the harbor was safe, but also difficult to access. For years they had been disagreeably opposed to each other and kept their distances respectively. The rich only ever came into Port Royal for slave auctions and audience with the governor when requested. The pirates stayed in Port Royal because that's where all the entertainment was; Kingston offered them nothing in the way of licentiousness or gain.

So, it was strange, that some haggard brethren of the coast had made their way into town, and many of the locals were left feeling a bit vulnerable. Smee and his entourage attempted to have an easier air to them, but they were just an off-putting bunch of dregs. Simcoe and Foggerty were gnarly-heads and Smee the older, weathered salt. They were out of place, and the locals crossed their eyes at them to make sure they didn't feel welcome. But this was in vain, because the townsfolk did still have a legitimate fear of these types of characters.

When Smee and his men would approach anyone to ask their questions, they would scurry and avert their eyes, or even just ignore them and lock themselves inside. No one was forthcoming with any information, and it was becoming a futile effort to keep asking around. They weren't welcome there and everything was turning to a dead end. Feeling they had exhausted their efforts trying to find this mystery plantation, they debated if they should venture further out of the township. This though, would prove a challenge because of how widespread everything was. They would need to split up and steal horses to fully encompass the various plantations, and even then, they risked their own necks charging on to someone's property. The owners and land managers weren't as shy to shoot intruders. Smee knew Simcoe might get himself in a spot with his demeanor, and Foggerty didn't take kindly to opposition, so it was possible for him to wind up in a disagreement over intentions.

In the square they stood scheming, trying to calculate any logical next steps. They didn't want to return to the *Jolly Roger* without any intel; Hook would gaff any one of them for insubordination. Perhaps they could venture over to Spanish Town in the morning, but that held little appeal. Of course, not as little as the wrath of their captain.

They decided to find a public house and settle in for the evening. This would prove its own challenge given the rebuke they'd faced all day just by being there. Figuring this to be the case, and knowing better than to strongarm anyone, for detriment to their mission, they weaved their way to the outskirts of the parish. Here they believed they might find better opportunity to find drink and a bed.

Spanish Town was a bit of a journey from where they were, nestled on the opposing shore across the bay. Thirteen miles away, it was unequivocally an entirely different town. There were many plantations spread out from the surrounding area there, but it was the seat of power in Jamaica. For what cold shouldered affect Kingston had to the pirates, they truly had no business in Spanish Town. It was Daniel walking into the Lion's Den with the questionability of the King's Pardon versus privateering versus outright piracy. If they showed any color of malfeasance, they could be jailed and hung for the birds.

Smee knew this, and while they need not be admonished, they needed to take real consideration to what they were about to risk. Hook was not one to be trifled with, and they dare not return without having exhausted every possible effort. However, they truly did not belong in Spanish Town. Kingston was one thing, neighboring Port Royal and being the only avenue out of there. However, they would make the trip in the morning and proceed with caution.

They managed to find an inn on the western edge who reluctantly allowed them in. It wasn't much to speak of, small, and it was unceremoniously quiet. The boys, accustomed to disorderliness, felt less than enthusiastic about the dimness, but the place had drink, food, and a place to catch rest. It was enough. As such, with nothing lively about, this made it easier to turn in early for the night. The next morning, they set off early, continuing west out of Kingston on the main, and only road leading to Spanish Town.

They arrived in Spanish Town just before midday, and for all the surprise of them appearing in Kingston, it was even more ghastly for them to be here. Entering the plaza, they were greeted by the rebuilt Anglican church, the King's house and many other Georgian architectures closing in on them like sentries along the checkerboarded squares. Most of Spanish Town had been rebuilt after the British burned it in the sacking and capture from the Spanish. It had some Spanish influences remaining, but by and large it was a stately British city nestled in an idyllic tropical landscape, contrasting the rest of the surrounding areas. The Kings House was regal, and every bit imperious as it ought to be for representing the crown's affairs afar. It was where the Governor conducted the parliamentary duties. The Port Royal mansion had served as a temporary court while Spanish Town was rebuilt, but now it merely served as a place to entertain – easily ignored for its distance away from the couth and pious.

Finding the area bustling, they did their best to fit in, keeping a low profile and their wits about them. Even more so than Kingston, very few people had time or interest in speaking with them. They were recognized as villains out of their place, and this made them spending any amount of time here perilously risky. As much, those milling about the town were no source of truth on the whereabouts of some sprat in the hills. They did however pique the ears of some, who had heard rumors of some lorn refuge in the hills, but nothing of consequence. Again, if they hoped to glean any fortune of information, they needed to seek the audience of the plantationers in the outlying areas.

Alas, the trio had little to show for their efforts. Belle's swain seemed to be the enigma of the island, a myth. But contrary to this, they knew he existed. They had seen him in passing and general hanging about back in Port Royal. What was odd though, was there was known to be a nest of maroons up in the hills, yet no one they had managed to stop had any info on that piece, most of all, or if they did, why weren't they sharing that information? Simcoe had grown very weary of being dragged across the island and now standing as a target in the city known to hang pirates. Foggerty wasn't far behind with the same feeling. Smee, undyingly patient, had begun to also feel the effort was going to turn up little in the way of report. He hadn't given up yet but knew at this point if they hadn't managed to gather any intel, it didn't bode well they would.

Knowing the longer they spent in plain view, harassing the locals, the worse it would be for their success and survival. It only took one cross individual to report them as outlaws, and they'd be clapped away without any chance of liberty. Knowing his men were edgy, Smee decided it best if they relocate to the harbor and lay low for a bit until they could devise any new scheme.

From the coastline, they could see the ships quiescent in the bay, their own ship huddled among the others. It was a tranquil scene, all the masts and spars crisscrossed in the sky, bobbing gently this way and that. As they sat watching from the banks, a villain of diametric significance was tucked away inside the hulking vessel. They answered to that villain, and yet still, the distance between them was palpable. Knowing their captain was so effectively predominant, the issue that they had turned up nothing began to concern even Smee. He grew anxious, his mind fumbling for some new strategy or plan to turn over stones and get answers. Returning to the ship without any report likely meant death for any of them, but most likely Belle. She was a casualty in all of this, and she, as a woman and a whore, was disposable. Though Smee had no attachment to the girl, he didn't care to see her (or anyone of the fairer sex) unlived on account of some superfluous exercise not of their making.

He sighed deeply and fidgeted with two coins between his fingers, his mind still mulling over what else could be done. Simcoe and Foggerty sat, weary of the fruitless mission, ready to get back to Port Royal and back to safe, familiar territory. As a distraction, Foggerty waxed fondly about Rosie back in Pixies and yearned for the feel of her body wrapped around his. The more he got to thinking about it, the more pent up he became, and subsequently more frustrated. By and large, Foggerty was an even keeled part of the crew, deadly, when necessary, but never unnecessarily pernicious. He was growing out of sorts presently, and the longer he was in this limbo, the more he strayed from his center.

All three of them were feeling it, but Smee most of all. His men were being dragged across all creation trying to dig up some sort of clue on the whereabouts of some girl, whom they had carted across the lower Atlantic, for their captain. This was not what they had signed up for as pirates, and while they feared or respected Hook, he didn't hold jurisdiction over them in this fashion. This was all just an exercise in duty to their captain, but truthfully, he was overreaching in his command and expectations. The longer this endeavor carried on unsuccessfully, the higher likelihood a revolt might occur. *This* was what Smee worried about almost as equally as their failing quest. If Simcoe or Foggerty returned scorned, it was not outside of their ability to call council among the men and oust Hook for this abuse. Smee's mind scurried like a starving rat eluding an even hungrier cat. And yet the more he envisaged, the cloudier his thoughts became. He needed clarity. He needed to stop, think plainly, and execute with intention. The best way he knew how to do this, was over a flagon.

They sat for a bit longer, resting their tired bones, watching the soporific scene before them. Smee acknowledged the issue they faced, and tried to offer some condolence to his shipmates,

"Fellas, I know this ain't been what'n ya signed on fer, sloggin' all over kingdom-come, looking for some coupla nobodies lost in the woods. I get it, I do. Cain't say I'm not feelin' the same rights about now. But the cap'n needs to find her, else we might'n not ever call Port Royal our port anymore. This, *she*, was our shot at taking this place over for our own, now, and forever. You and the others weren't in on the plan, 'cause'n it needed to go accordin' to plan, but it didn't, and now here we sit, tryin' like hell to scratch it out, and it's comin' out tits up. I hope ye can keep that in mind as'n we try to wrap this up, proper like. It ain't all the cap'n's fault, hell, anything it's that Wendy's fault really… but once we get where she's run off to, it'll all make sense. Giv'me a little bit more, and I hope I can swear, it'll be worth it."

The men internalized his words. It was true, they were already thinking about calling foul on this when they got back to town, justifiably. But Smee had a way about him that always seemed to ease and deescalate, so they just grumbled and laid back watching the few clouds hang in the sky. Smee felt he'd patched it for now, but if nothing else came soon, he couldn't hold it off again. These two would circulate the story and muster the support against Hook. Smee would remain ever faithful to him, but what good is a fearful captain without a crew? And all this of course, was predicated on them succeeding in conquering the fear of Hook among the men to even come to a mutiny. If they didn't, it probably didn't spell prosperity for them in the end. So, Smee offered to coax them along with another round of drinks and beds for the night. The men gladly obliged, and they crept back into town in search of another public house that would cater to the likes of them.

If it was a challenge in Kingston, finding a place to take the three in for a night was nigh impossible. They bounced from place to place, none of them willing to harbor pirates. Their reputation preceded them with some appropriate stereotype, but since Spanish Town was no Gomorrah, the likelihood of them getting into any trouble were next-to-none. Eventually, as they wandered the darkening streets, a young shadowy boy approached and led them to an establishment tucked away in the recesses of the city. The child had been sent to find them and bring them to the tavern, and when they were delivered, he was given a few pence for his efforts by another scrawny man waiting inside.

When the three of them entered, the few locals present made certain not to make eye contact, and shuffled away into various directions, all except for the one the boy ran to collect his earnings. This odd man waved the three over as the barkeep nervously eyed the entire engagement. Sitting down, they too were on-guard, uncertain what possible outcome this meant for them. This could have easily been a set-up for them to be captured and hung the next day, though if that were the case, why wait until evening, in a tavern, to arrest them? Why not make a spectacle in the streets, in broad daylight. It was all very odd, but here they were, with nothing else to show.

"I understand you three are the men lurking about, shaking the trees of my fellow townsfolk for answers on a particular runaway?"

Simcoe was the first to jump, but Smee quickly reeled him in so as not to give away any upper hand they held in this rendezvous.

"We're but passers through, looking to settle ourselves into the provincial humdrum. Who might you be, that asks such questions of men unknown?" Smee calculatedly replied.

"You are not men looking for such things, that much is clear. However, if you are not those men said to be looking for some girl in the hills with a curious lot of slaves, then forgive my presumptions. I will not keep you any longer, though, know that you are sorely out of place, and it is most advisable you return from whence you came before the day breaks on the morrow."

"I think you mean to tell us something, which is of value to both parties. It is not in our nature though, to discuss such affairs with strangers who might be dually represented. What assurance have you that we are of the same interest, and how might we trust some such as yourself?"

At this, the stranger waved to the barkeep to produce drinks for the men, that they were within control and manageable therein. Acknowledging, four frothy tankards were plunked onto the table post haste.

"Let this be a first step in trusting that you are who I have been looking for, and I am who you have been looking for."

"Let us see about that…" Smee raised his drink, offering a semblance of toast, signaling they were all vetted, and whatever conversation was about to occur could do so in the trust that all parties were satisfied with each's own safety. "Go on…"

"Rumor has it, you three have been seeking the answer to where has this wretch gone off to, is that right?"

"Perhaps… What information do you have on the matter?"

"Gentlemen, I represent a committee who wishes not to mingle with the likes of this woman, and as you are in search of her, I can tell you, I have visited her, and am here to provide you her whereabouts."

"So, you're going to sell her out for your own gain, then? Is that right? And you want to keep your hands clean so that nothing comes back to your little outfit, and you can profit more with her out of the picture?"

"Don't be smug. You have your own intentions. Why else would word have reached my stretches of you three vulturing about in Spanish Town and Kingston? Your lot has Port Royal, and no reason to venture this far out, so it is clear she is of importance to your design."

The three of them sat quietly, waiting for the man to go on. He was agitated now, and while it meant nothing to them that his partners gained from this, it did still come with some effort on their part, and likely some hazard. Smee weighed in,

"Aye. We're looking for a girl run off with a boy rumored to have a farm somewhere off in the hills. So, what have you on this?"

"As I said, I have visited her and seen the farm. I can point you to her. But you should know, her slaves are armed, the devils. They ran me off the land at gunpoint, and for that, it could not please me more to see her in your hands. She is something nasty, and if you were to reclaim her, I believe that alone, is God's retribution to her."

"And what of these slaves? Armed you say? That puts my men in danger, don't you think?"

"Once she is rid of the plantation, we will take care of those heathens. They belong to the various lot of us, and so they shall be returned. They only came back in a show of force after she had exchanged unkind words toward myself. It is a risk, yes, but are you not men who face such risks on the seas for reward?"

Smee contemplated what he was hearing, and what that meant, and how they might approach it. Simcoe and Foggerty, happy to have beverages sat at his sides, listening to what was being said, also plotting their conquest for having traipsed across the countryside, and now into the sweaty hills.

"So, if we are to succeed in rooting her out from her nest, what have you to offer for our risk?"

"As I said, it is of significant interest to all, that she is removed, and the slaves redistributed among their rightful owners."

"Yes, but what do we gain by doing your dirty work?"

"What do you deem fair? I have given you promise that I have seen her and can point you to her. She is the reward you're after, is she not?"

"She is not the only part of this. We are taking on the risk and danger, only to reacquire what belongs to us. Yes, you have here whereabouts, but we are doing all the work which benefits your deep pockets."

"You want to be paid for this."

"Nay, we have what is ours when it comes to coin, and your money is no more righteous than our own. So that there are no questions binding either of our parties, we shall not exchange contracts or payments. On the contrary, you shall secure the safety of my men in Jamaica, that we may walk without fear of our necks snapped up in a noose or hung in a gibbet for the crows."

"I alone cannot grant you that. Though, I am sure I can muster the support of my partners to speak up for your wishes. Understand I can only offer you that safety so long as our idiot of a governor reigns here. I am without power to negotiate any agreements with a new appointee. But you must already know, the King is intolerant of pirates these days. I cannot offer you safety outside of your port."

"Of course. We only ask that we are left to our own, and that if any of us do choose to acre out, we might do so without obstruction."

"Remove the thorn, and we will take the rest as it arises. I assure you on the first account, that your kind will remain at liberty in Port Royal, at least."

"On that, we will reclaim what belongs to us." Smee lifted his cup in contractual toast.

XVIII

"We got it cap'n. We know where she's hiding."

It had been days that they were gone, and while Hook understood it would take time, he had not expected it to take this much. He had grown quite insufferable as the clock ticked away the minutes and the hours, day after day. It pounded in his skull like a drum. TICK. TOCK. TICK TICK TICK TOCK. He had grown so loathsome of it, that he finally smashed it with his hook, and left it sitting in pieces on the floor as a reminder. So, when Smee and the men returned, he was more than eager to learn of the good news. Smee added the icing on the cake in telling him they had negotiated clemency for the foreseeable future if they were able to remove her from the farm.

"Excellent, my good man. Assemble a party. We leave tonight."

He was anxious to get on with tracking her down. So much time had lapsed since she had disappeared, that he reasoned all progress and opportunity were lost. It was quite a twist that they had gained their purpose all through the negotiation of locating her whereabouts. It was fortuitous, really. All burning rage diffused from Hook at this news, he began even wondering if there was any purpose to retrieving her at all. But he was reminded it all hinged on them capturing her, leaving the maroons behind, and staying clear of the cooperative in the process. It all seemed too easy.

Belle, on the other hand, had remained locked away in the sickening belly of the ship. She was fouled, having laid trapped in her cage with nowhere to relieve herself. No one had come to attend to her, except to bring her rotten scraps of food. As Hook's favor had expired for her, none of the other men gave any concern to her well-being either. Some days the even forgot (intentionally or not, is uncertain) that she was down there. It was miserable hell, and despite her cries for help, they went unheard, until her voice finally gave out. Broken, she wept, and the festering slash from his punishing blow stung from the salty tears. There was no easement in any form.

Smee, now returned, went to check on her, as soon as he was dismissed from report with the captain. He could not help her in the way she needed, but his old heart did beat a feeling for her condition. She was such a beautiful sprite, adored by so many – especially Hook. Now, here she lay macabrely, unable to even hold herself up, a victim of happenstance. Never could she

227

have predicted this, and it was unfortunate that it all stemmed from Hook's own animus. He brought her some water and turtle soup, hoping she could still digest any of it. He told her also, that it would all soon be over. She lay there nearly lifeless, not taking the food or drink.

"Eat child. You will need strength. You will be free soon. We have found Wendy and will be off in a few hours' time. When we return with her, I will see to it you are released, as your penance has been served."

Belle slumped over, barely able to lift her head toward him. Her eye swollen, the other distant, nearing the end of a dark tunnel. She wanted to thank him, but she couldn't. She wanted to scream at him, but she couldn't. She wanted to die, but she couldn't. Collapsing again, she knocked over the bowl he had brought her. A tear rolled out of her eye, stinging the wound again. Smee reached in to pick it up, but its contents had spilled out.

"I'll get you another one. But this time, you gots't' be more careful. You need to eat."

He didn't have time to attend to her, but he did care enough for her to survive. He needed to gather the hunting party for their imminent departure. There was quite a bit of preparation to manage ahead of their conquest, for which he was largely responsible. On the surface, it may seem simple enough to gather a horde of men and storm of into the night but there was certainly more to it. They would be leaving under the cloak of night, so they could gain as much ground in the dark and have the advantage of surveying the area to minimize casualties. They already knew they were going into an armed stronghold, so it could get very ugly very quick. A mission like this could easily be lambs to led to slaughter, though they had no real fear, much like taking a prize at sea. There were, however, ways to mitigate the risk, and if ever there was a lot to do it, it was this bunch.

They had outwitted, outsmarted, outmaneuvered some of the Navy's best ships, all while doing the same to claim prizes worth more than any pirate before them had lived to tell. They knew how to hunt, how to strike, how to succeed on water, this was a valley where men with less to lose were lodged in on familiar ground. Smee gathered the men and briefed them on what they were setting out to do. Many grumbled at the task, knowing this wasn't what they cared to devote their time or attention to. Smee was quick to remind them of the stakes, and politic the captain's efforts. He even gave them an out, but that out was permanent, and that meant they were blackballed – no crew was likely to take on a deserter. So together they stood, crowded on the main deck listening to Smee's words.

The sun was now setting, blinking its last rays of light behind the mountains. In all other days, those mountains were just a part of the landscape, blending into the view of their environment. But tonight, in the dusking shadows, it loomed darker than usual, rising like Olympus above the umbrous valley. They collected their weapons, braces of flintlocks, muskets, and swords and readied the boats to row across the bay. If the evening wasn't laced enough with tension, Hook stepped out onto the deck to face them, ready to lead the charge. He spoke,

"Men, I know this is not the glory you as the ablest cutthroats in all the Carib seek. This is a misfortune I have bolstered due to mine own folly. I dreamt of a way for our kind to exist here, where we so bountifully play, safely from the King's reach. That risk I took on this girl, has now spat in our faces, and condemned us. So tonight, much to your understandable dismay, we abscond to this hinterland to reclaim this badger, to keep her from promoting our damnation. If we are to succeed in reclaiming her, we thusly succeed in our endeavors to prosper here in Port Royal for what I surmise, is longer than the days you will count. So, for the privilege of walking freely through those streets, a tankard of ale, and a warm snatch to dally, we set off to finish this once and for all."

He was so calculated. Every syllable, pause or inflection orated with such craft. His speech enlivened the men so that they boisterously hosannaed him, forgetting all their waning faith in him. They leapt into the boats with fervor and rejuvenated mission ready to find this girl and return her to their ship for whatever awaited next. *This* was why James Bartholomew continued to reign as the king of pirates. He was erudite and knew how to inspire them over this prolonged snafu. Truly, if it weren't for this mishap, they might've already set sail again, off to capture more prizes or terrorize the Atlantic seaboard. This cost them and was something he was not acutely unaware of.

He belted his cutlass, clapped Smee on the shoulder, and with confident pride said,

"Let's go smoke out a fox, shall we, Smee?"

"Aye, lets."

They hopped into the waiting boat, and they all began pulling oars through the congested roadstead toward the Spanish Town river mouth, where they would stash the boats and head interior.

Gathering his bearings when they were landed, Smee led the party in the direction the man in the tavern had explained. The road led true as he'd said, and soon they were climbing, leaving the coastal lowlands quickly behind them. The evening turned sharply into night once they had ventured into denser canopy. The darkness in the jungle was unlike anywhere else. The trees eclipsed any light, making it atramentous like Hook's heart. Steeper they trudged onward.

After what seemed like ages in the wild unknown, they came to the clearing in the road, as the mystic had explained. Smee knew they were close, and that they needed to skirt the openness, sticking to the forest that concealed them. Cresting the hill, they could see the tired farmhouse sleeping in the night, unaware of their presence. From here though, they couldn't get a good vantage point of the outlying area, so Smee sent a band off to flank the farm and see what they could discover.

No signs of life were to be seen, which was good for them. They'd managed to sneak in just as planned, and so far, remained secreted away. Roughly half of an hour later, the scouts returned with their report. Just down the hill, on the other side, was a barn and what appeared to be the slave quarters. This was music to Hook's ears.

Devising their plan, Hook instructed the party to return to the far side where the barn was and set fire to it. This would wake the slaves and preoccupy them. Wendy would hear the commotion and inevitably come out to see what was going on. With the slaves attempting to curtail the fire, they would steal Wendy away and leave entirely unnoticed. This would be so dashingly easy it was almost too good to be true. With that, Scourie, Mullins, Turley, and Alf Mason slinked off to cause the distraction.

They reached the barn and crept along the backside to avoid being seen in the open. Thinking they were in the clear, they started to set the fire by using the powder and flint from their pistols. Unaware that several the slaves freely slept outside their quarters, in the open, they were not as quiet about it as they ought to have been. This woke those Lost Boys, who came running and yelling when they discovered the pirates. Because they had emptied their weapons of powder and flint, they were unable to fire back and instead clashed with the Lost Boys in fisticuffs and grappling. This in turn woke the others, who also came running out of the quarters, startled by the surprise, Nibs among them.

He and the others retreated to grab their guns and fired shots toward the barn as a warning both to the Lost Boys to clear out for a clean shot, but also to the pirates, that their jig was up. The fighters split apart, and the pirates ran like hell into the forest, but not before Adom got off a shot, striking down Scourie. The fire they'd started was growing but had not yet grown out of control, but it needed to be doused quickly before it exploded into uncontrollable magnitude.

From the other side, where the others hid, they awaited the sight of the smoke from the fire and the intended commotion to draw out their target, but instead heard the shots shatter the night's silence. This was not part of their plan and were now unaware of what was happening. Some of the pirates started to rush to action in solidarity, but Hook was quick to restrain them, knowing this would still result in Wendy running out as they'd initially strategized. It was just as important now, perhaps more so than before, they needed to remain hidden, because of this unexpected turn of events. If they rushed out now, their position would be known, and the plan might fail more tragically.

Sure enough, within seconds of the shots, Wendy came bounding out of the house. Now was their opportunity. Without hesitation, but a vengeance, Simcoe and Foggerty rushed out and scooped her up. She was blindsided, pummeled by the men. She let out a bloodcurdling scream that split the air like a peal of lightning. All sound disappeared from the earth, save for her cry in that moment. Nibs turned to see up the hill, two haggard pirates thieving her away, while they were in the field below, chasing off marauders, clearly a successful distraction. He yelled to the others, waving them to follow, and they ran as hard as they could to catch up. Behind them, the fire was able to claw its way up, until it had become a blaze illuminating the corner of the field.

Nibs and the others made it to the lawn above, where the gang of pirates were escaping with Wendy in their custody. The pirates fled into the darkness, firing haphazardly to deter pursuit, and when the shots were heard, the Lost Boys dodged, fell, and scrambled to avoid being hit by the invisible bullets.

They had been cowed; taken by surprise by those they least expected to challenge them way up here. It was too risky to give chase into the jungle against the pirates, and they now had a real problem to deal with the barn. Nibs cursed wildly, screaming into the void. The others pulled him back, needing his help putting out the fire and saving what was left of the farm before it spread.

For hours they tried to snuff out the inferno, but they had so little water to do so, it was almost as though their efforts just prolonged the pyre. The timbers blanching white hot, crackling into ash and cinder. Realizing they were fighting an impractical enemy, they shifted efforts to keep it from spreading to the forest, fields, and the main house. As the sky diffused from darkness into first light, the structure finally gave out, collapsing into a pile of smoldering rubble. So too did Nibs, exhausted, defeated, angry, and sad. The others looked on with similar faces and emotions, also exhausted and sooten from the efforts.

Tears welled in Nibs' eyes as he stared off at and past the heap of smoking remnants. The day had finally come that they would be beset, and for all the preparations they had ever made against the Masters, it came at the hands of the pirates, the type of men he knew, and yet never predicted as a threat. Too, they had taken only Wendy, and they were unable to protect her. This might have made him the most upset, for the fire and the barn were over and life would go on and could be rebuilt. The loss of Wendy was the loss of a member, and their creed was to keep and protect every soul among them. As the others began to clean up, he continued to sit as they moved around him. They left him be. They knew he was not okay, but there was little to do for him, other than keep on with what they were doing.

Morning had come, along with the humid blanket that seemed heavier than usual. Now they were shoveling loads of dirt on the coals so that nothing would reignite and spread. Nibs had gone up to the main house, separated from his mind while also inside it. He'd grown to adore Wendy. She was kind, fair, sweet, and always looking out for each of them as if they were her own children. His guilt turned to blame as he went through the rollercoaster of emotions walking through the house. He briefly blamed her for being the reason they had come but quickly cast that thought out. It wasn't her fault, any more than it was his. They had both escaped pirates for a reason, so he understood the whys and the risks. Touching the bric-a-brac on the shelf as reminders, he wandered aimlessly. The bed unmade from her bolting out into the night. Her scream echoed in his mind. The vision of her grappled and kicking wildly haunted him. He sat in the chair and drifted off both mentally and physically. He needed a fresh mind, so he allowed himself this, away from the others so they wouldn't see him weak and vulnerable. Eventually, they too took their rest under the shade of trees and elsewhere. The work had been done, and now it was quiet.

Hours had passed while the Lost Boys recovered. It was now late afternoon when Nibs stepped outside. He was ready to get back to work, rebuilding and figuring out just what to do about Wendy. His old life was returning to him, a vengeance blooming inside him. He'd left that life behind, having been cast away, and the rural farm life kept him pacified from it otherwise. But now he felt those pangs of fury and did not feel the urge to suppress them. The others didn't know his history, but they were about to. He was to rescue Wendy or die trying.

He roused the others and called them together at the main house to tell them his intentions. They all sat around on the steps and porch as he told them his history, many of them looking on in confused wonder. The others, also former pirates briefly, felt the fraternal kinship of the brotherhood, and stood with him, ready to rally behind him in this suicide mission. Those who were simply slaves felt the connection between the others, and though they were unequipped to fight against pirates, they would follow. They had no time to waste, as every hour brought on the possibility that Wendy would be killed, and their attempts would be for naught.

From out of nowhere, a small band of Taino natives appeared, walking up the dirt road. Natives weren't seen in this part of the island anymore, so this show was a nerve inducing sight. They were each of them, scarcely clad and were painted ceremoniously with markings across their faces, bare chests, arms, and legs. They were not known to be an aggressive lot, but to see them marching in parade toward the unsuspecting Lost Boys, was nothing short of concerning. Nibs finally recognized Piet, also painted and naked, leading the parade right toward them. He wasn't sure what he was up to, but he was going to find out. He wasn't in any mood to be toyed with at the likes of Piet's games anymore.

He stamped down and intercepted them. The Lost Boys all stood among the railings and steps anxiously ready for whatever was about to happen. All sense of decorum left Nibs as he squared up directly with Piet.

"Just what you think you're up to boy? You think you just dis'pear an' come back up 'ere like it's 'nother one your silly games? Why you bring 'dem here? You bring more people 'ere and more people find us. An' guess what? They foun' us, boy! They foun' us, an' dey burn't de place, an' dey took Wendy!" He was frothing mad.

Piet had never seen him like this and wasn't sure how to respond. No one had yelled at him so ferociously since his father. Though, in all of it, the news of Wendy's apprehending rang through.

"What? Who did? Why?" he bumbled. He had no expectation to come back to a discovery like this. His hope was to bring his native friends to the farm to commune with everyone and build a prosperity among them.

"She gone Piet. The one with de Hook. The one you mussed wit'. The one gon' kill her an' erry'body in 'is path. You took out 'ere to go play with the injuns an' lef her 'ere wit' us. She rebuilt dis place wit' her own two hands. It's her place now, not yours. You need to get on. Go back to town or go back with them. I don't care. You ain't fit for bein' 'ere!"

Feeling challenged and threatened, Piet immediately went on immature defense, unable to comprehend any valid truth to Nibs' outburst.

"No! Now you listen to me, Nibs! This is my family's farm, and it always will be! I brought all of you here and give you safe places to stay! You owe me!"

This did not land well with Nibs, who was feeling a rabid emotional rawness at this ridiculous parade before him. He couldn't believe how detached Piet was, so much that he saw red and wished to throttle him until his head popped off like a toy. Before he could get his hands on him though, a raven-haired woman stepped forward to mediate.

"I am Tiger Lily, daughter of the great chief. My father has passed, and we are on sojourn. Piet has brought us here only as we head east to the windward sea and rising sun. You are angry because you have been attacked. That is understandable, and I am sorry for you. Piet meant no harm to you by coming to us. It was good he did. He was cleansed by my father's forgiveness before he died. Now he is returned. We shall move on and not cause you any trouble."

Her grace defused Nibs. His being able to connect to people, made him see the honor and spirit she brought with her, and that she and her party were not to blame for this. He was still not yet so forgiving of Piet, who, unable to comprehend what the others had endured in his absence still lambasted his old friend at Tiger's interpolation,

"He can't talk to me like that. If it wasn't for me..." He didn't get to finish his gripe, and likely good he didn't, lest he say something despicable. Tiger interrupted him to quiet him and end the argument.

"A life is never easy. Do not make it harder for others along their way. The attack on them is reason for them to feel as they do. You were not here, and you cannot understand, but you could not be two places. You must allow them this anger so they may heal."

Nibs was appreciative of this woman's wisdom and ability to put Piet in his place so passively. He stepped back, welcoming them onward toward the house with her coterie. Piet still felt slighted but gave in and followed along behind. While Nibs introduced Tiger Lily to the other Lost Boys, Piet surveyed the fields below, taking notice of their improvements and growth, but also the charred graveyard where the barn once stood. Nibs was right... they had made the place over. It looked almost as it had when he was younger, and his parents actively cared for the place. He had no interest still, and so his swipe at Nibs for it always being his place was disconnected and unjust.

Looking now at the house, he saw the reclamation, and that it was a home. This too he had no interest in and never would, but the realization that Wendy wasn't here to welcome and greet him settled in. He had brought her here to escape and live out her days, and so of course her comfort in the house made sense. It looked lived in. It looked cozy, like a home should. But it wasn't his anymore, it never really was. But Wendy wasn't here. She had been stolen by Hook. Moreover, he had no idea that his nemesis had Belle as well.

That evening, everyone contributed to make a communal feast on the farm. The fire burned warm and bright, while emotions spanned the spectrum still. Tiger Lily was pensive, mourning her late, great father. Nibs and the Lost Boys were set on revenge and retribution. Piet was forlorn for the absence of Wendy and the loss of what he knew as his childhood home. The Tainos were out of place here and were uncertain how to compose themselves. Yet, they all joined as a collective in their adversities. Nibs approached Piet, sitting off to the side not quite by himself, but certainly removed from the scrum.

"We have to get her back, Piet."

"I know Nibs. And we will."

"She made dis place new. She made dis place a place for us again. I shouldn' have got at you earlier like I did. But you lef', a'd we all did this wit'out you. She brought it to life. She deserves to have this. I know it's yours by right, but when you show'd up after ery't'ing, I just couldn't help m'self."

"I know Nibs. We've known each other forever, and I never meant to abandon you, or the boys, or Wendy. You know I can't stay here. I never could. And I think now, I never will, so you're right... if... *when*, we rescue her, it'll be yours. Yours and hers, however."

This was the first grown up – and selfless – thing he had ever done or admitted to. It felt icky to him, but deep down, he knew it was the right thing. He may have been borderline feral, but his mother had raised him with a moral compass that shined through in the rarest of occasions. Hearing this melted Nibs' heart, and he put his arm around his oldest friend for reassurance and consolation.

"So now what?" Nibs asked.

"Now we go fight. We get Wendy back. I beat him once with nothing on the line. I'll beat him again."

"'s one thing to beat 'im by 'imself way back then, but we'll be up against the whole crew, Piet. I know my way 'round, but half dem boys don' got what it'll take."

"We won't need all of them to know, just all of them in numbers. The best of you can fight. The others'll be the numbers we need."

"I don' know, Piet. Not sure I's good wit' take'n dem down to fight pirates if'n they cain't fight at all…"

"They all know how to save themselves, Nibs, how else have they gotten on here with you? And for that matter, it's better to die fighting on your feet, than to survive on your knees."

"I think I'd rather live on my feet than die on my knees[5vi]…"

"I'd rather live forever, and I plan to. So, Hook will taste my blade for the last time."

"Jus' don' make your toyin' the cause of dem boys' demise. D'er's a difference."

"I'll go it alone if I have to, Nibs, but having all of you betters the odds."

"I won' let you go alone. Not for Wendy's sake, and dem boys won' sit back either. I'm just tell'n ya, don' send them to a senseless death."

"If we win, Nibs, it isn't senseless."

Nibs knew what he meant, but this was a dangerous way about it. Piet had blinders on that worried Nibs. Never in his life had Piet led a mission altruistically, and someone other than him always paid some sort of price. Though, he knew a fight to this degree would very likely come with casualties – they would be fighting pirates. He remembered clearly from his days as one what the combat would resemble, and most of the Lost Boys were not capable of wielding a weapon against one of the most notorious crews. This set his mind to thinking. They would have to outfox them, hit hard, and cause a lot of chaos. Piet was the integral piece to this.

As the two sat together, Tiger Lily had taken notice and came to see that they had mended their tempers and were getting along together again. She was so deft; they didn't hear her approach. When she spoke softly, it startled them that they didn't know she was standing there.

"Your hearts are one, bound together for goodwill against thieves, liars, and murderers. It is good to see you bonded once again."

"He's always been my deputy, and partner. I can never forget that." Piet said. Both Tiger and Nibs aware that Piet was boosting himself in that statement. Whether by intention or ignorance, it didn't matter, but they both knew Piet all too well, that this was as good a compliment as anyone might get from him.

"We're going to rescue her. Will you join us, Tiger?" He asked.

Dread flooded her, knowing the end result, but she didn't show any sign of her concern. She stood quiet for a moment before speaking.

"This is not our fight. I am sorry, my dear friend. We must continue to the shore, so my father may reach the spirits."

Piet wasn't expecting a decline to his invitation, which was more intended as an appointment, not a request.

"But they are a plague to us all! Surely you want to see them gone, as much as the rest of us?"

"Of course, I do. But we are so few in number that we may not survive to see them gone. I cannot lead my people into that death."

"But Tiger…"

"No Piet, she's right." Nibs interrupted. "This is ain't their fight, it's ours. You can't ask 'dat of 'dem. An' like she say, 'dey been wiped out. 'Dey's nothin' left of 'em. They only chance to survive don' start wit' fightin' pirates."

Of course, Piet didn't like being told 'no.' He began to pout, but since neither of them paid any attention to it, he gave up on it just as soon he started. Tiger Lily had changed in the wake of her father's dying and death. She had inherited the responsibility of the tribe, which included the burden of making decisions for their well-being. Her growing up (and away from Piet) had made her wiser and more risk averse.

"You are a good man, Nibs." Tiger responded in appreciation of him standing up for her and her people. "I am grateful for your understanding. You carry a heavy burden among your people too. I know you are courageous and wise. Do be careful with them. Your fight is more than this, I know, but do not be a fool that mistakes challenge for glory." She said this as she looked past Nibs, at Piet (who wasn't paying attention, and missed the intended message).

"Aye, miss Lily. My boys aren't warriors, but 'dey strong, and 'dey smart. Some may see their last day in this, but it's not one they wouldn't take over a whip or swingin' from a tree. But I know what ya' mean. Ain't no sense in leading them to 'dey death just for death's sake."

Tiger sat beside him, quiet in reflection. After a minute, she took a necklace from around her neck. It was a gorgeous loop of shells, rounded stones, and a golden frog shaped pendant. She handed it to Nibs as she spoke a blessing in her native tongue:

"In her favor, Atabey bless you and keep you; may the Creator shine favor upon you and be gracious to you; the Mother lifts up her countenance to you and gives you strength."

Nibs couldn't understand what she was saying but astutely recognized the symbolism of what she was doing. When she was done, she closed his hand over it and closed her eyes, still quietly mumbling too low to be audibly caught. Nibs felt the power, and now the gravity of the mission weighed heavy on him. He realized this all rested on his shoulders.

He looked at Tiger, their eyes now connecting in reverence. There was a respect between them, for different reasons, neither any lesser than the other. They understood the paths each would be taking tomorrow and silently wished the other nothing but peace and inviolability.

Nibs knew he couldn't count on Piet to stay in rank with him and the Lost Boys. He was hellbent on avenging Wendy and fighting Hook. Suddenly it all became clear: He needed to plan the attack, deliver Piet to Hook, fend off the remaining crew, and get Wendy to safety. It would be a nigh impossible mission, but he believed he had just the strategy to pull it off. He just needed Piet to stay in line long enough to set it all into action.

Tiger Lily excused herself after Nibs' and her supernal moment concluded. She felt the heaviness of Nibs' duty, knowing he was being led straight into danger by Piet's recklessness. Her heart panged, knowing she may never see any of them again. Having known the decimation of her own people, and the atrocities of man, she had seen too much in her life, and this deepened her sadness more than she already felt in mourning her father. She existentially mourned them, yet they were all still here in body with her. She glanced back at Nibs with adoration in her eye before she disappeared from the fire light.

Nibs turned to Piet and started to lay out his plan.

"Piet, I know you gon' go straight fo' that devil wit' de' hook, and I know ain't no way t'stop you. But I need you t'git us down d'ere, and we take care de res.'"

Piet stared off into the flames licking the night sky. He heard Nibs but hadn't given any signal he had. Nibs pressed further,

"Piet, d'is import'nt. We can't get down d'ere w'out you. Here's my thought – you march us down like you takin' us t'market, chain us if'n ya have to. This won't raise no suspicions. When we get to de watah, we git over to ya little island.' From d'ere we can get ready."

Piet turned to look at Nibs, now actively listening. "That just might work, Nibs. But when we get to the island, then what?"

"I know d'ese type. Once d'ey t'ink d'ey in d'e clear, d'ey gon' loose'n up d'eyselves. D'at Hook, he got wha' he want wit' Wendy. He gon' let d'e res' of'm back out inna town. Bes' we get to'm at night."

"Nibs, I'm not so sure. I'm around all of them in town. We should pounce on them there, after they've had their drinks and aren't fit to fight."

"We can't take all these boys into town like that, you know that. D'e minute we pick d'at fight, e'rryone of'm gon' come at us. We lost before we even start. An' he inn't gon' be d'ere anyhow. Plus, he gon' be on de ship w'it Wendy. No way he gon' leave her by herself."

Piet contemplated what he was saying. He wanted to be on familiar ground, and didn't rightly care about anyone else's fight, only his own. But Nibs was right; Hook was too smart to steal her away and go straight back into the place she came from. Truthfully, it would make sense that he would set sail again soon and take all of them away somewhere else. Piet realized the urgency of this and figured Nibs' logic made sense to attack them on the ship, if for nothing else, to keep them from escaping away with Wendy a captive. After some consideration, he spoke again,

"I think we should attack the ship. We stop them from getting away. We sneak in, attack the ship, then attack them, all at night when they won't see us coming."

Nibs knew his old friend well enough, that if he needed to believe it was his plan, he was even more likely to stick to it. He nodded in agreement, and replied, "I think you're right. You get us to d'e ship, we'll get you to d'e Hook."

And so, from there they began hatching the rest of their plan to get Wendy back. For some time, they sat together discussing options, strategies, knowledge, and approach. It all came to the utilization of Piet's little hideaway cay, and all the munitions, piraguas, and various accoutrements stashed away. They would leave in the morning, just as Nibs had propositioned, under the guise of them all being slaves. Anyone passing wouldn't second guess the procession, and this gave them a straight route to town. Once they had devised their plan they spit in their palms and shook on it.

Nibs stood, brushed off the dirt from his pants and left Piet to keep staring into the fire. Only now, he was watching an invisible vision of his heroics in the flames dancing in duel. How glorious the fight was going to be, a spectacle of spectacles. He was energized, eager for dawn to come. He could barely stand it so, that he wanted to take flight now, in this moment, but he swore an oath to Nibs. He couldn't go back on that.

Nibs however, had gone to corral the others, and inform them of what was going to happen tomorrow. He explained that those who were going would be tied up and they would all be led by Piet, the master, until they could all get to the island. From there they would separate and go in different directions in the darkness of night. He asked first for volunteers to stay back, but none of them were willing to miss out on this opportunity, so Nibs had to make a leadership decision, and instructed a select few of the men who were old and strong enough to tend to the farm – more specifically, keep it safe from usurpation. Next, he designated some of the younglings who were not skilled enough to go into battle and still had plenty of life to live without imminent threat of death in this manner. The selected bunch were still a variety of ages, as he needed the variety of skills and sizes of his battalion. These were not easy selections, but he needed to ensure he had the right men for the jobs, both in the attack, and the holding of the farm.

When he had finished telling them what they needed to know at this point, he ordered them all turn in and get rest. Tomorrow would be a long, arduous day, and they would need every bit of energy they could keep. Those selected dispersed and turned in, anxious about what was about to take place. Most had trouble falling asleep but eventually slumbered off in the stillness. Those who were staying behind went off to pack provisions for the others. Nibs however, stood in the field staring up at the stars above. The Taino visitors sat clustered together across the field, seeing him, alone looking upward.

Tiger Lily approached him quietly and stood beside him. He had a tear running down his cheek. She too stared up at the stars, not saying a word, just being there with him. He felt her heart beside his, and finally spoke, "D'ose my ancestors. Tomorrow, I may join them."

"Do not be sad," she replied.

"No. I'm not sad. I've lived many lives, an' I know my time a'come. Jus' did'n t'ink it come d'is a'way. Goin' back to d'e piratin' an' fightin'… trussin' Piet as much as I gotta."

"This Wendy… Piet has spoken of her adoringly. Is she worth your fight? Do you love her?"

"Nah, 's not like d'at. He bring her up 'ere to escape all a'd'at. We wasn' able to keep her safe. She treat us real kindly an' we let her down. She was gon' take over d'e farm 'ere. She don' deserve what comin', so 's only right we try'n bring her back."

"Your intention is noble. I can understand the need you feel but be careful. Those men are dangerous and wickedly crafty. I'd like to see you again on my return, safely back here as you are now."

She looked at him as she said this, and her soft words drew him away from the stars to look down at her. She blushed shyly when their eyes met and then looked down at her feet. He smiled, though she didn't see it, then reached to hold her hand. She looked back up at him, still smiling, and felt the amity stir inside her. Butterflies flittered inside her stomach, and she squeezed his hand back. They looked back up at the endless sky together taking in the celestial magnificence. After a moment, Tiger led Nibs to her tepee.

When morning came, it was oddly quiet. Everyone was observant of what lie ahead for each party. The Tainos had a long, onerous, trek across the Blue Mountains to the Eastern side. It was a difficult journey which would span days through the dense thicket of the jungles. The Lost Boys were apprehensive of their march down to an uncertain end. They knew the stakes but were willing to follow Nibs into the fire to get Wendy back. Piet was focused on Hook, and Hook alone. He had blinders on knowing this was his opportunity to combat the cur that stole Belle away from him all those nights. But also, he looked forward to battling the most notorious pirate, with whom he had already tangled with once to some mild, ironic success. His bravado was fueling his energy but clouding his mind. He was anxious to get going. The opportunity couldn't come soon enough.

Nibs and Tiger emerged from her tepee to find her people deconstructing camp, ready to pack hers away and load up for departure. They had shared an intimate night together, comforting each other for the days ahead, bonded now in mutually earnest respect. Before parting ways, she put her hand on his chest, closed her eyes, and then pressed her head to his chest. She had fallen for him, and wanted to make him hers, but their paths were leading in opposite directions, with only a sliver of hope they would meet again. Nibs spoke,

"Be careful on yah journey. I wish you an' your people safe passage to lay ya fa'tha' with yah ancestors. When you return, please come back 'ere. I will meet you once again, and you can all stay 'ere wit' us."

"You be careful on yours as well, Nibs. Do not fall for Piet's tricks. He can be just as dangerous as those pirates." Nibs chuckled, knowingly. She continued, "I hope that I will see you again, that you return here to your home, safely. And perhaps then I can meet this Wendy."

He hugged her tightly, laid his cheek on the top of her head as she held him. When they separated, they didn't belabor the moment, but simply, with heavy hearts, went their own ways. Tiger went to find Piet and Nibs went to round up his soldiers.

"Piet, thank you for allowing us this place to rest, and for understanding we are now separate people, connected by life but on our own paths of life. I hope that we will keep what we have between us forever, but I pray the spirits bless you today. I pray too, that you will be true to your men, and not lead them to death as you have before. Learn from those times. Be valiant but be careful."

"Tiger, you know I will defeat him. He is no match for my blade. We will run together again soon, you'll see!"

She knew she couldn't change him. No one could ever change him. He was selfish, arrogant, and reckless; all things catastrophic when heading into battle. She had to accept whatever came of this war, as the Fates had already determined the outcome. She showed no emotion to him, but inside she worried he would be cavalier with the others, just as he had been with her people all those years ago. She grabbed his hand and held it in hers for a moment, staring at it, doing everything she could not to think of all the bad things that could happen to him, Nibs, and all the others.

She finally looked up at him. He had a twinkle in his eye – the one she knew from long ago when trouble was afoot. He was eager to be on his way, and all this falderal was just delaying his ability to get onto his quest. Her heart fell deep into her chest as she let go of his hand and said her goodbye. Without further personal offense she joined her people, as they finished their collecting of things, and heading onward on their way. No more was said from her or her people before they quietly disappeared from the farm.

Meanwhile, Nibs had collected his men and was beginning to explain what was going to be happening. The ones staying behind all collected on one side, as he gave them instructions on what to do and what to look out for while they were gone. Those who were coming, he lined up separate from the stay-behinds. Explaining that he was going to lash them together to go, they were leery about the ropes that would bind them. Naturally, they had hoped to never be bound like this again, but Nibs reassured them it was only for show. They apprehensively complied, trusting Nibs, but a primal element hung in the back of their heads, worrying this could be some sort of trap. Many of them had tasted freedom before, only to be cast back into the lot of chattels. They had good reason to be on edge. Again, Nibs reassured them, that under his attention, this was all just to get down to the islet without cause for question. After he had bound them in a row, two-by-two, he passed around water for each of them to drink before they set off on the long walk to town.

When they were ready, Nibs went to fetch Piet to let him know they were set to go. Looking all around, he couldn't find him and began to worry that he had left without them, something that would not be uncharacteristic. Finally, he found him inside the house, which was the last place he thought to look. Piet had made it loud and clear that he would never set foot in his parents' house again, yet here he was, standing inside looking all around.

Softly, recognizing the soberness of this, Nibs said "We's ready."

Piet didn't reply right away, but after a brief silent pause, said, "You've really made this place into something better."

"Ah, we just refitt'd some t'ings. Made it strong again. 'S Wendy de one who made de' place a home again."

Piet looked from one place to the other, recalling certain memories, but pushing them away at the same time. He had no fond memories, as much as he tried to believe. "She really has. This isn't my home anymore, Nibs. Not that it was before, you know, but it's clear now, it's hers."

Nibs stood quietly, not wanting to belabor the thought. He didn't care that Piet didn't feel at home here. He hadn't called it home in years, while they all kept the place alive, if only by a thread. It bothered Nibs in a way, that Piet still felt he had any dominion here anymore. After what he felt was a solemn amount of time, he spoke again, aware they needed to get moving if they were going to make it to their hideaway by dark, "We ought'n'a get goin', Piet. Long road ahead, and de boys all tied up waitin'."

Piet turned to face him, walked past him back out onto the porch, and down onto the lane where the *slaves* awaited transport. He didn't stop to wait, but Nibs had followed him out and was only a few steps behind. He grabbed the lead he'd left on the train of his men, tied it around his own waist, and hustled themselves to keep a believable distance behind Piet. Looking back over his shoulder at his men behind him, and those standing back on the hill, his jaw clenched, and the enormity of this endeavor filled his chest and mind.

XIX

Hook stood at the fo'c'sle railing, staring out. He was deep in thought about what was to happen next. His men followed him for many reasons, mostly the profits he gained and the freedoms he afforded them in doing so, but they were growing agitated with his obsession over Wendy and the game he was playing with her. She was proving to be more his road to ruin. When they had returned to the ship with her, the men were happy to be done with the mission, and made it known with undercutting comments and gripes. The men weren't yet at the point of mutiny, but it wasn't out of the realm of thought to challenge his authority the longer this continued.

They had been in port a long while now, and many of them were near tapped out and were growing anxious to set sail again to refill their coffers. But Hook's plans kept them here indefinitely. And while Port Royal was nothing short of supreme distraction for them, they were, by nature, sailors, and the calling of the sea and prize grew louder and louder. He was running short on time to make any advancement on overturning Port Royal to the definitive pirate's republic.

His idea that he could transform the island to a haven like Captain Kidd had done in Madagascar seemed an unattainable dream now. As emigrants settled in, the demographics were shifting, and the economy was becoming more difficult to persuade. Sugar was controlling force in the Caribbean, particularly Jamaica, and with this came more slave trading and plantation sprawl. Other pirates had abandoned Jamaica for other outposts like Nassau, Tortuga, and even the eastern seaboard of America. Moreover, those who remained lived in a limbo state, where the Governor wasn't enforcing any of the King's decrees, but with rumor of a pardon flitting about, many felt safe enough here to possibly take it, and hang up their hat, should that opportunity ever present itself.

Pulling a slow drag from his long pipe, he contemplated this too. A pardon: from the king... Amnesty from all the barbarity he'd committed over the years. Though this was enticing and allowed a man willing enough to disappear into society, he was too great to be forgotten. He was too much a pirate to his core, that he could ever just walk away from the life he led full of fortune and freedom. He could never settle down on a farm like these others, it seemed so dull in comparison. Dashing his pipe over the rail, the cherry embers dropped to the water like falling stars. He pocketed the pipe and headed back to his cabin.

Inside, Wendy was bound and gagged on the floor. Her hair was a mess, barely pulled back, as strands hung down over her face. Her legs and bare feet marred with dried blood from the scratches inflicted from the branches and briars. She was every bit a disheveled captive, yet not a tear ran down her cheek. She was stronger than that now. Instead, she knelt quietly on his cabin floor, waiting for him. She knew this day might come, that she would have to face him again for deserting. Now here she was, come what may.

The cabin door opened, creaking of old hinges and salt weathered oak. The morning light poured in casting his long shadow toward her. Her stomach knotted instinctively in anticipation of whatever was about to occur. She took a deep breath in through her nose and let it out slowly through the twisted scarf choking her mouth. She glared at him, backlit from the light, dark and ominous. She knew his face well enough though, that she could see him clearly. His eyes seemed to glow ever so slightly in the shadow, making him appear like a specter. He closed the door, shutting off the bright light, and all became equal again.

"I have to admire your tenacity," he spoke calmly. "You tried, and you almost succeeded – getting away, that is – but you knew I would find you."

He paused, letting the dominance sink in. She was unmoved, still kneeling on the ratty, itchy rug.

"We had an arrangement, and you failed to uphold your end of the bargain. I warned you what would happen if you didn't. I went to great expense for you. Those gowns and baubles... those weren't cheap. So, here we are... On the side I so wished not to be."

He paced around her slowly, his leather boots creaking beside her with each step. Still, she remained undeterred, listening to his words. As he came around in front of her, he squatted to look her in the eyes. His hook glinted as he pressed it against her cheek. She made certain to bore into his soul, not dropping her glare at him. He looked her over, the mess she was, sitting tied on the floor, near naked and unpresentable – this thing that had caused him so much trouble. It seemed silly, now. For all her grandeur before, now she was nothing. Insignificant. He pulled the gag from her mouth so she could speak. He knew she wasn't going to scream or try to bite. What good would that do anyway?

He stood back up and walked over to his armoire. She wriggled her jaw to massage the ache. He opened the door and stared at himself the mirror.

For all the infuriation he felt before, and his infamousness for being what the devil himself feared, it was surprising he was so collected and calm. He could see her behind him in the reflection. He continued,

"Your letter... You said many things of interest toward my objective. It seems you were, indeed, able to acquire valuable details in a short span. 'Tis a shame you abandoned so brusquely."

"You are nothing but a scoundrel and a scallywag, like the lot of them, just as I said," she interrupted. She didn't mean to, but the words escaped her before she could stop herself.

"Yes, you did say that too. In fact, if I recall, you dared say I was of an echelon above the governor and his court. Flattered, of course." He paused, awaiting another retort from her, but she remained quiet this time. He sighed, not benefitting from another witty barb.

"I promised you greatness, should you succeed in setting me up to advance my objective here. Again, you have proved to have gained information I thought would take a much lengthier engagement. However, *you* determined your duties fulfilled and flew off with some chuckle-headed fool in the hills. That was not part of our agreement. *You* were not bestowed the authority to dismiss yourself from my employ.

Your letter exposed where power truly lies here, and how to best contain it. I must say, remarkable, really. Alas, instead of being patient and waiting for my reply, you disappeared, thinking yourself absolved.

Now, my dear Wendy, we find ourselves here in this predicament. I must confess, I am at a loss for what punishment is fitting your dereliction, and we shall never know if you could have been everything I had planned for you."

The memory of all that occurred erupted in her brain. She had suppressed everything living on the farm, having distractions to occupy her mind, but here, now, he was dredging up the past, forcing it all to resurface. It ripped open a hole in her that was near healed. She swallowed her feelings, knowing any emotional outburst would gratify him and make her appear weak.

"You set me out as nothing more than a strumpet, bleeding for the jackals to prey. Bait in your hunter's trap. You sold me as a whore, just like the others in that house, no better than them, for they at least received pay for their trade. Your intentions were despicable and duplicitous, and that is *not* what our agreement was. Therefore, any arrangements we had were nullified by your misappropriations. Despite that, and the abhorrence I endured, I still complied by providing you what you sought, and upon that, our compact was fulfilled."

Hook continued to primp as she spoke, hearing her words, but not allowing them to be justified in his mind. He polished his hook to a shine.

"In this place, there is little more purpose for a woman, and if you were in any way conceived as to establish yourself as more, I'm afraid that is where you failed from the start. You are a long way from London, and nary a soul knows you from anything of the sort from whence you came. Did you truly believe you would be welcomed as one of them? You had the social etiquette to carry yourself among them, yes, but you are nothing and you have nothing. What could you have possibly offered in status?"

It all caved in on her. He knew what he was doing the whole time, and she had believed his lies. As vulnerable as she was then, she had fallen for his savoir-vivre. Knowing now, his design, she could see it, and she hated herself for her ignorance and want to step right into the class she hailed from. In retrospect, that didn't exist here, like he said, and it became all too clear: she had been tricked and sold into prostitution for his personal gain.

She thought about Belle now, and how she had been condemned through no fault of her own either. She was always raised to treat people the same, but she had failed this time. Wendy had assumed herself superior to Belle, believing she was something she wasn't, something better than. All the sanctimoniousness Wendy displayed to her, Nena, and the others... Rosie... (*well, Rosie had it coming,* she thought). Everything unraveled in a matter of a few spoken words from this swindler. She sat back on her ankles. She understood now why Belle had been so protective and jealous of her relationship with Piet, and her false sense of freedom when she went off with him. She wished she could offer an apology and hoped that Belle would forgive her at this point.

"Belle... Was she part of your plan? Did you use her the same as me? Did you put her into that life too?"

"No," he said smoothly, drawing out the "o." "She was already established in her ways. She was just the *Pixie* what caught my favor so many years ago and has been mine ever since. Funny though, you should ask about her." He put his brush down and left the cabin.

He returned soon after, banging open the door, shoving a smaller person through the hatchway. The light was still bright outside, so Wendy couldn't see from the backlighting, but could see curves of the body revealing a female form. When he closed the door behind them, the light balanced, and she could see it was Belle. She gasped in surprise and struggled to get to her feet. She was still bound, making it problematic to get up.

The seductress Wendy remembered her to be was not who stood before her now. Malnourished, sickly, and dirty, Belle was a paltry specimen of what she once was. Her cherubic face was purpled and yellowed from the blow Hook had dealt her, her eye still puffy and swollen. The gash was oozing and showing signs of infection, and her clothing was soiled and foul. Iron cuffs chafed at her wrists.

To both of them, the sight of the other came as a surprise. Wendy was empathetically glad to see Belle. Belle on the other hand was incensed to see Wendy and stood in the entry half glad to see Wendy bound on the floor. Wendy cried out,

"Oh, Belle! What has he done to you?"

Not wanting to participate in any of what was happening, Belle didn't respond. Hook nudged her in further and walked over to his desk. Belle felt such animosity toward Wendy, that she wanted to pummel her for what she had had to endure at the cost of proximity to her, but she could barely stand as it was. Wendy pleaded to her again,

"Belle, I'm so sorry…"

"Isn't this touching?" Hook interrupted.

Belle held her shackled arms at her waist and stared at her feet. Wendy continued to kneel on the floor, staring at Belle to catch her eye. Belle wouldn't look at her.

"Now then… We all find ourselves together, though I wish under improved circumstances. You see, both of you have caused me trouble and a setback to my reputation. Neither of you is in any better grace, and as far as I reckon, are deserving of any punishments hereby fancied. The question is: what shall that be? I've a mind to strip you bare and leave you upon the rail for the men to do as they please while the sun beats you to blisters, and the gulls peck at your eyes and sores.

But I don't imagine that is entirely up to me. You have also cost me standing with my men, and while the treat of your snatch may satisfy some at the here and now, I hedge others may not be so concerned with that, having a cornucopia of choices just ashore. So, what am I to do... Methinks the decision's best left up to a court to please my men and restore faith in my interests." He pondered for a moment.

Since they had all recently returned from the raid, the crew were all still aboard the *Jolly Roger*. Hook hoisted Wendy off the floor, and marched both women out of his cabin onto the main deck. He yelled for Smee to gather the men. Belle and Wendy were tossed to the floor like rubbish, humiliated and told to stay put.

Slowly the men gathered before their captain. Some had been rousted from sleep, others from tasks and duties; none of them particularly pleased to be bothered by this again. They clustered in an arc around the captain and the two women at his feet waiting impatiently for what he called them all together for. Increasingly, they wanted nothing more to do with them, and the muted discontent rumbled among them incongruously. When it seemed they were all gathered, Hook began,

"It appears we have a quorum, and so I shall start by saying, it is not lost on me that you have become malcontent."

The grumbles filled the empty morning air a little louder at this observance.

"Yes... precisely. If you will allow me to elucidate, I will confess, that I was determined to convert this haven of ours, into a permanent establishment for the likes of us, and our brethren. I am not above realizing my endeavors have come at a cost, and that like pursuit of a prize unattainable, I must correct course. You have all endured my pursuits, and too, like taking a prize, we must determine our course together..."

The grumbles turned to agreeable mumbles.

"...and so, I've called you all here, to have a say in what we do now. I believe, that with more time and strategy, it could be possible to conquer this island as our own, but it will come at a higher price and a much longer fight against the crown. That means staying here indefinitely and pulling other crews to design a proper rebellion..."

The mumbles turned back to disagreeable grumbles at the thought of staying in port forever, and having other crews mix in.

"...But I am not so half-witted to recognize this is not in your interest. So, I lay it out to you. What is it you would have us do with these coquettes? What is it we shall endeavor on from here? Speak up now or hold your tongues evermore."

The girls sat awkwardly at the feet of all the men like a sacrificial offering. Belle was unmoved by the parade. She wasn't concerned about being passed around, but only hoped death would come soon. Wendy on the other hand had never found herself in this type of predicament and feared retribution from the men. Her brain was scrambling for evasive opportunity or wisdom to appeal to them. She was entering desperation but needed to maintain composure. The men muttered among themselves debating what to do.

Having chased Wendy for days, Simcoe blurted out, "I says we flay 'em, take'm ashore, and pike'm for the rest of'm to sees we don' mess around wit' no troublesome harlots. They ain't wor'f more, and surely ain't gon' be missed."

This garnered some agreeable murmurs.

Jukes offered up, "Oi, let's strap'm to the guns an' have a go wit'm and when we's done, then slit their f'roats and strap'm bare arsed to the prow as our figureheads, an' set sail on to somewhere's else..."

This proliferated more options as they felt more comfortable and willing to offer up. It appeared that they just wanted to one-up each other for the grisliest torture possible. There was a mix of thoughts ranging from macabre revenge to sexual degradations to public humiliation. Nothing seemed off the table, and Hook simply listened as they threw choices out wantonly. He even caught a chuckle at some of them for how impossibly and unrelentingly horrific the suggestions seemed. Belle sat uncaring of anything they spat out. She was ready to die. Wendy though, was not, and in a lull, offered out a plea bargain,

"Neither of us have caused you direct loss to your time or pocket. It is only I who is a nuisance and only to your captain, who has set his sights on the unattainable. He has only a gripe with me and has made her a casualty to not getting his way. Spare her and send her back to her place. She does not deserve such punishment you seek to dispense unto me. Do what you must with me but leave her be. She has endured enough already."

This made the men uproar in laughter. The thought of letting either of them go free was preposterous. This audience was offered carte-blanche retribution, and they were frothing. But not for any particularly appropriate reason. Wendy was right, in that she had caused them no direct offense; it *was* Hook's doing. However, he had stirred them and their groupthink into a frenzy, and the bloodlust needed sating. He stood idly by, watching as his followers fed off the caustic energy, ready to do his bidding and restored their fervor for him as their leader.

Finally, Smee stepped forward knowing that nothing constructive would come from this madness. He might've been the only one with a shred of compassion for the two spirited women, and offered an option that would appeal to them as men and as sailors,

"Lads, you are all eager t' punish these two lasses, an' our cap'n has given you the authority to do so. There is another option if you'll hear me. Y' all wish to return to sea an' plunder once again, no? Let us raise anchor and be gone then! These two are but a hindrance to that departure the longer you men bicker about the worst to be done to 'em. So let us be done and gone. We toss 'em over to the mermaids on the way out and let 'em meet their fate by their wickedness."

Cecco stepped forward in support of Smee's idea, "Aye. Let's be on men. Let's find a nice Spanish ship and fill our pockets again. We've been 'ere too long, and these two isn't worth our delay. Wendy came with us here and wasn't nothin' short of a part of us with her readin' and duelin.' It's her business wif the Cap'n what's got us held up 'ere, so let's just make way. Nuffin' lost but our days ashore, which I ain't so down about, an' I know most of you's ain't either. By the time the wind's in our sails, and Jamaica's at our backs, you won't'n've remembered 'em, or why we wasted any more time. I'm with Smee 'ere. Let's be on our way and leave them to the marmaids."

This was a surprising bolster of agreement from the heavy-handed warrior, but he too had recognized Wendy was only at fault because of the captain's plans. She never wanted any of this. What good came of them killing her, a girl they had come to know at sea when they stole her away from her parents. It accomplished nothing, and their code prohibited killing just for killing's sake without offense.

Hook continued to watch on as the assembly diffused from their adrenaline-fueled mania. In the most unlikely of scenarios, two of his trusted men stood into reason and convince them to leave the prisoners be, in essence. But the quick departure from port was the most agreeable action among them; the women were just a distraction from that. The mermaids were sure to dispose of them which satisfied them enough, and so it was agreed. When all of them had settled on the decision, Hook stepped forward again,

"It is decided then. We raise anchor and leave these creatures to their fates among the sea-devils. You have all come to this decision, and while I wish our time here was more prosperous for our futures, I shall not veto. Enjoy this last evening at liberty ashore as a gesture of my graciousness. Tomorrow, we have our duties to provision and prepare to set sail posthaste. Lock them away. Smee, a word with you in my quarters."

At this he turned and stomped off, slamming the door behind him. He was displeased at the decision, selfishly, but he couldn't go against the crew's decision at this point. He had given them the power to decide, and they had, but he hadn't expected Smee to be the voice of reason, allowing Wendy to go unceremoniously unpunished. Cecco lifted the women up and escorted them below deck to the brig. Smee had the rest of the men start working with Teynte to compile the list of supplies needed to be on their way, telling them he would dismiss them following his conversation with the captain. He then rapped on the captain's door, and let himself in.

"Captain…" he said simply, to announce his presence.

Hook stood again at his armoire, glaring into the mirror.

"Smee, I have trusted you as my mate since the day you found me relieved of my hand. You could have left me to bleed out and die in the gutter like any other scab. You have always been executor to my whims and desires, unfailingly. Yet, now, you undermine my chances to gain any future with that which I have in motion at present. And what's more, you have granted that contemptuous cunt reprieve from the men most deservingly suited to rid her of her precious life."

"It's not her the men give care about, cap'n. They're losing patience with you, and I'll tell you plain, they're not far from a mutiny…"

"Mutiny?!" he screamed now, unable to contain his anger. "For all I've done for these dogs? The lavish riches I've bestowed on them from our prizes? The exceptional life they've lived on the account, while others die at

253

the gallows in droves? Those scurvy knaves should lick my boots for all I've afforded them! The ungraciousness confounds me! Damn them all!"

"Might I be remindin' you; these men would follow you into the belly of hell for pastime, but they go to sea for pleasure, cap'n. It's where they belong. Your plans for taking this place for your own, that's your plan, not theirs. Nary a one of'm bought in on that, and they just been lett'n you be with it. But I hear what they whisper about when they think I isn't listen'n."

Hook heaved deep breaths, "And what's that they say, Smee? Do tell."

"Well, cap'n, they think you plumb silly for it all, and that's it. Ain't none of'm happy 'bout sittin' round here waitin' on the world to change for the likes of them. Them fancy pants sure isn't gonna let it happen here."

"They think me mad?" Hook asked, eyes burning.

"Truth is, cap'n, they ain't got no interest in settlin' down here. It's a jolly time 'ere, it is. But what're they gonna do when all this carryin' on dries up and they ain't got two coins to rub t'gether? Not'n a one of'm gonna make a life outta cane farmin'. That isn't nothin' of interest to'm. An' from what I reckon, not a spot for'm here to do so anyhow. Now, if you wanna stay an' see it out, I'll stick wit' ya. 'bout time I saw m'self outta this... lived a good life'n it wit' my head still on m' shoulders. But if'n you do, you need let them go on t'other things. Can't be havin' both."

"Those are my men, Smee. It stands that they should stick with me and do as I say as their captain."

"Don't work like that, an' you know it."

Hook snarled resentfully. Smee was right, but Hook didn't have to like it.

"And so that's that, I suppose? We just abandon all progress and leave? Those draggle-tails get nothing coming?"

"Aye, the vote said we set sail, an' that's what we'll do. Maybe best to get out an' come back 'nother time 'round an' try again. Though, can't say those girls won't get noffin', we said we'd set'm out for the mermaids. That'll be worse than I'd wish any fellow crossed me."

Still angry and disappointed, Hook sat on his bunk kicked off his boots and laid down. Before shanking the curtain closed, he told Smee,

"This isn't over, Smee. There's a lot of daylight between now and beef-headed decisions. Send them on their ways. I will readdress this after taking rest."

Meanwhile, Cecco had taken Belle and Wendy below, and tossed them in the locker. He'd stood for a minute, sizing up Wendy, recalling her choosing to duel him and the jest he'd taken with her. He thought about the nights she'd read to them and taught the others how to read. Now, here she was, fallen from high, locked in the hold. He may have been a cold-hearted killer of men, but he still had a soft spot for the fairer sex. He just couldn't do much more about it now. So, he left them be.

Belle curled up away from Wendy, not wanting anything to do with her. Wendy, on the other hand began scheming how to escape as soon as they were alone. She tugged on the heavy bolt, banged the iron bars, and pulled at the rusty hinges. Of all the things she had aspired to learn in hopes of sparing her life, nothing helped her in this situation. All seemed lost, and she cursed their predicament. Belle spoke without making eye contact,

"You can't get out. I've been locked in here for days. It's no use."

Wendy hadn't expected Belle to utter a word, given their interactions thus far, and was glad to hear her voice.

"We can't give up. There must be a way…"

"Enough, Wendy. You can't get out. This is a prison made for keeping pirates locked away."

Not to be deterred, she paused to talk *to* Belle, "Belle, I'm sorry. You must believe me. I never meant for you to get entwined in this… this mess. I was ignorant to all of it, promised splendor for his bidding. I know now, it was all a ruse, and I was not kind to you as I should have been. I'm sorry for treating you any less than you deserved. I am no better than you, and I want nothing more than to help get you out of here."

"I didn't think you any different than the others who came in entitled. It takes time. You're not the first one. What you did was take Piet away from me and run off with him. He chose you over me."

"Oh, Belle, No! I'm sorry… I know it looks that way… but I never… He… He was kind to me, and I trusted him. I never intended to steal him away from you. He was a friend to me – like you."

Belle turned now to face Wendy, increasingly angry, purging the hurt she'd pent up throughout this series of events.

"You ran off with him! Twice!" she cried. "He took you to his farm. He took you away from this place. He NEVER took me away!"

Wendy sat down and tried to hold Belle, but she rebuked her, and screamed at her, "No! You don't get to…" But Wendy shushed her and deflected her shoving motions.

"Belle, I asked him to get me out of there. You know what happened, and I asked him to help me escape. I'm sorry we didn't, *he didn't,* think to bring you with us. The whole thing was unplanned and sudden. That's why Hook is so angry with me and wants me dead. And do you know what, Belle? He didn't stay! He took me to his farm, and he left just as soon as we'd arrived. I've been up there this whole time with the Lost Boys all on my own."

Belle shifted quizzically, "What do you mean? Where did he go? Where has he been? Who are the *Lost Boys*?"

The missing pieces began to fall into place between them. Piet, as usual, had created a rift, and had left them assuming the other was the root cause.

"Yes, the same night we'd arrived, he disappeared. But that is because I refused to share his little hideaway fort. He doesn't use the house, Belle, he stays in a crude little shelter he made in the woods. I wouldn't spend the night in there, and I can only guess, his feelings were hurt, and that is why he left. I don't know where he went, but he was gone in the morning. If he didn't come back here, I haven't the faintest idea where he went.

The lost boys are Piet's slaves, but they are all free men. There is a band of them up there, all living together and keeping the farm. They are such wonderful souls. You will like to meet them, especially Nibs. He is their leader of sorts. He and the others helped rebuild the main house and allowed me to live in it. I would enjoy sharing it with you, away from all of this. If we ever escape this with our lives, I will take you to the farm myself."

"He didn't come back here. At least not before I was stolen. If he is here, he's made no efforts in coming to *my* rescue. But if what you're saying is true, there's no telling where he is, and as far as I care now, he can stay there."

"Belle, I am telling you the truth. I have no reason to lie to you. You must believe me."

Belle paused to think. She didn't know what to make of any of this. She had built up such contempt for Wendy, yet here she was locked up beside her, and all she could feel was hope; hope that they *could* escape and get away to the farm like she was describing.

XX

Piet and his gang of slaves debouched in the low plains below nearing Spanish Town. They had been on the road for hours now, making a rather quick pace to get to the harbor. But it was here they would encounter the most potential for opposition, so it was imperative they keep their eyes to themselves and act the part.

As expected, the closer they got to population, passers-by began appearing. Men on horses stared them down with supremacy and disdain, distrusting them as a generality. Though, for as many ugly looks as they received, staying in step with Piet, no one stopped them or said a word to them. Piet was so focused on his coming excitement; he perfectly ignored the men he led. This demeanor aided in the façade they were attempting to maintain as though he actually was leading an assemblage of slaves to whatever destination.

By early evening, they had put the outskirts of Spanish Town behind them and were fringing the bay toward Kingston. The sun bore on them most of the day, making them weary and dehydrated. They were close to the little inlet they would be able to duck out of once it was dark enough to go undetected. Until then, they needed to keep the charade up, but their pace as a collective was slowing. They needed to rest, and so they took shelter under a grove of mahoe trees. Knowing they couldn't move out to the island while daylight still shone, they would have to wait. Piet paced impatiently.

"Piet, sit. You gon' draw 'ttention to us. Only be a short while a'fore we get out dere."

"I can't sit Nibs. We need to get to Wendy."

This took Nibs by surprise for a moment. He had just said they needed to get to Wendy, as in, to rescue her, as a collective – the entire original plan. He hadn't said anything about Hook. This puzzled him but wasn't about to ruin the sentiment.

"Yes, I know. An' we'll get to her jus' as soon as we able. But 'til then, we gotta wait for de sun t'go down. Why don't we just go over de plan some more? Dese boys still a lil unsure just what we gotta do."

This quelled Piet enough to join the group and sit, but he did so with his back to them as he stared out toward the roadstead congested with all manner of ships. He was fixed on one ship in particular, mixed among the others, protected by those in the vicinity. He could see movement but couldn't make out anything discernible. Without looking back, he called to Nibs,

"That's it right there."

Nibs, unsure what he was talking about issued a, "huh?"

"That one," he replied pointing slightly off to the right of straight ahead. "The one about five ships back, surrounded by the others. No flags waving, with the three masts. Black with the red stripe. That's the one. Hook's ship."

Nibs sat up, peering across the bay, laying eyes on the demonic vessel. Piet's description made it easy to spot. From where they sat presently, Nibs couldn't get a great view, but he would be able to get a better look from the island this evening. Piet should even have a spyglass among the stores, which would benefit their spying. Seeing their target, and the protective obstacles surrounding it, he studied the ship and the locations of the others around it.

He sat surveilling, while the others lazed about, growing bored of inaction. Occasionally, he would grunt inquisitively, and a few of the Lost Boys would look up at him, then out at the ship, but never comprehending what he had noticed; nor would they. Nibs was observing the movements of each ship, and the crews on board from his perspective as a former pirate. He was calculating it all, from the current making them drift, to the shifting tide, to the formality to which any crew carried on – and none of them, he was noticing – was adhering to any sort of discipline while at rest.

The unplanned respite was giving him a superb ability of seeing and visually preparing for what they faced. The gears spun in his head of how to attack now that he had purview. It was all coming together in the most exceptional way. His sketch of an idea before might've resulted in real bloodshed, but now, he had a scheme coming together that would surely be more effective, deliberate, and destructive. He pulled the team together to set the motion.

"Piet, we all gon' need t' eat. Been all day, an' none'a us had a bite yet. We gon' need 'dat strength inna few hours. We also need'n a boat big enough to carry us all across de way. Les go back into town down there an' you keep actin' like you is. You get y'self a meal and set us up out back for whatev' they give us like they would. While you in dere, you talk'm up an' find us a boat, an' aft'a we's supped, we get ourselves on to dat island and make ready."

Piet nodded in understanding and agreement. Nibs was right about needing the transport, they didn't have a fleet of canoes stashed away for them to escape in, those were all still piled up on the island. He liked the plan, and the idea of swindling a boat from some unsuspecting mark added a little thrill to his agenda. And so, they all proceeded onward toward Kingston to find a place for supper.

Acting as a slaver, it didn't take much effort for them to walk into town and find a place to dine. Piet was allowed in the establishment, while the others were told to sit out back where the negroes belonged. There they were given what barely passed as a stew made of corn meal, scraps of stringy meat, and vegetables. Together they all sat, still bound together, as a watchful eye kept tabs on them from inside. In contrast, Piet was treated to a hearty meal and drink. He set to conversing with the few folks that were inside on simple things such as the latest ships coming in with provisions, slaves, and other privileged informational topics. Eventually, he slid into the conversation about seeking out a boat, and if anyone knew of any for hire. Those who had any intel pointed him toward the wharf, saying there were some dory men down the way who might be willing to ferry him to where he needed, assuming he was attempting to get out to a ship based on the conversations. This was all the info he needed. He now knew there were boats accessible nearby. He casually finished his meal, paid, and got up to leave.

By now, evening was creeping in, the stars in the sky beginning to twinkle through the fading light. The sideways smile of the crescent moon lit the land below with a dim glow. The lack of moonlight was optimal for their mission, providing a curtain to work under – with just a sliver of luminance to aid in their seeing what they were doing. Piet led the slaves down to the docks. There were still a few men milling about, jawing on about the day's events. They took note of Piet and the slaves, just as Piet took note of them. With them about, stealing a boat would be impossible, so Piet had to get creative. He approached two of the fishermen, who by now were a few drinks in.

"I say, I'm in need of hiring one of your boats. What do you say to an arrangement?"

They looked him up and down, before one of them replied insultingly, "Can't think'a any arrangement, what involves you and any of my boats, squib."

Not one to be deterred, Piet replied, "I'm an able waterman, friend, and I have this lot of slaves to deliver to the captain out there before nightfall. I shall return your boat and repay you 2% of the sale for your trouble."

The fisherman laughed at Piet's proposal. "10%, and you can take that one." He pointed to a dinghy bobbing against the seawall.

"That won't do, and for that matter doesn't seem fit to even get us all out there. You'd lose your boat and your recompense before we started out, I think." Piet scanned the lot, and pointed to a jollyboat, "That one, and 5%."

"Piss off, you're not taking that'n. That's one of me best, and I'll not have some bucket tosser run off with it."

"7%. That stands to make you a fetching wage for nothing more than sitting here slugging ales while I attend to the business what will pay you out for letting me borrow a boat large enough to ferry those creatures to sale."

The weathered drunk scratched his stubbled face considering the offer. The kid had a point. Assuming all went to plan, he wasn't out anything and was due a sizeable return for letting his boat for a few hours.

"Alright then. 8%, and you bring it right back to this very spot and tie it off when ye done."

To Piet, the amount never mattered. He would have agreed to any number, since there was never going to be a sale, and the boat was likely never to be seen again. So, he nodded in confirmation. "8% for your trouble, aye."

He ushered in the slaves and Nibs loosed the docking line. Piet sat in the bow, while two of the slaves wet the oars and began pulling out into the bay. The two fishermen watched them leave and went back to telling their tales and drinking. From Piet's perch, he could see the township – and the docks – disappearing. As they got further out into the bay, all sight of the men were lost as the coastline curved around. When he felt they were well out of sight, he instructed the Lost Boys to make for the hideaway cay as intended.

Skidding onto the tangled bines of the mangrove, the overgrowth had made the cay much wilder than it had been before. It had been a long time since Piet had spent any time here for maintenance, and the natural growth had begun to reclaim spaces that had been carved out. This would need attention, he thought, but for now, it offered supreme camouflage for them.

He hopped out, excited to see his old playground again, and inspect all the treasures he'd left behind. The Lost Boys followed. Some had never been here before, some had, but again, it had been years, so the memory of such a strange place was distant. Bits and parts were familiar, but now, in the dark, it looked spooky with the Spanish moss draping down. They unbound themselves, and tied off the boat on the slip, so it wasn't obvious and visible.

All of Piet's old things were still here, covered in dirt and leaves, abandoned long ago. The periaguas were still hanging among the trees, disguised as intended. Crates were falling into ruin from the dense tropical weather rotting them. Barrels crouched in the shadows, some of them water casks now turned rancid and burst. But the items most important, buried safely and still protected from the elements, were the stores of weapons, shot, and powder. Piet brushed off the trap door, exposing the cache like true hidden treasure. Swords, pistols, ammunition, among the stock all wrapped in cloth to keep them from spoiling, ready for battle.

The Lost Boys gathered around to see what was buried within. To their surprise a hoard enough to arm a throng was displayed, and Nibs was the first to reach in following Piet. The two of them handed the various weapons out so they could inventory what was usable, and what would need to be discarded or repaired. When it had all been sorted, a pile of swords and cutlasses lay glinting in the night, an orderly line of pistols and muskets lay beside the swords, and lastly a stockpile of gunpowder and ammunition was collected. All things considered; they had plenty of tools for war among them. The volatile gunpowder supply though, is what Nibs found most important. He inspected it closely to see that it was all still dry and useable. Piet picked at the scabbards and blades until he found the one that suited him. After he had chosen his, he invited the Lost Boys to take their pick.

When everyone had chosen their weapons, Nibs stepped in like a commander to authorize each with what they had selected. Most would be best suited with a blade because guns were unreliable and took too much time to reload in close combat. They would have one shot, and they needed to be true – or else. He assessed each one of them and then separated them into groups and began to layout his plan of attack. Piet continued to dig through his things looking for anything he could use to his advantage, though more accurately finding things he'd forgotten he'd stolen – a bird cage, for instance. Then he remembered, the last time he was here. It was that brief stop with Wendy in the rain. They hadn't stayed long, but he recognized the significance of being here again, and that was for her rescue. He turned to listen in to what Nibs was saying, and where he would play his part in getting to Hook.

By a show of hands, Nibs asked of the Lost Boys who could swim or at least felt comfortable being in the water around the *Jolly Roger*. About 6 of them raised their hands. This wasn't a strong number, but it would do. These men would be the start of the battle, and possibly the most crucial to its success. For the others, he kept them separated and paired the others off as best he could - one with a gun and one with a sword, until they were all counted. Then he began drawing symbols in the dirt at their feet. He carefully explained his plan of attack like an orchestra performing the finale of a Wagnerian opera. Detailing each premeditated and calculated step, each one compounded on the other in a mounting fury meant to confuse, debilitate, and defeat their adversaries.

When he had finished, he looked up at them all to indicate if anyone had any questions, now was the time to ask. In just a few hours' time, they would be creeping into the night, futures unknown whether they might live or die. The sobriety of this moment was enough to weigh heavily on them all. They each stood quiet, taking it all in, processing, memorizing. Seeing that no one was going to reply, he redirected their attention at him, and he spoke,

"My braddahs… Tonight we go into de dahkness to face an enemy of enemies. A devil like no otha'. I know summa you fret on if you gon make it to tomorrow. You know… you not promised a tomorrow, only guaranteed a yess'a'day. We gotta live for now. I know dere's a chance I mightn't make it, but dat's a chance I'ma' choose for Wendy. She been good to us, an' we gotta be good to her for dat.

'Cause'n the way I see it, any one'a us could be one'a dem souls at the end of a whip or worse. You don' die with worth in no field. No sir. But tonight, we're warriors, and if the lord choose to end me, well that's alright by me, 'cause I goin' out fightin' pirates for a purpose, not by some nasty masta' wit' a card to kill fa' nothin'. We's the ones gon' stand up against d'ese rascals. Even if'n we don' win, we still make'a try. That's not fa' nothin', ya see.

Now, we gon go out d'ere, and we gon' fight like it's our last day on this earth, 'cause even if we don' see tomorrow, we'll have seen today and today is good. And tomorrow, you'll be a hero no mattah what, and they'll talk about you for years to come. Might even write books about you! So, let's raise our heads, and let's go get Wendy back, huh?!"

The boys all lifted their chins a little higher and cheered. They all gathered the things they needed and began to prepare; even Piet lent a hand readying the canoes and the supplies. Soon, the battle would be waged, and there was no turning back. Adrenaline surged through arteries, fueling them, erasing fear from their minds. Piet was ready. He was anxious. He wanted to get out there and pick that fight with Hook. Nibs' speech had urged him on just as it had been intended to do for the Lost Boys. They all cohesively bustled together, many hands working as one team.

Everything was now ready, they only needed to wait for the signal. Standing at the waterline, they waited, camouflaged by the growth of the mangrove. Nibs peered out, using one of Piet's stolen spyglasses watching the movements on the *Jolly Roger*, but also on the surrounding ships. It wasn't just Hook's ship that he was targeting. The others would play a crucial part in the attack, serving as hiding spots in the water so they could sneak in for the kill. All the other ships had their own crews milling about, but it was nearing the hour they would all start to turn in or not be so present as they currently were. Piet began ticking, his leg shaking in impatience. Nibs reached over and put his hand on his shoulder to get him to settle. He needed Piet calm and focused.

After what seemed like hours, Nibs finally gave Piet the signal to go. He was going out to set the bait. If he were seen paddling around, it wouldn't raise any real concern, but if they had all gone out and been detected, all would be lost. If the coast was clear, he would give signal to Nibs who was watching his every move back on the cay.

Paddling his canoe, he weaved through the obstacle course of massive ships with a skill unrivaled. No one above on any of the decks seemed to take notice, and so he continued to cruise around between them all. Nibs would lose sight of him as he ducked behind a ship, and his pulse would quicken, but then Piet would reappear in another location, sliding through the water with ease. Finally, Piet felt he'd toured the area enough and gave signal to Nibs believing it safe.

The Lost Boys all processed from their refuge; a flotilla of canoes loaded with four men apiece. Two canoes carried only one person each but held powder kegs in the bow covered by branches. As they neared, they split off into different directions to gather alongside the hull of the *Jolly Roger*. The loaded canoes took a more direct path toward the mark and would tie up together on the rudder under the overhang of the captain's castle. They were trailed by two other canoes from the party as watchful support.

When they arrived, Piet was nowhere to be seen, which hopefully meant he had already accessed the ship, and was waiting. Nibs and the others quietly lashed the canoes together flanking the rudder on both sides. They wedged them in and tied them tight to minimize the banging from sway. The trailing two canoes came along on either side, and the men transferred into them once they had been secured, and paddled off, hugging the hull line forward. Nibs was the only one to remain and sparked the fuse. Once lit, he jumped into the water and swam as fast as he could underwater for as long as his breath could take him.

Under the cover of the branches, the fuses crackled in chaotic flash, racing toward the payload. The casks detonated violently, sending a ball of fire and shrapnel into the black night. The explosion was so powerful and concentrated by the aft balcony overhang, that the rudder was instantly eviscerated. Shards of burning wood floated in scattershot pieces, sizzling in the inky water. Fire climbed the remnants of the splintered rudder trying to escape the water, as the now compromised ship began to list, dousing the low burning tinder.

All ships and crews in the bay were now on high alert. The deafening sound of the explosion had attracted the attention of everyone, and they all began to panic. Nearby crews scrambled to see what was happening. Were they the next target? No one knew in the moment, but what they did notice, was a burning ship, and that meant they were in imminent danger. Instead of gathering their guns in retaliation, they hurried to flee, before the fire jumped to them, and reduced them to a charred heap at the bottom of the sea. But there was no room to maneuver, so ships began tangling themselves in their escape with rigging, spars, and lines crashing into each other in haste.

Meanwhile, on the *Jolly Roger*, the remaining crew who hadn't gone ashore earlier when dismissed, were rushing to protect their ship. They had sprung to action immediately, even before knowing what the situation was. The problem though, was the fire was unreachable. Smee, being the pragmatic leader that he was, sent a handful down into the ballast to contain any internal fire and try to stymie the flooding water. Topside, he and the others raced to extinguish the external fire before it could creep up into Captain Hook's quarters but more importantly, the highly flammable rigging and sails aloft.

At the shudder and deafening sound of the explosion, Hook bounded out of his quarters as well to see what was afoot. The whole ship lurched, knocking his things across the cabin. He was raving mad, a lunatic of fury. In the delegation of snuffing out the inferno, he was equally invested and aiding in the salvation of his ship. Flames licked the railings, inching toward the dry ropes. If they caught, the whole ship would burn to the waterline. He barked orders to his men to hoist buckets of water and drown the fire from all sides and soak the rigging lines. His attention was so fully occupied, that he didn't see Piet approach from behind.

Piet had every opportunity to run Hook through in that moment, and end his reign of terror, but there was no honor in doing that. Piet's vanity wouldn't allow for him to be cut down so easily. Killing a man like this from behind was cowardly, and Piet wanted the challenge, the game. He wanted the fight. He wanted to properly beat Hook and become the thing of legend. The one they talked about for years to come.

He called out to his adversary, "Hook! Your ship will burn to the bottom of the sea, you scurrilous scoundrel."

Hook wheeled around. At the sight of Piet, all the wrath from the devil's chasm roiled throughout him, and his eyes burned of vehement hellfire. "A pestilent puppy come to play! Damn ye, boy! I shall cut you down like the cub you are, and I shall piss on your bones!"

"You may try, you old louse, but I will best you again and take your other hand from you to feed to the crocs for pudding!"

Hook paused, trying to make sense of what Piet had just said, and what foggy memory Hook had of that fateful night suddenly burst into his frontal lobe with such blinding clarity.

"You unlicked cub! You're the urchin from the Inn; the one Belle is always so sweet on. I shall take great pleasure in killing you this time, but not before I have ended her life before your dying eyes."

"You won't have the chance, Hook. I've come to put an end to you and your shadow over this place. Give me Wendy, and I will see that your death is quick." At this he had his sword drawn, aimed at Hook, signaling the fight.

"Oh, I see! You have come for the other one. How delicious is this? Cecco, fetch our guests from the locker, and bring them to me. I do believe they should witness the death of this flea."

Cecco, reluctant to abandon the fire brigade, did as he was told. As he disappeared into the hold below, the Lost Boys ascended the ladders, swooping in from the fore once the pirates had gone aft. A swarm of black bodies crawled over the railing like a tangle of spiders. They drew their weapons, backing Piet in force. Hook was undeterred, but grinned malevolently, the red in his eyes glowing hot like the flames crawling upon his ship. He called over his shoulder to his men,

"Look alive, you swabs! The devils have come to play. Tis a shame they will die and hang from the bow for the gulls to peck them to pieces."

Shots exploded from the Lost Boys' pistols, dispatching flash, ball and smoke into the night's void. They wasted no time in setting the fight in motion, with every intent to cut the pirates down to improve their odds against them. Because the pirates were preoccupied with the fire, they had not had time to arm themselves and were easy targets, however the unskilled shots were not all landed. Most missed their marks, though of the salvo a few landed true clipping three of the pirates, but mortally wounding Alfred and Scourie. Alfred dropped heavily to the deck, immobilized from a chance hit to the back of his neck at the base of his skull, but Scourie took his to the chest just as he turned around. The blast was enough to knock him back over the railing, falling to the water below.

Nibs was worried now, because the shots were not part of his plan, but were the result of nerves of the Lost Boys, and when the first shot had exploded, the others followed in response. The battle was on, and now he could only hope that with the few pirates now aboard, his men wouldn't incur an overwhelming loss. As the pirates charged, the Lost Boys braced for attack, terrified of what was coming at them. Behind them, the flames reclaimed its grab and climbed higher, setting a nightmarish backdrop to the scene.

The smashing swords clanged loudly as bodies collided in combat. The Lost Boys were at a disadvantage in skill against the assailants but had the advantage in number. Valiantly they held their own the best they were able, but it was becoming evident they were unlikely to best the pirates by sword alone. Nibs called for the gunmen to fall back and reload while they continued to hold them off. On both sides, they took the occasional slice or stab, but onward they fought. When the gunmen had reloaded and were ready to fire, they couldn't find clean shots that didn't risk hitting their own men, so they scrambled around trying to find angles or openings.

Smee, had still been single-handedly attempting to quell the burning ship. He had been left alone to the effort and was not winning his own battle. He was hoisting buckets from below to toss on the flames, but they had grown unmanageable. The pirates below had succeeded in extinguishing the internal fire. The explosion had ripped a gaping gnarled hole in the stern just at the waterline. The jagged opening sipped the ocean in, and the men were able to use the water to extinguish the crawling flames. Once they'd put out the fire, they got hard to work at trying to temporarily repair the hole as best they could, so it would at least stop the ship from taking on more and more water. With all the urgency and barking they were doing; they hadn't heard the fight occurring above.

Meanwhile Piet had engaged Hook, and for all the enmity welling inside Hook, he knew he mustn't allow Piet the upper hand of a rash and impulsive attack. Instead, he toyed with him, cat-and-mousing him, leading him away from the others, so that he could control the fight in open space. This is where he would gain his advantage to kill the boy. With all the men clamoring away forward, the two of them circled each other midship.

"Let Wendy go, and I'll spare you Hook. You can leave this place with your life but never return again. If you refuse, I will relieve you of more than just your other hand this time."

"I will see to it, boy, that you will die a slow, wretched death – but not before you watch me rid this place of those two harlots whose tits you caudle before your bloody eyes." Hook said this with such a guttural snarl, it made Piet's blood run cold.

Almost too perfectly timed, Cecco appeared escorting both women. The detonation was terrifying to them in the dark recesses of the ship, jarring them into a panic. As Cecco lugged them out into the open, they assumed they were being dragged out to meet a torturous end Until now, neither of them had any cognition the other was on the ship. Piet stood dumbfounded at both Belle *and* Wendy as prisoners under Hook's charge. They too were equally surprised to see Piet and the tussle of black marauders.

Hook took a countering stab at Piet while he was distracted by the sight of them. In the last flash of a moment, he saw the attack coming, and parried, dashing the attack. If he hadn't, responded so quickly, the blade would have split his abdomen asunder. Instead, it sliced across his forearm cutting the muscle like soft cheese. Hook growled and reset himself. His one free opportunity to win had been spoiled. They now squared up, stepping carefully not to set themselves in danger of being off balance. Piet jabbed a couple times to provoke his adversary, but Hook merely slipped with panache, laughing at the feeble attempts. He finally stepped back from Piet, putting distance between them, and called to Cecco,

"Which one do you think he cares most about, mate? What say we find out? I do think he's not quite the paragon he feigns to be. He's come for Wendy but gets his milk from Belle. I am curious…"

"I came for you Hook. I came to finish what I started so long ago with your one hand. I should have finished you then but hoped that beast had done the job properly. You're nothing but a sorry excuse for a pirate and your time is run out. You don't scare me, and I will take them both in victory as you lie dead upon your back."

Hook scoffed, "I have found such devotion preparing this for the day I met the one that gave it to me. Here, now, to discover t'was you. This brings me such satisfaction to let you feel the pain it can exact, as I plunge it through your scrawny neck. But first, as I promised you will witness their lives slowly taken bit by bit. Cecco, you may begin. Do your worst but do make sure they are living enough to watch their beau's life dispatched."

Cecco heard the call and motioned to begin their suffering. Both were slopped on the deck beneath him, tied together by ropes like livestock for slaughter. Belle, still resolved to be rid of all this (and Piet), closed her eyes hoping it would soon end. Wendy twisted lamely in an attempt to fight off the brute above her. Suddenly her eyes stung with hot, sticky gore, and her mouth tasted of sour, salty guck.

In all the clamor, they hadn't been paying attention to the Lost Boys' overtaking the crew. In the firelit night, Nibs stood a few paces away holding a blunderbuss as a cloud of dense smoke wafted into the night revealing his ebony face. He had managed to break free from the skirmish and saw what was transpiring aftward. When he saw Cecco pull the cuttoe from his belt, he pulled his last braced pistol and fired. Notoriously inaccurate, the gun had blasted the ball low and to the right, a dangerous arc – which any lower curving might've struck Wendy – but took impact on Cecco's sternum and ribcage as he had leaned down toward her. The bullet exploded the bone and lodged in near his stomach. Not an instant kill, but it was enough to knock him backward, clutching the wound.

Piet took this opportunity to pounce at Hook. There were few men known that could best Hook at a sword, but just as he had nearly pierced Piet before, Piet had nearly run his blade through Hook now. This set off a fierce bout of swordery. Back and forth they danced, their blades smashing against each other. Piet would gain advantage, and in an instant Hook then had the upper hand. They fought ferociously, both hoping to be the victor over the other. The passion and determination made the fight a spectacle. Hook had not anticipated Piet's adroitness, but this only made him work harder toward triumph.

In the background Smee had given up and knelt in exhaustion as the crackling timber mocked him. Fiery embers of hemp fell from the sky like fireflies as it climbed into the rigging. As Smee acknowledged defeat, his attention was drawn to the duel occurring between his captain and the boy. The women were being aided by a dark-skinned fellow, and from his perch he could see Cecco's muscular legs kicking about in a trail of blood. He scampered down to aid his mate, but no sooner had he descended the ladder, Nibs aimed his pistol toward him. He threw his hands up and pointed at Cecco. Nibs kept his eyes trained on Smee as he finished cutting the women free.

By now, the Lost Boys had overpowered the crew, but not without loss of their own. They only eked out victory due to number, firepower, and the surprise of the attack Nibs had calculated exceptionally well. Only four of the nine pirates still stood. Seven Lost boys remained, Lutalo standing ahead of all of them with his pistol ready. They all stood eyeing the other in the event any further aggression was instigated. Typically, the pirates would have fought to the death, but in this case, it was more advantageous for them to live to fight another day and salvage their ship. The others on shore would surely see the beacon of fire on the blackened sky and come soon to their aid. This would turn the tables in their favor against the maroons.

As Nibs cut the women free, Wendy jumped up to hug him, and just as quickly asked him to attend to Belle.

"Take the others and get her out of here, now!"

"We not goin' w'out you, Wendy…"

"Go, Nibs, I'll find you. You must go, now before you can't at all."

"Aye… Find us on Piet's island. You know that one?"

"I do, now go!"

Wendy, then rushed over to Cecco who sat prone against the steps leading to the quarter deck, as Smee was fussing over him to stop the bleeding. She knelt beside him, taking both by surprise. Smee told her to hold pressure on him, and to keep him still. He ran off below, promising to return momentarily. Wendy pressed with all her might against his wound, so much that he howled at the added pain she was causing him.

Cecco coughed angrily, "Blast it all, get off me woman! I was going to slice you apart, bit by bit. Both you and the other one…"

"Yes, but only because he told you to. I don't believe you would have on your own will, or you would have done so upon all the other occasions we've had together. This is not between us, and for that I will do what is within me to help you. This is… I should say, was, between him and me. No one else should pay for that."

As she was finishing her thought, Smee returned with the surgeon's kit to try to dig the ball out of Cecco's belly, and said to her, "Miss Wendy, this's gonna get mighty ugly. You ought'n be here. Not a place for a lady. Go on now."

In the stalemate among the Lost Boys and the pirates, they backed off in their separate directions. The pirates dispersed and continued to stamp out the fire and tar up the gaping hole below. The Lost Boys backed off, waiting for a command from their leader, uncertain just what they should do now.

Nibs called to them and explained that they needed to get off the ship now, before the other pirates returned and waged another battle against them which they were sure to lose. He told Lutalo to stay with Wendy, but to get back to the island as quickly and safely as possible. Once they were off, Lutalo made Wendy aware he was with her and offered to help however he could. Smee took one look at his muscular frame and instructed him to hold his mate down; it was about to get very physical.

The remaining crew scrambled about on fire brigade. They began cutting the mizzen rigging down, so it would be free from the other shrouds, in hopes it wouldn't spread so wildly. If they were to lose the one mast, it was still better than the entire ship smoldering into the sea entirely. The remaining lines, tight under the pressure from the loss of the full distribution, snapped violently toward the sky as they were cut from their stays. The fire was still consuming everything in its path, as fire is ought to do, but once the rigging was freed, they swung like fiery vines. The furled sail was the imminent danger. If it caught, it would be the catalyst to bring the entire ship to its demise. The men turned to the base of the mast, and in a frenzy of orchestrated swings, began cutting down the mast. Sharp chunks exploded from the trunk as they hacked away. As the weight above towered unevenly, the maw began to cackle with splintering cries indicating it was nearing collapse, until finally it gave in. The mast was felled and came crashing down in a catapulting ball of flame streaking through the darkness. The wreckage had been minimized, but not without complete reprieve. As it toppled into the water below, the railing and stanchions were smashed and decking crushed. The splash was immense and cacophonic, the doused flames gurgled in the roiling water, steam, and smoke wafting in the night.

All the while, Piet and Hook were still dueling fiercely with the destructive opera a backdrop to their engagement. The impact of a heavy metal blade against blade, or hard treated wood is exceptionally fatiguing. The two of them fought with such intensity, it was a wonder they weren't exhausted from smashing sharply against another. But still, they fought deftly against each other, goading each other on with the hopes of one false move to make them the victor over the other. Hook was the devil incarnate, his eyes like cauldrons from the depths of hell. His black hair and beard matching the sky cast a sinister impression that for anyone who had never seen the likes of pure evil, this would have sent them straight to the altar for prayer.

Piet, however, was intently focused on every move Hook made. He was not afraid of the monster before him, even as the horrible hook sliced through the thick air toward him. He would simply block, jab, and swing with every counter offensive opportunity. He was determined to wear Hook down and end him, and this only propelled him to perform at his very best, anything less would have been his end. His lean physique kept him light on his feet, and his years of adventuring kept him nimble enough to be quick and dodgy. This gave him advantage over Hook in comparison.

As the mast collapsed, they both scrambled to avoid being crushed or tangled up the wildly swinging lines. Hook had rolled across the deck, and watched, aghast at his ship being destroyed before his eyes. Though, by the same measure, he was very much aware that the diminution was a necessary tactic for salvation for the ship as a whole; he was just further perturbed that this hellion was the root cause of it all. Once clear of danger, Piet pounced like a howler monkey toward a preoccupied Hook, landing a slicing blow. The hook caught the brunt, deflecting a mortal impact, but sent it downward toward his leg. It cut him passably, and he gnarled at the nicking bite. It was enough to draw blood, but the leather frog had prevented a deeper slice.

Hook lunged with an upward cutting drive of his sword missing Piet's throat by inches. When he felt the hilt pass unsuccessfully, he braced his momentum by digging his hook into Piet's side as Piet peeled away from the incoming blade. The hook gored his abdomen, but as the two twisted apart naturally, the hook was freed from the mark just as easily as it had landed.

Piet stumbled at the dull ripping pain, gripping his side, blood soaking his shirt. Both had now inflicted damage to the other and would wear them down. It also fueled them further to capitalize on the others' weakening state.

Cecco however, was writhing on the deck, fighting against the incomprehensible pain of Smee's surgical incapability. Sweat spangled his face. He wore gore more than he wore anything else. Lutalo pinned him as tightly as he could, holding him with all his might. He barked at Wendy telling her they needed to go. Wendy felt Lutalo's grip on Cecco's arm and looked up at him. Her eyes pleaded for permission to stay, but his stern glare made it clear they needed to leave now, or they might not be afforded another chance to do so. Smee had dug out the ball from the wound but was scoping for any amount of fabric which might've torn and lodged inside the wound. Cecco would survive the shot, but only if there was no dirty cloth or threads left inside to fester. An infection of that scale would be deathly, and most certainly miserable.

Smee patted Lutalo on the arm, signaling he could loosen the hold. They looked each other in the eyes, and with an unspoken understanding, separated. Cecco still wailing in agony, flailed at the awful pain. Any other man would have fainted, possibly died at the intensity of the surgery. Wendy stood slowly, invested in the wellbeing of this giant whom with she'd shared months at sea. He was a good man, despite his penchant for murderousness. Lutalo grabbed her arm to lead her away hurriedly. She looked back at Cecco and Smee, but they were too preoccupied. Without a word, they slipped away into the night, leaving them all behind, including Piet. From the canoa she could see him, and Hook still engaged in combat up above. Her heart was heavy, but Lutalo rowed them away toward safety putting distance between them and the ship as quickly as he could. Wendy lost all sight of them as they slipped between the ships back toward the cay.

Piet and Hook still carried on but slowing in their attacks. Piet's wound was dangerous because every time he shifted his abdomen, it squeezed the wound open again. He was losing blood fast, which meant he was losing energy even faster. Hook's cut wasn't causing him the same deficiency, so he was able to muster strength to overpower Piet by forcing him to continually crunch to the wounded side. This tactic exhausted Piet and the more he lost blood, the more he lost his wits. This was quickly becoming a losing battle for Piet. His efforts got slower, and weaker. It was a fight for survival now. Hook pounded on him relentlessly, intentionally wearing him down. Blow after blow hammered down on Piet, each one seeming to gain more energy than the last. Hook had found renewed fervor watching his nemesis punished by his effort. He took great merriment in prolonging the punishment, wearing Piet down to a husk.

With a quickness, Hook slammed a heavy strike down on Piet, reducing him to a crouched guard. He kicked Piet with his heavy boot, knocking him down upon his back, his sword falling out of his grip. Piet lay perilously vulnerable beneath Hook, who now towered over him, chest heaving with mad intent. He stomped forward, crushing Piet's arm beneath his heavy booted foot.

"Tut, Tut, Tut," he teased. "You were quite the adversary, boy. I must say you surprised me with your aptitude with a blade. You tendered a mighty fight I give you merit for that. Though, now, you pissant, to start, I will rid you of your hand, so you can feel what it's like to be without, just as I have." At this, he stabbed Piet's hand through to the deck underneath. Piet cried out as the blade pierced through his palm, tendon, and bone. Hook had him pinned still, moving his foot from the arm to the weeping wound on his side. The heft pushing down on the tender flesh was dull and miserable.

"Before I am done, you will beg to your feckless god for absolution. You have been nothing but a fly in the ointment all this time, and nary a soul on that shore will miss your bothersome existence. Indeed, I believe I am doing us all a favor by disburdening the world of you."

Piet was pinned, his hand tacked by the sword which Hook had left standing at attention unhanded. He was stroking his hook, pleased about the revenge he was about to fulfill upon the one who had bestowed him with the evil thing. All had gone quiet around them. Piet was near blacking out from the low pulsing pain burning his abdomen from Hook's weight, and his hand immovable without rending it in two.

"You see lad, I recount the mischief you have caused, not only to me, but to all of us in Port Royal. You have been a thorn in our side for years, yet right under our noses all this time. It was you stealing our things away. It was you stirring the pot among the brethren, galling them against each other. You... who ruined the life of that sweet morsel of a whore. Yet perhaps, I could thank you for that, because if it weren't for you, she mightn't have been such a gash for me to rip night after night."

Piet writhed at the insinuation he'd made of Belle, but the squirming only debilitated him more, the pain throttling into his spine. Hook chuckled and continued.

"Oh, but you see, you made the mistake of coming to rescue the other one – the one under my employ, who you also meddled with unpermissably. You made yourself a fool, stating you were here to wreak havoc on my men and ship for that courtesan, especially when both of them are victims of your fondness. Alas, they have both been stolen away by your henchmen, I will supremely enjoy turning you inside out for everything present and prior to fore. Do know though, that while you might or might not live to see them ended, I will find them, and finish what I started before your little interuptance. That bicche you've taken to is both the reason and result of…"

While Hook was monologuing, Piet mustered every bit of energy he could, pulling the stiletto blade from his belt and drove it deep into Hook's leg. He ripped it down the lateral line, digging a open gash from mid-thigh to just above the knee where the blade was rejected by the conglomeration of joints and bone. Hook stumbled backward, tripping over himself and Piet, and fell downward, clutching the slash. Piet was able to pull himself up and limp off to the railing where he dove (more accurately intendedly fell) overboard into the water below.

Hook roared into the night, "SMEE!!"

XXI

Nibs took a deep breath in as he looked out over the bay. For all the chaos and mayhem they'd just been a part of, here it was oddly quiet, with the only sounds of croaking frogs, lapping water, and rustling leaves in the branches above. His heart was heavy as he awaited the other canoes to rendezvous back on the isle with him. Within the plan, he had no real expectations of surviving – only hopes. He knew many had gotten off the ship, but many hadn't either. He anxiously awaited their return – most specifically Lutalo and Wendy – so he could survey the toll. In all the life he'd lived, it never got easier when those close were killed, especially under his charge and he was deeply concerned about their being left behind.

After what felt like an eternity, finally, in the fading darkness, Nibs could see them approaching. No more canoes could be seen or expected. The only one missing was Piet. He hadn't returned, and it was thought he likely wouldn't.

Helping to land the two of them, he continued a watchful eye on the water for any signs. Wendy had told Nibs she had seen him still fighting with Hook as they rowed away. Nibs grieved over this but wasn't specifically sure what he should feel – or why. Normally, Piet was always missing, absent, or away. Was this for the possible loss of his old friend because Piet's vanity had finally caught up with him? This just felt different; a bad gut feeling and an emptiness in his chest.

With feet on the ground, Wendy vaguely remembered this place, having visited with Piet so long ago in the rain. She found Belle scared, utterly exhausted, and confused. The poor thing had no idea who these men were, and why she had been stolen away again by strangers. While she had fleetingly attempted to resist, she had been quieted by Nibs' ability to defuse and by the connection between him and Wendy. He had told her as they were rowing away from the ship that everything would be fine, and to trust him, but understandably, the font of trust wasn't something flowing freely.

Wendy consoled her. She spoke quietly, motherly, "I made you a promise, that if we got of that ship, I would take you away. I will make good on that promise, Belle. We have been rescued against all possible odds against our favor. These men are Piet's freed men who live on the farm. That is where we will go, all of us, as soon as we can.

You must rest. They will keep watch over us. It is a long way back to the farm, and it won't be easy."

Belle could only nod in understanding, her exhaustion was turning to expiration now. Belle shifted to curl into Wendy's embrace and closed her eyes. It took no time for her to collapse into fitful sleep.

Here they would shelter themselves in the hideaway until they could flee back to the farm that coming evening. They needed to rest and prepare for what would be a very dangerous, and risky escape back to the farm. Without Piet, they were nothing more than a band of escaped slaves running in darkness. If they were caught, it would be ruin for them all. They would be taken to the other plantations and pressed into actual slavery; that is assuming they survived any punitive whipping, beating or even the possibility of death. It didn't matter at all if Wendy and Belle were with them. In fact, it would most certainly spell death for them also, appearing as the conspirators of the escape, regardless of the truth (which, of course, wasn't any better).

Nibs found Wendy cradling Belle and sat down beside her. She could sense he was uneasy, and she put her free hand on his, gripping it tightly. He didn't look at her, but squeezed his fingers on hers gently, reciprocating the connection.

She knew the loss of his men and Piet missing weighed on him. There was little she could do for him right now, but she felt it too. She leaned her head back, weary herself, and closed her eyes. She still held his hand and Belle, but squeaked out a frail, "Thank you Nibs. For everything."

She fell hard asleep with Belle curled up in her lap, Nibs at her side, though Nibs didn't sleep. He kept vigilant watch over the bay. He kept a dim hope in his heart that he would be reunited with Piet, just so, if nothing else, he could know if he was alive. The mystery of it bothered him. There was no closure, and the thought of him reappearing one day in the future, while not abnormal, was too much to bear. The stakes were too real and personal this time.

So too did the remaining Lost Boys sleep in the crooks of the intertwined roots. Piet had dug and carved these out for just this reason, so they all fit perfectly. Nibs continued his watch while they all rested, taking shifts with Lutalo throughout the day. Hidden away, they were almost frozen in time from everything else happening across the bay and in town. Nibs kept his eyes trained on the listing ship, watching to see any movement of, or action on it occurred. Nothing of interest transpired, and so it simply sat, an awkward blemish on the landscape.

As the sun burned into retirement, everyone began to roust to prepare for the next campaign – the return to the farm, the haven, the sanctuary, the never land. They managed to catch some fish and prepare them with a low ground fire to cook them. This didn't produce any significant smoke to give away their location and was enough to give them sustenance for the next jaunt to safety. Wendy took some to Nibs, who was still on watch, and sat with him again.

"I worry this isn't over, Nibs. If Hook is still alive on that ship, and Piet is not, our troubles are still very real."

He grunted reactively. He wasn't sure what the answer was either. He replied, almost mechanically,

"'Aven't seen much'a anythin' happenin' over d'ere. Don' make sense. I reckon dey lost too much'a dey ship to be worryin' on comin' t'find us again. That don' mean it i'n't possible."

He wasn't trying to worry her any more than she already was, but his answer didn't ease Wendy's apprehensions. With all she'd been through, she couldn't not keep her guard up now. It would take a sustained duration of quiet for her to ever feel at ease again – if ever she could. He was just as concerned but didn't want to show it. The fact that he hadn't seen anything, not even anyone else coming or going from the *Jolly Roger*, concerned him. He expected, at a minimum, that others would return to the ship in aid. Lutalo hadn't seen anything either during his watch either. And still no sign of Piet.

While they waited for prime darkness, the group sat telling stories to pass the time, many of which were retellings of how they arrived here, and how they came to become part of the "Lost Boys" gang. Belle had only heard snippets of these tales long ago from Piet, but never fully listened, because she wasn't yet attached with him. She thought them just to be tales made up to impress her and gain her attention, a show of bravado. She heard stories all day and all night from customers and had learned to only half listen. Once they were partners, he didn't spin these yarns like he had before but instead boasted of his newest excursions and conquests. Because he was always telling stories of fantastical feats, she grew more and more platitudinal whenever he returned from his latest adventure.

When the others had told their stories, she listened quietly. Having been rescued by all these men, she was staggered at their selfless efforts to do so after hearing so many atrocious experiences. She was astounded that all of them were the rescues of Piet's efforts. Their collective existence was the result of a rebel seeing through the systems of powerful and dominant men and bucking those systems, standing up for humanistic intent. Piet was an unbridled rascal, but his thievery and mischief was well-intended. As she considered all the things he'd done to hurt her over the years, this gave her pause and she questioned her contempt for him.

Before she could go too far down the rabbit-hole of second-guessing the minutiae, she was encouraged to tell her story. She never had and was reluctant to do so now, so she shied away, attempting pass it off as inconsequential. Her real story was a tragic and heartbreaking, but she had the wherewithal to know *that* was not the version to tell, when so many of them had endured worse. But they cajoled her enough to tell a condensed, watered down version of her story, and how she was never meant for anything other than the whorehouse, where she met Piet.

What she failed to recognize in her modesty, was that their stories were not so different. Some details and experiences varied by degree, but she, as a half-caste, was no better received as a human than they were. In many cases, the mulattoes were hated by both the whites and the blacks, and this made for a very hard life. But this was not about prevailing hardships and who had it better or worse. Her lot was cast, and she had accepted it long ago: she was never going to succeed in anything beyond her promiscuous profession.

The truth was she only knew one way of life, though, for what life she led, she was quite well placed at Pixies under Nena's care and didn't take that for granted. In dreams, she hoped she might inherit the establishment and become the madam herself, but this was a fool's dream she just realized. Nena would sell the place before she would turn it over, and then what? She might find herself in another establishment, but she wouldn't be the top girl anymore, and this was a status she very much intended to maintain. All these factors began to sink in heavily. It occurred to her that her future was directly dependent on Nena, and not of her own. This instability suddenly gripped her with a fear of uncertainty, and how it could all come to an end without warning. And it had all been upturned in a flash, at the hands of the very scoundrels she knew.

She got up and excused herself from the group to join Wendy and Nibs. The solemnity she approached with could be felt, and so they stood looking out, with her beside them. But while they were watching for signs of danger, she cast her eyes toward the town. From here, it seemed a different world now, the light illuminating the darkening night sky. By now, she thought, the house would be filled, and she would be running her game. Everything would be as it ever was, day in, day out. She then thought about all those she'd catered to, and how they were so easily ready to kill her for nothing but the wishes of a madman.

Breaking the silence, she spoke, "I can never go back, can I?"

"I don' 'magine so…" Nibs said apologetically.

Wendy wrapped her arm around Belle, and simply said, "Give it time, Belle. It will all seem normal soon. From here we create our own adventures."

She had dreamt of being free, and here it was before her, an opportunity to change into something new. But change is difficult for those not ready for it. From here, the courage was on the other side of trying; disaster was on the face of familiarity.

Acknowledgements & Gratitude

Throughout the course of this, I did my best to not tell everyone "I'm writing a book!" mainly because I was worried it might never come to completion. However, there are a few people I let into the circle, and for that I do want to thank those who supported me, inspired me, and encouraged me to follow through with this and see it through to finish:

My endlessly supporting wife for so many reasons I cannot begin to list. She is my biggest cheerleader and has believed in me in everything I've ever attempted – as simple or insane as my meandering brain has concocted.

Our daughter whose tuned-in social calibration helped me learn along the way – as well as our shared interests, humor, and snark (another reason to thank my wife for putting up with me/us) helped keep me creatively pursuing this goal.

Our son. Our son has autism, and the obstacles in life he has overcome have been nothing short of an inspiration, and it has been a joy watching him become the man he is today. His diagnosis has pitted him against so many challenges, yet he has persevered and broken through barriers time and time again. He has taught me so much and I cannot imagine who I would be without his part in my life. There have been many instances in the original story and this one, where I wondered if Peter Pan may have had some spectrum in him too…

Brian Payton and Damien Eyersmann – two amazing individuals who are geeks like me (in their own right). They were nothing short of encouraging and excited about the concept (and knowing my love for pirates, tiki, Disney, and the like). They often casually reached out to ask how it was coming along, something I appreciated, even if I never expressed it.

Dr. "Skipper" Marley for taking the time to help me get a handle on how to publish this, for his books, his wildly entertaining podcast, and the on-point tiki bar recommendations. You could've easily ignored me, but you didn't, and in doing so got me here - perhaps a little fuzzy on the edges - but it was worth the adventure!

Disney – I know… I am giant manchild and still reminisce fondly on the old (and some new) Disney. But seriously, without Disney's original animated adaptation, I wouldn't have thought to pursue this project. I grew up on that movie, and it always stuck with me.

The late Robin Williams – the adaptation he portrayed is hands-down, possibly the best versions of this story. That movie is a timeless classic, and his life brought so much to that character. He is gone too soon, and I wish we could've had him longer, but the world couldn't contain such a bright star. I get goosebumps if I ever see the pinball machine, and I will never not play it.

The Chesapeake Bay and Outer Banks (+Ocracoke Island) – Growing up on the bay, I was privy to a rich history, specifically in my case – pirates and colonial history. I was and still am, a voracious lover of piratology. The stomping grounds of real pirates and the battles that occurred in those very waters I called home were real, and I couldn't get enough. Had I not had that experience or proximity to that history, I wouldn't have had the ambition or background to write this story.

And finally, J.M. Barrie – without his original story, absolutely none of this would ever exist. Thank you for your literary contribution to the world and inspiring so many iterations before this.

I'm certain there are more people and things to thank, and this may be amended accordingly… but I want to share this last bit:

I want to thank YOU for purchasing my book, reading it, and getting to this point to understand how grateful I am for your part in making this book a reality.

-S.C. Poteet | ©2025

ABOUT THE AUTHOR

S.C. Poteet was born and raised at the mouth of the Chesapeake Bay, where pirates flourished in the early 18th century. Having spent decades studying their history, visiting their haunts along the Chesapeake's tributaries to the Outer Banks of North Carolina, and the scattered islands of the Caribbean, they are more than just a pop-culture fad to him. Now residing in San Diego, CA., S.C. found inspiration through a childhood tale, to craft a story marrying the two where pirates were real, the world was small, and life was less than fantastical. In his first authored book, S.C. has woven a story told time and time again, only now with historical accuracies befitting the realms of kings and thieves.

Footnotes

---

[i] *Peter Pan, JM Barrie*
[ii] *William Shakespeare, As You Like It, Act 2 Scene 7, lines 139-40; Jacques to Duke Senior and his companions.*

[iii] *Peter Pan, JM Barrie*
[iv] *William Shakespeare, Hamlet, Act 2 Scene 2, lines 213-17;*

[v] *Adapted from The Mata Hari by Paulo Coelho*
[vi] *Emiliano Zapata (1879–1919), Rise Against – Survivor's Guilt*

www.ingramcontent.com/pod-product-compliance
Lightning Source LLC
Chambersburg PA
CBHW020542020726
47494CB00006B/1885